Desert Critter Friends

Crabby Critters

Mona Gansberg Hodgson
Illustrated by Chris Sharp

CPH.
SAINT LOUIS

Dedicated with love and great respect to Pastor Jim
and Celia Huckabay, who were my youth pastor
and his wife when I attended Grace Baptist Church
in Riverside, California. With Special thanks to
Sherri Crawford for her critique of this story.

Desert Critter Friends Series

Friendly Differences	Jumping Jokers
Thorny Treasures	Campout Capers
Sour Snacks	Sticky Statues
Smelly Tales	Goofy Glasses
Clubhouse Surprises	Crabby Critters
Desert Detectives	Spelling Bees

Scripture quotations taken from the HOLY BIBLE, NEW INTERNATIONAL VERSION®.
NIV®. Copyright © 1973, 1978, 1984 by International Bible Society. Used by
permission of Zondervan Publishing House. All rights reserved.

Text copyright © 2000 Mona Gansberg Hodgson
Illustration copyright © 2000 Concordia Publishing House
Published by Concordia Publishing House
3558 S. Jefferson Avenue, St. Louis, MO 63118-3968
Manufactured in the United States of America

Library of Congress Cataloging-in-Publication Data

Hodgson, Mona Gansberg, 1954–
    Crabby critters / Mona Gansberg Hodgson ; illustrated by Chris Sharp.
      p.   cm. — (Desert Critter Friends ; bk 11)
  Summary: Because Nadine the javelina fails to show respect to her animal friends, they respond in a crabby way to her. Additional text
explains that God wants us to show respect to others.
    ISBN 0-570-07074-0
    [1. Respect—Fiction. 2. Behavior—Fiction. 3. Desert animals—Fiction.
4. Christian life—Fiction.] I. Sharp, Chris, 1954- ill. II. Title.
PZ7.H6649 Cr   2000
[E]—dc21   99-050660

1 2 3 4 5 6 7 8 9 10   09 08 07 06 05 04 03 02 01 00

Nadine, the javelina, opened her sleepy eyes. "It's already evening," she said to herself. "Almost time for the talent show!"

She usually slept until dark because she is nocturnal. But Nadine had other plans for this evening.

3

She s-t-r-e-t-c-h-e-d, then plopped out of bed. She needed to get to the desert critter friends clubhouse. After all, she was in charge of telling about each act before it went on.

Nadine stopped on the path to the clubhouse to snack on a cactus. *CHOMP! CHOMP! CHOMP!* While she chomped, she thought about the different acts in the talent show. Wanda was going to juggle cactus apples. Quincy was going to draw a picture of Fergus. Jill was going to sing with Rosie. Of course, Jamal was going to tell jokes. And ...

"Hey, Nadine," Jamal, the jackrabbit, shouted as he hop-hop-hopped up to Nadine. "Have you heard the joke about—"

"Not now, Jamal!" Nadine said. "I'm busy thinking."

Jamal twitched his nose. "I was going to practice my—"

"You can't practice on me," Nadine said. "I'm thinking about what I'm going to say at the talent show. That's more important than your jokes."

Jamal frowned. "You didn't have to be rude," he said as he hopped away.

"He's sure crabby today!" Nadine whispered to herself.

As Nadine walked on, she came
to Myra's house. Myra's yard was
full of plants. Another snack
sounded good to Nadine. She
began to dig-dig-dig in the dirt with
her long snout. She was munching

on roots when Myra suddenly raced out of her house toward Nadine!

"No! Not my garden!" Myra, the quail, shouted. "You didn't ask me if you could eat my plants!"

"I was hungry," Nadine said as she gulped down the roots.

Myra flapped her wings at Nadine. "Well, you could have shown me some respect by asking me if I cared," Myra said. "You've pulled up most of my beautiful flowers. You destroyed my garden!"

"Mmph! You sure are crabby today!" Nadine said as she walked away.

cabbage

beans

11

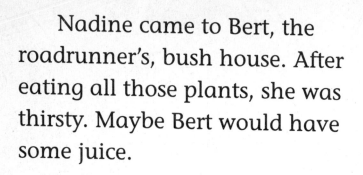

Nadine came to Bert, the roadrunner's, bush house. After eating all those plants, she was thirsty. Maybe Bert would have some juice.

KNOCK! KNOCK! KNOCK! Bert didn't answer when she tapped on his door with her hoof. Nadine pushed the door open with her snout. "Bert, are you in here?" she called.

Nadine decided to go inside and help herself to a drink. That's when she saw something red sitting on Bert's shelf. It had shiny metal sides with holes in it. She put her snout on it to get a better sniff.

SNIFF!

"Humm ... ONK!"

SNIFF!

"*Humm ... ONK!*"

Each time she sniffed, the holes made a noise. And so did Nadine.

Suddenly, Nadine heard a booming voice behind her.

15

"What are you doing to my harmonica (*har-mon-i-ca*)?" Bert shouted.

Nadine was so surprised, she jumped. She bumped the shelf with her snout. The harmonica went flying.

"Oh no!" Bert cried. He dropped
his backpack on the floor. *ZOOM!*
He raced toward the harmonica. He
caught it just before it hit the floor.

"Bert! Don't surprise me like
that!" Nadine said.

"I'm the one who is surprised,"
Bert said. "Why were you in my
house and snooping in my stuff?"

Nadine grunted. "I was thirsty,"
she said. "And you weren't home."

Bert put the harmonica into his backpack. "Well, you could have shown some respect and waited for me to get here."

"Mmph! You're crabby too," Nadine whispered.

Bert pulled his backpack on. "I've got to get to the clubhouse," he said.

"I do too," Nadine said. "We can walk together."

Bert was still frowning as he pulled his cap down on his head. "Not this time," he said. "I have to zoom so I can practice before the show starts."

"I don't zoom," Nadine said. "I'll see you later." She watched Bert zoom-zoom-zoom away.

20

Nadine headed toward the clubhouse again. She thought about her crabby friends. First Jamal called her rude. Then Myra said she had destroyed her garden. And now Bert had called her a snoop. They were all crabby critters!

As Nadine walked along the path, she heard someone call her name. "NADINE!"

Jill, the ground squirrel, scurried up to Nadine. "Hi, Nadine," she said. "I want to show you something."

"Hi, Jill," Nadine said. "Shouldn't you be practicing with Rosie?"

"I will," Jill said, "but I want to show you my great idea about a big ending for the talent show!" She pulled a tablet out of her bag.

Nadine stared at the sky. "The moon is starting to rise," she said. "I should be going."

Jill flipped pages in her tablet. "Just a minute," she said. "Here's my first idea."

"You don't need to bother with your idea," Nadine said. "I have my own plan for the ending." *DIG! DIG! DIG!* She dug up a root with her snout.

"But ... but ... I think you'll like my idea," Jill said.

"Don't worry, my ending will be plenty big," Nadine said with a mouthful of roots. "I need to get to the clubhouse now," she said.

Jill stuffed her tablet into her bag. "You could have at least shown me a little respect and listened to my idea!" Jill said before she scurried away.

Nadine grunt-grunt-grunted. "Jill is crabby too," she said to herself. What was wrong with her friends? This wasn't going to be a very fun talent show if they were all crabby.

When Nadine reached the clubhouse, she could hear her friends practicing for the show. She stopped in the doorway to watch and listen.

Nadine watched Myra twirl around in her ballet clothes. She watched Fergus put film into his camera. She listened to Bert trying to play a song on his harmonica.

Nadine listened to Jill and Rosie practice their song in a corner. She listened to Taylor read from his poetry book. She watched Fergus, the owl, pose on his perch. Then she watched Quincy, the porcupine, set out his drawing pad and pencils.

"Oh no!" Nadine yelled. She watched Toby doing flip-flip-flips right toward her.

CRASH! Toby smashed right into Nadine. He flopped to the floor. Nadine went down on her front legs.

"OUCH!" Toby said, rubbing his head. "Are you okay, Nadine?"

"I guess so." Nadine grunted.

"Well, I don't know about the ending," Jill said with a giggle. "But that flip, flip, flip, crash sure would make a big opening act!"

"I'm sorry, Nadine." Toby said. "I didn't see you there when I started flipping."

Nadine stood back up. "I wish all of you would show me some respect!" she said. "Like not crashing into me."

Jamal jumped over to Nadine. "Funny you should mention that word *respect*," he said. "You didn't show me respect when you were rude to me on the path."

Myra stared down at her ballet shoes. "You were not respectful of me when you destroyed my garden," she said to Nadine.

Bert zoomed up. "What about when you walked right into my house and snooped in my stuff? Were you showing me respect?" he asked.

"And what about me?" Jill said. "You weren't respectful to me when you wouldn't listen to my idea."

Nadine hung her head. "No wonder you were all being so crabby," she said. "It's because I wasn't showing you respect."

Nadine looked up at her friends. "I have a lot to learn about showing respect to others. Thanks for showing me that I was wrong. Will all of you forgive me?"

"Of course," her friends said.

41

Bert blew a note on his
harmonica. "*HUM-M-M-M!* On with
the show, everyone! And let's not
do that big opening act with
Nadine and Toby!" he said.

"Right!" Nadine said, rubbing
her head. "I respect your idea!" She
smiled at her friends.

God loves you so much that He sent His Son, Jesus, to die for you. God wants all of us to show love and respect to others. This is why He gave us the Commandments. Ask God to help you be considerate of others and to help you value other people, their property, and their privacy. Ask Him to help you respect others so you can show them His love.

Do to others as you would have them do to you. Luke 6:31

Hi, kids!

Help Nadine take the path of respect for her friends on her trip to the clubhouse.

For Parents and Teachers:

Each of us, including our kids, longs for respect. We want other people to appreciate us and our ideas. And we want them to show consideration for our property.

Yet disrespect runs rampant in our society. Like a virus, it infiltrates and weakens our families, our neighborhoods, our schools, and even our churches.

Nadine focused only on herself and her own role in the Desert Critter Talent Show. As she did, the needs and feelings of those around her—Jamal, Bert, Myra, and Jill—became insignificant to her. She demonstrated her lack of respect for them in her rude attitude toward Jamal and Jill, in her invasion of Bert's privacy, and in her disregard for Bert and Myra's property. Sound familiar?

As you know, a lack of respect is at the root of countless sibling spats, playground squabbles, and even parent/child conflicts. We can help our children understand respect by demonstrating it in our own behavior toward them and toward others. Children will learn what is modeled for them, but they will also learn through discovering what is required of them. After offering them your respect, require the same in return.

Another vital part of teaching respect is to show your child the many faces of and consequences of disrespect. In Nadine's case, it created serious problems in her relationships with her friends. As a result of her disrespectful behavior, they became crabby and treated her with disrespect. Help your child see that God wants us to treat others as we ourselves want to be treated.

Help your child see that a healthy understanding of respect begins with a deep respect for God the Father and how much He has loved us through Jesus. Jesus is the ultimate example of respect, following God's will by loving us enough to die for us. As we seek God's help in placing others first, we will better appreciate others and show love and respect for them and their property. We will learn that respect flows from love and love flows from God.

Here are some questions and activities you can use as discussion starters to help your children understand these concepts.

Discussion Starters

1. Why did Nadine wake up in the evening? Can you name five other animals that are nocturnal?

2. Why were Jamal, Myra, Bert, and Jill crabby to Nadine?

3. Has anyone ever been disrespectful to you? What did you do? Were you crabby to them like Nadine's friends were crabby with her?

4. Have you ever been disrespectful to your parents or anyone else? Are you sorry? If you are sorry, ask God to forgive you. If you hurt someone's feelings because you didn't show respect, ask that person to forgive you too.

5. Can you think of some things you can do that will show respect for your parents and teachers?

6. Can you think of some ways in which you can show respect to God?

Pray together. Thank God for loving you so much that He sent His Son to be your Savior. Ask God to forgive you for those times when you haven't shown respect for Him or for the people He has placed in your life. Ask Him to help you show respect to Him and to be considerate of everyone around you.

God will help you show respect for others. How will you show respect for the people around you? Tell me on these lines.

_____

_____

_____

_____

Journey in North America, 1831

Journey in North America, 1831
Sándor Bölöni Farkas

Translated and edited by

ARPAD KADARKAY

ABC-CLIO, INC.

Santa Barbara, California
Oxford, England

Library of Congress Cataloging in Publication Data
Farkas, Sándor, 1795–1842.
  Journey in North America, 1831

    Translation of Utazas Eszak Amerikaban.
    Includes index.
    1. United States—Social life and customs—1783–1865.
2. United States—Description and travel—1783–1848.
3. Farkas, Sándor, 1795–1842. I. Kadarkay, Arpad,
1934–   II. Title.
E165.F2313   973.5'6   77-19145
ISBN 0-87436-270-9

American Bibliographical Center—Clio Press

2040 A.P.S., Riviera Campus, Box 4397
Santa Barbara, California 93103

European Bibliographical Centre—Clio Press. Ltd.
Woodside House, Hinksey Hill
Oxford OX1 5BE, England

Manufactured in the United States of America

To Ray Billington
Donum est magnum

Acknowledgments

*M*y *debts are* many and, in part, intangible. I owe a great deal to the generous help of the research staff at the Huntington Library, that *instauratio magna* of Americana so greatly conceived and greatly achieved.

I wish to acknowledge my gratitude to a host of Hungarian scholars. At various stages of this work, Ferenc Fehér, Ágnes Heller, Charlotte Kretzoi, István Gál, and Pál Pándi provided me with valuable help. Twin-sceptered in literature and philosophy, Ferenc Fehér, in his knowledge and his unfailing readiness to forward much-needed archive material, has been a model of international scholarly cooperation.

On these shores I received encouragement from many quarters. My principal debt is to Professor Béla Vardy, and Professor John Lukacs, whose knowledge of Tocqueville I came to value highly. I received valuable encouragement from Daniel Boorstin and Stephen R. Graubard. On a personal level, the friendship and understanding of Professors Kenneth Atchity, Lawrence Caldwell, the late Edward Mill, and John Rodes sustained me.

I owe a special thanks to Professor Robert Nisbet, who read the introductory essay. Professor Harry Jaffa's works instructed and improved my labors. I was privileged to receive assistance from the renowned Goethe scholar, Professor Stuart Atkins, in whose presence I felt like Goethe's crickets that fly by leaping from the grass and then fall back to sing the same old song—about the grace and intellect of the human mind.

Among my colleagues my principal debt is to Professor Gordon Baker, whose patient and wise guidance in American political thought has been an inspiration and an enrichment. Unknown to himself, Professor Herman Pritchett taught me that the enduring strength of American democracy is its ascent to the Constitution. My thanks are also due Professors Peter Merkl, Robert Wesson, Michael Gordon, Thomas Schrock, Dean Mann, and Wolfram Hanrieder.

For editorial help I am indebted to Lloyd Garrison, whose reasoned, blue-penciled advice meant movement from darkness to light.

A special gratitude goes to my wife, Leone, for teaching a library cormorant the language of flesh and roses.

Finally, an appreciation to Mr. and Mrs. Fred Oakley, in whose house, and among whose friends, I learned that to be an American is almost a moral condition, an education, a reasoned commitment to ideals.

Contents

List of Tables

Journey in North America, 1831

Introduction

This is America!
This is the New World!
Not the present European
Wasted and withering sphere...
This is no graveyard of Romance,
This is no pile of ruins,
Of fossilized wigs and symbols
Of State and musty tradition.
—Heinrich Heine

Happy Hungary, if she
does not let others mistreat
her any more.
—Dante

*I*n a remote Transylvanian village cemetery, Házsongárd, where men are dust and dreams, an ornate tombstone carries the inscription: Sándor Bölöni Farkas—North American Traveler—1795–1842. Not many people even in his native village know that entombed under the simple inscription rests a contemporary of Alexis de Tocqueville. A century and a half after his *Democracy in America* appeared, the classic of all democratic ages, Tocqueville is emerging as the "greatest political thinker of the nineteenth century,"[1] and his book complimented as the "most illuminating commentary penned by a foreigner, and one which comes closest of being immortal."[2]

Tocqueville and Farkas met in September 1831 at the Charlestown state penitentiary. In his *Journey*, Farkas refers to two French magistrates, and the Charlestown prison logbook on the same date reads: "Two German [*sic*] Noblemen from Transylvania visited and inspected the Prison." This refers to Farkas and Count Ference Béldi. Tocqueville's American visit was a celebrated occasion and his *Democracy* was a European event, proclaimed as the greatest philosophical analysis since Montesquieu. Reviewing the first volume of *Democracy*, John Stuart Mill said that Tocqueville's object was to "inquire what light is thrown, by the example of America, upon the question of democracy; which he considers as the great and paramount question of our age."[3] Mill goes on to state that all who in Europe debate the issue of democracy versus aristocracy "are prompt enough in pressing America into their service."[4] Tocqueville himself, in a letter to his friend, Kergolay, admitted: "In my work on America . . . though I seldom mention France, I did not write a page without thinking of her, and placing her as it were before me."[5]

Tocqueville's statement assumes added significance in light of Farkas's *Journey*, published one year before *Democracy* appeared. Farkas also analyzed American democracy by pressing it into service to counter the despotic regime of Metternich. But unlike Tocqueville's book, *Journey* has never been translated into English even though it complements the acclaimed classic. A close analysis of Tocqueville's and Farkas's work, their treatment of Jacksonian Democracy, their contrasting intellectual backgrounds and philosophical presuppositions which bear on their assessment

[5]

6   of American democracy, must await a separate work. By and large, the
immediate contrast between *Democracy* and *Journey* resides in Tocqueville's
Catholicism and Farkas's Unitarianism. In the former, Pascal looms large;
in the latter, the presence of Rousseau is felt inescapably. Pascal prevents
Tocqueville from seeing the emerging industrial democracy, while Rousseau, partly refracted through William Ellery Channing, enables Farkas to
grasp intuitively the emerging democracy of steam and steel.

Tocqueville wrote *Democracy* with France in mind, and Farkas
produced his *Journey* as a democratic primer for feudal Hungary, where it
became a best-seller. The book was unprecedented in early-nineteenth-
century Hungary, where, as one wit put it, books were valued so highly as
to be placed on the master beam, next to the smoked ham. A contemporary
of Farkas, reflecting on the unknown author's overnight success, wrote:[6]

> When the modest Chancellery secretary left his country no one thought it seeds
> an event that in a few years will electrify the nation. As a writer, Sándor Farkas
> was completely unknown. Only his gangling figure, prominent forehead,
> aquiline nose, the sunken face, and thoughtful stroll as now and then he stopped
> in the marketplace have suggested that in this man a Cassius pursued his hidden
> thoughts.

And, as Shakespeare described that character:[7]

> Yond Cassius has a lean and hungry look;
> He thinks too much: such men are dangerous
> ... He reads much;
> He is a great observer, and he looks
> Quite through the deeds of men ...

Sándor Farkas was born on December 14, 1795, at Bölön, Háromszék
County, in Transylvania. His family belonged to an impoverished Székel
nobility, which in the nineteenth century comprised the lumpen nobility,
poverty-stricken nobles of good birth, and sometimes brain, but no means.
His family employed four landless cottagers and when Farkas enrolled at
the Unitarian College at Kolozsvár (today Cluj in Rumania), he wore the
toga or uniform *(societas togata)* compulsory for poor students. Students
from well-to-do families dressed as they pleased. Thomas Hobbes said that
fear and he were born twins, and this natal circumstance of danger and
disorder colors his masterpiece, *Leviathan*. By extension, poverty and
Farkas assumed a Janus face. Indeed, Farkas could intone with Juvenal:
"Slow rises worth, by poverty depressed."

But Farkas's poverty was neither grinding nor absolute. Rather, his
was a psychological awareness of meager economic means in a society
lorded by magnates and aristocrats who lived in conspicuous splendor and
wallowed in wealth. In 1820, at age twenty-five, he wrote to his friend: "My
politically sublunar and urban wanderings taught me that those living on
porridge and onions can be happy or happier than those who eat white
bread."[8] This signal example of high thinking and low living presaged the
stoic detachment of Farkas which was a social problem rather than a
personal choice. In 1821 the theme reappeared: "I am poor, have no high

contacts, and cannot crawl. And can I help it for not being born a Catholic?"[9] His letter to another friend in the same year struck a Rousseauean tone: "How I wish to be with you and not tread the hateful Kolozsvár treadmill. My friend, how I feel the burden of poverty. Without means I cannot forsake the cemetery of my honor. *Det vitam, det opes.* Live happier and more secure than I. May heaven protect you."[10]

There is a striking parallel between the backgrounds and careers of Rousseau and Farkas. Both lost their parents early, both became homeless wanderers, both were bruised yet sensitive and unable to relate to the conventional world. Both were at odds with the regnant ideas of their times. Rousseau began his famous *Confessions* with a burst of challenging eloquence:[11]

> I am forming an enterprise which has had no example, and whose execution will have no imitator. . . . Let the trumpet of the Last Judgement sound when it will, I shall come, this book in hand, to present myself before the Sovereign Judge. I have told the good and bad with the same candor. I have concealed nothing of evil, added nothing of good . . . I have shown myself as I was: despicable and vile when I was so, good, and generous, sublime, when I was these; and I have unveiled my inmost soul . . .

On January 1, 1835, already acclaimed and celebrated for his *Journey,* Farkas began his own confessions—the diary of a broken soul. Unlike Rousseau, Farkas never intended his memoirs for publication. Not even his closest friends knew they existed. Unfortunately we have only his confessions spanning January 1835 to January 7, 1836, and the rest is irretrievably lost. There is a hint in Farkas's personal writings that he burned his manuscript. But the remnant establishes that Farkas was a worthy imitator of Rousseau. Had he lived to the ripe age of his intellectual mentor, Farkas would have emerged as the great biographer of Everyman in Metternich's wasteland empire.

His confessions begin:[12]

> Of all the moments of life when we reflect on man's mortality, look back on our career, and sigh for the future, perhaps the waning moments of last year are the most interesting. Willed or unwilled, we are surprised in spite of their fleetingness by the images of the past which unveil, as it were, the shadow of our sins. We anticipate with uncertain feelings and sigh with presentiment at the approaching year.
>
> I had such a moment on the last evening of 1834, when I entered the fortieth year of my life. I feel that not much is left and how little I have accomplished. I survey my past year's history, its feelings, my existence and intern myself in the remembrance of things past. I examine my deeds. Yes, I found some pleasing to my soul, as an honest man and patriot. But I also discerned traits that shamed my soul. I discover I was not honest in everything, vanity spurred many of my activities, and indolence excused many of my private and public responsibilities.
>
> I have also discovered the nature of my heavy sufferings; condemnation, official slighting and humiliation, joined by a deep anxiety over my country's misfortune and by fate's unpredictable moods, last year I won the esteem and attention of many patriots and prominent men. My last year also chronicled the

8

painful losses of the feeling heart whose memory storms my breast, and suppressed sadness weighs down on me. Fate has plucked from me the dearest to my heart, for ten years the object of my desires and dreams, eternal preoccupation of my feelings and thoughts. Even my coldness may have saddened her hours. Due perhaps to the strange constellation of events, she died because of me before I could ask her: "Forgive me for I hurt you!"

In the midst of the soul's stormy recall of the past, finally I can pity myself that after so many years I was compelled to carry so much hidden pain. And something intimated consolation: "So much suffering sanctions your mistakes." In my introspective sorrows I have found some bittersweet bliss and wished to recapture its moments. But they fleet before me veiled, never to be recaptured, regretfully, in their vivid completeness.

This realization affirms my long-standing resolve to jot down important events of my life, activities, feelings, and deeds which would comprise a depository where my past—good or bad—I could view as in mirror.

On January 9, 1835, Farkas continued his confessions:[13]

Since I wrote the above lines a few days have passed and kept me preoccupied with my resolution. Reflecting on my spiritual power to execute the plan, with blush and despair I recalled many similar attempts that came to naught. I feel the challenge of my resolution. I know it demands a total soul to depict honestly our innermost being, confess every motive of deeds, overcome vanity, and describe accurately feelings and thoughts which, in our sober moments, conscience accepts unqualified.

I interrogate my mind, heart, and soul: have you the strength not to shame me before my Self? As I write, my hand appears supplicant toward the invisible reality and my soul entreats help, for strength and steadfastness. Are they in sacred religious feelings? Are they in the divine inspiration of prayer? Or perhaps the sighs I heave in my happiest and saddest moments invoke these thoughts and feelings? I feel they bring me spiritual solace and strength to steel my resolve. Yes, from this day on I will try to write down very honestly the important events of my life as if relating them before God's Judgment seat. I shall purify my heart, and, if within my power, overcome its base impulses. I will seek to ennoble my feelings and, by describing my deeds, critically examine the knowledge of my soul.

This inward searching of a sensitive, lyrical soul bears the imprint of Rousseau, whose magnetism Farkas could not escape. The introspective self-revelation, the recording of fleeting moments to preserve them for the reconstruction of knowledge—all this is Rousseau. Farkas's candor and sincerity are disarming and moving. Beyond them lurks Rousseau's *dédoublement*, or splitting of a self, which Farkas exhibits in his confessions. Part 2 of Rousseau's *Confessions* is darkened by his complaints of persecution and conspiracy, imagined and real. Farkas had every reason to suspect that his well-known republican sympathies, and a head "crammed with American nonsense," marked him as certainly as though he were plague-infected, avoided by even close friends—especially when Emporer Francis II (1768–1835) suspended Transylvanian home rule and introduced the militaristic *Machstaat* which suppressed every germ of free thought. During this dark period, the actions of Baron Miklós Wesselényi, a fiery, popular Transylvanian reform leader and a childhood friend of Farkas, became

suspect in Vienna. The fear-gripped atmosphere produced this entry in
Farkas's diary:[14]

> I frequently visited Wesselényi. I share his destiny. I fear for him because he is the object of the philistine time-servers' hatred. I watched him closely. He appears also restless but not dispirited. Every moment is precious for him because any moment he can expect his arrest. I implored him to leave, to withdraw for a while and stop playing Egmont. Whenever I visited Wesselényi before, his house was crowded. To my great surprise nowadays only one or two people can be found there.
>
> At noon the royal commissioner in full pomp visited the Gubernium. In the street and around the Gubernium there were many spectators. The councillors came down the steps to meet and pay homage to the commissioner. Dignitaries and important people were ordered to stand on balconies to enhance the occasion. In the council itself the commissioner's rescript was read, giving him unlimited power. I have never seen more contrasting faces than when the royal commissioner arrived and left. People stood by silently. Some faces radiated hidden pleasure, others appeared to gaze into their private depth of sadness. Still others resembled Homer's Achilles, who, after the killing of Patroclus, rolled his uncrying eyes in agony. Others just stood there, shrunk in their nothingness, ready to bend their necks to any yoke destiny offered . . .

After the royal commissioner assumed arbitrary power, silent fear spread through the city. The "atomization" of the community, the psychic syndrome of unbounded power, which created quailing individual islands of separateness, is masterfully captured by Farkas:[15]

> Wesselényi has left. Being emotionally overwrought, I deliberately did not visit him to say good-bye. It was as if a stone rolled off my heart when I learned he was allowed to leave.
>
> I started to think about my fate. Kept to my room all day, examined myself, and catalogued my political sins. I pressed my memory to reexamine my political activities, writings, and speeches in the last five years. Reviewed them one by one from a strictly legal viewpoint, and judged myself as if a stranger. Found myself completely innocent before the nation's laws—if justly interpreted. Then imagined myself before the seat of tyrannical power and felt my vulnerability as a poor, solitary man, as a bureaucrat and writer.
>
> Before the sentencing I saw myself dragged through a thousand anxieties. The invisible mercenaries of darkness shadowed my footsteps. I feel their presence everywhere, among friends and acquaintances, at social gatherings and in private meditations. Even at my desk they peer over my shoulder at the paper in front of me. My ordinary statements were given a thousand riddled explanations. Progressively my work comes to a stop. Invisible forces preyed on my plans, and cold, suspicious faces stare at me. Suspecting enemies everywhere, I grew silent in company. At times abject fear seized me. Then I erupted in anger but no one was there. I wanted to cross swords with my enemies, but no one stepped forward. Fully convinced of my innocence, I wanted to open my heart and refute the charges. But there were no accusers and no charges. Everywhere my name was vilified. I trembled from concocted sins whose source nobody knew. In the end I drew completely silent, a misanthrope. In a country I live and suffer for I lead a life of bitter uncertainty, forever severed from happiness.
>
> Finally, I was summoned to the tyrant's castle—by a secret decree and conducted through a secret gate. They cited a black book against me, even though no one read the accusations and there were no accusers. Defense denied,

the sentence was declared without anyone to appeal to. In vain did I state my innocence, requesting justice and fair laws. Nobody listened. Deprived of everything in life, humiliated and unfree, I suffered every spiritual and physical torture devised by the tyrant. Then I saw my ultimate punishment—exile from my native land!

But what are my offenses? Am I guilty that after years of reflecting on my experiences here and abroad, I strove for a constitutional government, based on natural law and common sense, where the king is the people's first servant and not its tyrant; where law protects and punishes equally all citizens; where strict but impartial laws, rather than personal tyranny, constitute the government. Am I guilty because my country's demoralizing backwardness, and its oppression and intellectual infancy, have pained me deeply? From my youthful years on I hoped, dreamed, and strove resolutely for a national rebirth. Despised every privilege, monopoly, and discrimination. Loathed the aristocracy's ignoble arrogance, and whenever possible I ridiculed it. Bureaucratic pedantry I hated, disclosed, and cursed its overbearing insolence. In deeds, in words, in writing I have spread democratic ideas. My heart bled at the slavelike oppression of my countrymen. Fought with them against feudalism and summoned freedom for the whole nation. I lived and died for the nation's language, which, by suppressing other languages, I sought to make dominant in the country inhabited by free Hungarians. Hated cold cosmopolitanism, the greatest poison of nationality. Despised beyond measure, hated with vengeance, those who retarded the nation's cultural and linguistic progress or were indifferent to it. I considered ungrateful villains those for whom the national language is not the language of heart and social discourse. Laughed at the sycophants of royal favor and splendor. Considered religious bigots, of whatever creed, the basest creatures, and heaped ridicule and contempt on them. In all creeds I despised the priestly cast, which aspired to a separate status in civil society. With all my strength sought to vanquish its hydra head that oppressed enlightened philosophy, free inquiry of ideas, and civil liberties. I did not worship my God blindly, or according to the script and instruction of those who are just as helpless as I. I neither feared, burned incense, or crawled before my God. From childhood I have never turned to him in formal prayer. But in sorrow or hope, in church or in the open field, when feeling an inner need, I opened my soul and turned to him as a close friend.

This is the *summa* of my political sins. Insignificant as my career is, my life narrowly confined and obscure, it will attract the slander and attention of tyranny which consign me to be branded. But what can any despot do to me to cure my sins? Strip me of office, which has consumed my health and wealth, and cast me out into the world as a beggar? It cannot deprive me of my spiritual power and pride in poverty. I have earned my bread with the sweat of my brow. Schooled in unyielding fate and want, as long as my health allows I can secure my existence anywhere. They can pierce me and take my life and liberty. But not my conscience and the proud conviction that I strove only for goodness, truth, and sought public and national happiness. I stand innocent before God and my conscience. Unashamed before my Self, I will never renounce my previous feelings and thoughts.

This lengthy quotation from Farkas's confessions reveals his escape into his self and is the most autobiographical of his private writings. Farkas was guided by a Rousseauean concern for retaining his individual identity as it passed through the needle's eye of conscience and faced daily his self-willed responsibility to live. But he went one step beyond Rousseau by insisting that it is not enough to live; one must live nobly. His search for authenticity also unmasked society and its ascribed privileges. Aristocratic Hungary and aristocratic France placed an unbearable burden on sensitive men who came from the lower depths of society like Rousseau and Farkas. There is a clearly implied conflict in Farkas which stemmed from his low origin and his lifelong quest for personal recognition in a status-conscious society where tinsel and decorum counted more than human worth. Like Rousseau, Farkas believed that a feeling heart could overcome social conventions and create its own world of conscience. In a sense, Farkas escaped his birth by escaping into himself to listen and live on the stilled and soft *travail et combat* of suffering.

In the mendacious feudal society, the world of pretenses and glittering surfaces, such confessions are acts of self-affirmation of things unspeakable and unthinkable. The confessions of Rousseau and Farkas are like the sea under starlit nights—they ponder deeply their own unfathomable being. The two Romantics knew their own suffering and distilled intuitive knowledge from it, but few can share their knowledge. Still, such confessions should not be dismissed as privatized feelings that yield no historical information. Historically, other sensitive beings who by deed or creative effort suffered and then gained public acclaim also confessed—St. Augustine, Rousseau, Farkas, and even Sartre—because the social layers they scaled were unresponsive. By confessing, Farkas stood still, as it were, and by trying to capture himself, he sought to persuade society that naked conscience is more natural than a social mask.

The nearest analogy of such a naked conscience, which unfolds in Farkas's diary, is Sören Kierkegaard, that hunchbacked genius who laid bare his solitary being to contingent realities. Christianity has always managed to paper over the deep cracks between secular existence and the eschatological demand of its creed. But no one opened these cracks more explosively than Kierkegaard. His fantastic moral requirements mocked and undermined mundane values. Farkas was a contemporary of Kierkegaard and, like him, was sealed off in a difficult language and isolated in a rump country. Nonetheless, Farkas elevated suffering to an uplifting and edifying exercise of will enabling him to face the Creator and his destiny with unblinking eyes and a purity of heart. Farkas's natural prayer parallels Kierkegaard's inward prayer of "speaking with one another."[16] Both were dedicated to installing the voice of conscience forever in the individual. Conscience is an exacting taskmaster and Kierkegaard noted that it is only in eternity that "each shall render account as an individual."[17] This concept is identical to the thought expressed by Farkas, "I am not ashamed before my Self." The two philosophies were mostly entombed in their respective languages and inaccessible to a larger audience, yet Farkas and Kierkegaard shared a striking inward reformation.

There is at least circumstantial evidence that Farkas, like Kierkegaard, reacted against Hegel's philosophical system, in which the individual is but a passing point, a mere moment in the impersonal and infinite cosmic

12 process. Kierkegaard once said of himself, "I stand like a lonely pine tree egoistically shut off, pointing to the skies and casting no shadow..."[18] During his college years, Farkas referred to himself as a "lonely cliff-pine." His close friend János Kriza, the Unitarian bishop of Transylvania, studied under Hegel at Berlin, so Farkas became well acquainted with Hegel's philosophy—that vast conceptual expanse which tends to shrivel the human intellect. Kriza used to say that he could not understand Hegel's philosophy in spite of his German education. There are two principal reasons for this. First, Kriza was imbued with the Rousseauean notion that reason flows through the heart. Second, Kriza's religious views were colored by the libertarian-rational spirit which Unitarianism owes to the writings of Channing, Priestley, and Parker. Kriza's philosophy is summed up by his statement that "feeling is everything. But we must teach rational religion that gives strength to reason and warmth to the heart."[19] Farkas, like Kierkegaard, sought an exclusive and all-absorbing unity with his self, thus affirming the primacy of the *principium individuationis*, which countervails the impersonal Hegelian system.

Unfortunately, less is known about Farkas's intellectually formative years than Kierkegaard's. But Farkas's school years at the Unitarian College reveal a consistency in his intellectual-political outlook. His searching for purity of heart and conscience led directly to a search for a polity in which the individual and society could cooperate for the public good. But this intellectual portrait of Farkas is incomplete without an understanding of Transylvania in the late eighteenth and early nineteenth century.

Transylvania was a small replica of America. It was part of the Kingdom of Hungary nominally under Hapsburg rule and also a rebellious principality, a Protestant thorn in the Catholic body politic. During the reign of Leopold I (1655–1705), Jesuit press-gangs roamed Transylvania and sent many Protestant ministers to the galleys in Naples.[20] Leopold's successor, Emperor Joseph I (1705–1711), rescinded these inquisitorial methods and forbade the persecution of Protestants. However, under Emperor Charles VI (1711–1740), the ill-famed Hapsburg principle of *divide et impera* (divide and rule) was reintroduced in its Machiavellian self-consciousness on religious grounds, and Maria Theresa (1740–1780) attempted to make her realm uniformly Catholic and German. To press anything and anybody into the Hapsburg dynastic and patrimonial ideal meant a constant struggle between Catholic universalism and Protestant particularism.

Under Hapsburg ascendancy, Transylvania included three nations comprised of Hungarians, Székels, and Saxons, and four "received" religions. These separate nationalities and creeds never merged to form a national identity. Instead they spent their energies in a Hobbesian war of all against all without any moderation or restraint. Under the centralizing drive of the Hapsburgs, some unbalanced rulers, like Ferdinand II, preferred a desert to a country with heretics, and a cruel war against the

Protestants continued until the end of the monarchy. The Hungarian Puritans comprised an enclave of sanity in this crucible of dynastic religion. There is a historical link between Puritanism and democracy[21] just as there is between Puritanism and empirical rationalism.[22] The Puritan demand for direct religious experience and Bacon's experimental spirit, the anticlassical postulate that free inquiry means opposition to received knowledge, are close correlates. As George Fox said: "You will say, Christ saith this, and the Apostles say this but; What canst thou say?"[23]

The Hungarian Puritans had extensive contacts with English Puritans. Many Hungarian Puritans actually sided with the Glorious Revolution. The enormous distance between these groups was bridged by a common creed and by students who studied at Oxford and brought home to Hungary ideas such as the separation of church and state; a democratic ecclesiastical organization; public education in the native language; and piety unmediated by clergy and dogma. Milton's *Areopagitica*, after complimenting the Lords and Commons for refusing to bow shaven heads to popery, says:[24]

> Nor is it for nothing that the grave and frugal Transylvanian sends out yearly from as farre as the mountaneous borders of Russia, and beyond the Hercynian wilderness, not their youth but their stay'd men, to learn our language and our theological arts.

The Unitarians of Transylvania were on the brink of extinction under the despotic centralist drive of the Hapsburg rulers, and documents of the period record their unremittent hardship and suffering. After being occupied for a century and a half by the Unitarians, the great church in Kolozsvár was taken away by the military in 1716. Soldiers were billeted in the homes of prominent Unitarians. Ministers were evicted from their homes, endowment property and the church press were confiscated. Unitarian students were scattered and forced into Jesuit schools. During the reign of Maria Theresa, Unitarian students could not study in Protestant universities abroad. These were the catacomb years. But the congregation persevered and through sheer will and faith it survived. The Unitarian community in Farkas's hometown, centered around the church and the college, was a small beacon of light in the long feudal night. As a student, Farkas complained of the "Boeotian backwardness"[25] of his district. In the 1790s, the city's 10,660 inhabitants included only about 850 Unitarians. Yet the closely knit congregation made inordinate sacrifices to maintain its church and school, both of which were community-supported and self-administered. Dating from the 1560s, the school first modeled its curriculum on the German Lutheran schools and later on Holland's theological schools. Otherwise there were few schools in Transylvania, and they generally offered little education. The Unitarian College, in the eighteenth century, offered courses in jurisprudence, geography, philosophy of metaphysics (called "senior philosophy"), experimental physics, mathematics, Hebrew, Greek, and Latin. Most important, it

14   taught biblical criticism, which the Unitarian students picked up during their studies at Jena and Göttingen. Farkas thus had learned the Bible by heart when he was only twelve years old.

During the early nineteenth century, the Hungarian Unitarians reestablished the links with the English Unitarians that were severed by Hapsburg despotism. The curriculum then began to reflect the influence of Parker, Priestley, and Channing. János Kriza (1811–1875) transmitted Channing's ideas to Hungary. He was a prominent folklorist and a close friend of Farkas. Under Francis II, whose reign as emperor of Austria (1804–1835) spans Farkas's career, the Unitarians were declared equal before the law, the seizure of church property was prohibited, and the freedom of an uncensored press was restored to them. But the inquisitorial policies of the past left deep scars in Farkas's intellectual outlook. On top of the religious persecution, Transylvania was swept with plagues and famine during the eighteenth century. The Unitarian College register for July and August 1710 recorded the burial of 75 to 82 plague victims daily and the church decided against tolling the bells, to avoid panic. Only pallbearers were allowed beyond the city gate and everyone else was confined to the city. On July 12, 1710, in the city alone, 105 people died from the plague and during the year Unitarian students attended 360 funerals. The plague returned in 1712 and students were confined to their classrooms; food was hoisted to their windows twice a day. In August the student body was moved to Házsongárd. The military command erected a gallows at the city gate of Kolozsvár, posted with the stern warning:

> Traveler, entering Kolozsvár
> You approach plague and death
> Unless you wish to swing from this gallows
> Heed our advice: reflect and retreat.

The citizens recovered from the plague only to face the famine of 1717, in which the poor subsisted on boiled tree-buds. The plague returned again in 1719 and Farkas's home district was hard hit. Some villages were reduced to a few dazed survivors after the plague took its toll. The dead were buried in trenches, infested houses were barricaded with thorn bushes, and students roamed the streets begging for food. One contemporary wrote: "This generation's tears could not be described either by Cicero's pen nor conveyed by the oratory of Demosthenes."[26] The plague- and famine-swept district became a wasteland, but this was hardly a new experience. The great educator, Comenius, who taught in a Hungarian college between 1650 and 1654, in his memoir dedicated to the prince of Transylvania, described the wretchedness of the people devastated by plagues and famine (*Abundamus mendicis et squalore*). Comenius noted: "Hungary is a country which devours its own inhabitants . . ."[27]

The will to survive obviously taxed the energy of the hardy Unitarian community. They neglected their school. The front wall sagged from neglect and "frogs could easily jump through the windows." The students themselves cast bricks, and built four classrooms in 1765. Farkas himself witnessed a famine in his hometown in 1817. He observed students huddling vacant-eyed, spectral figures in rags, under gate arches begging for food. At night the moan of the dying filled the streets. In the mornings the survivors stumbled over corpses, and during the day the bells tolled as the city buried its dead in a common grave, without religious services. One contemporary wrote of the famine-gripped city: "I saw a dead mother by the roadside. Her child crawled over her breast, grinning, trying to knead some nourishing milk."[28] The famine and plague had an impact on Farkas which explains why he was so taken in America by public education, and the equality of condition that prevailed there. As a student, he was exposed to the Enlightenment idea that happiness and progress are inherent rights of man. He believed that aristocratic privileges, clerical wealth, the jarring contrast of riches and famine were unreal and contrary to the law of nature. At the same time, as the delayed impact of the French Revolution reached remote Transylvania, linguistic nationalism began to surface and also left a strong impression on Farkas. During the revolutionary years, the students sang Jacobin songs in Latin.

> Ah, ibit hoc, ibit hoc, ibit hoc
> Aristocratae vobiscum ad laternam!
> Ah, ibit hoc, ibit hoc, ibit hoc!
> Aristocratae, vos pendebitis!

But in 1800, Unitarian College students signed a petition requesting that they be allowed to sing and play Hungarian music on weekends. The director of the college was reprimanded by the city fathers for allowing the students to read French radical literature, in particular Helvétius's *La Vrai du système de la nature*—its materialism was thought to poison mind and soul. Kolozsvár was greatly affected by the radical currents of the French Revolution. The Gubernium warned the city council in 1794 against the "unknown wanderers," itinerant Jacobins who spread revolutionary ideas among the people. Some French prisoners, brought to Transylvania, spread the Jacobin heresies among the people of Kolozsvár. The governor informed the mayor that "many officers among the prisoners have distributed buttons among the people on which the daring and insolent French symbol of Freedom is illustrated by the words *Liberté et Egalité.*"[29]

A Jacobin pamphlet and the work of Helvétius were secretly translated and distributed among students. The translator unknown to the officials was József Gedö (1778–1855), a student at the Unitarian College (1791–1798) and a lifelong friend of Farkas. Gedö and Farkas were devoted bibliophiles who later turned over their private libraries to the Unitarian College. Its holdings of sixteenth- and seventeenth-century first editions of Unitarian writers, including rare medieval works, made it a unique depository of Protestant literature. Unfortunately the Unitarian church was taken by the military, and many rare books were carted away and burned. "For three days the precious books and MS collection burned and

16   smoked."[30] That painful memory haunted Farkas and was reflected in his comments on American public libraries which noted enviously the love of books among Americans, rich and poor alike.

Farkas's love of books paralleled Machiavelli's. Like the Florentine secretary, Farkas escaped from his daily cares into the soothing world of books. Farkas, when beset by illness and poverty, loved to retire into the ancient court of ancient men. In collecting, lending, and buying books, Farkas forgot the world, his worries, troubles, and poverty. He gave himself entirely to books. No wonder that he kept a lifelong friendship with Gedö, who amassed a private library of 5,300 volumes, while Farkas's personal library consisted of only 1525. The collection of a private library in those days when books were rare, and when even book publishers kept on their shelves more "mugs of red and white grease"[31] than books, indicates that the collectors had more than ordinary antiquarian interests. Farkas undoubtedly believed that books collected, read, and shared were a means to national rebirth and public education. Farkas and Gedö alike valued books not because of their worth as first editions but because books imprisoned living intellects—reading released those intellects and put them to work. Farkas was called the "second Franklin"[32] in reference to his ceaseless civic activities. He set up reading rooms, organized library loans, solicited funds for a fencing school, and was a charter member of the first savings and loan association in Hungary.[33] He also sought to disseminate useful knowledge by creating the Transylvanian museum, and was a moving force behind the publication of the *Nép Lap* (People's Journal) and the *Nép Ujság* (People's Newspaper). Both were devoted to civic education, the spread of rational ideas, and the unveiling of superstition and bigotry. There was virtually no end to his civic undertakings. Like Franklin, who returned from Italy not with a glowing description of Michelangelo's *Pietà* but with a recipe for Parmesan cheese, Farkas translated German menus into Hungarian and tried to convince German restaurant owners in Kolozsvár to use them. He affixed a copy of *The Times* to the door of a printer's shop to demonstrate the latest printing techniques. Influenced by Saint-Simon, he tried to convince a hotel owner to introduce an English-style cab service so that the social classes, in riding together, would learn a sense of equality. Farkas was a century ahead of his time in feudal Hungary, and hence a tragic figure.

To Farkas nothing was too small or insignificant when it served a civic purpose. Civic knowledge, and its widest possible dissemination, was his overriding ambition. He shared Milton's view that "he who destroys a good Booke, kills reason itself, kills the Image of God . . . . Many a man lives a burden to the Earth; but a good booke is the pretious life-blood of a master spirit . . ."[34] Farkas once wrote that he would give half of an estate for a good book. In Paris he witnessed the February uprising when an angry mob stormed Notre Dame and, with the cry "A bas l'Archevêque!," broke into the library. "It contained about 50,000 old books," wrote Farkas, "and rare ecclesiastical works. They were ripped apart and what the mob could not destroy was heaved through the windows and mutilated in the street, and then cast into the Seine."[35] Farkas watched the carnage with infinite sorrow.

Although he was rather shy, if not reclusive, Farkas shared his love of books and deep interest in literature with his friend Gedö. They were both devoted republicans. While in college Gedö was inordinately proud of his nickname, "Citoyen Gedö." Similarly, Farkas believed that to be a citizen was man's highest accomplishment as *zoon politikon*, or political animal. Because he was a homeless wanderer who wished to be a citizen of a republican society, Farkas especially understood Rousseau's pride in being a citizen of Geneva, even though the city fathers were not exactly enamored of their prodigal son. When Farkas landed in America, he saw only citizens. He wrote from Kolozsvár, which played a role in Transylvania somewhat similar to that of Geneva in Switzerland, to inform a friend:[36]

> You ask me how I am doing? Think of a man who, after many fugitive years labors for years to build a house only to find, upon returning from a walk, it is burned to the ground. And then he resumes his homeless exile.

Farkas's homelessness was personal and political. He craved the citizen's surroundings, but in Hungary there were only privileged aristocrats and impoverished peasants living in a kind of Hegelian master-slave relationship. There was no middle class except for a few reform-minded individuals like Farkas. Unlike the English, the Hungarian aristocracy never developed an independent power base against the monarchy. Actually the Hapsburg rulers reduced Hungarian aristocrats to courtiers. Farkas, despite his meager income, was tirelessly and selflessly pursuing civic activities; Hungarian aristocrats squandered fortunes in Vienna, millions on castles and summer festivals, all the while convinced that it was their "historical" privilege not to improve the public weal.

Some Hungarian aristocrats had personal libraries stacked with books by Voltaire and Rousseau. Some, like Count János Fekete, corresponded with Voltaire. The Sage of Ferney had a high opinion of Count Fekete's poems and encouraged him to send more; they arrived packed in cases of Tokay wine. But the Hungarian nobility regarded people as "simpleminded but useful bees." Whig aristocrats were nation builders, interested in commerce and trade and many were blessed with genius and vision. In contrast, the vast majority of Hungarian aristocrats were indolent, immersed in luxury, lethargic and cold toward public life. They read Rousseau merely to affirm that the historical nobility embodied the general will according to his theory of the social contract. The leading Hungarian reformist-aristocrat, Count István Széchenyi, suggested that the claim was like asking the "wolf to protect the lamb."[37]

The Hungarian nobility nonetheless typified the general will in two respects. The nobility codetermined power and right and by definition could not err. Thus, since their authority was proclaimed beyond good and

18   evil, the Hungarian nobility embodied the general will. Second, Rousseau's notion of the general will implied, at its sinister worst, an orgiastic fraternity for which the Hungarian nobility was renowned. If Rousseau's general will was an ideal norm, which combined the merits of Hobbesian political realism with a Lockean government by consent, then the general will was a reality in aristocratic Hungary. In fact, the nobility almost constituted a majority. On a comparative basis, the nobility in Hungary was the largest, per capita, in Europe. In 1789, France had 26,000 noble families; Hungary, 75,000. In 1840, the population was 11.4 million, of which 0.5 million were nobles, 1 noble per 22 commoners. In Austria the ratio was 1 to 350.[38]

After traveling in Hungary in the mid 1830s, John Paget left an unforgettable picture of the feudal conditions that prevailed. Paget (1808–1892), educated at the Unitarian Manchester College at York, married Baron Miklós Wesselényi's sister and settled in Transylvania to promote scientific agriculture. He endowed an English chair at the Unitarian College in Kolozsvár in memory of his son.[39] His firsthand knowledge of the Hungarian nobility led Paget to note that it was completely denationalized. "They know," he wrote, "almost any language of Europe better than their native one."[40] In the Diet the Hungarian nobility clamored for privileges and at home they were content to smoke their pipes and "flog their peasants to prepare them for the great change."[41] The Catholic prelates and princes of the church were even worse offenders. These seigneurs of the soul enjoyed more privileges than the seigneurs of the soil. Voltaire rightly scorned the Hungarian nation as a *regnum Marianum*. The Catholic church in Hungary was not in the state, the state was in the church. Next to the nobility, Catholic priests were the most numerous estate. According to John Paget, there was one priest for every five hundred peasants. They drew good salaries, collected fees for sacraments and burials, and possessed thirty to forty acres of land, while millions of peasants had only God's acre.

In theory the spiritual and temporal orders composed the Hungarian state. In reality the most important political, military, and feudal customs were stamped with the seal of the Catholic church. Little wonder that Herder, a passionate Protestant, regarded Hungary as a model of a degenerate polity under whose aristocratic-ecclesiastical arches there was little light of reason. "The whole constitution of Hungary," wrote Herder, "the relations and condition of its inhabitants . . . all floated on the ocean of the church; the episcopal power formed the starboard side of the vessel, the feudal system, the larboard, the king, or the emperor, served as a sail; and the pope stood at the helm."[42] When Farkas visited the Harmonites in Ohio, he was particularly taken by George Rapp, whose *Thoughts on the Destiny of Man* was influenced by the writings of Herder.[43] Herder had an impressive capacity for *Einfühlung*, or empathy, released by romanticism.

Farkas himself borrowed Herder's idea that all cultures and nations are equal in the eyes of God. This excited Central European intellectuals suffering under the Germanizing drive of the Hapsburgs, and particularly Farkas, since he was supercharged with love of country. Herder stressed linguistic identity, through which the national genius unfolds and reaches its climax. Herder's emphasis received a sympathetic hearing from Farkas. Although a national and linguistic identity can be disrupted by foreign rule, it is seldom eradicated from the hearts of the people, and nationalism was emerging in Hungary in the 1830s. To illustrate, when the holy crown of St. Stephen was returned to Hungary, the chief justice asked in German for the key to the crown box. A Hungarian aristocrat turned to him, gravely, "Your Excellency, it is not a German crown, it doesn't understand German. Try Hungarian and it will open."[44]

Farkas's national consciousness was pronounced. Because of their origin, the Székels were pressed into the border militia under Austrian officers to patrol the northeastern frontier of the empire facing the Ottomans. Every Székel male had to serve in the border guard. Only by becoming priests, professors, or schoolmasters could Székels be exempted from duty in the military frontier force. By custom the oldest son in the family succeeded the father in military service. A Job-like cry issued from Farkas as he recalled the hated custom: "Destiny made me to be born in this circumstance. But why me with such a temperament? Oh, but who can stand before the wheel of destiny and complain to the Creator? My brother died in 1811 and it was my turn . . ."[45] Farkas, however, secured a military release and continued his studies, even though he could have been called to arms at any moment. The uncertainty weighed on him and the border guard, set up by Maria Theresa in 1764, created havoc with teachers and students in his native city. In 1800, Székel students were allowed to attend classes only if they possessed a passport from their regiment. In principle the Székels served for life, but after twenty years they could be discharged.

The border units drew a cordon around Hungary's Turkish frontier. In peacetime about forty thousand men were on duty along eight hundred miles of frontier, and in war the number swelled to two hundred thousand. Each family head who served in the guard received thirty to forty acres of land in the frontier district, and each family had to furnish and maintain, depending on its size, one or more men-at-arms. The Farkas family was required to equip one male, mounted, for the border guard. When not at war, the border guard families repaired roads and bridges, drained swamps, fixed public buildings, and, in some areas, served as educators. Paget estimated that about seventy-eight hundred of the nine thousand children on the Turkish frontier, between the ages of seven and twelve, were educated in the special schools there. The Székels resented German instruction.

Many Székels refused to serve in the border guard unless commanded by native officers. But Vienna, for obvious reasons, put Austrian officers in charge who acted as press-gangs in the Székel villages. In 1764, many

20   Székels fled to the mountains from an approaching press-gang. The government evacuated a village in the middle of winter, hoping that the starving families would force the fugitive males back to their frontier duties. They refused and instead drifted back to their villages. Thereupon Austrian troups surrounded a village during the night and opened cannon fire on the sleeping villagers. In the ensuing bloodbath, two hundred Székels lost their lives, and more than a thousand were wounded. The commander explained that bloodletting restores discipline in the army as well as in medicine. After the massacre many Székel families escaped into Moldavia to avoid enlisting in the frontier guard. The Székel refugees in Moldavia built villages called Godhelp and Welcome, which became monuments to the folly of unenlightened man.

This background informed and influenced the commentaries Farkas made on military issues in America. Even in the France of Napoleon, Farkas noted that the system of conscription was civilized. He held that military service is a patriotic duty and that men should not be driven to it by "ruse and whip." After observing the lottery for military draft in Paris, Farkas wrote[46] bitingly that in Hungary they pounced upon a youth

> like robbers, remove[d] him from the family, and drag[ged] him by chains and ropes to defend the country with honor. He faces·an unknown future, and can perhaps never escape his destiny where he is under the whim and rod of foreign speaking and thinking officers. How could the Hungarian soldier love his fate! How can he serve the country he does not know? Can he sacrifice his life and blood for a country he is not part of and where he has no rights? He despairs and despises the military.

In a letter to Ferenc Kazinczy (1759–1831), the Hungarian counterpart of Noah Webster, Farkas wrote: "I am a conscript of Mars to whom the Muses close their eye."[47] Farkas's soul belonged to the Muses, not Mars, and yet he memorized military manuals. "At twenty Schiller," he wrote in the same letter, "has accomplished much, I have done nothing. The realization of it drives me to despair."[48] Rather than face the possibility of lifelong border guard duty, he decided to make a virtue of necessity and applied for admission to the Hungarian Noble Bodyguard in Vienna.

In a letter accompanying the application Farkas said, although only twenty, "I pledged my life to Hungarian literature." He reiterated his sad destiny of not being born "free," meaning of course the ever-present possibility of being called for border duty. After stating his fluency in German, French, and Latin and why he wanted to join the Hungarian Noble Bodyguard, he added:[49]

> The young Cato's talents would have been lost if he didn't meet Sarpedon in Caesar's kitchen who showed him the career to follow. I do not wish to compare myself to Cato, but I know that many souls can accomplish good and useful things if given space and field to express themselves.

In a separate letter, addressed to His Excellency the Administrator, Farkas made a poignant point: "Your Excellency . . . will recall that Greece and Rome didn't close the road to their public spirited youth whom they judged worthy, which saved them for long from decline."[50] The Farkas pledge to literature was no doubt influenced by György Bessenyei (1747–1811), a Hungarian nobleman who resigned his guard commission to devote himself to literature. In Vienna, Bessenyei was exposed to the ideas of the French Enlightenment, which influenced his literary writings. Farkas no doubt hoped that he too could serve the Muses and Mars simultaneously and, like Bessenyei, make the most of it. By joining the Noble Bodyguard, Farkas sought to escape the hated military frontier service—his "unfreedom." His stoic demeanor broke down when he wrote about his "unfreedom":[51]

> Destiny made me a soldier-boy! I sigh with Don Carlos: why me among the millions? I feel deeply what it means not being born free. It keeps me back and dashes my plans at my feet. The future is closed, I cannot transcend it because I am a Unitarian, and a poor, penniless Székel conscript. My hopes for the Muses are soul-destroying.

The theater and literature claimed Farkas early. The dour, rather puritanical Unitarian College students were strictly forbidden to attend city-theater or to read Hungarian plays. But students are nonconformists everywhere. Even St. Augustine sowed his wild oats and let the "briers of unclean desires" grow rank over his head under the burning African sun. Augustine found school to be a dreadful bore and tried to make life miserable for his teachers. Young Augustine went to plays, tossed dice on the hot pavement, and walked "the streets of Babylon" at night, flesh bent on pleasure while his soul begged, "Give me chastity and continency, only not yet."[52] Augustine wrote the confession of all nineteen-year-olds on his nineteenth birthday: "I loved not as yet, yet I loved to love ... I searched about for something to love, in love with loving, and hating security, and a way not beset with snares."[53]

Farkas was no different, and although he was forbidden to attend city-theater, he sneaked out from the college and caught stage fever. He became acquainted with a stage director and tried a couple of Schiller roles on stage. The rector of the college spotted him on stage and mercilessly hauled him off in costume and paint to prison. Farkas admitted that Schiller transported him to a "different world." Farkas was attracted to the theater by the Hungarian language, and the director asked Farkas to translate Shakespeare's *Julius Caesar*—clearly an impossible task for a young student. The assignment meant locating an English copy of *Julius Caesar*. Farkas then sought out Gábor Döbrentei, the editor of *Transylvania Museum*, a literary journal. The friendship which developed had semitragic consequences for Farkas.

Döbrentei was a founding member of the Hungarian Academy (1828), chartered for the "cultivation and development" of national language. The leader of the linguistic renaissance in Hungary, Ferenc Kazinczy, conceived national language to be a weapon against despotism and feudal privilege. Kazinczy believed that the translation of Voltaire, Rousseau, and other philosophers would inject an enlightened culture and ideas into Hungary. His manifesto, published in *Orpheus*, the first Hungarian literary

22   journal, read: "I made resolute efforts to tear the bloody dagger out of the hand of superstition and unmask its horrifying face."[54] The Hungarian Enlightenment lived on borrowed ideas, and so did the fledgling national literature. Farkas wrote to Gedö in 1828:[55]

> Let's admit honestly that our literary output is only mawkish, a sweet flattering of a nation whose self-assured fledgling attempts only appeal to us the enthusiasts! And this literary constitutional struggle enlisted our passion and support. But can our journalistic literature and the current of time appeal to others?

The quest for national identity and collective imagination through literature and re-creation of the inherited language, spearheaded by Kazinczy, paralleled the role of Noah Webster in America. The daring venture in making the American republic was followed by a process of vocabulary making. Political creation was accompanied by the creation of new words and expressions in the American common speech. Efforts of men like Noah Webster gave Americans the courage to break free from their cultural colonialism and assert their identity and independence in spelling and pronunciation. In America the political release from colonialism was accompanied by a cultural release too. Daniel Boorstin noted that linguistic legislation has a counterpart in "an American passion for a written constitution and for almost every other kind of legislation."[56] Farkas talked about the "literary constitutional" struggle which enlisted his enthusiasm. After 1776, linguistic nationalism began to express the American quest for a national identity. The idea of a single "proper" speech, which any person can learn and use, carries an unmistakable political message—that one justice, law and fairness in politics, should be learned and followed by all. Linguistic nationalism, in America and in Hungary, coded political reform in an age stamped by eclectic, personalized privileges and "influence." The code was used by the crown and ministers in England, and later in Vienna, to manage politics in their colonial spheres. In Hungary the linguistic nationalist memorized the political axiom of David Hume that force is always on the side of the governed:[57]

> The governors have nothing to support them but opinion. It is, therefore, on opinion only that government is founded, and this maxim extends to the most despotic and most military governments as well as to the most free and most popular.

Kazinczy knew that by changing the climate of opinion through a cultural renaissance, he would sap the support of despotic power. Thus he rejoiced when he found a talented devotee and eagerly enlisted Farkas in the cause. When his application to join the Noble Bodyguard was turned down, Farkas was reduced to a sense of nothingness. Döbrentei wrote to Kazinczy: "Sándor Farkas graduated from the Unitarian College last June. He is a Székel conscript from Háromszék county and must join his regiment. Write him, and include my letter, so he can rejoice."[58] Döbrentei knew Kazinczy's weak spot and he told him: "Love him [Farkas] because he

is aflame with you." Kazinczy eagerly hailed his newly discovered
admirer:[59]

> My esteemed friend, Döbrentei, informed me of your letter concerning me.
> Since you love not my person but love me because of my endeavors, and because
> what our esteemed and influential friend in Transylvania wrote about your
> *Decius* and *Janus*, and because your written lines reveal and sketch a man and
> writer, I am delighted by our acquaintance and will boast to friends about you.
> Esteemed youth, you understand what so many good heads, and the ignorant do
> not comprehend: what our language will gain by my resolute efforts...

Farkas was metamorphosed just as all aspirants of the Muses would be
in receiving a letter from a literary deity. Dazed by his transformation, he
wrote to Kazinczy:[60]

> I received your letter of October 8 [1815], the auspicious beginning of my life.
> Each day I ask myself, am I not dreaming? I feel my pulse... if my soul is not
> intoxicated by the much hoped for surprise.

He was intoxicated; after all, Kazinczy was the acknowledged literary
figure of the reform era. One can hardly blame young Farkas for feeling like
a "fugitive in the burning sands of Asia, prostrate" before the prophet. But
more was still to come; Farkas's life was drawn taut like a bow ready to snap
or to overshoot the mark. Kazinczy's next letter was heady:[61]

> My esteemed friend, your lips were inspired by God, your language beautiful,
> your imagination soaring on flaming wings. Start creating, give us original
> pieces...

He offered spiritual kinship yet he had never laid eyes on Farkas. "You are
mine and I am yours—we are one." Kazinczy's panegyric peaked in his
poem dedicated to Farkas:[62]

> With splendid run you begin your career
> On the Olympian field the dense
> Multitude shouts Paean to the great Darer...

Kazinczy also praised his new discovery in literary circles. He wrote to
Miklós Wesselényi: "If our nation could only have ten like him, our
literature would shine. You will see, my friend, what will become of him in
a decade. I expect everything from him."[63] Farkas was hardly twenty-one
and had yet to publish a single line, but he was already proclaimed as the
remaining hope of Hungarian literature. So he tried to live up to his
reputation by ransacking libraries for Lessing's works, *Letters on Modern
Literature* and *Hamburg Dramatic Journal*, to learn how to "start creating."
Lessing's works, using Aristotle's *Poetics*, offered guidance in how to make a
creative work easier, surer, and finer.[64]

These premature garlands began to feel like a crown of thorns to Farkas
and his pragmatic self surfaced in a letter to Kazinczy in 1819: "Your praise
would make me vain if I did not know my insignificance.... It is a burden
to be esteemed higher than what we really are."[65] Farkas's integrity,
humility, and religious resources are his most enduring qualities. The
searing experience imbued him with a taste for literature, which never left

24   him. If he was uncreative at least he felt he could translate. He translated Goethe's *Sorrows of Young Werther* (1818), Schiller's *Don Carlos* (1819), and Madame de Staël's *Corinne* (1821). During the day he was an ordinary secretary in the Gubernium, and at night he was transported to the world of Goethe and Schiller. Somehow he also found time to complete his legal studies at the Royal Lyceum in Kolozsvár. He took his oath as a jurist in November 1816, and remained a bureaucrat out of necessity. He recalled his nineteen years of treadmill office life:[66]

> I entered the 19th year of my Chancellery career. During my school years, as I contemplated my future alternatives, it never entered my head that I would become a dicast. In jest I took an oath of office lest I bum around nameless in Kolozsvár. The jest became my destiny.
>
> I found a great difference between 1816, when the graduate enters the world, and the present. The era is full of indolence, luxury, narcissistic immersion in vanity, complete indifference and coldness toward the public good. Effeminate sentimentalism, rowdy bravado, aristocratic haughtiness, glory in piling up debts, famine among the poor, conspicuous waste at the table of the great, sophistry gleaned from pulp literature, sparkling conver- sationalism, small gossip, ridicule of nationalities, and German spoken by those who wished to appear cultured, and eternal do-nothingness. This is the hallmark of the era. In such period and amid these circumstances, I left school, became a jurist in 1816 and came to Kolozsvár in 1817. Because of my contact with the Wesselényi family, I was introduced to the leading families and the pace-setting youth. Possessing a middle-sized estate, and an appealing sophistry called education, I had opportunity to observe the seductive play of time. But slowly the school nourished ideals began to fade. And the dreamer of great deeds, a heart burning for the nation, and embracing mankind has opened itself to vanities. Indolence replaced the love of reading, flirting with women, carousing with friends, city chronicles and office gossip, vanity and rank pleasures have preoccupied me. I drifted in the world and imperceptibly turned into a dicast.
>
> Sometimes my better genius has awakened. When it demanded an account, I recoiled from my nothingness. I felt lost unless I changed my situation. This demanded great decision. Tired and soul-sick as I was of my job and much as I hated the riff-raff company, the female intrigue tied me down. Finally in 1821 I broke the circle and left for Vienna to study military and Austrian law in order to start a new career. With iron discipline I sweated and struggled. Realizing my mistake that this profession would turn me into a programmed machine of absolutism, still I was ashamed to step back. Pressed toward my goal even though daily I swallowed hard, and suffered the insults of the riff-raff for my country just because I was a Hungarian. Finally, the bitter cup filled to the rim. I lost my temper and turned on my tormentors who banished me abjectly. My long term plans went up in smoke and, once more, I became a Chancellerist, glued down forever.
>
> In the morning I reflected on my 18 years career, my present low status, the ever-worsening future, declining health, advancing age, sacrificed wealth, the wilted flower of imagination and enthusiasm, and the soul's sagging power— and all this I sacrificed for the Chancellery. Just thinking about it, despite my will, I gritted my teeth in desperation. Called myself a fool, and would have cursed had I not been ashamed before my Self.
>
> Self-tortured, I tried to rationalize my restlessness. I am aware of Horace's adage that every man is dissatisfied with his fate. I know it and do not dispute

him. I too preach this soothing science to others. But can I help it if this nice philosophy is a mere palliative cure of my sickness?

There was a time in my career when, as a matter of conscience, I was punctual, honest, and diligent. In those years I lived for the office, suppressing my true inclination and better passions. What did I gain? It awakened my colleagues' secret envy and invited their calumny. Finally I realized that all diligence and attempt are futile without higher favors. But higher favors are bought at the expense of character. So I hunted favors, and blush sitting here recalling how I demeaned myself for bread and glory. Bowed to people my soul could not respect. Approved plans I considered harmful, kept silent the mistakes of others, and overlooked their profiteering. For that I will never forgive myself, I helped to smear those they smeared, and pretended to flatter their vanity. Then they accepted me as useful, diligent, and an honest man.

In the end I despised myself for playing the role. Then I took off the mask, resolved to be overlooked and poor rather than hate myself. Made a vow that, trusting only my judgement, I will do the right things without begging the favor of others. I do my office duties with dispirited, routine boredom, but honestly and with conscience. Now they treat me as useless, an eccentric political dreamer whose head is crammed with American nonsense, a secret cohort with liberals, despiser of office, and a suspicious character. In short, they dislike me. I do not know how long it will last, but I feel very depressed.

This revealing confession sketches Farkas's duality—he was both a man and a social person—and both constantly dueled in him. Farkas's life exemplified what Pascal once called "the internal warfare of man." In addition to his internal conflict, Farkas was inclined toward introspection, and his frail health caused him to be unduly preoccupied with his mortality. His journal entries verify his discordant inner life, and they also hint of a kind of Kafkaesque preoccupation with the invisible yet truly evil forces in Metternich's empire. His diary suggests abnormal psychological visitations arising from his nearly simultaneous persecution and summons to secret power—as though he was conducted through a secret passage to the seat of judgment. Yet his contemporaries confirm that Farkas had a brilliant mind. His protean personality, flights of spiritual inwardness, frequent surfacings in the marketplace, his feverish civic activities were more a response to the age he lived in than the product of his intellect. He was charged with a personal outrage against the ascriptive values of society ruled by nobles and priests. Like Rousseau, Farkas could plunge into complete emotional rejection of society. His whole being was an anguished cry: "I am myself, myself alone."

The duality of Farkas, at once sick from the privileges of the age and yet seeking to relieve man's estate, created a tenseness of intellect and style. He was born of romanticism, and his writing is colored by the influence of Goethe and Rousseau. Although the word "romanticism" refers to any number of things, it has two primary referents: first, a general and permanent characteristic of mind, art, and personality found in all periods and in all cultures; and second, a specific historical movement in the early nineteenth century. Our concern is only with the second of these two meanings. Farkas was under the dominant influence of historical romanti-

26   cism, characterized by the celebration of emotions, feelings, and moods that are in opposition to reason, intellect, and order. Hegel associated romanticism with a slavish subservience to the senses. It would be more accurate to say that the Romantics sought to reproduce and transcribe the sensations proper to existence. Herein lies the importance of Farkas as representative figure of romanticism. He illuminated and drew attention to a more realistic, or tough-minded, aspect of historical romanticism, whose hero was Faust. In ordinary usage, "Faustian" denotes egotistical and destructive drives. But to the romantic generation of Farkas, Faust typified activity over happiness.

    Faust dies only upon perceiving that his happiness lies in the hope of helping men to build a great dam. Equally important, Faust's last words affirm what the Romantics stood for: a desire for individual liberty within society, and pursuit of intellectual and religious life without superstition or intolerance. Faust symbolizes to the romantic generation that social improvement comes within the bounds of individual freedom—a theme which undergirds Farkas's whole life. In a real sense, historical romanticism is a vehicle and medium for the nineteenth-century desire for political reform. The tough-mindedness of the Romantics to move from fixity of status to a world of change and freedom is expressed by Faust:[67]

> Thus here, by dangers girt, shall glide away
> Of childhood, manhood, age, the vigorous day:
> And such a throng I fain would see—
> Stand on free soil among a free people!

    The Faustian striving for freedom was accompanied by a romantic search for a mind free from superstition, tyranny, and priestcraft. Farkas gravitated toward Madame de Staël, who perceived that the romantic view of life is basically Christian because it combines the infinite value of the individual self in its power and weakness with other free human beings. Farkas's intellectual orientation and reaching out for Goethe and de Staël illustrate that historical romanticism marks a profound revolution in the nineteenth-century European mind. Briefly, romanticism is the redirection of intellect from a static concept of the world to a world that is organic, changing, and progressive. The values of Romantics are change, imperfection, growth, and diversity. The debate between classicism and romanticism, the issue between Tocqueville and Farkas, is really a contrast between two different concepts of reality. To the classical mind, the empirical world—natural and social—has meaning and purpose independent of the perception of the individual. To Tocqueville, there is value and order in the world. Romanticism asserts that value and order emerge from the perception of the self. The classical mind of Tocqueville refused to separate the social role from the self, for a civilized political man must play a social role.

    The romantic Farkas, as is evident from his confessions, strips bare the self or, more accurately, invents the self to establish his sense of identity in the ecclesiastical-feudal world he is alienated from. Hence the loneliness and social alienation of Farkas, or loss of relatedness to the perceived world at large. From this dramatic sense of the self as the source of order and identity flows romanticism's tough-minded realism. The romantic self, particularly the poet whom Channing and Farkas conceived of as the primary and exemplary source of value, redeems the world. The self is its own redeemer and the model for the redemption of mankind. But the romantic self can only redeem this world, which means that privileges, brutality, and social evil must be faced with unblinking realism. The flowers of value are plucked by Farkas not from sunny spots of happiness but in the abyss of sorrow and despair. The preoccupation with sorrow and sadness, symbolized by Goethe's *Werther* and Farkas's confessions, is the romantic recognition that the tinseled and titled world is absurd, unnatural, and ugly. The Romantic's tragic fate is that he has to strive against a world that lacks his concept of order and meaning. In such world, only the self can be recognized and assert its existence in another fellow man. This emphatic affirmation that all men possess a self—defined by Romantics as a basic human desire for order and sense of value—is the basis of romantic social morality. It enabled Farkas to discover value and meaning in Negro slaves, among savage Indians, and in the Gospel-glutted Shakers.

From this perspective and perception of the self, the Romantics reacted to the rational model of the world symbolized by Newton's world machine. With the great impact of Rousseau after 1760, the heart claimed its moral kingdom against the cold empire of reason. A man moved from trust in the Newtonian universe to a period of doubt and despair of any meaning in the universe. Reason itself was suspect:[68]

> If abstract reason only rules the mind
> In sordid selfishness it lives confin'd;
> Moves in one vortex, separate and alone,
> And feels no other interest than his own.

This vaunted reason could neither explain the French Revolution nor say anything moral about the universe working as a clock. A clock reports the now, but it cannot chime the future. To the Romantics the mind cannot voyage forever through the solitary universe of thought—alone. Hence the Romantics turned away from the universe and made their concern man and his soul. There is something profoundly Socratic, then, in the romantic turning from the universe to man and his soul. And turning to man, the romantics also turned to nature. Between the creative mind and nature there is a mutually ennobling interchange of action. Nature helps the sensitive mind, as Wordsworth put it, to "see into the life of things." Standing at Niagara Falls, Farkas felt that nature was a living voice which induced an act of confession. Thus Wordsworth[69] can discern in the moon ... the emblem of a mind

That feeds upon infinity, that broods
Over the dark abyss, intent to hear
Its voices issuing forth to silent light
In one continuous stream . . .

To Farkas the universe and society were alive, pulsing, and active. It was not a perfect clock but something which lived and spoke to man, directly to the creative mind and its senses. To affirm the living universe is to affirm becoming over being. The Romantics conceived of society as an organism striving for perfection under the oppressive layer of civilization. The essential aspect of man and society is what roles and masks conceal. Though man cannot live without masks, nonetheless the vital and essential quality of human experience resides in what the masks hide.

Here we are concerned only with the political implication of Farkas's quest for the hidden self as the datum of order and value. Alfred de Musset associated romanticism and republicanism and thereby implied a common concern for honesty, integrity, and devotion to the pursuit of individual excellence. Farkas perceived in the lineaments of historical romanticism some elements of republicanism, particularly since the Romantics rebelled against privilege. As already indicated, romanticism denotes a shift in European thought. The very language of Romantics, the paradigms they used, indicates a reordering and redefinition of political reality. For one thing, in Rousseau's works the language and thought are inseparable. Herder, the prophet of German romanticism, said that "the thought clings to the expression." Herder's postulate does not imply that political thought is but an exploration of the conceptual and perceptual frameworks used by the Romantics. What Herder and Rousseau convey, and what is manifest in Farkas's private writings, is that the political ideas of the Romantics, or, more accurately, the pattern of ideas about political values, authority, and concept of change, are contingent upon the way the Romantics used language. To Rousseau, the language evinced a "body" of its own. Once more it was Herder who summed it up when he declared: "We live in the world we ourselves create."[70] This makes Herder not only the oracle of Sturm and Drang but a conscious critic of Kant's attempt to compartmentalize human faculties into "reason," "imagination," "intuition," and "will." Farkas accepted Herder's dictum that every nation has a distinct cultural identity which cannot be expressed in Kant's cosmopolitan terms. Like most Romantics, Farkas repudiated the classical effort to impose one common speech, culture, and reason on all Europe. Farkas's pronounced cultural nationalism was incompatible with Kant's distinction between intuited necessity and observed contingencies.

Farkas believed that human experiences, artistic, political, and social, are facets of *Einfühlung*, which implies that personal emotions formalized in language count as much in political life as does cold rationalism. The romantic mode of perception, which strove to bridge the gap between the self and the world, denied the validity of Kant's conviction that there is an order and meaning immanent in the natural universe, even though the understanding cannot reach it and feelings cannot transcribe it. The Romantics categorically denied the validity of the Kantian *Ding-an-sich*, the existence of the thing in itself.

Farkas understood that the emotionally expressive language of Jacksonians, though it might lack what Tocqueville called "the deeper combinations of intellect," reflected the emergence of a pluralistic society based on public opinion. This explains the Jacksonians' dislike of specialized, abstract language, or a philosophically one-sided habit of mind. A democratic society has an addiction to inflated language, which was noted by Tocqueville. The political thought of the romantic period (1760–1832) cannot be separated from its literary expression. To the romantic mind, particularly to Rousseau and Farkas, what is said cannot be divorced from how it is expressed. Rousseau's political theory and style of writing are the triumph of romanticism. As Judith Shklar said: "Political theory was a distinct literary form also, and inherently so. All political theorists must, among other things, be competent rhetoricians.... Political theory meant to be persuasive."[71]

Farkas's literary ambitions and his early disappointment in failing to fulfill the expectations of his mentors are related to these views. Yet his love and appreciation of artistic accomplishments, and their role in shaping national identity, remained firm. He wrote to Gedö:[72]

> I cannot express how pleased I am, my friend, that you retained your love of literature. The passions of life have receded and waned in me, but this one, though silent for long, continues to be the joy of my life. And what joy it is! My prospects, wealth, and health are its victims. Yet I would not wish to live if I lost my literary interest.

Farkas's translations of Goethe, Schiller, and de Staël reflected stages in his elective affinity for creative minds. His translations have never been published, despite the effort of Döbrentei and the promise of the publisher, but they show that Farkas was a master of Hungarian prose. He translated *Werther* and *Corinne* under the influence of romanticism that attained the zenith of its growth about 1830. Whatever its irrational and mystical tendencies, romanticism attempted to build a system of belief dedicated to social progress. Romantics were rebels against stubborn conservatism and employed their talents in passionate appeals for justice and freedom. They proclaimed the holy innocence of moral "I," at once mystical and wandering off into vaporous abstractions and also combating repression in many of its social forms. The Romantics were zealous advocates of the common man's nobility, and tended to associate the coming age of happiness and freedom with republicanism. Even Tocqueville's classically sovereign mind betrayed his personal and emotional involvement in the unfolding drama of democratic civilization—providential in its advance.

Farkas's translations of Goethe and de Staël reveal that these authors spoke to his felt needs to transform the existing world of conventions and privileges into a higher judgment of individual conscience, or, as in his *Journey*, to teach it the republican grammar of politics. Farkas, in rebelling

30   under the feudal yoke, gravitated toward those who were caught in the web of his fate; a sensitive being hurling bitter invectives against social cruelty and seeking redemption in civic activities and suffering. This is evident in his translation of *Corinne*. A Genevese Protestant like Rousseau, Madame de Staël was, in the words of Goncourt, "A *man* of genius." She and Benjamin Constant were the leading European advocates of a representative system. Both held the rights of man to be a divine right of birth. In *Corinne*, de Staël praised ancient Rome and its republican virtues over Christian ones. She dismissed the Basilica of St. Peter as an "ill-built barn," and declared the catacombs beneath the Appian Way to be "tortures of existence" forever banished from the sunlit world.

De Staël's travel novel struck two themes which played a dominant role in Farkas's political thinking. To her, Italy's greatness resided in its language, which, more than statecraft, created the nation. Thus she regarded Tasso, Dante, and Petrarch to be the true statesmen of Italy. Appropriately Machiavelli, the patriotic and passionate admirer of republican Romans, detested the foreign domination of his beloved Italy, and concluded his famous book, *The Prince*, by quoting Petrarch:

Valor against wild rage
Will take up arms, and the combat will be short,
Because ancestral courage
In our Italian hearts is not yet dead.

Farkas, who similarly detested the Hapsburg domination of his beloved Hungary, agreed with de Staël and Machiavelli. At the same time, the linguistic nationalism of Farkas included the Nietzschean notion that when a nation is on a political sickbed—and Hapsburg Hungary was sick—then cultural revival is the quickest and surest cure. This view has no historical relevance in Anglo-Saxon countries, where nationhood and cultural identity are concurrent. William James persistently asked just one question about an idea or institution, "What difference does it make?" What difference, indeed, did it make that in Central Europe, and in Hungary in particular, the bards and writers embodied the missing aspects of politics—centralization and solidarity.

The poets in Hungary were the acknowledged legislators of national identity. The English model of political development contrasted sharply. Despite the Norman conquest and the incursion of the French language, a common language, called English, emerged by the time of Chaucer, though 48 percent of its vocabulary was taken from Latin and French. Consequently by the early fourteenth century, England developed a distinct cultural identity. In dramatic contrast, Latin was the language of politics and administration until the 1840s in Hungary. If those who command the language also wield political power, then power was in the hands of the church and the landed nobility in Hungary. This specifically explains the extraordinary role poets played in shaping the national psyche in that dark period. The poet portrays, he does not analyze: "A poet," said Herder, "is a

creator of a people."[73] Hungarian poets were indeed creators, since the
body politic was often dissolved under successive foreign invasions. The
nation, for all practical purposes, lived in a world created by its poets. Lord
Macaulay, in a brilliant essay on Milton's role in English national life,
wrote: "In proportion as men know more and think more, they look less at
individuals and more at class. They therefore make better theories and
worse poems."[74] Macaulay's penetrating insight summed up the difference
between England's and Hungary's national development. About the latter,
Gyula Illyés, Hungary's great contemporary writer, once remarked that
"poetry preceded politics" in the 1840s.

The English genius is marked by social classes and political theories.
English classes managed a variety of social situations and most knew how to
surrender with grace. Tocqueville noted repeatedly that English history—
and England was Tocqueville's second intellectual home—was distinguished because the British political class maintained contact with the
"other classes." Even Conservatives pictured conservative workingmen in
the inarticulate mass of the English populace just as Michelangelo perceived
David in a block of marble. In contrast, Hungary never developed a middle
class and it is tragically apparent that the people never did anything in
common or forgot anything. Unlike the English, the Hungarian national
character perfected its images but not its political theory. For this reason,
the vocabulary of enlightened English society is philosophical, that of
Hungary is poetical.

Farkas borrowed a second theme from Madame de Staël—religious
freedom. She perceived aesthetic sensitivity and religious feeling to be
complementary, especially in great works of art. That is why the Vatican
enlisted the genius of Michelangelo, Titian, and Rubens. But de Staël and
Farkas preferred the anthropocentric Greek concept of religion to that of
Catholicism. "The Greek religion," wrote de Staël, "was not, like
Christianity, the solace of misery, the wealth of the poor, the future of the
dying: it required glory and triumph; it formed the apotheosis of man."[75]
Farkas believed the Catholic church had lost its credibility, and treated
Catholicism with disdain. The *regnum Hungarium* was a joint product of
miter and crown and it proved to be a barren combination of fraud and
force.

In an extant fragment of his projected history of Transylvania,
Farkas made Matthias Corvinus (1458–1490) a model to dramatize the
political degeneracy of the Hapsburg Empire. Corvinus was truly a
Renaissance figure—a born soldier, first-class administrator, linguist, and
lover of the arts. His private library (Corvina) was famous throughout
Europe. His leadership abilities were characteristic of the fox and the lion.
Corvinus followed Machiavelli's political precepts. Foxlike, he recognized
the traps set by the aristocracy and he frightened the wolves by creating the
Black Army, a dreaded force subservient to his needs. Corvinus's reign was
popular. Like Machiavelli, who said: "I will only say, in conclusion, that it

32 is necessary for a prince to possess the friendship of the people; otherwise he has no recourse in times of adversity,"[76] Corvinus also observed constitutional forms. He encouraged trade and commerce and, most important from Farkas's standpoint, he "elevated into office unknown people with talent." Corvinus surrounded himself with unknown, talented commoners, and thus anticipated Machiavelli's warning:[77]

> He who becomes prince by help of the nobility has greater difficulty in maintaining his power than he who is raised by the populace, for he is surrounded by those who think themselves his equals, and is thus unable to direct or command as he pleases.

Farkas unfortunately never completed his projected history of Transylvania. It was useless as history but it was a trenchant and impressive commentary on society and political power. It demonstrated a critical knowledge of Tacitus and Machiavelli. According to Farkas, Corvinus's reign manifested the first glimmer of reason outside of musty monasteries. Under Corvinus, justice reached and swayed everyone in the realm. In contrast, the despotic rule of Francis II denied the peasants an identity with the country. It belonged to seigneurs and the land was plowed by peasants on corvée assignment; instead of justice, the peasant suffered rod and dungeon. Farkas blamed the Hapsburgs for the religious wars which squandered national resources on persecution and hatred.

The theme was revised during his visit to Canada, with its indelible imprint of the Catholic church and vestigal feudalism. After traveling through the countryside outside Saint Johns, he wrote:

> The monotony of travel is not relieved by settlements, orchards, gardens, or the variety of roadside buildings of prosperous farmers. Only plowed fields, divided by furrows, meet the horizon. The peasants, clad in coarse, homespun garments, work in groups. Their very appearance, submissive greetings, vacant stare, and listless movement indicates that they are engaged in corvée work."

After observing the pattern of emigration in Canada, Farkas concluded: "Most immigrant settlers prefer Upper Canada, where feudalism is absent and where the settler can claim his purchased land as his private property." Lower Canada invoked his Protestant animus against the Catholic church and the clergy's mystical hold over the populace. He wrote:[78]

> It is undeniable...that original Christian religion progressively assumes a mystical direction under the exclusive care of the clergy who wrap it in cunning, ignorance, and remove it from the human condition.... Natural rights become a double-edged weapon; to suppress popular liberties, disrupt family tranquility, and cunningly fish away middle class property, and that of the nation. This proves that religion, originally woven from the loveliest flowers of Greek and Roman mythologies, and the wise principles of classical moral philosophy, is twisted. It no longer imparts happiness because it is an incomprehensible mystery peddled by a sect.

Farkas viewed the Reformation as a response to the people's weariness at being other-directed in their worship of God. Just as Rousseau's gospel of the "feeling heart" and sentiments of sociability are a response to the limitations of reason and scientific humanism in the Age of Reason, Luther's religious primitivism and bibliocracy breached the walls of Christianity. Luther's battle cries *sola Scriptura* and *sola fide* leveled the "walls" that stood between the believer and God. The radical egalitarianism implicit in the doctrine of "by faith alone" is also a claim that a community can function without a hierarchy and become an assembly of one faith. The political element in Protestantism that appealed to Farkas was its anti-authoritarian religious thought. Luther's vocabulary was colored by an accusatory imagery. He denounced the practices of priest as oppressive *(tyrannicum)* because they denied the believer's right *(ius)* to full participation. He attacked the papacy as a Roman dictatorship *(Romana tyrannis)*, to which good Christians ought to refuse consent *(nec consentiamus)*. [79] All this suggests that Farkas, in rebelling against dogmatic Catholicism, wanted to return to the unglossed wisdom of the Scriptures. This simplistic imperative, the uninhibited and unmediated directness with God, was destructive in a society based on hierarchy. Farkas categorically rejected monarchy and church hierarchy. He wanted to strip Christianity of its mystical and ritualistic aspects and a creed contingent on cloister mentalities. "The human mind," wrote Farkas, "could not comprehend why the pleasure of the flesh, and the earthly things should be rejected with the sour, cloister mentality."[80]

According to Farkas, religion authenticated by the Gospel alone gave peace to the soul and flight to reason. He traced the Protestant revolt as a sequel to the "unswaddled human soul" nursed on natural law. To him, the Protestant spoke a new language—the democratic language of the Gospel—and he singled out the Renaissance and Reformation as two solvents of the traditional Christian world. They were they terminal points of ecclesiastical authority, and marked the emancipation of the individual. The Renaissance detheologized politics, while Protestant reformers de-politicized religion. Each side enhanced the cause of national particularism that preoccupied Farkas. To Farkas, the Renaissance and Reformation marked a "rebirth" of literature and piety. As a linguistic nationalist, he particularly emphasized reading the Bible in Hungarian so that believers could communicate with the Creator in the "mother tongue." The translation of the Bible into his native language was to Farkas a meeting of the people and their history. *Historia vitae magistra.*

Influenced by Rousseau, Farkas was conscious of the emotional and psychological needs of the people. All of his private writings reveal a suppressed anger against aristocratic epistemology—the notion that truth and knowledge are the inborn gifts of a few. He advanced instead the democratic concept that "simple faith" in religion and "opinion" in republican democracy were meaningful alternatives either to the metaphysical subtleties of philosopher-kings or the theological mysticism of priests. His political concept of a good community revived the Aristotelian notion that the pooled judgment of the citizenry is superior. Farkas really believed

34   that plain men were worth studying. The brooding figure of Farkas, described by contemporaries as a walking encyclopedia, frequently talked to the simple people of his native city. He was compassionate with a keen eye for life in the cottages huddled in the shadow of palaces. He despised the monarchy and was contemptuous of its sceptered and unlawful sway. His attatchment to the common people, celebrated in the pages of his *Journey*, might be paraphrased in the words of Goethe:[81]

> ... What you the spirit of the ages call
> Is nothing but the spirit of you all
> Wherein the ages are reflected.

There is no conclusive textual evidence in his manuscripts deposited at the Cluj branch of the Rumanian Academy of Sciences that Farkas consciously connected Rousseau and Goethe. But a careful reading of his diary entries, letters, and translations indicates that he intuitively moved from Rousseau's *La Nouvelle Héloïse* to Goethe's *Werther*. Farkas experienced in his personal life a tragic denouement similar to that of the pining lover in *Werther*. He fell in love with a German governess, Jozefa Polcz. She became his "Alpine violet" never to be touched; she married an American, James Swain, while Farkas was traveling in America. She died (1833) in Philadelphia, in childbirth. As in most flaming romances, their differences were irreconcilable. The demands Farkas made on himself, his concentration on the fullness of being, and his perceptual reliance on metaphysical solace scared away the governess who sought security in matrimony rather than immolation. His diary entries indicate that he loved Jozefa but his mercuric temper, unbending convictions, and his offer of an ordinary family life were beyond her.

Jozefa remained Farkas's "Alpine violet" sans marriage. And just before he died, he wrote, "Plato hid himself in a cave to live for wisdom. And sickness is often the soul's ethical cave, with its repose, darkness, and solitude."[82] In facing death, Farkas sought a deeper solution and actually contemplated a book on marriage and women. The memory of Jozefa constantly inspired his theoretical interests and after losing her, Farkas continued to feel that their relationship was his *vita ante actum*. In his translation of Goethe's *Werther*, he prefaced Book 2 with the words:

> You pity me, crying youth?
> Protect my memory against infamy
> From the depth of the soul I caution you:
> Be a man! Do not follow my footsteps.

Farkas also grasped that Goethe, like Rousseau, bestowed final authority on the individual, the microcosm that reflects the universe. To Farkas, *Werther* was an unfolding drama of his own self—a young man at odds with a confining society. Like most Romantics, he endowed the individual with a high moral authority, uncorrupted by conventions and opinion. Influenced by Rousseau and Goethe, he wrote: "I feel the remote and insoluble secrets of my secret self, and I too crave happiness."[83]

Happiness to him meant individual and social fulfillment. Like Rousseau, he held that society can be formed only on the principle of transparency, that is, all individuals consent to open themselves to one another, and thereby remove the antinomy between the private and public person. In sum, Rousseau and Farkas both carried the private practice of confession into a political context. The projection of the private self into the public realm blurs the distinction between creativity and politics. Just as Rousseau's self-revelations are read both as literature and as political theory, the fragments of the Farkas diary can be construed as literature and social theory. But there is a difference between Rousseau and Farkas. Rousseau's use of the "general will" implied that one individual unit is as good as the next and is therefore replaceable by units of the same kind. The general will is thus analogous to a sheaf of wheat, where one unit is as good as another. Farkas pictured the general will to be a composite of individual units where individuality, as in a work of art, prevails. Nonetheless, their common denominator is a concept of the self treated as the road to knowledge. The importance of the self in romantic thought is the assumption that civilized and primitive men enjoy unity only to the extent that each is capable of self-understanding. It has been said that Rousseau loved the noble and distant savage only to save himself the trouble of having to love his fellow citizen—Voltaire. Similarly, Farkas's diary indicates that he disclaimed any love for his fellow clerks, the bureaucratic riffraff. But he did love the downtrodden, the primitive, and the persecuted. He repeatedly raised the issue that splendor might endanger republican simplicity. He preferred unpretentious simplicity in society and politics to pomposity and affectation. Farkas shared Rousseau's romantic notion that conscience is more often heard in nonsocial settings, but he did not make a sharp distinction between freedom and community. The classic recognition of this dichotomy is described by Chateaubriand, who visited the virgin wilderness in America looking for "primitive liberty." Chateaubriand observed in the midst of an American forest: "I went from tree to tree and indifferently from right to left, saying to myself: No more roads to follow, no more towns, no more cramped houses, no more presidents, republics, kings, especially no more laws and no more men."[84] Farkas saw enough trees and wilderness in Transylvania not to succumb to romantic simplicity. He preferred simplicity in civic and political matters. His attachment to simplicity extended to religion and he preferred the Quakers to all other religious communities. He stressed conscience as a guide to human conduct, conscience independent of reason and rational judgment as a virtue binding on individuals and the community in every republican political system. He believed virtue to be the principle which animates and nerves republican social structures. He did not deny that aristocratic society might be motivated by virtue, or by human passions which set society in motion. Farkas defined the virtues of republican society to be a love of equality and frugality framed in laws, and he noted that in

36   aristocratic societies, virtues are personal, eclectic, and lack the universality
of law. Virtues merely contingent on the goodwill of the aristocrat are a
slender reed indeed.

This is brilliantly illustrated in Goethe's *Werther*. The indignities
Werther suffered in aristocratic circles are central for Goethe, and he
masterfully portrays the unpredictable outcome of interactions between a
social structure and the individual (Werther) who follows the dictates of his
own conscience. Farkas was born in a society where the arrogant assertion
"I am a nobleman" had a Leviathan quality, and he suffered the fate of
being born "unfree." He fell in love with America because there men were
free and their actions, under government by law, had a predictable
outcome. In Hungary legions of conscienceless Leviathans dominated
society like the colossus portrayed by Shakespeare:[85]

> ...he doth bestride the narrow world
> Like a Colossus, and we petty men
> Walk under his huge legs and peep about
> To find ourselves dishonorable graves.

While visiting Niagara Falls, Farkas stood at the edge of the cataract, and
wrote:

> What a chilling view. One step, one resolute move, and then the dreadful plunge
> into the gorge whence no mortal has ever returned. There are moments in life
> when the despairing heart counsels such a step.

His thought of a "dishonorable grave" revealed the many inner hurts and
humiliations suffered in an aristocratic society. The humiliations were real
to Farkas and so was his indictment of the Hungarian aristocracy:[86]

> The vast majority of the Hungarian nobility has a terribly misguided concept of
> liberty. They cannot get into their heads the principle of natural law that liberty
> is secure when we swear not to violate each other's liberties.... As a free
> nobleman he wants to be free everywhere, but violates at will the liberty of his
> fellow man. He craves a refined, cultured, and to him deferential society. But he
> himself is rowdy, and his language vulgar. How sad it is to listen to the debate of
> the liberal-despots, these splendidly poor noble-rowdies.

Farkas faulted the criminal indifference of the aristocracy to the public
welfare, and singled out its congenital inability to comprehend the concept
of civil society. His radicalism and resentment can be summarized in one
Rousseauean phrase: we will not become men until we are citizens! But as
already indicated, Farkas derived his judgment from actual experience
within the model Renaissance polity of Corvinus. Farkas consistently
invoked the conceptual scheme adopted by Corvinus—that a good polity
can be created by rational design. The reign of Corvinus was marked by the
civic humanism powerfully sketched by Machiavelli. Its pagan features
have scandalized Christians ever since. Machiavelli was neither an anti-
Christian nor a cold technician. He did project civic humanism as an
alternative to Christian ethics extrapolating its antecedents from the Roman
republican tradition. This is precisely what Farkas did by maintaining that

Corvinus's rule was a model of good society as compared to the degenerate Christian empire ruled by Metternich. Farkas equated civic humanism with the style of thought that prevailed in republican and constitutional forms of government. He maintained that the self-fulfillment of the individual is only possible when the individual acts as a citizen. He defined the citizen as an informed being who consciously participates in civic matters. Professor Pocock cogently analyzes civic humanism and its seminal influence on Anglo-American thought: "Civic humanist thought strongly implied... that the republic and its citizens were somehow capable of this mastery...."[87] The individual can fulfill his moral and rational nature in a republic.

Farkas depicted American constitutionalism as a model which fulfilled and cultivated the individual's moral and rational nature. Farkas could never agree with Rousseau's model of citizenship in raising Cato over Socrates, which implied that there should be an obedient identity between a ruler and a citizen. The Unitarian Farkas perceived such a polity as merely a body politic without a soul. Given a choice, he would opt for a democracy with a soul, even at the price of his own life. In his essay "Sickness, Suffering, and Death," Farkas movingly and trenchantly defined civic humanism: "Many among us have neither wealth, talent, nor extraneous privileges that could be sacrificed for humanity. But all of us, rich and poor, mighty and low, possess one thing in common—we can sacrifice ourselves."[88] Socrates sacrificed himself for Athens, where the *polis* and its citizens were an integrated whole. Farkas admired Greek civilization because its greatest triumph was the transformation of men into citizens. Farkas often expressed his wish to be transported to classical Athens and so confronted his full share of an anguishing dilemma: "...Wandering between two worlds, one dead, the other powerless to be born..."[89]

Farkas continued to be troubled by the aristocracy's irresponsible secession from the body politic; its self-love and the gratification of individual ego at the expense of the public welfare were despotism in the classical sense. Despotism negates freedom because human relationships become a kind of master-slave dependency, which cancels law and civic love. The Hungarian aristocracy was despotic because it lacked an identity of interest with the public good. The Hungarian nobility even refused to be taxed. Farkas insightfully juxtaposed the English and Hungarian aristocratic stages of development by comparing Magna Charta (1215) with the Golden Bull (1222). The latter was drawn up by Hungarian nobles to restrict the king's prerogatives (e.g., not to appoint foreigners to office without the consent of the council).

Magna Charta marked the beginning of the English tradition that the life of every individual is a matter of importance. That great political principle, "What touches all should be approved by all," profoundly affected British society. Unfortunately, the Golden Bull had no parallel influence on Hungarian society because the nobility failed to develop a

38   moral conscience in opposition to royal absolutism. It is interesting to note that the Hungarian greetings—*szervus*—derives from the Latin *servus*, which implied in its original meaning that the individual should consider himself fortunate if he was reduced only to slavery and was not killed. Being a slave, in the Latin sense, remitted the death penalty which he deserved. Farkas indicted the Hungarian nobility for allowing the Golden Bull to lapse through disuse "until we allowed ourselves to be dependent on his majesty's pledge of conscience."[90] The English aristocratic stage, in contrast, was marked by the establishment of civil rights according to the rule of law and legal protection against arbitrary arrest. The English aristocracy precipitated and participated in the commercial and industrial revolutions. In Hungary the nobleman's privileges depended on a pliant and subserviant attitude toward Vienna. Thus English nobles were empire builders with vision—their Hungarian counterparts lacked national habit, culture, language, and outlook. They were reduced to the role of courtiers and so were estranged from their native land.

One Hungarian historian wrote: "The enormity of the historical crime of the Hungarian aristocracy is that they ruined themselves financially in Vienna and by thus losing their independence deprived the nation of one of its principal supporters."[91] Farkas scathingly indicted the nobility for this betrayal of the national interest. A few Hungarian peers, however, conceived of their role in terms of the English model. One of them, István Széchenyi (1791–1860), was an important and fascinating architect of the reform age. His intellectual mentors were Benjamin Franklin and Jeremy Bentham, and he had a practical mind. Farkas was greatly impressed by Széchenyi. Farkas wrote to a friend in 1829 that Széchenyi was a "classical man" who spoke to his own heart. By "classical," Farkas meant that he would subordinate private interests to the public good, and, like Aristotle, Farkas tended to equate a "divine" nature with the common good. To him anything divine was incorruptible and imperishable. Civic-mindedness was both "classical" and "divine." Thus Széchenyi, in Farkas's own words, was an "immortal man" because of his selfless devotion to public affairs. He used his enormous wealth for cultural, political, and economic reforms.

Their concern for national reform and improvement focused the attention of Széchenyi and Wesselényi on America. Széchenyi's diaries document that although he was an aristocrat, he was the complete antithesis of Metternich. Széchenyi said: "Metternich's system ceases with his life. Mine will begin only after my death."[92] Széchenyi dreamed of visiting America, "das werdende Land,"[93] in the early 1820s. A Hungarian historian wrote of Széchenyi's intellectual development that he wanted to adorn the "inhabitants of the country with civic virtues as stated by Franklin, so that freedom would become part of human existence."[94] Széchenyi borrowed Bentham's notion that the greatest happiness for the greatest number is the fundamental principle of morality and added that happiness is predicated on human toil.

But human toil in Hungary after the Congress of Vienna was enervated by doubts concerning the viability of Western civilization. Central European intellectuals displayed general frustration concerning the decline of the West under the lengthening shadows of the Holy Alliance. Intellectuals like Farkas were aware that enormous energies were wasted on policing society, and were vaguely exasperated while waiting for the *ancien régime* to collapse. No string of quotations or volumes of statistical data could recapture the revolutionary excitement of Farkas's generation. The private adventure of ideas and spirit unleashed by the French Revolution was sustained until 1815. The Napoleonic Wars quickened the pace of events and human sense of time. The letters and diary fragments of Farkas and his contemporaries record that the deep and prolonged crisis changed the human rhythm of perception and tenor of life profoundly. Immanuel Kant, that philosophical clock, was late for his morning walk when he heard of the fall of the Bastille and the decision of the republican regime to rewrite the calendar of human affairs. Farkas and Gedö watched the spread of French republicanism with a sense of glory. Wordsworth found it a bliss to be alive and very heaven to be young while the French were making their new constitution. Farkas believed that the Old World was about to shed its worn and tattered skin, and that injustice and poverty would be eradicated forever.

But by 1815, European intellectuals were discontented when the Holy Alliance again corked the bottle which had released the spirit of the Revolution. Farkas visited Paris following the July revolution in 1831, to stand before the tombs of Voltaire and Rousseau, the geniuses who "set the tone of the century." Farkas wrote: "I picked up fragments from the crumbling coffins of both, in eternal memory that I stood over their bodies. Rest in peace, sacred souls."[95] *Lumières* like Rousseau undoubtedly lighted the Revolution and his notion of the people's sovereignty briefly illuminated Transylvania—before disappearing. By 1815, Europe was guided by *Ruhe and Ordnung* (calmness and order) and many Central Euro0ean intellectuals began to look across the Atlantic, where the Old World ideas of liberty and equality were turning into political reality. At the Congress of Vienna, Széchenyi was nicknamed "der Amerikaner." That suggestive title implied that European circles were aware that Americans were a distinct political species, neither noble nor peasant. In the Old World, nobles and peasants virtually lived on two separate planets.[96] But in America there was an "equality" of condition reported later in detail by Tocqueville and Farkas.

While traveling in England and Europe, Széchenyi declared Hungary, so shamefully backward, to be a "respectable" competitor of the Turks—the sick men of Europe. Széchenyi visited Transylvania in 1821, became friends with Wesselényi, and planned a joint visit to America. On being informed of their plan, Emperor Francis, in response to the Hungarian quest for constitutionalism, exploded with indignation: "The whole world has gone crazy, and abandoning its good old laws, is searching for idealized constitutions."[97] Metternich opposed the trip:[98]

> Those United States of America . . . in their indecent declaration they have cast blame and scorn on the institutions of Europe most worthy of respect, on the principles of its great sovereigns . . . they [Americans] lend new strength to the apostles of sedition. . . . If this flood of evil doctrines and pernicious examples should extend over the whole of America, what would become of our religious and political institutions, the moral force for our governments, and of that conservative system which has saved Europe from complete dissolution.

Metternich turned down Széchenyi's visa application, and the latter noted in his diary: "Metternich findet meinen Wunsch bizarr, nicht unausführbar."[99] Széchenyi and Wesselényi visited England instead and returned impressed by the working of that constitutional monarchy. The Hungarian Diet was composed of two houses, but, unlike the English Parliament, had no precedent to yield to numerical majority. The upper and lower houses were considered to be one body in relation to the king and joint resolutions were presented to him in the form of humble representations *(humillimae representationes)*, which were either accepted or rejected. The Hungarian judicial system was medieval. The landowners in many places retained the right of jurisdiction *(ius gladii)* as late as 1790. The seigneurs retained powers of life and death over the serfs. Little wonder that Farkas was greatly impressed by the American judicial system.

Prior to Farkas's travels in America, the American democratic experiment attracted the attention of liberal reformers in Hungary. Széchenyi wrote: "Every day I am convinced that Herder is right; the Hungarian nation will soon cease to exist."[100] He described his own class as "vampires" who reduced the peasantry to a "vegetating animal." Both he and Farkas expressed the conviction that it was the ordinary people who made America great. After reading Harriet Beecher Stowe's *Uncle Tom's Cabin*, Széchenyi noted:[101]

> The poor Hungarian is an outlaw even if he is given amnesty and is not persecuted and hunted, so beautifully depicted in Uncle Tom's book . . . because everything described there perfectly applies to Hungary.

The cholera epidemic of 1831, followed by the peasant uprising in northern Hungary, was reported in Philadelphia and the report compelled Farkas to terminate his American visit. John Paget traveled through the cholera-stricken areas in 1835 and wrote: "We noticed in many parts of this country, but particularly in this neighborhood, a great number of gibbets, from each of which several bodies were dangling."[102] The Hungarian nobility were still hunting down peasants four years later. After the epidemic and the uprising, Széchenyi tried to convince Metternich that reforms were overdue and necessary. Metternich preferred to blame the uprising on Russian agents. In this charged atmosphere, Széchenyi contacted the American Philosophical Society in search of a model for reform. He wrote to the president of the society:[103]

The qualities of the soul do not recognize time. Although the angel of Light has taken up quarters but a short time ago in the rugged wilderness of America, yet it has lent its radiance to those who, languishing for centuries under more adverse circumstances, like us, had hardly been able to extricate one leg from the disgusting feudal confusion debasing mankind and particularly our fatherland. Under more fortunate circumstances we ought to blush on account of such backwardness which, however, has not completely suppressed, thank heaven, all vestiges of our nationality. The national quality upon which our existence has been based is still alive, and sometime in the future, we shall be able to stand our ground among the ranks of advanced free generations.

Metternich made sure that Széchenyi and Wesselényi did not travel to America and see the "pernicious example" of liberty. But Farkas, the tutor and friend of Wesselényi, did visit the land of the future. Interestingly enough, his trip was financed by Count Ferenc Béldi, a close friend of Széchenyi. Other members of the group included Farkas Wesselényi, younger brother of Miklós Wesselényi, and Pál Balog, Széchenyi's personal physician. Széchenyi was fascinated by America all his life because of its demonstrated ability to throw off the yoke of oppression and undertake rapid economic development, and because he was interested in the fall and decline of civilizations. "In ancient times it was Phoenicia," he wrote, "that occupied the place, then Venice, and Genoa, later Holland, Britain . . . and now it is the turn of Yankee America."[104] Széchenyi and Farkas were aware that "republics have always failed" the moral test of hearing the cry of helots and slaves. They were thus deeply interested whether America would hear the cry of its Negro slaves. The most compassionate and moving passages of the *Journey* deal with the issue of slavery. Farkas stated categorically that America would attend to the cry of Negroes.

The historical aspect of republicanism tested on a large scale in America was of particular interest to Széchenyi and Farkas. They were also keenly interested in America's technological progress. Széchenyi kept in close touch with American ambassadors in Vienna, particularly Francis Barber Ogden (1783–1857), a mechanical engineer and close friend of Fulton. President Jackson appointed Ogden as the American consul in Liverpool in 1830 and Széchenyi consulted with Ogden on bridge building. Farkas and Széchenyi viewed American democratic and economic progress as empirical proof that prosperity and progress are built on constitutional foundations. Specifically, they noted that constitutional freedoms create a society where everyone works through persuasion rather than coercion, and nobody is really governed. They believe that internal motivations—the result of persuasion—were more effective and longer lasting than coercion "from without." Farkas again extrapolated his knowledge of a feudal economy and compared it to the compelling principles, values, and dispositions of a market economy. Farkas was on a sound sociological foundation when he correlated constitutionalism and economic progress. The American political mind has always associated autonomy within its political institutions with productive efficiency. The principle of autonomy

42   suggests that what can be done well by a smaller and lower unit must never be taken over by a larger one. That is what Jefferson meant when he said: "The less government is the better." The application of that maxim, of course, requires people trained in the art of self-government. Széchenyi was cognizant of that: "Hungary will be neither happy nor of exalted position until the people are admitted to the ranks of the nation."[105] He was convinced that America could be of considerable help to reform-oriented thinkers. "I would also extend my attention," he wrote, "to distant America to become acquainted with the conditions of that country."[106]

Széchenyi's search for a "developmental" model for Hungary presaged Farkas's American visit. But Farkas also had contingent and personal reasons for traveling to America. He hinted of his intention to visit Asia to search out Hungary's missing ethnic kin in 1828. Ever since the appearance of the Magyars in the Danube basin in the ninth century A.D., this strange diaspora was soliloquized by Hungarians. The Hungarian problem— Asian roots and a Western mentality—imprinted Hungary's cultural life and literature with ambivalence. The awareness that its roots were non-European while its social life was leavened and shaped by the West was unmistakably recognizable in Farkas's outlook. He accepted the Hungarian destiny by renouncing the backward past and embarking on a soul-searching quest to lift the yoke of foreign invaders. The history of the wasting invasions and occupations by Tartars, Turks, and Hapsburgs—and the effort to dissolve imperial ties—significantly influenced Farkas in his search for the nation's Asian roots, and his visit to America. Had it not been for the Hungarian ethos, Farkas's planned Russian journey might have been construed to be a Tocquevillean recognition of "two great nations," the Russians and Americans, looming on the political horizon. But his friend, Döbrentei, was less than enthusiastic about Farkas's travel plans. "Dear friend," he wrote, "leave alone travel. It is not for a single and sick man . . . . Do not take your genius elsewhere, use it for the nation here . . ."[107] Farkas did not make the Russian trip, but he did not give up because his restlessness needed outward space. He regretted not being informed earlier of von Humboldt's travel so that he could have joined him. When Döbrentei learned about it, he wrote sarcastically: "Where do you want to wander off this time? Obviously some public good drives you. But pray, do not search the Asian desert for Hungarians."[108] When Farkas received Döbrentei's letter, he informed Gedö:[109]

> In the autumn I plan to travel for a year or two. Heaven listened to my plea, and perhaps I will accomplish the greatest wish of my life even if it means sacrificing part of my fortune. But never will I spend on a more worthy cause. Like a student, I am cramming geography, statistics, constitutional history, and learning languages.

In July 1830, the vice-governor informed Farkas that he could take a year-and-a-half leave of absence and approved his European travel plans. Farkas received his passport on October 31 and left Transylvania on

November 3, 1830. After touring Europe, he and three companions crossed **43** the English channel and sailed on the *Columbia* for America on July 27, 1831, returning on December 14, 1831. Farkas kept a detailed notebook of his November 1830 to January 1832 tour, but only *Journey in North America* was published. The slim volume appeared in 1834 and the eleven hundred copies sold quickly. The second edition appeared in March 1835—an unprecedented event in unbookish Hungary. By September the *Journey* appeared on Vienna's index of forbidden books and Farkas noted in his diary:[110]

> The catalogue of indexed books arrived at the Gubernium and it lists my work.... What a great distinction! There must be something in it that took effect. But it is too late. I think the poison took hold and the proscription merely titillates.

Farkas became an overnight *cause célèbre*, and he was showered with acclaim and distinctions. Széchenyi was deeply moved by Farkas's book. "Thank God that this book appeared, its value is inestimable for the nation."[111] Wesselényi headed a special delegation to honor the author and addressed Farkas in a magisterial tone:[112]

> What beautiful fate to see with your own eyes the giant of natural rights and liberty. Shed tears on the grave of the great Washington; touch the soil from which, mixed with the challenger's sacred blood, sprung the new age of reason, embrace the uncorrupt sons of that happy country, inhale the air of liberty—the breath of God—unspoiled by privileges and despotism.

The Hungarian Academy elected Farkas as a corresponding member, and awarded his book the grand prize of two hundred gold pieces. The membership genuinely embarrassed Farkas and he returned the money and informed the secretary that, although he had little money, he was honored to place it on the "nation's altar." At the height of his greatest personal triumph, Farkas wrote this lacerating comment:[113]

> Why can't I enjoy the distinction? I fear to reveal it to anyone because few would really understand. Indeed it is nice, very nice, and surpasses my greatest young dreams. But when I think of the state of our literature, my hand trembles touching the laurel crown.... Now I really know what I refused to believe for so long: we have not progressed very far when in one year my work is acclaimed the best, whereas in England or America it would be a commonplace thing. Indeed, we have not progressed very far! ... I would be ashamed to tell an Englishman or an American that no better book than mine has appeared here in the whole year.

This disarmingly honest and introspective indictment did an injustice to a book which had so galvanized moribund Hungary. Statesmen, students, and intellectuals alike praised the book and sought honors by lauding Farkas for having written a republican grammar of politics. Polite society craved to see the man who shed tears on Washington's tomb, shook hands with Andrew Jackson, and walked the streets of Franklin's birthplace. The book had a powerful appeal to the parliamentary generation of the 1830s, a seedtime for the Hungarian Revolution and War of Independence (1848–1849).

44   Farkas, like Thomas Paine, possessed the rare combination of humanism and intense personality which, on colliding with reality, illuminated the age in which he was born. Farkas was a polemicist and catalyst, and his writing, like Paine's, became a beacon in dark times. Farkas, despite illness and approaching death, upheld the principle that the human challenge is not only to live but to live nobly. He remained true to the conviction that human suffering and social backwardness could be eradicated if the people were instructed in the grammar of democracy. Above all, he was convinced that government had to be based on the consent of the governed. His translations of the Declaration of Independence, the lengthy New Hampshire Constitution, and selected articles of the Constitution clearly stated these convictions.

Farkas cited Jefferson, the Constitution, and President Monroe to demonstrate to Metternich that the true greatness of a nation is founded on the principles of natural rights and religious freedom. Farkas masterfully made his point by adopting a technique reminiscent of Thucydides. He imaginatively reported a speech President Monroe might have delivered before Congress. The speech (see page 162 of the text) expressed Farkas's belief. By quoting Jefferson and Monroe, Farkas accentuated and lent authority to his dearly held ideas.

The ideas and principles expressed in the *Journey* are the essence of his political and social philosophy. Tracing the origin of his ideas and thus identifying his book as one of the genre of foreign comments, analyses, and interpretations of America is a provocative and difficult pursuit. No other nation has attracted, unsolicited, so many analysts. No country has so incessantly had its political portrait painted, its customs and manners scrutinized, its character dissected, its soul probed, and its historical achievement evaluated. America has always fired the imagination of Europe in a peculiar and unique fashion. The Old World, comprising a haphazard sequence of human policies reaching back to the smoke of human sacrifice rising from the Pantheon, is hardly a persuasive experiment when compared to the American experience. The United States is the first great nation born free of the hazards of countervailing forces out of the conscious design of human beings. This prodigious widening of human possibilities arising from human initiative intoxicated Farkas with the thought that humanity was finally escaping from the iron laws of history. He was convinced that America differed significantly from the anguished old Europe. He visited America during the maturing of a classic democracy built on the ideas and principles which represented to early-nineteenth-century minds a conquering force that held great promise for the future. The optimism of classic democracy was clearly expressed in the American dedication to progress.

Other factors compound the difficulty of assessing Farkas's interpretation of American democracy. As indicated before, the thematic spokesman for Hungarian historical development and the pursuit of national happiness

is literature, rather than politics. Early-nineteenth-century Hungary
lacked a cumulative, systematic philosophical tradition from which to judge
the American reality. In this respect Tocqueville enjoyed a definite
advantage over Farkas. Farkas had a good command of Western political
thought, including the Greco-Roman, English liberalism, and Continental
radicalism, but his temperamental predisposition toward Rousseau's
intuitive individualism sharply distinguished his views in comparison to
Tocqueville's. It may have been coincidence that focused their attention on
Jacksonian Democracy, and they had a brief personal encounter. Their
intellectual differences are written into *Democracy* and *Journey*. Farkas
landed in America and immediately announced the nature of the "science"
of politics he would be looking for in the New World:

> For sixty years the watchful eyes of Europe and the world have been on
> America. For centuries liberty and oppression met on the battlefields of the Old
> World. Though a thousand times disappointed, its weary cheated hopes
> counseling surrender, in final listless resignation Europe has turned to America,
> destined by Fate to answer the question: Can man and mankind create a just and
> good government through self-determination and free election? And is man's
> political destiny forever decreed by history and tyrannical power?

This passage established the tone of Farkas's *Journey* and it is grounded on
presuppositions totally opposite to those of Tocqueville. Farkas was a
radical and, in many respects, a revolutionary. Students familiar with the
writings of Thomas Paine will find passages in Farkas directly traceable to
Paine, particularly his paradigm of despotism and aristocracy as conceptual
opposites of constitutionalism. There is an ongoing scholarly debate
whether Tocqueville's treatment of democracy disguised an aristocratic
viewpoint, but there is little doubt that his individualism was linked to
classical precepts and that he was ambivalent about democratic man's
pursuit of economic interests.

Tocqueville's *Democracy* is comprehensive and architectonic. He
employs the normative values of philosophy to explicate the "laws,"
"causes," and "truth" of the rising democratic civilization. It has been said
that Tocqueville deliberately refrained from reading books on American
democracy lest they color his judgment and force him into another's
interpretative groove.

There is, for example, no record that he consulted either Captain Hall
or Harriet Martineau. In contrast, Farkas disagreed with Hall both in his
Journey and in private correspondence. In response to a friend who
complimented his *Journey* while commenting favorably on Captain Hall,
Farkas wrote: "I am well acquainted with Hall's American book, and used it
as a handbook during my travel . . . but I have also discovered that, though a
learned man, he is not a friend of republican ideals."[114] Tocqueville
deliberately refused to be influenced by others, and Chevalier's first letters
from the United States made him uneasy, yet he did not deviate from his
strict procedure. Consequently Tocqueville missed, barely noted, or

46   merely bracketed a number of cogent observations. He operated in a kind of
speculative exclusiveness which illuminated and brilliantly focused some
facts and values, and obscured the rest by placing them in an omitted
background. Hence Tocqueville was not unlike Plato. He sought the logic
and psychology of democracy apart from its aristocratic elements. The
ideal typology in *Democracy* sets high abstract standards which Tocqueville
used to evaluate the realities and future trends of mass democracy.

The individualism Tocqueville associated with democracy, as distinct
from the great chain of being in aristocratic thought, assumes that
democratic man is deficient of "mind" and perverse in "heart." His fear that
excessive individualism would pull society to the brink of dissolution is
Platonic, and his association of democratic society with the atomization of
individuals, and aristocracy with the solidarity of class, has Burkean
overtones. Tocqueville suggests that the democratic bond of human
affection extends and relaxes, so "the woof of time is every instant broken,
and the track of generations effaced."[115] Thus, in contrast to Paine and
Farkas, Tocqueville postulated that democracy and despotism are related
because the snapping of ties between individuals is "more particularly to be
feared in a democratic age."[116]

Tocqueville's fame was derived in part from his being the first to
articulate a theory of "mass age," and from his drawing critical attention to
the inevitable effects of the French Revolution on the emerging industrial
society. It was the latter that pushed ostensibly democratic systems toward
conformity and mediocrity. This great sociological insight leads to the
Tocquevillean principle that acquisitive individualism, by utilizing universal suffrage and the legislative branch, paves the way to an egalitarianism
having normative values related to the subjective wants of the masses.
Historically egalitarianism and centrism are connected in that egalitarian
drives stimulate the extension of state power. This theory was recently
revived in terms of the "democratic distemper" thesis cogently argued by
Samuel Huntington.[117] Huntington theorizes that in a democracy the
rising demand for goods and services from the government, accompanied
by a growing mistrust of politics, creates a democratic distemper. The
"distemper" is an excess of democracy based on a "welfare shift" with a
corresponding decline of public trust in government and cynicism toward
politics.

The theory has antecedents in the writings of Tocqueville. However,
his original concept failed to consider the notion of popular sovereignty that
maintains that freedom of the press, universal suffrage, and representation
are not agencies of the government. On the contrary, these are the means by
which the sovereign power of the people is exercised in government.
Tocqueville's axiom that egalitarianism paves the way to centrism suffers
from biased rationalism. To him the executive and legislative branches of
government were merely a means of securing economic satisfaction for the
people. Tocqueville failed to note that as long as basic human rights,

freedom of the press, and constitutional checks and balances are maintained, they would counter the expansive power of the state in its egalitarian
tendency. Tocqueville's great classic is marked by an uneasy concern that a
democratic framework cannot accommodate both economic self-interest
and leadership.

The *Federalist Papers* also influenced Tocqueville, who referred to them
frequently and spread their fame in Europe.[118] The language of the
Federalist, like that of Tocqueville, is theoretical and legal, and both
approach politics from the pragmatic viewpoint of statesmen. The *Federalist*
writers consistently evaluate events and ideas within the framework of
certain rules. One such rule is that ethical behavior, while possible in
principle, is not expected from men who pursue power in politics. The
most important principle guiding the *Federalist* and the writings of
Tocqueville is the balance they strike between liberty and authority. David
Hume, who influenced the work of Hamilton, Jay, and Madison, said, "In
all government there is a perpetual intensive struggle, open or secret,
between Authority and Liberty, and neither of them can ever absolutely
prevail in the contest."[119] Finally, the Federalists and Tocqueville made it
abundantly clear that they did not want to exchange absolute monarchy for
absolute democracy. Hence Tocqueville's statement that "a new science of
politics is needed for a new world" also implied a warning that if democracy
became the medium for expressive mass politics, then the new age of
democracy would herald "soft totalitarianism."

Tocqueville underrated the special features of American democracy as
they emerged during the Jacksonian period. He noted the emerging
assertiveness of the people but judged that it would have a negative impact
on government. His central thesis throughout *Democracy* was that public
opinion would become the arbiter of republican destiny. He viewed the
"multitude" as the rock upon which public opinion would build a
democratic church of commercial and business interests which would
enervate, extinguish, and stupefy the people, "till each nation is reduced to
nothing better than a flock of timid and industrious animals, of which the
government is the shepherd."[120] In Tocqueville the multitude is presumed
to have an exaggerated taste for physical gratification, hence he was
critically ambivalent about the voluntaristic aspects of democracy. The
aristocratic point of view, in contrast, assumes that certain historical
verities—e.g., God and human nature—are permanent despite historical
change. Voluntarism reverses that point of view by assuming that human
needs and wants are bases of political legitimacy. In sum, the "pursuit of
happiness," which implies that economic gratification is legitimate and
desirable, cannot be reconciled with Tocqueville's a priori postulate that
defines the "wholeness" of man in intellectual rather than socioeconomic
terms.

Contrary to Tocqueville, Farkas recognized the restless economic
desires of the multitude as legitimate in a popular democracy. Farkas thus

48   parallels John Marshall's view that every man has a natural right to the fruits
of his own labor. Farkas explicitly argues that the incentive to work, acquire
property, trade, and produce is fundamentally protected in the American
political system. The system, he believed, does not serve the interests of the
leisured aristocrat as well as it does the restless enterprise of the
businessman. In short, Farkas argued that self-interest promotes the larger
interests of the community. To him freedom and economic progress were
dynamic, desirable, and complementary. To Farkas, American constitutional law was the unique American accomplishment because it facilitated a
remarkable increase in the means of production. He was impressed by
America's technological progress and predicted the United States would
surpass England as the workshop of the world. After Farkas visited
England and took a "steam wagon" ride from Liverpool to Manchester, he
enthusiastically anticipated the coming age when wheels would roll
"everywhere along iron rails." In Pittsburgh he visited a bakery and nail
factories and celebrated the age of steam as did Robert Southey, who
captured the Jacksonians by writing that "an American, when he speaks
colloquially of power, means nothing but a steam-engine."[121] Farkas
observed the impact steam had in reshaping agrarian America and noted
that material progress was desirable and positive. His concept of progress
was predicated on the belief that it was facilitated by science, government,
and the efforts of individuals living in freedom. Despite the dynamic
progress that was turning arcadia to industry, Tocqueville wrote that
American men were in perpetual motion but "their minds are almost
unmoved."

This analysis is intended not to denigrate Tocqueville's brilliant
accomplishments but to note that he did misjudge Jacksonian society. Even
Emerson, who was no lover of machines, acknowledged that every age has
its "own distemper." And there was distemper in the 1830s. Jacksonians
liquefied power so that it began to flow in a nontraditional direction toward
what Tocqueville called the "unlimited power of the majority." The
Jacksonians exceeded the Jeffersonians in trusting the common man to the
extent that the government was no longer "an engine for the support of the
few at the expense of the many."[122] Harold Laski analyzed a similar
contribution of the American system to democracy and reached a similar
conclusion. He wrote: "By the time of Andrew Jackson the claim was
broadly conceded" that the masses shared political power.[123] It was
conceded that, to borrow a phrase from George Bancroft, whose *History of
the United States* proved that Divine Providence had sponsored the
American nation, "the day for the multitude has now dawned." Tocqueville, however, disdained the catchpenny reality of the Jacksonian
period and ignored the workbench primitives busy introducing a new
industrial age. Tocqueville was more interested in empirically affirming the
effect on American society as it departed from traditional values. Farkas
was more interested in studying how the constitutional republic would

adjust to new industrial realities. Tocqueville minimized and merely bracketed the emergence of an industrial-urban America, while Farkas sought to transcribe it.

Robert Dahl pointed out that Tocqueville devoted six sentences in his two-volume *Democracy* to show how "it can be strictly said that the people govern in the United States."[124] James Bryce made a similar observation that Tocqueville understated the "purely local and special features of America."[125] Thomas Hart Benton earlier took exception to Tocqueville's characterization of the Congress as "vulgar" as well as his statement that "in a country in which education is very general, it is said that the representatives of the people do not always know how to write correctly."[126] Tocqueville ignored two fundamental strengths of American democracy, the expansion of franchise as the source of popular self-government and the constitutional provisions that vested Congress with the power of originating revenue bills and the sole power of impeachment.

Paradoxically, Tocqueville had little knowledge of the American colonial period. Lord Acton noted that he had failed to grasp the full significance of the key English influence on the development of American political tradition. Bernard Bailyn's incisive analysis, *The Origins of American Politics*, traced the "linkages" of English and American politics to eighteenth-century Whig opposition politics. According to Bailyn, the intellectual environment of eighteenth-century politics, or, more generally, the "greater political culture," is the backdrop against which the American political tradition should be analyzed. Tocqueville surprisingly ignored political culture despite his recognition that the intellectual atmosphere and political science are interdependent. "The political sciences," wrote Tocqueville, "form a sort of intellectual atmosphere breathed by both governors and the governed in society, and both unwittingly derive from it the principles of their action."[127] Since Tocqueville glossed over the enlargement of suffrage in America, it is worth quoting Bailyn on the importance of the franchise:[128]

> But of all the underlying characteristics that distinguish the process of politics in America from that of the English model, the breadth of the franchise was perhaps the most dramatic—and in its origins the most circumstantial.

Tocqueville was undoubtedly a genius and his *Democracy in America* is a work of lasting significance. But where his perceptions were weak, those of Farkas were strong. Tocqueville's limitations can be traced to Pascal's insistence that ideas and social values be evaluated in terms of the conceptual "wholeness" of man. Like Pascal, Tocqueville judged the Jacksonian common man from that larger perspective. In Pascal, man is God dependent; in Tocqueville, democracy and its advance were providential. Pascal postulated the immense facticity of the world and the finite spirituality of man. In a letter to Eugène Stoffels, a boyhood friend, Tocqueville expressed amazement concerning the dual world of morality-order, and liberty-equality:[129]

This strikes me as the most extraordinary and deplorable spectacle ever offered to the eyes of man; for all the things thus separated are, I am certain, indissolubly united in the sight of God. . . . It seems to me that one of the finest enterprises of our time would be to demonstrate that these things are not incompatible; but that they are bound up together in such a fashion that each of them is weakened by separation from the rest. Such is my basic idea.

Tocqueville's statement is the clearest transposition of Pascal's concept of the totality of man into democracy. Tocqueville regarded democracy as nothing if it suppressed or fragmented the wholeness of man. Whether that suppression came from a single despot or from an elected majority was irrelevant. He expressed this succinctly to a close friend:[130]

To indicate to men, if it is possible, what they must do in order to escape from tyranny and degeneration while becoming egalitarian, such is, I think, the general idea which epitomized my book and which will appear on every page of the one I am writing . . .

Tocqueville had, nonetheless, strongly influenced other foreign analysts of American democracy: Bryce, Laski, Brogan, Myrdal, Aron et al.[131] The exception was Farkas. His *Journey in North America* appeared before *Democracy in America* was celebrated in Europe. In *Democracy*, the self-evident truths of the Declaration, the Bill of Rights, and the federal and state constitutions are passed over in virtual silence. The *Journey* is unique, since Farkas noted that the principles of American politics are contained equally in the Declaration of Independence and the Constitution.[132] Farkas thus rightly deserves to be considered the Columbus of democracy. The Farkasian political science is summarized in one sentence: "To me," he wrote, "the declaration of the rights of mankind, noted by so few, is the most significant, and the rest is just a frame around it . . ." If Farkas had never written another word, his *Journey* would still have reserved him a modest niche in the democratic pantheon.

Yet it would take a separate work to establish Farkas's proper place in nineteenth-century liberal thought. He was the first to draw attention to the Declaration of Independence as the accepted American article of faith, the truest expression of the American mind. Any inquiry into the meaning of equality must begin with Jefferson's "self-evident" truths. Farkas understood that slavery tested the principles of the Declaration. While entering Maryland, Farkas wrote:

As soon as we entered Maryland we saw more Negroes than in any other states. Everywhere blacks worked in the fields. The reason did not dawn on us until we saw a notice posted on an inn door which read: "On October 28th this year the goods of Jacob Caldwell debtor, including two male and one female Negro slaves will be sold at an auction to the highest bidder." Reading this, I felt as if an icy hand gripped my heart. I sighed in sorrow—we had arrived in the land of slavery!

During our travels we heard a lot about slaves, the constant topic of controversy between the free and the slave-owning states. Having observed the unprecedented free civic life secured by this great country's Constitution, based on the principle of natural law . . . I found the contrast between noble ideals and despicable praxis always incomprehensible. . . .

To me the saddest and most shameful aspect of moral philosophy is man's willingness to abuse power and reason when wielding intellectual and political power over the powerless and the uneducated. Perhaps no individual and no nation can be considered truly enlightened unless they irrevocably renounce or curb this tendency, and pledge to respect the rights of the uneducated and powerless as their own. But how many individuals and nations can boast of the abrogation or at least the disuse of this evil tendency so that we have a guarantee against relapse? If approaching an ideal can be scaled on a thermometer, then America, including her treatment of slaves in historical perspective, has reached the highest degree of esteem in my heart.

Farkas then boldly prophesied that the "awakened human conscience" would shortly end slavery in the United States. He was convinced that if America was to achieve the ideals expressed in the Declaration, its principles must be applied to the enslaved Negroes. Yet Farkas was under no illusion that the emancipation of slaves would automatically usher in a more perfect union. He noted that several organizations had been formed in various states to emancipate the slaves, and raised the question:

But one difficult and vexing question arose: What should become of the already freed and the yet to be freed slaves? Once more this presents a delicate issue, inconceivable to a European mind. The white man shows a certain reserve even toward the freed Negro, who possesses equal natural rights. Is this nature's ploy and play on color? Or is it more plausible that the white man finds it humiliating to socialize with those hitherto treated as beasts of burden, and under the sway of his absolute power. Behold! One more instance of the weak side of the human soul which sways some American citizens just as it sways the proud European aristocrat.

Farkas nonetheless reaffirmed his faith in the Declaration of Independence:

This document, the cornerstone of American faith, despite its simplicity is strikingly original and unique. Its uniqueness becomes apparent when compared with European historical declarations of rights and charters of freedom which, by and large, were royal grants of historical rights. In essence the royal charter proclaimed to the people, this much will be yours and the rest belongs to us. At best, these charters of freedom, full of contrived smooth clauses, are but compacts between two contending parties. But this document summons Americans to a political creation, to the framing of a just government. It declares that just power derives from the consent of the people who entrust some rights to the government. The language of the Declaration is not the language of diplomacy but the language of natural law.

The majestic opening of Lincoln's Gettysburg Address—"Fourscore and seven years ago our fathers brought forth upon this continent a new nation, conceived in Liberty, and dedicated to the proposition that all men are created equal"—states poetically what Farkas said in prose that the Declaration "summons Americans to a political creation." Farkas's brilliant insight preceded Lincoln's address by more than twenty years. In the last year of his life, Jefferson called the Declaration "the genuine effusion of the souls of American society."[133] Lincoln stood in Independence Hall on

52   February 22, 1861, ten days before his inauguration and said: "I am filled with deep emotion at finding myself standing here in the place where were collected together the wisdom, the patriotism, the devotion to principle, from which sprang the institutions under which we live."[134]

Farkas also associated the unique qualities of American democracy with the principles of the Declaration. He considered its theory of politics to be the single most important statement on government. Most political writers in the nineteenth century avoided deriving the right of the majority from the natural-rights philosophy formulated in the Declaration, while Farkas treated natural rights as articles of American democratic faith. The most sophisticated interpretation of majority rule prior to the nineteenth century was fashioned by Bentham, whose *Fragment on Government* appeared in 1776. The antirevolutionary mood which evolved during the nineteenth century was more receptive to the utilitarian concept of majority rule than to the natural rights of the Declaration, which could be used to justify revolutionary movements.

For half a century after the French Revolution, most of Europe feared a new Reign of Terror and Tocqueville seemingly wrote *Democracy* as though the Jacobins were peering over his shoulder. The classic eighteenth-century natural rights embodied in the Declaration were a standing invitation to insurrection. So Tocqueville judiciously avoided them and associated the Declaration with America's "breaking" its commercial ties with England.[135] Given his knowledge of the French Revolution and its aftermath, it is understandable that Tocqueville was only a venturesome conservative. Yet it is something of a paradox that Tocqueville, who advanced the maxim that governments which are founded upon a single principle are the strongest, ignored the greatest principle of American democracy.

Farkas, in contrast, understood the importance of the Declaration and the Constitution as the founding and the completion of the republican edifice. He translated the Declaration to demonstrate to Emperor Francis that the truths it announced were self-evident, and he documented the excellence of their results in his *Journey*.

In modern America the unique principles expressed in its founding documents are in danger of being replaced under the pressure of a decadent middle class unfamiliar with the edifice constructed by the Founding Fathers two centuries ago. Thus it is refreshing to read Farkas's bracing vision of immutable constitutionalism in a still-democratic society in constant search for a more perfect union. The American Revolution, according to Farkas, was unique because it established civil liberties and the preservation of certain inalienable rights as the primary principles of government. Here Farkas again differed with Tocqueville's view that the American Revolution "proceeded hand in hand with a love of order and legality." Farkas analyzed the American Revolution as a search for principles that did not end at Lexington, Saratoga, or Yorktown. To him the search had worldwide significance. Paine first announced this theme in

Common Sense, where he justified the American rebellion on the grounds that it was a special American mission. This concept received the seal of approval from Emerson, who wrote: "[America] is the country of the Future... it is a country of beginnings, of projects, of designs of expectations. Gentlemen, there is a sublime and friendly destiny by which the human race is guided."[136] Lincoln observed the worldwide significance of the American Revolution by saying: "This is the sentiment embodied in the Declaration of Independence."[137] On leaving America, Farkas spoke for Emerson and Lincoln when he wrote: "Farewell once more, glorious country! Remain mankind's eternal guardian and haven! Stand forever in stern warning to despots! May you remain forever the inspiring beacon to the oppressed."

After suffering under the despotic rule of Emperor Francis, Farkas naturally saw the Declaration as an affirmation of a right to revolution just as Lincoln did when he said that the Declaration "gave liberty not alone to the people of the country, but hope to all the world, for all future time."[138] This interpretation was consistent with Farkas's reading of Paine, Joseph Priestley, and David Ramsay. He had read Priestley's *Doctrine of Philosophical Necessity Illustrated* (1777) and his *Lectures on History and General Policy* (1788). Priestley openly advocated the French Revolution and wrote a brilliant rejoinder to Burke's famous jeremiad against it. He linked the French and American revolutions because they signaled a change from "darkness to light."[139] Farkas was therefore greatly attracted to Priestley because of Priestley's Jeffersonian views and because he was the most articulate and influential exponent of Unitarianism. Jefferson's regard for Priestley was amply demonstrated when he tried to induce Priestley to settle near Monticello and Jefferson described his friend as matchless "in religion, in politics, in physics."[140] However, Priestley's view of the American and French revolutions as a passage from "darkness to light" is antithetical to Tocqueville's neo-Burkean view that "the American... has arrived at a state of democracy without having to endure a democratic revolution..." Coleridge summarized the exchange between Priestley and Burke by writing: "The severest punishment I wish for him [Burke]—that he may be appointed under-porter to St. Peter, and be obliged to open the gate of heaven to... Priestley!"[141]

Farkas accepted the Jeffersonian concept of the Revolution as well as Ramsay's view that in America "the sovereignty was in the people."[142] This was but a shorthand version of Paine's theory that government has of itself "no rights"; they are altogether "duties." Farkas was, unlike Tocqueville, a radical. Their contrasting assessment of Lafayette is sufficient as an example. Tocqueville wrote: "In general they consider the hero of two worlds, as a fine man who lacks judgement and who wants to apply political theories to a people whom they don't suit."[143] Farkas wrote:

> Ever since the fall of the Greek and Roman republics, history cannot attest to greater and truer democratic men than Washington, Lafayette, and Bolívar.

The American revolutions they led are important and famous not because they established a new form of government, but because they transformed the prevailing theory of governing and have inspired mankind to new ideas.

Farkas was in Paris in December 1830, when the rumors began to spread that Lafayette had resigned his commission in the National Guard and the king had accepted. Some students decided to send a delegation to Lafayette to convey their sadness and Farkas reported:[144]

> I joined the delegation and when we reached Lafayette's place on the Rue d'Anjou news spread that he was at the Chamber of Deputies. The cry went up, "A la Chambre!" We were about to set out when the old man drove up in a carriage. . . . He could hardly alight in the throng. The crowd shouted with one voice: "Vive Lafayette!" In the meanwhile he went up to his room. We gathered in circles in the yard. Then the grand old man came down and joined us. Respect shone on all faces with religious devotion. One youth conveyed the purpose of the delegation. When he finished, the old man kissed him with passion. What an enviable kiss! The first love kiss couldn't have been sweeter. Then the old man addressed the youths and conveyed his appreciation for their devotion. Tears streamed down their faces and only a stone-heart would have been unmoved. . . . No emperor and conqueror could have inspired such respect, and a thousand politicians couldn't have induced such celebration. He shook everyone's hand and we left the place and the great man with a sacred, noble feeling.

This moving portrayal of Lafayette reveals much about Farkas himself. His diary entries and private writings confirm that he was attracted to revolutionary figures. His seemingly timid and introspective surface masked a rebellious spirit which, had opportunity presented itself, would have erupted and translated theories into action. He despised absolute monarchy. The fatherly Emperor Francis died and the papers spoke of him in almost idolatrous veneration. Farkas's diary reads:[145]

> I cannot remember from my history whether prior to the spread of the Bible it was claimed that God orders, elevates, and deposits kings on earth as his vicars. To my knowledge it contradicts the legal tradition *(iuris publici)* and coincides with the Pope's claim that he is God's vicar.

Farkas comments on the divine right of kings by writing: "You Greeks and Romans, English and French, and stubborn Americans and all those who fought despotism, opposed God's will. What a pity we cannot discourse on this topic without bayonets." Farkas conceded that Emperor Francis was a good Christian. But like Austria's greatest poet, Grillparzer, he believed that Francis would have become a Turk overnight if it would help his despotic regime. According to Farkas:

> The most unfortunate and painful situation is when under despotism liberty awakens in one's soul yet that soul must try to extinguish its sacred flame—without much hope. What a bitter, despairing existence this is for a proud soul who, without hope of betterment, endures at every step abject humiliations, and struggles in solitude with the passions of his poisoned life! He sighs and queries bitterly the future: will it be forever the fate of nations to be but the inheritence of monarchs, and pass on as commodities or beasts of burden?

Farkas referred to hereditary monarchies as the "great lottery of nations" against whose outcome there is no appeal on earth, except a Lockean appeal to "God in Heaven." When Francis suspended the constitution, Farkas confided in his diary:[146]

> And oh, Creator, not even our ardent prayers' invocations reached the steps of your judgment seat? We only wanted to reclaim your eternal laws and nature's sacred rights. We only sought the divine reign of Justice. We merely wished to be free to worship you as free men. But now, Creator, our faith is shaken by doubt. Our patience is wearing thin. Can you blame us if, exhausted by your long and unremittent punishment, we approach you in bitter desperation, requesting: deliverance or destruction.

Farkas's relation to God intimated here is akin to that of Paine, Priestley, and Jefferson. Farkas conceived God to be all-wise, compassionate, simple, and accessible to human reason. He affirmed the Unitarian principles that God endowed man with will and reason to be utilized in leading a moral life and devising a good government. Farkas was repelled by theological portrayals of an awful God who reduced man to nothing more than a vehicle of depravity and sin. Yet he considered himself to be a good Christian and an adherent of the morality of Jesus. In his diary he wrote:[147]

> Among other things this year, I have realized that no positive religion can provide moral principles that would satisfy reason. Not prayer, or the blood of Jesus, or even God himself can absolve our sins. Only we ourselves can do it by ceasing to be sinners.

Farkas had a rather novel concept of Jesus, completely consistent with his political philosophy:[148]

> Jesus perhaps didn't even intend to give mankind, man, and the educated classes a general religion. He saw only his own oppressed nation.... He saw the political oppression and nothingness of his nation and knew that only moral force can save it.

Jesus the great reformer was part of the Jeffersonian concept of Christian religion. Priestley, in a book entitled *Socrates and Jesus Compared* (1803), interpreted Jesus as an ethical propagandist to be imitated rather than worshiped. Like the Jeffersonians, Farkas projected his own activist-reformist qualities onto Jesus.

In adopting the role of activist-reformist, Farkas had to have a strong sense of duty and compassion for the oppressed. He had no difficulty in symbolizing Lafayette as a champion of the cause. He summarized Lafayette's role in the American Revolution:

> He came when the chances for a successful outcome were small, when liberty was banished from the face of the earth, and the oppressed, servile people were scared even to think. He came here when reason itself and the free, unshackled expression of an idea were signs of rebellion. And the mere mention of or sympathy to the rights of man was persecuted and often rewarded with exile or death.

Farkas was haunted by the image of exile or death. When the Greek War of Independence broke out in 1821, the flower of Greek youth—the Sacred

56   Battalion—was routed, although a few managed to escape across the
Austrian border. Four of them turned up in Farkas's hometown, and he
wrote to a friend:[149]

> An exciting event occured which I want to share with you. Four important
> refugees from Ypsilanti's vanquished army arrived here, and took up residence.
> One is secretary to Ypsilanti [Skufto], the second is the young prince
> Soutzos . . . the third is the adjutant of Ypsilanti [Riso], the fourth a well-known
> Greek patriot [Mano]. Friend! They awe and astonish me. . . . Every day I am a
> regular visitor at their place. They gave me so much pleasure and satisfaction,
> and I have spent so many exciting hours there, that I part with them as a lover.
> To praise and sum them up, I say with Shakespeare—These are the men. . . .
> Skufto has a handwritten poem by Goethe, whom he met in Jena. Who knows
> whether we shall not share their destiny. I told Soutzos that if I deserve to live, I
> shall turn to him. Whereupon he embraced me and said in tears: "Remember the
> poor Greeks!"

Goethe gave Skufto his handwritten and autographed poem, "Kop-
tisches Lied" (1796) or "Ein Anderes," i.e. the second Coptic song.[150]

> Geh! gehorche meinen Winken,
> Nutze deine jungen Tage,
> Lerne zeitig klüger sein:
> Auf des Glückes grosser Waage
> Steht die Zunge selten ein;
> Du musst steigen oder sinken,
> Du musst herrschen und gewinnen,
> Oder deinen und verlieren,
> Leiden oder triumphieren,
> Amboss oder Hammer sein.

The moral drawn from the poem for the Greek revolutionaries was the
choice of being an anvil or a hammer ("Amboss oder Hammer sein"), a
choice which Goethe did not leave open to doubt.

Farkas also faced that choice, and hence he remembered the Greeks.

While in Boston he called on Edward Everett, a philhellenist known
chiefly as the orator whose peroration at Gettysburg was eclipsed by
Lincoln. Philhellenism was a strong intellectual current in the third decade
of the nineteenth century and many contacts Farkas made in England were
members of the philhellenic circle. They included Sir John Cam
Hobhouse, MP, eventually Lord Broughton, a radical celebrated for the
invention of the phrase "His Majesty's Opposition." While in Canada,
Farkas also met William Lyon Mackenzie, the fiery Scot who called on the
people of Canada to strike a blow for liberty and independence. So it is not
surprising that the contacts made in England among the members of the
London Greek Committee were mostly Whigs, Radicals, and Indepen-
dents. Bentham and David Ricardo were members, but John Stuart Mill
was not. Mill and Tocqueville disliked radicalism in any form.

The idealized Greeks inherited a romantic tenor from Byron and
Shelley. Even Goethe could not resist the legend of Prometheus. Romantic
minds, like that of Farkas, are attracted to rebels whose fire and knowledge

defy Zeus. In his dramatic fragment, *Prometheus* (1774), young Goethe
revealed how Prometheus appealed to the Romantics:[151]

> Sieh nieder, Zeus,
> Auf meine Welt: sie lebt!
> Ich habe sie geformt nach meinem Bilde
> Ein Geschlecht, das mir gleich sei . . .

The myth of Prometheus assumed special reality for Farkas, because he sought justice and progress in a country ruled by a foreign despot. His urge to give the gift of knowledge to a backward society and infuse it with justice for all was shared with Széchenyi. But Széchenyi and Wesselényi were scions of ancient families with wealth and power. They could afford to rebel against Metternich and consort with other members of the European nobility. Even so, they were revolutionaries, peers of other prominent rebels like Byron. Their titles and wealth lifted their Promethean defiance to a higher plane. Bertrand Russell, himself a peer-rebel, described all three when he said of Byron:[152]

> It must be understood that the freedom he praised was that of a German prince, or a Cherokee chief, not the inferior sort that might conceivably be enjoyed by ordinary mortals.

Farkas himself had already indicted the Hungarian nobility for its congenital inability to understand freedom in the ordinary sense—only the nobility could flap liberal wings under Metternich.

At the height of his personal triumph, Farkas was visited by a delegation, headed by Wesselényi, which intended to honor him as the Columbus of democracy. Farkas recalled the visit in his diary:[153]

> The delegation was approaching my quarters. To me the billowing heron feathers on hats appeared like engulfing ocean waves. I felt I was sinking. Wesselényi led the goblet-bearing procession. My room soon filled with people, and I stood before them like a condemned man. Wesselényi spoke with such a solemn expression as though he were not my childhood friend but a stranger standing before me. His speech was long and I was unable to concentrate on its content in order to respond. I was preoccupied with my feelings, and under the cataract of praise my surging emotions became ever more confused.

The delegation departed and again Farkas confided in his diary:[154]

> After the delegation left, I felt completely exhausted, fatigued in body and spirit as if I had completed a long journey. But under the fatigue I felt indescribably happy that once more I could be alone without battling my confused feelings. As if a burden, carried for long, was cast off my soul. Glorious moments of success! I have paid a high price for your fleeting moments.

Farkas's emotional response was more than a personal idiosyncrasy, perhaps best explained in the words of Byron:[155]

> Sorrow is knowledge. They who know the most
> Must mourn the deepest o'er the fatal truth
> The Tree of Knowledge is not that of Life.

The "fatal truth" was simply that Széchenyi was an aristocratic Prometheus, while Farkas knew that he himself was of the lumpen aristocracy and

58   thus an unlikely Columbus of democracy—especially in Metternich's despotic empire. Farkas also knew that the unwritten law of feudalism forced him, Széchenyi, and Wesselényi to live on virtually separate planets. Farkas wrote of Wesselényi:[156]

> In political life he has one big flaw. He believes, and rightly so judged by the results, that he is a master orator. He refuses to believe that he faces a crafty enemy who dissolves behind his back with mocking laughter his rhetoric. He refuses to admit that the enemy is as cunning as it is stupid. Oh, my country! When will end my anxious suffering for you? At times you inspire noble hope, full of radiant and bright future. Then the clouds seem to disappear. But then a new storm thunders over and lays you prostrate. We are aroused from our dreams to face a new, ever refined and crafty tryanny. Oh, what a depleting existence the sufferings of a hopeless lover.

The "sufferings of a hopeless lover" could have been written by Farkas as his own epitaph. He was in love with republicanism, sick unto death of the feudal order, and considered citizenship to be man's highest achievement. He echoed the Aristotelian dictum that the *zoon politikon* is the true social character of man.

Farkas's perception of citizenship as the answer to political problems influenced his socialist sympathies, and some Hungarian Marxists have claimed Farkas was the precursor of socialist thought in Hungary.[157] However, Marx believed citizenship was a mode of alienation, a preliminary to the final "human" emancipation, free of political, social, and economic attributes. This interpretation is based on the suppressed Táncsics manuscript and Farkas's own diary entry about the meeting between Farkas and Táncsics, who was a Marxist. There is no doubt that Farkas was strongly sympathetic toward utopian-socialist thought. But if he had expressed his view on this subject, it would have been identified with solitariness rather than solidarity. He was prevented from going over by his Unitarian faith, which could not blend with the solidarity of Marxism. Farkas never sought to redeem mankind but only to lead "servile Hungary" to a new age of secular republicanism. Besides, Farkas asserted proudly that he was a masterless man and he agreed entirely with Jefferson that the mass of mankind was not born with "saddles on their backs" to be ridden by the few. After his first few days in the United States, Farkas wrote:

> Only ordinary citizens live here. Converse with members of leading families, meet the higher and lower nobility—they are but citizens. Priests and soldiers, police and judges, scholars and bankers—so many equal citizens! . . . No privileges. No nobility. No titles, no feudal orders, no guilds, no secret police. Oh, how exhilarating each of these are to us.

This passionate celebration of the political freedom of equal citizens is linked to Rousseau's notion of the general will. The general will in Farkasian terms is exemplified by citizens having equal political rights in a constitutional democracy. Compare that with Tocqueville's thesis that America was a democratic society without a democratic government. Tocqueville associated the principal strength of American democracy with a diffused democratic spririt rather than with a broadening of popular suffrage during the colonial period. Tocqueville also stressed the intellectual spread of democratic values and its impact on public opinion. To Tocqueville the success and viability of democracy were dependent on an image of man schooled in traditional aristocratic values. Tocqueville's philosophical conservatism was rooted in the concept of authority, tradition, and sanctity.

Farkas, on the other hand, welcomed the widest possible dissemination of untutored public opinion facilitated by newspapers and communication networks, which brought together in one agora the citizens in Jacksonian Democracy. Farkas captured the latent romanticism of the Jacksonians, the fluidity of power and swift economic changes that were undermining traditionally sacred values. The inquisitive and innovative restlessness of America in the 1830s sought shortcuts to economic prosperity. But American romanticism was a more pragmatic and pronouncedly more interested in enlarging political space and freedom than its European counterpart. European romantic thought was more of a threat to every form of government based on anything but the will of the governed.

The European Romantics emphasized the Hegelian concept of "becoming" more than his conservative "being." Whatever the "secret" of Hegel's philosophy, Farkas associated the mainstream of European political theory with constitutionalism, democracy, and progress. Hegel did not hold in high regard any of these concepts. He rejected the concept of "the people" as an abstraction, and considered universal suffrage as the "French libertarian madness." Farkas, on the other hand, believed that the inborn goodness of man entitled peasants to political rights. Here Farkas borrowed from Rousseau the radical view that titles and privileges violated the law of nature. This explains Farkas's anticlericalism. He had seen the same falseness in religion and in politics: one preached rites and the other upheld titles. What was needed was to undo this reign of deception. Hence the Romantics in general, and Farkas in particular, attached considerable importance to the power of the printed word to inform the suffering people of their decadent oppressors.

Farkas continually marveled at the proliferation of published knowledge in America. Truly, Rousseau's prophecy that the future will be under "the empire of opinion and the appeal of pleasure"[158] had become a reality. Pascal's similar observation on the power of opinion over men's minds[159] leads directly to Tocqueville's postulate of the tyranny of the majority. Farkas did not reach a similar conclusion. He did not share Pascal's view that opinion rules the world. Rather, Farkas dealt with opinion as a sociological aggregate. Farkas's individualism premised the coalescing of religious and economic activities in the public realm. He believed that citizens were characteristically well informed about and interested in the res publica. Farkas associated government—rooted in a constitution and based on consent of the people—with the competitive pursuit of happiness

60   without a corresponding neglect of public affairs. Farkas, in his fragmentary but deep-thrusting way, conceived of the state as a humane institution for the promotion of public welfare which operated by the principles of economics and politics. He did not commit the fatal error of many of his contemporaries of separating economics from politics as though the production and distribution of wealth and goods could be divorced from the civil and constitutional law under which the process operates. Hence Farkas was more attuned to Jacksonian realities than was Tocqueville.

The point is that the romantic Farkas was also a tough-minded realist, more at home in the expansive and seething democracy of Jacksonians with its loud nationalism, fluent and free citizens, than was Tocqueville. The highly volatile Jacksonian generation—a nation of farmers and mechanics—was worrisome to many people who wondered whether a republic of principles could survive the emotional Jacksonians and their worldly interests. And philosophers of the Old World who were accustomed to cast horoscopes of the future took note of that Jacksonian Democracy which the *British Foreign Quarterly* called "horn-handed and pigheaded, persevering, unscrupulous, carnivorous . . . with an incredible genius for lying."

Though Farkas himself was a European, he did not suffer from one-sided pedantry in reflecting, with few strictures, on the American experiment in democracy. Most European Romantics escaped from practical politics into a created world of aesthetics and metaphysical abstractions; Farkas, when it came to democracy, was a man of practical common sense. He did not display the refined contempt for society that sharpened "the depth of Pascal's thoughts."[160] Even as a man of letters, he considered himself to be part of society and hence able to transcribe the Jacksonian reality. American romanticism supplanted the democratic Enlightenment and was schooled in the imperative of "We, the people." In contrast, the European Romantics were defiant titans battling the tradition of the "aristocracy." That is the fundamental difference between European and American romanticism, as well as the difference in their political traditions.

"We, the people" played an indispensable role in developing the American political tradition. "We" included the intellectuals with a strong attachment to the Constitution, but European intellectuals were not conditioned by constitutional history. With the appeal for a "natural" government, the essence of democracy, as distinguished from an artificial and ceremonial monarchy, there was also the leveling process of democracy in arts and letters. But this was only true of Jacksonian Democracy. Emerson may have preferred the poetic genius to the steam engine, but he never questioned the efficacy of happiness under the constitutional framework. Thoreau said, "The only government that I recognize—and it matters not how few are at the head of it, or how small its army—is that power that establishes justice in the land, never that which establishes injustice."[161] American Transcendentalists, unlike European Romantics, did not attack politics and society in the name of "culture." Robert Southey's *Colloquies* clearly shows that the romantic mind prefers rosebushes to steam engines.[162] Of course Santayana classed the Declaration of Independence as a "piece of literature" and called it a "salad of illusions."[163] But Santayana's roots were deeply European and he could not accept democracy as only a method of finding proximate solutions for insoluble problems. He was European to the extent that he preferred men of letters who would starve in garrets rather than test their ideals in the world of dust and sweat. While European intellectuals distinguished themselves in the world of ideas and literature, American intellectuals were creating a nation.

Jefferson's cabinet was composed entirely of college graduates in 1801, twenty-seven of fifty-six men in Philadelphia with college backgrounds supported the Declaration, and twenty-three of thirty-nine committed themselves to the Constitution.[164] During the Jacksonian period, American intellectuals mounted pulpits, stood on public platforms, and disseminated useful knowledge. It was this civic spirit and commitment to the *res publica* that caught Farkas's attention in America.

Farkas welcomed the industrial dawn in Europe and in America. In Europe the march of bricks across meadows invited a romantic defense of a homespun gothic past, and produced an aesthetic distaste for the leveling forces of industry. Many Romantics preferred daffodils and snowdrops to the naked new cottages of the manufacturers. In America, there were few literary attempts to dismantle the "dark satanic mills," or the "malevolent spirit, Mechanism." Jefferson was full of Doric values, and preferred an agrarian arcadia not corroded by industry. He believed that industry begets cities, hence mobs had a certain historical validity. The republican virtues espoused by Jefferson were contingent upon an expanding frontier, settled by people uncorrupted by commerce or industry. The Jeffersonian thesis that finite space filled with an infinitely expanding trade and commerce would doom America as it had Europe was summed up by Channing, who saw Europe filled with "improved fabrics but deteriorating men."[165]

Farkas, however, was sympathetic to Saint-Simon's "religion" of scientism and progress. He did not envision a machine-dominated civilization devoid of spiritual and cultural values. Farkas's common sense was manifest in his concept that the worlds of fact and spirit evolve together—this, incidentally, makes him attractive to Marxist humanists. His writings convey clearly that the changing circumstances that mark the economic and social development of nations also give periods to the improvement of arts and letters. It is one of the significant phases of history that political democracy during its formative centuries was accompanied by the rise and development of science and invention. When Rousseau was writing the *Social Contract*, Watt was putting the steam engine on an operating basis. Farkas revived Hume's practical view that expanding commerce and

62   industry not only enlarge the choices available to man, and thus the sphere of human experience, but become a "second" nature of man. Farkas understood the complementarity of an expanding economy exemplified by the steam engine, steamboats, and the railroads. These technological developments were a means of disseminating information to a democratic citizenry which could only bring its opinions and votes to the agora. Farkas farsightedly knew that technology would produce a national identity tied to the common pursuit of progress. Washington Irving may have wished to blow up "all the cotton mills" and make picturesque ruins of them; Emerson could prophesy that "machinery is aggressive" and dangerous; but, as Robert Penn Warren noted recently, American literature mostly celebrates a miraculous feat:[166]

> Two hundred years ago a handful of men on the Atlantic seaboard, with a wild continent at their back, risked their necks and their sacred honor to found a new kind of nation, and thus unleashed an unprecedented energy that succeeded to a power and prosperity beyond their most fantastic dreams.

Warren calls attention to the difference between Europe and America. In Europe, there was an irreconcilable quarrel between the artist and the world, but the American artist did not quarrel "with this world but with what had been made of his world."[167] This ideal was expressed in the two documents that Farkas associated with the guiding genius of America, and so Warren apparently agrees with the Farkasian thesis that the concept of the self is proclaimed in the Declaration and the Constitution, and later embodied in "the very structure of the government which was to depend upon the vote of 'single men spoken on their honor and their conscience.'"[168]

According to Farkas, what was unusual about America was not an "equality of condition"; rather, it was the will-to-change of the common man. He remarked that in America, reality simply outstripped statistical data, and predicted that the avocation of ideals and the vocation of practical democracy would be combined in constitutional republicanism. He wrote:

> Opponents of republican principles who claim to see the rebirth of a national aristocracy, and to whom administrators are the necessary product of a higher power's secret decisions, find this system incomprehensible. Convinced that the electorate is always faction-ridden, they prophesy the collapse of the whole system. Yet in America no one seems to fear this for the simple reason that here the people constitute the government and not the government the people.

Farkas also discerned that republican America wove a new pattern of life. After visiting Lowell, he wrote:

> The textile mills give jobs and livings to about two thousand workers. Newly arrived immigrants comprise most of the labor force, particularly the poverty-driven Irish immigrants, who, if they are thrifty, can save enough in two to three years on their high wages to buy a few acres of very cheap land, and thus become farmers. To a settled and propertied citizen every opportunity is open. According to the latest science of politics, high wages are a sign of a prosperous nation because where the number of wage earners increases, the number of poor declines.

While in Lowell, Farkas pronounced wage labor preferable to
serfdom, and in Boston he discovered that industry and culture are
compatible. He leaves no doubt of his conviction that wealth and progress
are the product of freedom. Farkas, under the influence of Channing,
caught glimpses of the intellectual ferment in Boston as English rationalism
made its symbiotic yield—*sic transit gloria mundi*—to European romantic
thought. "About 1820," wrote Emerson, "the Channing, Webster, and
Everett era begun, and we have been bookish and poetic and cogitative
since."[169] Like Tocqueville, Farkas visited Channing. Tocqueville confided
to Channing that he was frightened at "the distance that the human spirit
has travelled since Catholicism," and objected to making reason a common
denominator of the great "mass of man." Then Tocqueville added:[170]

> It seems to me that Catholicism had established the government of the skillful or
> aristocracy of Religion, and that you have introduced Democracy. Now, I
> confess to you, the possibilitiy of governing religious society like political
> society, by the means of Democratie does not seem to me yet proven by
> experience.

The statement is instructive. While Tocqueville saw Catholicism as a
positive thing in Canada, Farkas treated it as a brake on progress and
antithetical to liberal democracy. Tocqueville declared: "I don't believe
there is a happier people in the world than the Canadian." Farkas said:

> But no matter how attractive the English government's settlement policies are,
> Canadian settlers are still attracted to and look with undisguised yearning at the
> constitutional life of the neighboring free states. Despite the debt of gratitude to
> the mother country, they cannot hide their feeling of political nonexistence.

Catholic Lower Canada was the opposite of Farkas's Unitarian and
republican ideals. He had a natural affinity with Channing which
transcended religion. Both shared a deep interest in literature and were
under the spell of Rousseau, of whom Parrington said:[171]

> Changing its name and arraying itself in garments cut after the best Yankee
> fashion, the gospel of Jean Jacques presently walked the streets of Boston and
> spoke from its most respectable pulpit, under the guise of Unitarianism.

The influence of Rousseau on Channing was evident in the Unitarian
notion that the soul transcribes God and his natural goodness. Unitarianism
was a humanistic religion, or what Paine called the Religion of Humanity.
Farkas's commitment to rational intellect and man as free moral agent was
coupled with broad social sympathies. He gave many instances of his
compassion for the bruised and maimed left behind by progress or history.

The other Americans—the Indians—elicited his empathy. Though
Jefferson and his generation hoped that the Indians might merge into white
society, by the 1830s it became clear that nature's man would never become
a farmer. Farkas saw the tragedy as missionaries, without real knowledge of
Indian tradition and culture, wrecked and demoralized a proud race. The
well-intentioned attempts to integrate the Indians merely hastened the
disintegration of red culture. One year after the Congress passed the Indian

64 Removal Bill (1830), Farkas commented: "Poor Indians! Strangers in your
own land! Your enemies, who murdered your forefathers, already treat you
as foreign intruders!" Although there was a good deal of romanticism in this
treatment of Indians as a vanishing race, which was part of the literary
sentiment of the 1830s, it also expressed Farkas's Unitarian concern for the
crushed and scorned. Unitarianism in Boston may have been the self-
celebration of the arrived, but Farkas, coming from the crucible of races and
religions, had a fine-tuned social conscience for the psychological needs of
others.

Farkas's Unitarianism, like that of Channing, was not a pulpit creed
but the disposition of a sensitive mind. During his European tour,
Channing visited Wordsworth and Coleridge. Wordsworth agreed with
Channing that nothing in original Christianity rendered it unadaptable to a
progressive society based on civic order and administered by just laws. In
turn, Channing was taken by Coleridge's poetic genius constantly striving
for higher truths. Channing attributed a divine power to poetic genius,
whose plasticity, iconic imagination, and unmediated creativity are close to
God. In Milton he saw the archetype of poetic genius:[172]

> We agree with Milton in his estimate of poetry. It seems to us the divinest of all
> arts; for it is the breathing or expression of that principle or sentiment, which is
> the deepest and sublimest in human nature; we mean, of that thirst or
> aspiration, to which no mind is wholly stranger, for something purer and
> lovelier . . . than ordinary and real life affords.

Romantic philosophy came to America on the rhymes of Wordsworth
and Coleridge and, sublimated, in Channing's lyrical sermons. To Channing and Farkas, literature had a public utility that had antecedents in
Rousseau, who told the Poles to remain culturally Poles and thus
indigestible to Russia's imperial appetites. Farkas's cultural nationalism
was also a means to escape the Hapsburg embrace. As Romantics,
Channing and Farkas saw religious utility in poetry due to its ability to
penetrate the soul, where, according to the Unitarian view, the apotheosis
of religion occurs as an adoration of goodness. Equally important, literature
was socially useful because its expressive ideals sustained moral values,
preferably republican and libertarian. In Channing's Unitarian theology,
there was a pronounced animus against the ruinous European idea that lofty
social ranks and respectability go together. To Transylvania-born Farkas,
where unmerited privileges flourished like a rank weed, this was a
revelation. But Channing accepted, at least implicitly, the Lockean notion
that property and wealth, though given by God to mankind in common, are
based on industrious merit. Farkas expressed the same convictions by
coining the term "meritocracy." The Hungarian phrase, *igyekezet arisztok-
ráciaja*, literally translates "the aristocracy of endeavor."

Attending a dinner party given by Mr. Winthrop, lieutenant governor
of Massachusetts, Farkas wrote:

> The wealthy Boston citizen's life recalls the privileged few in England and
> France. Those who believe that the comforts of life, secured and attained by

wealth, will erode republican values, and sooner or later introduce aristocratic luxury, can indeed fear that people who walk on English and Chinese rugs in rooms decorated with priceless art, whose table sparkles with the choice wines of Spain, Portugal, and the islands, such leisure class will not maintain for long its independence.... But in America wealth and property are the legitimate offspring of Freedom, Enterprise, and Industry. In America only the aristocracy of endeavor and individual resourcefulness will perpetuate themselves.

Though unabashedly laissez-faire in attitude, Farkas also showed strong interest in utopian socialism and religious communalism. In the midst of boastful Jacksonian materialism, full of cant and avarice, Farkas sought out communal enclaves where sincerity and simpler ways of life glowed contagiously. It is a historical pattern that the thundering facts of the new economic order based on capital and labor release an outburst of utopian enthusiasm. The Shaker and Harmonite communes Farkas visited were havens for those whose religious needs were no longer satisfied by the historical faith of pulpit and pew. The English industrial revolution produced not only machines and wordly goods but religious visions and prayers. The atomized society of machines, and a life disciplined by factory whistles, created not only captains of industry but John Wesley and his religious ecstasy. When English society felt the impress of the machine age, with its clocks, timetables, factory whistles, ordinances, rules, and the lockstep of industrialism, Wesley's call for religious rededication reaped a rich harvest of neglected souls. By the 1760s, Methodism emerged as the religion of those whose emotional needs were unmet by factory life. Unlike the machine's steady monotony and chill clangor, Methodism encouraged emotional outpourings of sobbing and weeping, laughter and hysteria. Farkas captured in the Jacksonians' acquisitive drift this neurotic edge of life undergoing rapid change. Though theology was being forced to reform its verbal modes under the imperatives of industry and technology, and the clerical profession began to scour the Bible for pertinent truths applicable to capitalists and mechanics engaged in creating a new economic order, many people could not adjust to a society swollen with the proceeds of commerce and speculation. It was no accident that Jacksonians who were emotionally or intellectually unfit for everyman's democracy, or who resented its subversion by the uprush of plutocracy, leaned toward the soothing confines of theoretical and spiritual brotherhood.

Farkas wrote:

The Shaker, Rappite, and Owenite communities are three unique phenomena in human history. If they can maintain themselves for another half a century, they will distill great philosophical lessons, and refute many political theories. In all respects the honor for what may follow belongs to the American Constitution, which allows time and gives testing ground for diverse thinking and ideas. It sanctions the soul's many-sided quest without fear of imperiling the system of government and the Constitution.

Taking leave of George Rapp, the patriarch of Economy, Farkas offered a philosophical introspection on man's utopian adventures:

Economy is the great school of practical life and pragmatic philosophy. What is done here is clear and logical: these simple morals, this bucolic domesticity, this disregard of worldly luxury, balanced by full enjoyment of life's rich offerings—all this would seem pious dreams had we not seen it to be convinced of its existence.... I left this place in awe, enriched by a new philosophical discovery: I rejoice in and prefer what I have seen to the secrets that can be learned in all salons.

Farkas's preference for observed reality to the "secrets" of salons was a Rousseauean reaction against the *philosophes*' egotistic gossip conducted in the moral void of salons where "Helvétius had told everybody's secret." To Farkas the affected wisdom of salons was mere froth even if it bubbled with Voltairean wit. He treated enlightened despotism and *res publica* as conceptual opposites. The former denoted a personal rule, the latter a system of law. The antinomy was stated by Paine:[173]

What is called a republic, is not any particular form of government. It is wholly characteristical of the purport, matter, or object for which government ought to be instituted, and on which it is to be employed, *res-publica*, the public affairs, or the public good; or, literally translated, the public thing.

Thus to Farkas what Athens was in miniature, America was in macrocosm: a government that unfolds in the public realm, where private and public interests intersect and where the community seeks a good life under laws. By contrast, the Hapsburg monarchy was based on the medieval notion of rulership. The king or emperor not only ruled as the supreme dispenser of justice but conceived of the realm as a piece of real estate to be fleeced at will. Rulership meant the right to extract income from the realm for a conspicuous style of living. Analyzing the 1830 budget of the United States, Farkas wrote:

The simple secret of national welfare is that no conspicuous court, indolent officialdom, useless army, and secret police are kept at public expense.

The importance of Farkas's place in nineteenth-century liberal thought was his consistent republicanism. Ever since the fall of the Roman republic, the main political tradition of Europe was monarchical. If we add that political thought is for the most part the product and not the cause of political conditions, then we begin to appreciate the historical importance of Farkas as perhaps the only nineteenth-century figure, next to Benjamin Constant, who attempted to draw up a comprehensive republican program in monarchical Europe. Though the voice of Kant sounding across the sandy plains of Prussia proclaimed the French Revolution as the advent of permanent peace and federation of European republics, it was Farkas who, suffering the paralyzing social and political conventions of the Hapsburg monarchy, conceived of the republican form of government as the alternative to the rampant militarism of monarchies.

Tocqueville sought to establish some "secret" connection between democracy and militarism when he wrote: "No kind of greatness is more pleasing to the imagination of a democratic people than military greatness, a greatness of vivid and sudden luster, obtained without toil, by nothing but

the risks of life!"[174] Farkas, by contrast, associated militarism and its
squandering of public wealth with monarchical polity. He knew well what
crushing debts the Hapsburg monarchy imposed on society. During the
Napoleonic Wars, the monarchy had an army of 371,000 men out of a
population of 16 million, or one soldier for every thirty-two persons. By
1814 the army swelled to 619,000 men. Empress Maria Theresa started to
roll the presses to cover with paper money the enormous military debts. By
1811 paper currency reached over one billion florins. The Hungarian
nobility, schooled in the medieval theory that the realm is the ruler's real
estate, left the finance and currency to the divine reason of rulers. The
taming of royal authority by controlling purse strings in England had
widened the scope of freedom and introduced the policy of bargaining with
the monarch for redress of communal grievances. This was totally
unknown in the Hapsburg model of government. No wonder Farkas was so
taken by the "happy country" of the Jacksonians, whose frugal government
was a "disheartening lesson for Europe." Farkas may have remembered
Tacitus's maxim that "the whole point of autocracy is that the accounts will
not come right unless the ruler is their only auditor."[175]

Partly under the influence of David Ramsay, Farkas attributed the
uniqueness of America to the sovereignty of the people and the concept of
representation. He wrote:

> In a constitutional republic the electoral laws are the bedrock of the governmen-
> tal system and the cornerstone of civil liberties. The fall of Greece and Rome
> resides in the class restriction of the electorate, the disfranchisement of the
> people, and the establishment of permanent officeholders. These historical
> lessons greatly influenced the framers of the American Constitution, who with
> one stroke of the pen established the self-evident truth that in civil society
> individuals enjoy equal rights.

Unlike most radical liberals of his time, with the possible exception of
Benjamin Constant, Farkas conceived of community as *civitas*—that is, an
association of individuals who are partners, under a constitutional
framework, in the practice of civility whose rules apply equally to rulers
and ruled. In European liberal tradition the state is understood as an
association of persons (*cives*) in terms of a law recognized as a system of
prescriptive conditions (*res publica*), but which are more applicable to the
subjects than to the rulers. In fact, the rulers can be indifferent to the
satisfaction of the people's substantive wants. Farkas's contribution to
liberal political thought was the theory that government is the custodian of
res publica, founded on the spiritual and material well-being of citizens. A
republican government is contingent not on the virtue of its rulers, though
they may be à la Machiavelli benefactors of mankind, but on the pursuit of a
common goal in accord with certain principles.

According to Farkas, it is fear which defines a despotic regime. The
despot's utterances are commands and he gets his way by the exercise of
force. And what is called "government" is but the personal gratification of
the ruler. To Farkas despotism was an outrage against natural law because a

68   despot, whether armed with the rosary or the sword, reduced men to obedient subjects. By contrast, the republican form of government was based on the rule of law sanctified by individual conscience and reason. The republican "science" of politics was not identical to the rulers' self-gratification whether they managed the realm or saved souls. Rather, it was a constitutional commitment to a good society which Farkas understood as a common interest or purpose.[176] This point was best articulated by Constant, whom Farkas admired. Constant understood the important characteristic of the republican form of government to be[177]

> the right to be subject only to the laws, the assurance of being neither arrested, nor detained, nor put to death, nor in any way mistreated, by an arbitrary act of will of some one individual or of many. It is for each the right to express his opinion, to choose his occupation and ply it in peace; to dispose of his property, ... to come, to go, without any permission and without rendering any account of his motives or steps. It is for each the right to assemble with other individuals, either to confer with them upon common interests, or to practice the religion of his choice, or merely to use his leisure conformably to his inclinations or indeed his fancy.

Farkas's *Journey* is permeated with this spirit. His republican theory of government was marked by two insights. He associated the genius of American politics with the two "founding documents." The Declaration expressed the ethical commitment of the nation, and the Preamble to the Constitution stated a sociological fact. The ethical commitment—Lockean and Jeffersonian—bounds the power of government in maintaining authority and order. The Preamble stated the conservative Aristotelian notion that because the nation, "We, the people," is an aggregate of many members with diverse interests and values, it must seek under the constitutional framework a "more perfect union," "justice," and "domestic tranquillity." To reconcile and weld together the people into a cohesive national identity, and herein lies Farkas's second great insight, is the true art of republican government.[178]

Farkas was convinced that America had conclusively demonstrated to the Old World that a more perfect union is attainable and within the compass of human achievement. He attributed the success of the American political enterprise to the creation of a form of government that was neither strictly republican nor democratic. America was not a rerun of Europe—Milton's ideal republic was an aristocracy, Cromwell's commonwealth a hybrid of aristocracy and dictatorship, and the French republic oppressively unitary—but something breathtakingly new. The Republic had replaced European tyranny based on privilege with an American constitutionalism based on individual liberty, conscience, and popular rule. Farkas's human-conscience-oriented republicanism was captured in Wordsworth's lines: "By the soul / only the nations shall be great and free."[179]

Though philosophical idealism was pronounced in Farkas, he realized that American constitutionalism undermined Rousseau's version of the general will. The Constitution was designed to prevent the emergence of a tyrannical majority and anything that smacked of the notion of the general will. As a Unitarian, which in Hungary meant belonging to a persecuted and slighted minority, Farkas could not accept that whoever refuses to obey the general will can be "forced to be free." Democracy is neither rule by majority nor rule by a minority, but rule by a constitutional government based on persuasion. To Farkas both the majority and the minority are permeable by reason and attend to the common good.

In America, Farkas learned that only in a democracy, based on persuasion, can the minority accede to majority rule. Even the Congress was designed to resist the unprocessed waves of democratic sentiment reaching the legislative chamber. Consequently the Senate was not apportioned according to population growth—though Farkas noted the phenomenal growth of cities and population. The congressional process was a formal safeguard against the potential tyranny of the majority. Slowing the democratic and legislative process meant there was time to discern the sense of community that inevitably emerges. In addition, there was one powerful guard watching over the civil liberties of citizens. Farkas put it this way:

> Here too, despite the strict electoral laws and a strong sense of justice, vanity, hunger for power, and cunning could twist elections to ends to which they are twisted in many places in Europe, despite flawless laws. But a powerful guardian watches here over civil liberties and laws, ready to strike with its sharp weapon the violator of the law making his first move. That guardian is the freedom of the press.

To Farkas the freedom of the press was an informal yet powerful curb on the tyrannical tendency of power. Though influenced by Rousseau, Farkas was reluctant to endow "the people" with unlimited power. His model was the American concept of popular sovereignty—conditional and bounded by checks and balances. Unrestrained power was like dice, whose outcome is unknown and hence to be feared, from whatever hand they are tossed.

A product of the nineteenth century, Farkas reflected his own time. That century was noted for its intense search to devise a formula to reconcile the individual and society. There were many attempts to integrate man and society in a political formula—among the seminal ones, Rousseau's general will as revived by Hegel, the English utilitarians, Tocqueville's "new science of politics," and Marx's apolitical classless society. Did Farkas possess a model to reconcile man and society? His *Journey in North America* carries the conviction that American democracy was the model to reconcile individual liberty and the social order. Unlike John Stuart Mill, and to a lesser degree Tocqueville, who objected to the inclusion of the emerging industrial order under a democratic framework, Farkas welcomed the ascendancy of a democracy of steam and steel.

The emerging industrial reality in America predisposed Farkas to the great challenger of nineteenth-century liberalism. While in Paris, Farkas

70   attended a gathering of Saint-Simonians, who preached the gospel of science, progress, and the amelioration of the condition of the poor. Saint-Simon sought to reconcile God and Industry. He advanced the theory that God's will and scientific progress are identical and beneficial to society. Opposed to the political philosophy of Plato and Rousseau, Saint-Simon vested his hopes in the science of production. Not surprisingly, the philosopher of progress, Saint-Simon, who fought under Washington in the American Revolution, looked upon America as the possible theater in which to carry the new idea to full fruition.[180]

According to Farkas, the American Constitution was not only an array of devices to hold men in check but also a vehicle of human aspiration. The Constitution was unique because it recognized that progress is generic to man. In American experience, activism and republicanism have generated a near-irresistible pressure to make confidence in progress the keynote of the legal order. The Constitution did not confine society to a "static" austere existence. On the contrary, to Farkas, the American legal order opened the door to future contingencies by presupposing that change is the business of living and that social reality is always active, questing, problem-solving men.

Although Farkas had lit a candle in the Saint-Simonian church called Progress, his Unitarian conscience recoiled from reducing politics to a mere technical ordering of production. But he accepted and applied four Saint-Simonian criteria in measuring progress. All four are evident in his *Journey*. First, Farkas judged the United States by the socioeconomic arrangements which produce the most efficient means to satisfy society's basic needs. Second, he correlated good government with the degree to which advancement in society was based upon ability rather than privilege. Third, he used population increase as an index of prosperity. His fourth standard of progress was the degree to which society valued scientific and technological achievements. Though sympathetic to the Saint-Simonian criteria of progress, Farkas rejected its messianic humanism leading to the unification of all men in one "great age." Farkas was indifferent by temperament and philosophy to any grandiose world civilization that would efface individual uniqueness. He suspected all gospels that promised to cure this sad planet of all ills and misery, now and immediately.

To Farkas, the American republic was like a many-colored glass dome which stains the immortal radiance of the Declaration and the Constitution. He predicted that America would remove the "stain" by abolishing slavery and thus bring reality closer to its radiant ideals. He affirmed that in the mutable world of democracy, only the Constitution is immutable. Progress and the Constitution are the twin resources by which American democracy extends its scope, deepens its commitments, and disciplines its aspirations.

This generation, heir to many broken hopes and somewhat cynical of America's "uniqueness" when it no longer is the Athens of democracy and the Rome of power, might learn something from Farkas's book. He came to

America when Europe was fired by the reality of *novus ordo saeculorum*. Many Europeans wanted to see with their own eyes how this new republic translated the utopian idealism of the European Enlightenment into political reality. They wanted to know whether the American experiment would endure beyond the Old World's transient republics. To this, Farkas gave a resounding yes.

It is altogether proper that Farkas's *Journey in North America* reach the American people when, once more, this nation is affirming and returning to its founding principles. To Farkas, America was unique because it enlarged mankind's vision of the politically possible. Farkas's book, in drawing a sharp contrast between the Republic and European tyranny and between American democracy and European aristocracy, revives that concept of American uniqueness which was treated in the works of Arthur M. Schlesinger, Jr., Daniel Boorstin, Louis Hartz, and Henry Steele Commager.

The translation of *Utazás Észak-Amerikában* is based on the original first published in 1834. The original text of *Utazás* was composed of twenty-nine chapters. The first three sketch Farkas's European travels and the Atlantic crossing and have been omitted. The English text begins with the concluding part of chapter three. Most of chapter thirteen, which contains Farkas's translation of the New Hampshire Constitution, has been excluded. Also omitted, from chapter twenty-six, is Farkas's narrative of Captain Smith's heroic exploits against the Turks in Hungary, his ambush by Indians in America, and how he was saved by the chief's thirteen-year-old daughter Pocahontas. Other than this, the original chapters are reproduced intact.

Notes

1. Raymond Aron, *Main Currents in Sociological Thought* (New York: Basic Books, 1965), 1:184.

2. Quoted by Jack Lively, *The Social and Political Thought of Alexis de Tocqueville* (Oxford: Clarendon Press, 1955), p. 12.

3. See John Stuart Mill's introduction to Tocqueville's *Democracy in America* (New York: Schocken Books, 1970), 1:VL.

4. Ibid.

5. *Memoirs and Letters and Remains of A. Tocqueville* (Boston: Tickner & Fields, 1862), 1:392.

6. László Kőváry, "Bölöni Farkas Sándor életrajza" [Sándor Bölöni Farkas's life], *Napkelet*, no. 105 (1859): 104–105.

7. Shakespeare, *Julius Caesar*, act 1, sc. 2, lines 194–95, 201–03.

8. See Farkas's letter of August 23, 1820, published in *Keresztény Magvető* [Christian sower] 19 (1884): 358. Hereafter cited as *KM*.

9. Ibid., p. 359.

10. Ibid., p. 360.

11. Rousseau, *The Confessions*, trans. J. M. Cohen (Baltimore: Penguin Books, 1965), p. 17.

12. Elemér Jancso, ed., *Farkas Sándor naplója* [The diary of Sándor Farkas] (Kolozsvár-Cluj: Minerva, 1944), pp. 1–3. All translations by the editor.

13. Ibid., pp. 3–4.

14. Ibid., p. 14.

15. Ibid., pp. 15–19.

16. *The Journals of Kierkegaard*, ed. Alexander Dru (New York: Harper Torchbooks, 1959), p. 55.

17. Kierkegaard, *Purity of Heart* (New York: Harper Torchbooks, 1956), p. 185.

18. *Journals of Kierkegaard*, p. 55.

19. Quoted by Kelemen Gál, *A Kolozsvári Unitárius Kollégium története* [The history of the Kolozsvár Unitarian College] (Kolozsvár-Cluj: Minerva, 1935), 1:91–92.

20. See E. M. Wilbur, *A History of Unitarianism in Transylvania, England, and America* (Cambridge: Harvard University Press, 1952), 2:127.

21. For a classic treatment of this, see R. B. Perry, *Puritanism and Democracy* (New York: Harper Torchbooks, 1944), esp. pt. 3.

22. See T. L. Underwood, "Quakers and the Royal Society of London in the 17th Century," *Notes and Records of the Royal Society of London* 31 (July 1976): 133–50.

23. George Fox, *A Journal or Historical Account of the Life of . . . George Fox* (London: Thomas Northcott, 1694), p. 11. Fox advised the people to stand "fast in the Liberty, wherewith Christ has made them free, and not to be entangled again with the Yoke of Bondage" (p. 621). Fox sought to persuade "all kings and princes, to give liberty to all tender consciences in matters of religion and worship, they living peaceably under every Government" (p. 631).

24. *The Prose of John Milton*, ed. J. Max Patrick (Garden City, N.Y.: Doubleday, 1967), pp. 319–20.

74   25. See Farkas's letter of December 26, 1815, to Ferenc Kazinczy, in *Kazinczy Ferenc levelezése* [Correspondence of Ferenc Kazinczy] (Budapest: Magyar Tudományos Akadémia, 1903), 13:369–71. Hereafter cited as *KF*, and appropriate volume.

26. Gál, *A Kolozsvári Unitárius Kollégium története*, p. 206.

27. Quoted by Oscar Jászi, *The Dissolution of the Habsburg Monarchy* (Chicago: University of Chicago Press, 1929), p. 222.

28. Quoted by Ferenc Kanyaró, "Inség 1817-ben" [Famine in 1817], *KM* 40 (1905): 92.

29. Károly Borbáth, "A Jakobinus káté kolozsvári másolójárol" [The Kolozsvár copier of the Jacobin catechism], *Korunk* (Kolozsvár-Cluj) (1963): 259–61.

30. Gál, *A Kolozsvári Unitárius Kollégium története*, p. 189.

31. György Lajos, *A magyar regény elözményei* [The beginnings of the Hungarian novel] (Budapest: Magyar Tudományos Akadémia, 1941), p. 33.

32. Elek Jakab, "Bölöni Farkas Sándor és kora" [Sándor Bölöni Farkas and his era], *KM* 5 (1870): 321.

33. On Farkas's charter membership and activities in the savings and loan association, see József György Oberding, "A Kolozsvári Gondoskodo Társaság [The Kolozsvár Friendly Society], *Erdélyi Muzeum* (1934): 79–104.

34. *Milton*, p. 272.

35. Sándor Farkas, *Nyugateurópai utazás* [West European journey], ed. Elemér Jancso (Kolozsvár-Cluj: Minerva, 1943), p. 133.

36. *KM* 19 (1884): 362. Farkas's aphoristic statement is reminiscent of letter twenty-one in Goethe's *Sorrows of Young Werther:* "My condition is that of a ghost who returned to the burnt-out, ruined castle he had once built, equipped with all the gifts of splendor, when he was a flourishing prince, leaving it, at his death, full of hope to his beloved son." *Sorrows of Young Werther*, trans. Harry Steinhauer (New York: Norton, 1970), p. 58.

37. Homan Bálint and Gyula Szekfü, *Magyar történet* [Hungarian history] (Budapest: Királyi Magyar Egyetemi Nyomda, 1936), 5:25. For an excellent treatment of Voltairism in Hungary, see Béla K. Király, *Hungary* (New York: Columbia University Press, 1969), ch. 12.

38. George Barany, *Stephen Széchenyi, and the Awakening of Hungarian Nationalism 1791–1841* (Princeton: Princeton University Press, 1968), p. 101. See also Béla K. Király, *Ferenc Deák* (Boston: Twayne Publishers, 1975), p. 32.

39. János Kovács, "John Paget Esquire élete" [Life of John Paget Esquire], *KM* 28 (1893): 96–103.

40. John Paget, *Hungary and Transylvania* (London: John Murray, 1850), 1:177.

41. Ibid., p. 178.

42. Johann Gottfried von Herder, *Reflections on the Philosophy of the History of Mankind* (Chicago: University of Chicago Press, 1968), p. 332.

43. For Herder's influence on the Harmonites, see Karl J. R. Arndt, *George Rapp's Harmony Society 1785–1847* (Philadelphia: University of Pennsylvania Press, 1965), pp. 251 ff. Isaiah Berlin, *Vico and Herder* (London: Hogarth Press, 1976), examines the work of Herder and its impact on the nineteenth century. Herder had a great influence on romantic thought by setting in motion the idea that since each civilization has its own outlook and way of thinking, including feeling, it creates its own collective ideals by which it must be judged. Herder also prepared the Romantics for rejecting history as a linear progression. Instead, it was conceived of as a succession of distinct and heterogeneous civilizations, each unified internally, and above all, intelligible in its own right.

44. Bálint and Szekfü, *Magyar történet*, p. 55.

45. *KF*, 13:369–71.

46. Farkas, *Nyugateurópai utazás*, pp. 114–15.

47. See letter of November 6, 1815, in *KF*, 13:264.

48. Ibid.

49. Dénes Bogáts, "Adatok Bölöni Farkas Sándor életpályájához" [Data on Sándor Bölöni Farkas's life], *Erdélyi Muzeum* (1944): 177.

50. Ibid., p. 179.

51. *KF*, 13:209–11.

52. *The Confessions of Saint Augustine*, trans. Edward B. Pussey (New York: Collier Books, 1972), p. 125.

53. Ibid., p. 36.

54. Antal Szerb, *Magyar irodalomtörténet* [Hungarian literary history] (Budapest: Magvetö Könyvkiado, 1958), p. 218.

55. Quoted by Jakab, "Bölöni Farkas Sándor," p. 275.

56. Daniel Boorstin, *The Americans* (New York: Vintage Books, 1958), pp. 281–82.

57. *David Hume's Political Essays*, ed. Charles W. Hendel (New York: Bobbs-Merrill, 1953), p. 24.

58. *KF*, 13:87–88.

59. Quoted by Lajos Hatvány, *Munkák és napok* [Works and Days] (Budapest: Kaldor Könyvkiado, 1934), pp. 50–51.

60. *KF*, 13:209.

61. Ibid., p. 240.

62. *Kazinczy Ferenc eredeti munkái* [Original works of Ferenc Kazinczy] (Budapest: Heinrich Gusztáv, 1826), p. 151.

63. *KF*, 13:509.

64. On Lessing's Germanized Aristotelian precepts, see J. G. Robertson, *Lessing's Dramatic Theory*, ed. E. Purdie (Cambridge: Harvard University Press, 1939), esp. pp. 489 ff.

65. *KF*, 16:264.

66. Jakab, "Bölöni Farkas Sándor," pp. 33–36.

67. Goethe, *Faust*, lines 11577–81.

68. Alexander Pope, "Essay on Man."

69. William Wordsworth, *The Prelude*, bk. 14, lines 70–72, 101–02.

70. Johann Gottfried von Herder, *Sämtliche Werke*, ed. Bernhard Suphan (Berlin, 1877–1913), 8:252.

71. Judith Shklar, *Men and Citizens* (Cambridge: Harvard University Press, 1969), p. 225.

72. Jakab, "Bölöni Farkas Sándor," pp. 276–77.

73. Herder, *Werke*, 8:33.

74. Thomas Babington Macaulay, *Critical and Historical Essays* (London: Longmans, Green, 1883), p. 3.

75. Madame de Staël, *Corinne*, trans. Isabel Hill (New York: Harper & Brothers, n.d.), p. 140.

76. Niccolò Machiavelli, *The Prince*, ed. Max Lerner (New York: Modern Library, 1950), p. 33.

77. Ibid., p. 36.

78. Manuscript no. 1021, at the Cluj Branch of the Rumanian Academy of Sciences.

79. Cited by Sheldon S. Wolin, *Politics and Vision* (Boston: Little, Brown, 1960), p. 145.

80. Manuscript no. 1021.

81. Goethe, *Faust*, lines 577–79.

82. Manuscript no. 779.

83. *KF*, 14:87.

84. *Oeuvres complètes* (Paris: Panthéon Littéraire, 1837), 1:206.

85. Shakespeare, *Julius Caesar*, act 1, sc. 2, lines 135–38.

86. Jancso, *Farkas Sándor naplója*, pp. 9–10.

87. J. G. A. Pocock, *Politics, Language and Time* (New York: Atheneum, 1973), p. 86.

88. Manuscript no. 779.

89. "The Grande Chartreuse" (lines 84–85), in *The Poems of Matthew Arnold, 1840–1867*, ed. A. T. Quiller Couch (London: Oxford University Press, 1930), p. 272.

90. Manuscript no. 1021.

91. Henrik Marczali, *Hungary in the Eighteenth Century* (Cambridge: Harvard University Press, 1910), p. 93.

92. *Gróf Széchenyi István naplói* [The diaries of Count István Széchenyi], ed. Gyula Viszota

76 (Budapest: Magyar Történelmi Társulat, 1925–1939), 3:30. Hereafter cited as *Diaries.*

93. Ibid., 1:612.

94. See Béla Iványi Grünwald's introduction to Széchenyi's *Hitel: A taglalat és a hitellel foglalkozó kisebb iratok* [Credit: The analysis of minor works dealing with credit] (Budapest: Magyar Történelmi Társulat, 1930), pp. 182 ff.

95. Manuscript no. 959.

96. R. R. Palmer, *The Age of Democratic Revolutions* (Princeton: Princeton University Press, 1962), 1:138 ff.

97. Cited by Jászi, *Dissolution of the Habsburg Monarchy*, p. 81.

98. Halvdan Koht, *The American Spirit in Europe* (Philadelphia: University of Pennsyvlania Press, 1949), p. 32.

99. *Diaries*, 2:227.

100. Ibid., 3:320.

101. Ibid., p. 487.

102. Paget, *Hungary and Transylvania*, 1:450.

103. Original text in Barany, *Stephen Széchenyi*, p. 330.

104. *Diaries*, 2:417.

105. István Széchenyi, *Világ vagy is felvilágosito töredékek némi hibás elöitélet eligazitására* [Light or enlightening fragments to straighten out some mistakes and prejudices], in Kálmán Szily, ed., *Gróf Széchenyi István munkái* [Count István Széchenyi's works] (Budapest: Magyar Tudományos Akadémia, 1904–05), 1:84.

106. *Diaries*, 1:656.

107. Jakab, "Bölöni Farkas Sándor," p. 290.

108. Ibid., p. 291.

109. Ibid.

110. Jancso, *Farkas Sándor naplója*, pp. 54–55.

111. Jakab, "Bölöni Farkas Sándor," p. 297.

112. Ibid., pp. 298–99.

113. Jancso, *Farkas Sándor naplója*, pp. 53–54.

114. *KM* 20 (1885): 228.

115. Tocqueville, *Democracy*, 2:119.

116. Ibid., p. 123.

117. Samuel P. Huntington, "The Democratic Distemper," *Public Interest*, no. 41 (Fall 1975): 9–38.

118. For a comprehensive treatment of Tocqueville and the *Federalist*, see Gottfried Dietze, *The Federalist* (Baltimore: Johns Hopkins Press, 1962), esp. ch. 1.

119. *Hume's Political Essays*, p. 41.

120. Tocqueville, *Democracy*, 2:381.

121. Robert Southey, *Sir Thomas More, or Colloquies on the Progress and Prospects of Society* (London: John Murray, 1831), 2:155.

122. Quoted by Arthur M. Schlesinger, Jr., *The Age of Jackson* (Boston: Little, Brown, 1953), p. 46.

123. Harold Laski, *The American Democracy* (New York: Viking, 1948), p. 717.

124. Robert A. Dahl, *Preface to Democratic Theory* (Chicago: University of Chicago Press, 1956), p. 32.

125. James B. Bryce, *The Predictions of Hamilton and de Tocqueville* (Baltimore: Johns Hopkins University, 1887), pp. 24–25.

126. Thomas Hart Benton, *Thirty Year's View* (New York: Appleton & Co., 1862), 1:205.

127. Tocqueville, "The Art and Science of Politics," *Encounter* 36 (January 1971): 30.

128. Bernard Bailyn, *The Origins of American Politics* (New York: Vintage Books, 1968), p. 86.

129. *Oeuvres complètes d'Alexis de Tocqueville*, ed. Gustave de Beaumont (Paris: Michel Levy, 1860–1866), 5:429 ff.

130. See G. W. Pierson, *Tocqueville in America* (New York: Doubleday, 1959), pp. 455–56.

131. For a concise analysis of American values treated by foreign commentators, see Kasper D. Naegele, "From Tocqueville to Myrdal, a Research Memorandum on Selected Studies of American Values," *Laboratory of Social Relations* (Harvard) (October 1949).

132. For a broad treatment of this theme, see Harry V. Jaffa, *Equality and Liberty* (New York: Oxford University Press, 1965), pp. 114–39.

133. Cited by Caroline Robbins, "The Pursuit of Happiness," in *America's Continuing Revolution*, ed. Irving Kristol et al. (Washington, D.C.: American Enterprise Institute, 1975), p. 133.

134. *Collected Works of Abraham Lincoln*, ed. Roy P. Bassler (New Brunswick: Rutgers University Press, 1953), 4:240.

135. Tocqueville, *Democracy* 1:506.

136. Quoted by Daniel Bell, "The End of American Exceptionalism," *Public Interest*, no. 41 (Fall 1975): 199.

137. *Works of Abraham Lincoln*, 4:240.

138. Ibid.

139. Joseph Priestley, *Letters to the Right Honourable Edmund Burke* (Birmingham: Thomas Pearson, 1791). Priestley finds it strange that an avowed friend of the American Revolution like Burke should be an enemy of the French Revolution, "which arose from the same general principles, and in a great measure sprung from it" (p. 4). Priestley rejects Burke's theory of "passive obedience and resistance" and affirms that from Locke on, it is a maxim that all power in any "state is derived from the people," which, according to Priestley, is one of the first "elements of political science" (p. 23).

140. Quoted by Daniel Boorstin, *The Lost World of Thomas Jefferson* (Boston: Beacon Press, 1948), p. 19.

141. R. J. White, ed., *The Political Thought of Samuel Taylor Coleridge* (London: Folcroft Press, 1970), p. 44.

142. David Ramsay, *The History of the American Revolution* (Philadelphia: R. Aitken & Son, 1789), 1:355–56. For a critical evaluation of Ramsay's theory of America the Promised Land, see Lawrence J. Friedman, *Inventors of the Promised Land* (New York: Knopf, 1975).

143. Pierson, *Tocqueville in America*, p. 47.

144. Manuscript no. 959.

145. Jancso, *Farkas Sándor naplója*, pp. 25–27.

146. Ibid., p. 20.

147. Ibid., p. 61.

148. Ibid., p. 62.

149. *KM* 20 (1885): 33.

150. Goethe, *Sämtliche Gedichte*, ed. Ernst Beutler (Zurich: Artemis-Verlag, 1949), 1:92. Although in Goethe's collected works there is no reference to Skufto, in his *Tagebüche* (July 1828) Goethe makes reference to Ypsilanti. See *Goethes Werke* (Weimar: Hermann Bohlaus, 1900), 2:246.

151. *Goethes Werke*, 39:205, lines 243–46.

152. Bertrand Russell, *A History of Western Philosophy* (New York: Simon & Schuster, 1945), p. 748.

153. Jancso, *Farkas Sándor naplója*, pp. 8–9.

154. Ibid., p. 9.

155. Quoted by Russell, *History of Western Philosophy*, p. 750.

156. Jansco, *Farkas Sándor naplója*, pp. 6–7.

157. Pál Pándi, *Kisértetjárás Magyarországon* [The specter of a ghost in Hungary], 2 vols. (Budapest: Magvetö Könyvkiado, 1972). Pándi devotes considerable attention to Mihály Táncsis (1799–1884), whose suppressed manuscript, "Buda-Pesti levelek" [Buda-Pest letters], was inspired by Farkas's *Journey in North America* and its treatment of the Owenite and Rappite communal experiences. The Táncsics manuscript is deposited at the National Archives, Budapest, under the general collection *Centrale censurae collegium* (1842), document no. 616.

Pándi makes an interesting connection between Robert Owen and Prince Pál Eszterházy,

78 Austrian ambassador in London from 1815 to 1842. Though a friend of Metternich, Eszterházy also visited Robert Owen and expressed great interest in his communal plans, and in particular in Owen's ideas on how to eliminate poverty, ignorance, and misery. In fact, Owen says that the prince became his "friend," and upon "subsequent occasions was most useful to me." See *The Life of Robert Owen: Written by Himself* (London: Effingham Wilson, 1857), 1:134. Eszterházy supported the radical Hungarian opposition to Metternich and may have been instrumental in securing the visas for Farkas and his group. Farkas had letters of introduction from Wesselényi and Széchenyi to Eszterházy at the Court of St. James's.

158. Rousseau, *Lettre à d'Alembert*, ed. M. Fuchs (Lille: Giard, 1948), p. 22.

159. For a general treatment of this concept, see Paul A. Palmer, "The Concept of Public Opinion on Political Theory," in *Essays in History and Political Theory in Honor of Charles H. McIlwain* (Cambridge: Harvard University Press, 1936), pp. 230–57.

160. Hannah Arendt, *On Revolution* (New York: Viking, 1965), p. 119.

161. *The Writings of Henry David Thoreau* (Boston: Houghton Mifflin, 1906), 4:430.

162. Southey, *Colloquies*, 2:157: "Bad as the feudal times were, they were less injurious than these commercial ones to the kindly and generous feelings of human nature, and far, far more favourable to the principles of honour and integrity."

163. Alpheus Mason, "American Individualism: Fact and Fiction," *American Political Science Review* 66 (March 1952): 2.

164. Richard M. Gummere, *The American Colonial Mind and the Classical Tradition* (Cambridge: Harvard University Press, 1963), pp. 65 ff.

165. Arthur W. Brown, *Always Young for Liberty* (Syracuse: Syracuse University Press, 1956), p. 186.

166. Robert Penn Warren, *Democracy and Poetry* (Cambridge: Harvard University Press, 1975), p. 30.

167. Ibid., p. 34.

168. Ibid., p. 33.

169. *The Complete Works of Ralph Waldo Emerson* (New York: Houghton Mifflin, 1903–1904), 8:339.

170. Quoted by Pierson, *Tocqueville in America*, pp. 287–88.

171. V. L. Parrington, *Main Currents in American Thought* (New York: Harcourt, Brace, 1930), 2:322.

172. W. E. Channing, *Discourses, Reviews and Miscellanies* (Boston: Carter, Hendee, 1830), pp. 6–7.

173. Thomas Paine, *The Rights of Man* (Garden City, N.Y.: Doubleday, 1973), p. 413.

174. Tocqueville, *Democracy*, 2:234.

175. Tacitus, *The Annals of Imperial Rome*, trans. Michael Grant (Baltimore: Penguin Books, 1962), p. 33.

176. Farkas's juxtaposition of despotism and republican democracy bears the influence of Montesquieu. In *The Spirit of the Laws*, Montesquieu defines political liberty as essentially security, the ability to calculate the consequences of one's actions (bk. 12:2). By legalistic criteria, men can enjoy freedom within virtually any political system, so long as certain procedural standards are observed (bk. 12:4). But despotism precludes freedom because despotism is regulated by the "momentary will of the prince" (bk. 4:16) and has no "fixed constitution" or "settled laws" (bk. 3:8). See Montesquieu, *The Spirit of the Laws*, trans. Thomas Nugent (New York: Hafner Publishing Co., 1949). Farkas was familiar with the writings of Montesquieu, and he shared the latter's extraordinary insight—patterned perhaps on Aristotle's analysis of the techniques of despotic rule—concerning the method of how to break the spirit of men in order to make them manageable.

177. Quoted by Michael Oakeshott, *On Human Conduct* (Oxford: Clarendon Press, 1975), p. 246. On Constant's critical acceptance of Rousseau's general will that influenced Farkas, see John Cruickshank, *Benjamin Constant* (New York: Twayne Publishers, 1974), esp. ch. 2.

178. The doyen of American political thought, Alpheus Thomas Mason, traces the Unfinished Revolution to the Declaration of Independence and the federal Constitution of

1787. Both embody the special character of American political thought. According to Mason, "The first takes into account human aspirations and ideals; the second builds on man's shortcomings, his inordinate greed, his drive for power." A. T. Mason, *Free Government in the Making*, 3d ed. (New York: Oxford University Press, 1965), p. 133.

179. Wordsworth, "Inland, within" (line 14), in *Wordsworth's Poetical Works*, ed. Thomas Hutchinson (London: Oxford University Press, 1971), p. 243.

180. Charles A. Beard, *The Rise of American Civilization* (New York: Macmillan, 1939), 1:731–32: "It is one of the curious but neglected facts of history . . . that a French army officer, who proudly wrote himself down as 'a descendant of Charlemagne and a soldier under Washington,' gave the nineteenth century the doctrine of socialism as the goal of progress. That officer was Count de Saint-Simon."

Journey in North America, 1831

Sándor Bölöni Farkas

F or sixty years the watchful eyes of Europe and the world have been on America. For centuries liberty and oppression met on the battlefields of the Old World. Though a thousand times disappointed, its weary cheated hopes counseling surrender, in final listless resignation Europe has turned to America, destined by Fate to answer the question: Can man and mankind create a just and good government through self-determination and free election? And is man's political destiny forever decreed by history and tyrannical power?

These feelings carried on a dialogue in my soul as we approached the shores. The magnificent trees, the country homes along the blooming shores were already American. The Fort Lafayette fortress loomed majestically in the middle of the bay, and opposite it Fort Richmond and the telegraphs. We sailed into the bay. And what a splendid panorama greeted us. The mighty Hudson stretched before us with its romantic islands and shores, and beyond the forest of masts loomed New York City. At eight in the morning we anchored before the Staten Island quarantine house. Soon a boat approached with a doctor aboard to check if there were sick among the passengers. In a quarter of an hour the whole inspection was over.

As the tide has just turned, leaving our baggage on the *Columbia*, with the captain we boarded the steamboat *Bolivar* and in half an hour reached New York—the dry land of freedom. I would never be able to make an orderly account of my true feelings on this occasion. Enthusiasm and fantasy, childish joy and excitement, and all the emotions characteristic of life's perfect moments swelled and blended in my soul.

[*83*]

III. New York—American Police—Institutions—Schools—Wesselényi and Balog

*T*he very moment a European traveler first lands in an American port he steps into a new world. Negroes and whites, mulattoes and mestizos bustle and crowd the port, offer their services to a foreigner to carry his luggage and guide him to a hotel or some desired place. The new, strikingly colorful faces offer a strange sight to the foreigner's eyes. He immediately realizes he is on the other side of the globe. Strolling along New York's Broadway, we were spellbound by the beautiful buildings, rich stores, the overflowing abundance of fruits, the colorful diversity of passers-by and, in general, we were awed by the ceaseless hustle and bustle of the neatly dressed pedestrians. After checking into the enormous Hotel American, we decided to clear our luggage at customs. Here all we had to do was to declare that our luggage contained only personal belongings and nothing for sale. Permission promptly given, we removed our belongings from the *Columbia* and said good-bye to our captain, the crew, and the ship familiar to its last mast.

*   *   *

From the first, fairy-talelike days in America, when in the evenings I recounted and reflected upon my day's activities, two things struck me forcefully. First, upon entering America nobody demanded our or for that matter any other passenger's passport. In fact, no one even asked our names, and our arrival went unnoticed. Second, at customs the traveler's word is sufficient guarantee to clear his luggage. It is not opened, rummaged through to check upon the passenger's honesty. Even duties on merchants and their goods are based on a simple declaration of faith. Even

86   though it is hearsay, those who have not traveled in those parts of Europe
will have some inkling why I was impressed by these things. And those who
have traveled there will share my admiration for the American method.

Nothing frustrates and humiliates a traveler more than duties and
passport regulations. When the fatigued and completely unknown traveler
arrives at some European border without any letters of introduction,
instead of hospitality he is greeted with men armed with steel. He is ordered
from his carriage as a suspect, his papers are taken away and he is
scrutinized, cross-examined, and watched suspiciously. Then they pounce
on the helpless traveler's possessions, mercilessly rummaging through and
scattering them. In vain can he state his true intentions. A clear conscience
will not save him from the shameful treatment and the humiliating
questions, let alone prevent this lawful brutality. To forestall or at least
mitigate these unpleasantries, the wretched traveler must resort to the
disgraceful practice of choosing between his purse and his honor. Then
there is worry upon leaving, lest he be reminded of his expected
magnanimity. No traveler in Europe can recall without bitterness such
embarrassing predicaments.

This, then, is what first impressed me in America. When I inquired
about it, Americans gave a natural explanation. I reviewed in my mind the
European police systems and concluded that most assume man is either
born a crook or society makes him dishonest. What a welcome contrast in
America. The American Constitution declares that all men are born equal
and honest. American law assumes the honesty of most travelers. To
subject all to regulations designed against a few crooks would violate human
dignity and personal freedom. In America everyone is free to enter and
leave the country as he wishes. People can travel, pursue their happiness,
and live where they want without anyone officially so much as asking their
name. What a great contrast between the mentality of the Old and the New
World. European police for centuries have racked their brain and issued
secret and public directives on how to spy on human perfidy. Both human
deceitfulness and the method to cope with it were subject to scientific
analysis. Conversely, the people are just as ingenious in subverting and
eluding police methods. In the process society become corrupt. Moral sense
can be stifled and man dehumanized not only by tyrannical laws but by
laws which deny any human faith in virtue and abrogate human dignity. As
the Latin writer put it: *Multi fallere docuerunt dum timent falli at aliis suspicando
fecerunt*, "Many sinned fearing sin, but made others sin by suspecting
them."

***

The next day we presented our letters of introduction. The addressees
in turn introduced us to their friends and acquaintances. We have hardly
spent three days in New York and already enjoy a wide circle of
acquaintances. At first we attributed the warm welcome of our stay to our

hosts' social importance, or to our just being foreigners from a distant place. Later, however, we learned that such a cordial welcome and boundless trust in foreigners, despite many abuses, are marked characteristics of North Americans.[1] One or two letters of introduction to some leading families are sufficient for a stranger to gain access to all social circles because the original host not only recommends you to others but he secures and writes letters of reference to towns you intend to visit. Consequently the traveler, provided his character merits trust, is passed on from town to town.

Among our acquaintances Baron Lederer, the Austrian consul, was unsparing in his effort to make our stay in New York pleasant and memorable. First he introduced us to some leading persons and then took us around the city, showing its buildings and institutions. The nearly three-miles-long, arrow-straight Broadway, with its magnificent and luxurious shops and beautiful buildings, vies with the best streets in London and Paris. Midway down Broadway is the august, white-marble City Hall, surrounded by a fenced-in lawn, which is intersected with promenades. The other buildings were private residential homes or belonged to different associations. And although they are not so interesting as the historical buildings in Europe's ancient cities, nonetheless their utilitarian and original design can satisfy even eyes used to antiquity.

***

The New York area was discovered by the Dutch captain, Hudson, in 1609, hence the origin of the name of Hudson River. The original settlers of this untracked wilderness were the Iroquois Indians. In 1610 the Dutch, in constant struggle with the Indians, built the first shacks along the Hudson. Later on, the English pushed out the Dutch, and by 1673 the area was in English hands. At the outbreak of the War of Independence, the English occupied the city and held it until the signing of the peace treaty. Though favorably located, the city did not expand and progress until independence.

Table 1. New York Population Growth[2]

1697	4,302
1756	13,040
1790	33,130
1800	60,489
1810	96,373
1820	123,706
1825	166,086
1830	207,021

Each day we visited some of the numerous institutions whose description alone would fill a separate book. All were built by private associations; the government neither backs them financially nor intervenes in their affairs. In New York alone there are more than fifty different associations founded for the purpose of advancing science, trade, professions, or philanthropy.[3] Annually great sums are spent on the maintenance of these institutions. Our visit coincided with the Horticultural Society's annual meeting. At the beautiful Niblo's Garden, on stands were displayed fruits, flowers, and different products from the surrounding farms. Every fruit basket, containing peaches, grapes, watermelons, pears, and apples, was labeled with the grower's name and locality. Visitors thronged around the display stands laden with countless species of peaches, watermelons, pears, apples, and different kinds of table and uncultivated grapes. The society's chosen judges determined the three best products in each category and the growers were then awarded the year's prizes. The event concluded with a splendid ball.

New York has many such associations whose purpose is to encourage and advance human enterprise. Coming from that part of Europe where the government acts and thinks for the people, a traveler can hardly comprehend how these associations can exist without public money and without governmental supervision and meddling. But in America the people govern, look after their own welfare, and make sacrifices, neither by borrowed power nor by catering to the privileged few, but through the free exercise of self-government—the greatest pleasure of citizenship.

***

Among New York's most successful institutions, with the largest membership, is the Public School Society. The Republic's greatest strength resides in a population whose members are educated to their fullest potential, and who know and understand their own laws. The Americans are fully aware that education not only is the key to individual achievement but it also leavens national welfare. Just as education and knowledge ensure individual superiority, only an enlightened people can rise and maintain its position over other nations. They know that where enlightenment and knowledge of laws are class privileges, there the educated rule with ease the uneducated masses. Hence the Americans devote great effort to ensuring that even the poorest members of society acquire some learning.[4]

Despising every kind of personal tax, the American is not easily taxed. School is the only thing for which in every state they willingly pay progressive taxes, from which a principal is built up to cover school expenditures. In New York private donations have created a large capital fund whose interest earnings, together with the lottery revenue, cover the $58,625 annual school expenditure.

Table 2. Basic Data on New York Schools (1830)[5]

	Schools				Total
	Public	Charity	Incorporated	Private	
Number of schools	11	19	3	430	463
Principal teachers	21	25	6	432	484
Assistant teachers	24	5	23	259	311
Children 4–5 years	—	197	33	1,013	1,243

Table 2. Basic Data on New York Schools (Continued)

	Schools				Total
	Public	Charity	Incorporated	Private	
Children 5–15 years	6,007	2,297	1,008	12,631	21,943*
Children above 15 years	—	50	40	676	766
Total number of children	6,007	2,544	1,081	14,320*	23,952

*These figures are the correct ones. Farkas copied the mistakes as they appeared in *The New York Annual Register*, 1831.

As the figures indicate, in 1830 the city of New York's 463 schools had an enrollment of 23,952 students, of which 805 were Negroes. In addition, the Sunday schools enrolled 16,441 students.

The less government interferes in the citizen's private affairs, his institutions, and his religion, the greater his interest in education. The government makes prodigious efforts to expand public schools in the United States, and in turn the states endeavor to secure at least through the early grades education for even the poorest. To this effect the state governors submit a special annual report on school issues to the public, which shows great interest in public education.

Table 3. Extracts from New York State Governor's Message (1831)

Number of school districts:

New York state		9,062
New York City		463
Albany		40
Utica		27
	Total	9,592
Number of students in lower grades		499,424
Number of students in colleges		50,576
Total enrollment in 1830		550,000

The population of New York state is 1,923,522, and the student-population ratio is 1 to 3.5.

Table 4. Revenue Sources of New York Primary Schools (1830)

Voluntary tax ($1)		239,713
Revenue from common school fund		100,678
Funds possessed by certain towns		14,095
Percentage of lottery earnings		200,000
Donations		160,412
Matching state contributions		239,713
	Total	$1,061,699*
Adding the revenue of N.Y. schools		58,625
Capital interest of colleges		302,779
	Total	$1,423,103*

*The first six items total $954,611 and not $1,061,699, which Farkas copied from the original. The total, with that correction, is $1,316,015—not $1,423,103.

90   Of the many institutions in New York, public schools alone convincingly demonstrate the Americans' public-mindedness and the importance they give to the advancement of public welfare. Astonished as I was daily to discover New York's thriving schools and institutions, I could not suppress a sigh recalling my country's schools. A Hungarian traveler, burdened with the memory of his country, sighs frequently.

***

One of the pleasant surprises of our New York visit was meeting Baron Farkas Wesselényi,[6] and my friend, Pál Balog.[7] We parted in London, since they sailed for America from Liverpool on the *Sylvanus Jenkins*, and their ocean crossing lasted forty-five days, even longer than ours. The New York summer heat is so oppressive that we decided to tour the northern states in September and then go down to the South in October.

***

From my first days in America the busy schedule of seeing people and visiting places hardly left time to reflect in private on impressions whose jumbled accumulation resisted any orderly sorting out. The traveler's first impressions of America are not unlike some fairy tale read in younger years. The faces, appearances, customs, and language—all portray brilliantly the New World. Even more revealing is that appearance and formality, considered indispensable in Europe, are nonexistent here. One searches in vain for titled persons, mighty magistrates, and strutting, preening officials. Only ordinary citizens live here. Converse with members of leading families, meet higher and lower nobility—they are but citizens. Priests and soldiers, police and judges, scholars and bankers—so many equal citizens. On top of it, how incomprehensible to a foreigner that of the forty-eight denominations none dominates, but all are equal. The clergy does not constitute a separate class. No standing army. No privileges. No nobility. No titles, no feudal orders, no guilds, no secret police. Oh, how exhilarating each of these are to us.

IV. New York Harbor—The Steamboat *Cinderella*—Hudson Shores—Sing Sing—Peekskill Village—Newspapers in America—Fulton, the Inventor of the Steamboat—Major Arnold's Treachery

We left New York on September 9 with the intention of returning later. Because of its favorable location, three-fourths of New York is surrounded by water, and in almost all directions one must travel by boat. Despite centuries of harbor improvements, neither the London, Liverpool, or Amsterdam and Le Havre harbors can compare with that of New York. Its natural location and size make it the world's leading port. From Sandy Hook to Fort Washington, on either side of the city, more than a thousand large vessels can dock safely.

Table 5. Ships Entering New York Harbor (1830)[1]

From foreign ports	1510
From American ports	1,352
Fishing trawlers	1,110
Coastal merchant vessels	487
Local ships	527
Scheduled steamboats	75
Total	5,061

On the average seven hundred to eight hundred ships are tied up at piers, loading and unloading quickly, unlike at London, where it takes days to clear a dock.

The city's seventy-five steamboats run a regular schedule to different places. The steamboat *Cinderella* was ready to depart when we arrived at the harbor in the morning, planning to visit Sing Sing state prison. Our company included Baron Wesselényi, Balog, and Baron Lederer[2] and his

92   family, who traveled to Fishkill. At the third bell, the proud *Cinderella*, its
flags fluttering, paddle-wheeled to the middle of the Hudson, right past the
lovely Hoboken countryside. I only knew America, its people and customs,
from one town. Steaming upstream on the Hudson, I was greatly surprised
at the vast expanse of nature. Before the Hudson's majestic natural beauty,
Europe's cultivated scenery, with its palaces and ruined feudal castles
forlorn on riverbanks, is completely dwarfed. Like a proud fledgling youth,
the untamed, expansive nature here inspires respect and presages great
promise. The so-called Palisades are a unique product of nature. On the
western bank the cliffs form high towers for two miles, while on the eastern
side the lovely country homes, gardens, forest, and meadows keep the
traveler captivated. The shores are also rich in history. The War of
Independence left many memories here, and Americans traveling the
Hudson proudly point to different historical spots.

As New York receded far behind, gray cliffs began to tower
perpendicularly from the water's edge and in places, where the water
wedged between huge rocks, it gave the appearance of lakes in Scotland. On
these high cliffs, under English rule, once stood the aristocratic castles and
below, the shacks of slaves. But the triumphant Revolution, having
abolished primogeniture, removed all traces of privileged aristocracy and
today one can see on the high banks and below only the abodes of citizens.
In less than three hours after leaving New York the steamer dropped anchor
before Sing Sing state penitentiary.

In the last half a century the formerly much-abused, maligned, and
patronized America has surpassed Europe in many ways. In America many
institutions attract the admiring attention of even the envious English,
particularly the prison system. Nowhere in Europe is there anything
resembling the American penitentiary system, either in design, method or
purpose. The humane approach to crime and criminals, and the philosophy
of rehabilitation, are unique American inventions and differ completely
from ours, based on different penology. I wanted to visit Sing Sing.
Unfortunately, due to the absence of the warden, we could not receive
permission to enter. Mr. Balog and his company left us at Sing Sing and
returned to New York to visit Pennsylvania and we, accompanied by Baron
Lederer, traveled by coach along the Hudson to Peekskill.

***

Peekskill was the third village I visited in America. Although from
books I had already formed an ideal picture of American institutions, I fully
expected its newly settled towns and villages to be rather backward and
could not even dare to compare them with European ones. But what a great
surprise to find a completely original and in appearance markedly
un-European village. Peekskill, located thirty miles from New York on the
banks of the Hudson in Westchester County, was a settlement barely eighty
years old with a population of 1,250. The village comprises two streets with

120 houses and yet in style and comfort the houses were no different from middle-class homes in London suburbia. The streets are lined with two rows of beautiful catalpa trees, there are several denominational churches, one public school, and some attractive stores stocked with basic goods. Even more astonishing, twice a week this village publishes a newspaper *(The Westchester Sentinel,* edited by Mr. Marks).

In Europe we would consider a miracle the ways and means by which America has so quickly raised the individual and national level of education. In America, however, the explanation is obvious and natural. So simple and obvious, in fact, that when the foreigner learns its secret he wonders whether to pity and condemn or to marvel at his own country's purblindness. The Constitution guarantees the undisputed right of every individual to set up a printing shop where and whenever he likes. As long as he does not infringe on the rights of others, he can print and disseminate any writings without official permission or censorship. By this simple method newspapers are born and multiply in America, spreading useful knowledge, learning, and culture simply and cheaply. According to official figures, in 1831 there were 1,015 newspapers published in America, 237 in New York state alone and 54 in New York City.[3]

The population of Transylvania is close to that of New York state. Yet Transylvania publishes one newspaper, compared with 237 in New York state. The population of the two fatherlands [Hungary and Transylvania] nearly equals that of the United States. However, in the two Hungarian fatherlands only 10 meager newspapers and periodicals vegetate, whereas the United States supports 1,015 newspapers. In Peekskill a newspaper has been published for a long time, while in Maros-Vásárhely and Debrecen, in fact in most of our Hungarian towns, the Hungarian citizen still considers the newspaper a letter of lies.

***

At Peekskill's wharf we crossed the Hudson and Baron Lederer took his leave, leaving me with Count Béldi.[4] We decided to board a fishing sloop and on it we soon sailed on the nearly mile-wide Hudson opposite Fort Montgomery. The weather was lovely. While our sloop bobbed among the big vessels that ply the Hudson, the ferryman regaled us with stories about the river and the Revolution. What a scenic view unfolds on the Hudson; everywhere boats, sloops, and proudly whistling steamboats. Poor Robert Fulton! If you could only see from above what your invention brought to man you might forgive the ungrateful world that lined these very shores first to mock, then to admire your invention. In the end, persecution and bankruptcy hastened your bitter death. Fulton's statement, commemorating his steamboat *Claremont's* trial run in 1807 from New York to Albany, is a noble testament of the human soul:[5]

> In the spring of eighteen hundred and seven, the first Fulton boat, built in New York, was launched from the shipyards of Charles Brown, on the East River.

The engine from England was put on the board of her. In August she was completed, and was moved by her machinery from her birthplace to the [New] Jersey shore. Mr. Livingston and Mr. Fulton had invited many of their friends to witness the first trial. . . . Nothing could exceed the surprise and admiration of all who witnessed the experiment. The minds of the most incredulous were changed in a few minutes. Before the boat had made the progress of a quarter of a mile, the greatest of unbelievers must have been converted . . . [the] complacent smiles gradually stiffened into an expression of wonder. The jeers of the ignorant, who had neither sense nor feeling enough to suppress their contemptuous ridicule and rude jokes, were silenced for a moment by a vulgar astonishment, which deprived them of the power of utterance, till the triumph of genius extorted from the incredulous multitude, which crowded the shores, shouts and acclamations of congratulations and applause. The boat had not been long under way, when Fulton ordered her engine stopped. Though her performance so far exceeded the expectation of every other person, and no one but himself thought she could be improved, he immediately perceived that there was an error in the construction of the water wheels. . . . The power of the propelling boats by steam is now fully proved. The morning I left New York, there were not perhaps thirty persons in the city who believed that the boat would ever move one mile an hour; or be of the least utility. And while we were putting off from the wharf, I heard a number of sarcastic remarks. This is the way in which ignorant men compliment what they call philosophers and projectors.

This, then, is the history of the first steamboat and also a revealing, sad human lesson that daring, innovative individuals, who rise above others in intellect and skill, are fated for envy and abuse under all skies.

Originating in the mountains between Ontario and Lake Champlain and dividing New York state, the Hudson River courses 306 miles before it joins the ocean at Sandy Hook. The river's navigability, in addition to its location and its straight course, enables the ocean tides to reach Albany 160 miles inland about twelve hours later than in New York. Previously it took four to five days on land and nine to ten days on water to travel the 145-mile distance between New York and Albany. But what a difference since Fulton invented the steamboat! The same distance now is usually traveled in fourteen to fifteen hours. In 1825 the steamboat *North America* set a record time of ten hours thirty minutes from New York to Albany.[6]

***

What is commonplace today, only thirty years ago would have been considered impossible. Since inventing the steamboat, the Americans have surpassed Europe in harnessing and utilizing steam power, whose potential very likely they will perfect. The American steam engines are better and more efficient than the English ones, and each day they introduce new inventions. The American steamboats resemble a smaller frigate built in a luxurious style and comfort that are completely unknown in Europe. Superimposed on their main deck is an upper deck (the promenade), a unique American invention, on which twenty to twenty-five passengers can stroll with ease. The steamboats' interior would do credit to any fashionable European salon: carpeted steps, mahogany doors and furniture,

white-marble fireplaces, gilded columns, walls hung with well-known
landscape painters' oil paintings, beds screened by silk and satin curtains,
and almost on every steamboat a small library.

We arrived at Montgomery in the early afternoon. The West
Point–bound steamer not being due till 9 P.M., we had time to inquire from
the waiting passengers about the locality and look up in our travel books the
famous historical sites. Many Revolutionary events took place on these
shores. Benedict Arnold betrayed his country here and the English major,
John André, was executed near Montgomery in 1780. Arnold's treachery is
a sad lesson to Americans, who mention his name with a curse as they pass
the historical spot with heavy hearts. The steamer *Philadelphia* arrived at 10
P.M. and in an hour we arrived at West Point.

V. American Educational System—West Point Military Academy—Kosciuszko Memorial—Hudson Bank Towns—Steamboat Passengers—General Van Rensselaer—American Aristocracy—Albany—Courts—Population Growth and Its Causes—Erie Canal

*T*he United States Military Academy is located at West Point. Compared to its population, American has certainly more educational institutions than any European country. With the exception of England, most European educational institutions are directly or indirectly government-funded or -supported. European governments are vitally interested not only in who and how many in society are educated but in supporting, not challenging, the status quo. The exact opposite is true in America. Empowered by the Constitution to be guardians of the government, the people also reserve the right to determine how and by what ideals to educate the youth.

To a foreigner the contrast between European and American laws and institutions is so striking that he attempts to attribute it to a unique historical accident. But a closer study of the Revolutionary era and constitutional history convinces him that America's uniqueness is not accidental. On the contrary, years of deliberation and debate made America unique and different from Europe. This is also true of education. Many diverse opinions have contributed to granting the people control over their own education. The West Point Military Academy is the only institution in America maintained by public money which also enjoys complete governmental support.

On President Jefferson's recommendation, in 1802 the Congress established the West Point Military Academy. The congressional charter's main designation was not only the military training of youth but through the cadets the dissemination of military discipline, good taste in literature

and science. The number of students enrolled is two hundred fifty; they
come from the various states and must be recommended to the president to
fill vacancies. The applicants, aged fourteen to seventeen, have to read and
write and know some mathematics. Only after half a year of strict character
training and intellectual tests are the students admitted.

The instruction lasts for four years. The curriculum consists of
mathematics, drawing, the French language, natural sciences, chemistry,
artillery, geometry, civil and military ethics, tactics, physics, weaponry,
aesthetics, and constitutional law. Thirty-two professors teach classes in
different departments. In addition, every day the cadets engage in military
exercise, and every year they spend three months camping. Discipline is
strict and demanding. Every two cadets share quarters, with a separate
study and bedroom, where they also keep their weapons that must be kept
as clean as their uniforms, which they wash themselves. On graduation the
cadets can join the military or, if they wish, return to civilian life.[1]

The superintendent of the academy, Colonel Thayer, to whom we had
a letter of introduction, received us very cordially and showed us all the
buildings. We attended some classes and listened briefly to some lectures.
In the academy's magnificent library one can find new and old maps of all
descriptions, countless charts on military strategy, and leading newspapers
available to all cadets. Colonel Thayer has transplanted the best ideas of
European military institutions he has visited.

West Point has an ideal location as an educational institution.
Overlooking the magnificent Hudson banks, the West Point peninsula,
rising 188 feet above the river, forms a plateau on which the buildings are
located. The view is magnificent: above, wooded mountain ranges; below,
the lovely Hudson, dotted with ships. In this place remote from big cities,
surrounded by raw scenic wilderness, rich in historical memories, the ruins
of Putnam fortress nearby, the mind cannot but reflect.

Taken by the scenery, unaware, we came upon a lovely monument
screened by the trees. On a simple white-marble pyramid the inscription
read: KOSCIUSZKO.[2] The cadets erected the inscribed monument to the
brave Kosciuszko. Behind the monument lay a small fenced-in plot—
Kosciuszko's private garden, which he cultivated while he lived at West
Point. His garden tools, rickety rake, hoe, and pots still lay there, sacred
relics to the cadets. Rest in peace, Kosciuszko, ye guardian of Liberty and
Humanity. Your memorial is simple. Yet looking at it, the traveler feels his
heart beat faster, for he remembers liberty and the rights of man.

***

At West Point we boarded the *Albany*. Mountains line both shores up
to Newburgh, where the so-called Highlands end. During the Revolution,
Washington had his headquarters on the shores of the Hudson at
Newburgh, whose citizens later distinguished themselves by giving a
rousing welcome to Lafayette in 1824.[3] Every half an hour or so the

98   steamboat stopped before a thriving community or town to disembark and take on passengers. Fishkill, Poughkeepsie, Kingston, Red Hook, Catskill, and Hudson are all attractive, busy towns with seven thousand to eight thousand inhabitants, whose numbers and prosperity grow daily.

The constant change of passengers makes the Hudson journey interesting. The larger steamboats, on daily runs between ports, take aboard one hundred to two hundred or even more passengers. The exchange of passengers at villages and towns unfolds a fascinating portrait gallery of faces and characters on the steamboat. If the traveler is not interested in conversation, he can still enjoy himself on deck as he could in any bustling town. The efficient and smooth embarkation and disembarkation of passengers is quite a sight for a foreigner.

***

In the evening we reached Albany, the state capital of New York. Next day we first called upon Mr. Stephen Van Rensselaer[4] to present our letters. The old general not being home, his son received us. The European aristocratic splendor and luxury at the Rensselaers' home surprised me. Located on the outskirts of the town, the house, both inside and outside, with its English driveway and surrounding park, recalled an English lord's mansion. I could hardly reconcile this splendor with republican simplicity. But seeing more such homes, I realized that everywhere wealth and intellect have their own aristocracy, if wealth and talent's universal love of comfort and family security can be called aristocratic.

Mr. Van Rensselaer is the descendant of the oldest Dutch pioneer families who settled here in 1630 under Dutch rule. The original Van Rensselaer family was granted a large estate, called a patroonship, around Albany. During the feudal period here, the oldest member of the family carried the title "The Patroon of Albany." Though the Revolution abolished the patroonship, the Van Rensselaer family continued the tradition of primogeniture. Consequently the family estate still stretched intact for twelve square miles, to be inherited by his son. Possessors of great wealth, the Van Rensselaer family, like their predecessors, enjoy great public respect for their philanthropy.[5]

After we took a turn in the garden, looking at the rare species of plants and the Erie Canal at the edge of the garden, Van Rensselaer Jr. took us in his carriage to town to show us its historical sights. First we visited the state house or capitol. The Ionian-columned white marble capitol, located on a hill downtown, is the seat of the two branches of state government, the supreme court, and also contains other august assembly halls. The court was in session and since in America it is open to the public, we decided to watch the procedure for a while. The presiding judge was flanked by the jurors, and opposite him sat the court clerks at a desk equipped with ink and paper. At the hearing both parties are present, accompanied by their lawyers, who sit in front of the presiding judge. The citizen can either state his own case or hire a lawyer. If the points are obscure, the judge or even the jurors will ask for clarification. After both sides declare they have presented their case and the submitted documents are all read, the judge briefly summarizes the issues over which the parties contend and then reads the law applicable to the case. The jurors withdraw for deliberation and, upon reaching a verdict, return and it is declared to the court.

Leaving the court, we took a stroll in the streets. Albany is one of the oldest cities in America. Its first log cabins were built by the Dutch in 1612 [1614] on the banks of the Hudson, and in 1623 [1624] they built a fortress called Fort Orange. The English took possession of the area in 1664 and renamed it Albany in honor of the York and Albany princes. The city's oldest section, built by Dutch settlers, resembles German and, in many respects, the older Transylvanian Saxon towns. But the new section is built in contemporary style. Its central location made Albany the state capital of New York, even though New York itself is more populous.

In Albany eleven political and literary journals are published, it has one university and several Lancaster schools.[6] Hitherto sparsley populated, but becoming the state capital, and particularly after the opening of the Erie Canal, Albany underwent tremendous population growth.

Table 6. **Population Growth in Albany**

1820	12,630
1825	15,971
1830	24,238

In the last forty years the state's population also underwent rapid growth. At the outbreak of the Revolution, the state population numbered less than 200,000, but since then it has increased steadily.

Table 7. **Population Growth of New York State**[7]

1790	340,130
1800	586,050
1810	959,049
1820	1,372,812
1825	1,616,458
1830	1,923,522

According to the European science of politics and the combined laws of logic and metaphysics, America and its fast-growing population, composed of diverse nationalities with different religions, languages, customs, and political traditions, cannot live and coexist in unity. Yet how different reality is. Despite all combinations, America prospers and progresses. Once more it is accomplished by a simple method. People hasten to a place where the original sacred natural right is constitutionally guaranteed, where government is based on consent not mysticism, where man thinks and speaks freely, where conscience and reason worship God, and where birth and riches do not tip the scale of justice. Indeed, to such a place people go in a breathless hurry and subordinate their ancient

100 prejudices and interests to the common task which unites them as equals. A man emigrates if the political system he lived under is flawed, and if his natural rights were violated or even nonexistent there. Perhaps his soul was hurt and bruised, or he was deprived of something he could not even dare to express. These are the simple reasons for America's phenomenal population growth.

***

With the opening of the Erie and Champlain canals, in the last ten years Albany gained such a key commercial position that soon she might vie with New York. With the ocean tides large vessels can sail 160 miles inland up to Albany but the Hudson is not navigable beyond the reach of ocean tides. The area from here to Lakes Erie and Ontario, including the St. Lawrence waterways, comprising about 360 miles, was closed to commerce. The produce of the inland states could not be hauled on water, so it had to be carried for hundreds of miles overland to find water routes to sell it to distant neighbors, who suffered similar trading disadvantages. Not unlike my country, the inland states literally suffocated in their own fat, without any prospect for development. In these thinly populated areas, there was neither the need nor the desire to cultivate the land. But one magnificent thought of the human mind in 1818 has transformed this area into one of the most prosperous in the United States. In place of the impenetrable wilderness suddenly populous towns and villages began to flourish, giving prosperity and security to their inhabitants.

It was an old dream of New York state to link by canals[8] the Ontario-Erie-Champlain-Cayuga lakes and the St. Lawrence River, and through the Hudson reach the ocean The plan was inspiring and its future advantages virtually unlimited. However, the physical obstacles were considered almost insurmountable and unprecedented in the world. Lake Erie, wedged between rivers and mountains, is 565 feet higher than the Hudson, not to mention the nearly six hundred miles' distance connecting the three [four] lakes, which made the cost of the project virtually impossible to estimate.

But the old dream, considered for a long time a mere pious wish, turned into reality in 1817, when the daring and courageous De Witt Clinton, state governor and canal commissioner, accepted the plan and convinced the public that the undertaking was feasible. The plan received enthusiastic public support and immediately sacrifices were made for its realization. The land for the canal route was partly financed by public subscription and partly by government-guaranteed canal bonds, and from revenues derived from customs duties of the Salina salt operations. On July 4, 1817, the digging of the great canal began simultaneously on the Hudson and Erie sections. In 1819 the Utica to Rome 15-mile canal was already open to boats, thus providing further incentive for the project. In 1823 the customs revenues of the completed 283-mile route had almost covered the

remaining cost. The Grand Canal celebration on November 4, 1825,
marked the completion of the project. On November 24, when the first ship
reached Buffalo on Lake Erie, the northwest opened to commerce and
trade. In 1828 the Oswego-Cayuga Canal was added, linking Ontario and
the St. Lawrence with the Erie Canal.

The great canal system is the triumph of human reason, of cooperation
and noble ideals of enterprising citizens who, without burdening society
with additional taxes, in eleven years accomplished a feat unprecedented in
human history.

Table 8. The Great Canal System

	Length	Rise and Fall
1. Erie Canal (Albany to Erie, 4 feet deep, 83 locks, 566 bridges)	363 mi.	698 ft.
2. Champlain Canal (21 locks)	72	188
3. Oswego Canal (linking Ontario and Erie Canal, 14 locks)	38	123
4. Cayuga-Seneca Canal	20	73.5
Total	493 mi.	1,082.5 ft.

The cost of the canals:

1. Erie	$ 9,027,456
2. Champlain	1,179,781
3. Oswego	525,115
4. Cayuga-Seneca	214,000
Total	$10,946,352

The canals, linking the northwest with the ocean, teem with canal
boats. The traffic is heavy and annually increases due to the lower shipping
costs. In 1829 the Erie Canal was served by 178 boats, in 1830 by 215, and
the increased customs revenue defrays the construction cost. In 1829 the
canal's toll revenue was $813,127; in 1830, $1,056,799.

As is evident from these revenues, half goes toward the repayment of
debt whose principal, $7,825,035, is to be paid off in ten years, when the
debt-free canals revert to the states.[9]

The success of the great canal system sparked a canal boom in several
states, which drew up plans modeled after the Erie Canal. In New York
state alone ten private companies were authorized to dig canals at different
places, and thirteen other companies were chartered for railroad construction.

VI. Shaker Religion and Worship—New Lebanon—Methodists

*F*rom Albany we planned to visit New Lebanon to witness the Shakers' and Methodists' strange worship. We crossed the Hudson by horse-boat, a typical American invention. At Greenbush we took a stagecoach and, after passing through Union, Stephenstown, and Canaan, we arrived at the hot springs of Lebanon and the Shaker village. So many strange things are written and said about the Shakers' life and religion that they attract many visitors, both domestic and foreign. Originally the Shakers settled here after coming from England. The sect's religious creed was formulated by Ann Lee, the daughter of a Manchester blacksmith. She herself was the wife of a blacksmith named Stanley in the same city. After devoted reading of the Bible, she had several revelations and claimed the Holy Spirit possessed her. On such occasions she preached and prayed in public places, performed miracles, predicted Christ's second coming, the millennial church, and other mystical things. Most of Ann Lee's followers were common people, whom she led in ritual dancing and worship. Persecuted and imprisoned for the noisy worship rituals, in 1774 Ann Lee and her family had to emigrate to America from Manchester together with her noisy disciples.

After divorcing her husband in New York, obsessed with her visions, she found her way to Watervliet, where she settled with a small group of believers. During the Revolution the sect was subject to constant harass-ment. Consequent to the signing of peace, and as a result of religious freedom, Ann's sect expanded and, together with other like-minded believers, bought property at Niskeyuna and settled down. After her death

in 1784, some members of the sect, now numbering several hundred, built a
community at nearby New Lebanon.

The Shakers' main principle is communal ownership. Property is communal rather than private. The fruits of labor are communally stored, from which members receive their food, clothing, and other necessities. Celibacy is a precondition for joining and members of the sect, men and women, enjoy equal rights. The Shakers renounce worldly pleasures, luxury, and fame. The sexes live separately. Part of the Shakers' religious worship consists of ritual dances, since the Bible makes several references to the Jewish practice of worshiping God by dancing, e.g., King David danced before the Ark, and when Solomon said, "There is a time for every purpose," obviously he meant dancing too. In addition to these biblical references, the sect's founding prophetess has taught that not only the tongue but the whole body must honor God. Hence the ritual gesturing and dancing at religious services gave the sect its name—Shakers.[1]

As soon as we entered the Shaker village, we were astonished at the orderly cleanliness and the uniformity of houses, the lovely orchards, the vegetable gardens, the well-stocked barns, and the immaculate streets planted with two rows of trees. We came to the village full of prejudices, but its external appearance inspired in me a growing respect for this sect.

We sent our carriage back to the hot springs, for the Shakers do not keep any inns. We stopped at the church to watch as the faithful from the village gathered into two lines, men separate from women. The big-windowed, plain church's interior resembles a nice hall. Unadorned and bare of any attributes of religious deification, it hardly suggests a religious place. One side of the nave is lined with chairs for many visitors from the "world," who, like us, frequent the strange worship. On the other side were some white wooden benches for the believers. They entered in pairs, each sex through a separate door, and sat down facing each other. The men were identically attired: calfskin shoes, white stockings, breeches, long gray-colored vests, narrow white collars, old-fashioned dark coats fastened with big buttons, and white hats. The women costumed themselves in long black or brown gowns, tight under the armpits, white linen vests, bonnet caps shading their faces, and in each hand a white handkerchief. Though plain, the garments of both sexes were clean and gave a very pleasant appearance.

Gathered in the church, the believers stood up and remained silent for a quarter of an hour. Then they began a strangely original song, doleful and fraught with sorrow, accompanied by swinging arms as if preparing for flight. Then they fell into deep silence. Later an elder Shaker seemed to pray in a trembling voice as if expressing his inner agony. His prayer done, someone intoned, "Brethren, let us work," which sounded like "Brethren, let us pray" of other religious sermons. Thereupon they set to work in earnest. Men solemnly took off their coats, hung them on pegs, and then pushed the benches against the wall. Their shirts loose, they lined up in the center of the church, facing the women. The elders and the children lined up against the wall and began even stranger song, accompanied by swinging arms. The men and women began to dance. The song quickened as did the dancers' movements, whose changing pattern appeared to be an adaptation of the gavotte. Despite the twirling mass confusion, the dancers were so well rehearsed, their steps so accurate, that there was no chaos. But it was impossible not to suppress a smile at the incredibly bizarre dance, the sacred seriousness of waving hands and those leaping bodies in tune with trembling, whining voices. I saw on the faces of others, and felt myself, the smile was partly the smile of pity.

I have witnessed and attended many religious services in England and America. But never could I imagine anything like this. The dance completed, the believers once more formed a line. An elder stepped to the center of the nave and, turning to the visitors, related the sect's history and its main religious principles. Then they struck up a new song and resumed an even more complicated dance. At times a handclap signaled change in the dance figures. When they appeared near exhaustion, they lined up and remained in suppliant meditation for about a quarter of an hour. Finally they dressed and filed out of the church, solemn and calm, as if their supplication was answered.

So ended this incredible religious ceremony. I stepped outside and watched, filled with pity and sorrow, as the line of believers moved toward their homes. In my mind I recalled the countless religious disputes that have torn human souls apart since the dawn of Christianity. Maybe I am misguided myself when I laugh and pity them. Unshaken in their conviction that dancing leads to salvation, they left the church pure in heart and calm, convinced they pleased God. Even in public life they are the most peaceful people, never commit any immoral act and never offend or quarrel with anyone. They are honest, hardworking, and decent people. Their homes and farms are models of resourcefulness and cooperation. And who dares to stand in judgment between God and the Shakers' conscience! Might not their faith be misguided? But it makes them happy! And can anyone vouch that his own faith is not self-deceiving?

***

We left the Shakers to see New Lebanon. Its beautiful location makes it a popular summer resort. Wealthy Southerners spend the summer in the northern states, frequenting the springs at Saratoga, Ballston, or Lebanon. None of the hot springs here can compare in mineral power, as is evident from their analysis, with the Hungarian mineral spas. The pure and abundant Lebanese springs, with a temperature of seventy-two, have the same mineral content as those at Ballston and Saratoga, and are also used for bathing.

***

In the afternoon we took a carriage and drove to see what some claim is an even stranger religious group than the Shakers. Every fall and spring the Methodists hold their eight-day camp meeting. The local Methodists' camp meeting was just two hours' drive from here. Traveling on bad roads through virtually untracked wilderness, we finally reached the place the meeting was said to be. Approaching the edge of a clearing, we came upon a wagon-camp. Horses grazed around and thick smoke filtered through the trees. As we came closer there appeared a large number of tents, gleaming white among the trees, rent with tremendous noise mingled with moaning and crying as if someone were being tortured. The tents, spread out in a wide semicircle with staked-out walks, were crowded with men and children, but mostly with women. In the middle of the camp rose a big, high-framed pulpit made of planks. The interior of the camp tents was divided into two sections; in the rear stood the staked camp-beds, and at the entrance carpeted with straw stood a plank table piled with cooking utensils and clothes. And in the middle of the tent was a bench, and a couple of chairs.

To peer into such tents completely unprepared, and not to be shocked, would have required great composure. We stopped before one tent with the most horrible noise. At the entrance a young man, his head kerchiefed, knelt on the straw and cried bitterly, clutching a chair. His face plunged into the straw, then jerked skyward and his clasped hands thrust upward as if to pluck down the heavens, and he howled hoarsely, "O my Jesus, bless me. O Holy Ghost, come upon me!" He repeated it in convulsive groans. In the rear of the tent, hysterically sobbing women and girls, prostrate in the straw, repeated in convulsive groans his words. One women cried bitterly, another covered her face, a third lay in delirium in her neighbor's lap, eyes bulging at heaven, while others beat their breasts, shrieking and screaming heartrendingly. They fainted, revived, and sighed with beatified faces at the heavens. As we walked among the tents the incredible and wild comedy repeated itself with different gestures and convulsions. The most loudly articulate moans were: "O my Lord! O my Jesus! Bless me! O Holy Ghost, come upon me! Bless me!" One almost felt physical pain at the sight of these incredibly misguided soul-flagellants; one almost pitied all the hoarse throats, raspy voices, and all the tearstreaked faces, in which the leading role belonged to women and girls.

The Methodists' strange dogma derives its scriptural sources from the passage: "Raise your hand to God. Knock, and you will enter. Cry on God's mountain." Their own ministers attend these camp meetings and their plank-pulpit preaching, according to eyewitnesses, is something to behold. The Methodist sect has many followers and they are recruited mostly from the uneducated. I left the camp meeting shaken and again seized by compassionate sorrow as I reflected on religion. The Methodist throws himself to the ground and hoarsely howls to God. The Shaker dances to

106   please his God. The Quaker is silent in church as he contemplates his spiritual and social duties. But, God, whose prayer pleases you most?

It was already getting dark when with great difficulty we made our way to Lebanon on the road jammed with carriages of other curiosity-seekers.

VII. The United States—The First Settlers in North America—English Colonial Oppression—Tea Tax—Battle of Lexington and the Revolution

*F*rom New Lebanon we journeyed to Boston, the capital of Massachusetts. At Pittsfield we crossed into Massachusetts, or New England, the colonial name for this part of America. The Union is divided into four areas:

A. New England, or the Eastern states: Maine, New Hampshire, Vermont, Massachusetts, Rhode Island, and Connecticut.

B. Central states: New York, New Jersey, Delaware, Pennsylvania, Ohio, Indiana, Illinois, and the Michigan Territory.

C. Southern states: Maryland, Virginia, Kentucky, Tennessee, North and South Carolina, Georgia, District of Columbia, and the Florida Territory.

D. Western states: Louisiana, Mississippi, Alabama, Missouri, and the Arkansas Territory.

Originally only thirteen states formed the Union. The rest were purchased either from the Indians, Spain (Florida), or France (Louisiana). Eleven other states joined the Union when their population reached forty thousand. The District of Columbia, Michigan, Florida, and Arkansas, still under forty thousand inhabitants, are not members of the Union.

***

After the discovery of North America (1498) [1492], Virginia and Massachusetts were first settled by the English. In many respects Massachusetts, then the most populous state, became the cultural and political leader of North America, particularly since it became the cradle of the Revolution and marked the first triumph over the English. By the early 1600s the Boston area in Massachusetts had settlements, and some Pilgrims settled at Plymouth on Christmas Day in 1620. In Europe this coincided

108   with religious turmoil, in particular reformist England persecuted its
dissidents. The reigns of Elizabeth, James I, and Charles I are marked by
religious persecution, intolerance, and fanaticism. Suffering under the
yoke of persecution, their faith proscribed, many families, whose character
was shaped in adversity, left England and sought a haven in the New World
to find freedom of conscience.

The more the Old World persecuted its best people, the more
populous became the New World, whose settlers founded Massachusetts,
New Hampshire, Rhode Island, Connecticut, and Pennsylvania. The early
settlers' resolute resourcefulness changed the environment, and their new
experiment in living spread prosperity among them. They created
completely new laws based on free and equal popular rights. But the early
settlers' progress and success aroused the envy of England, which wished to
profit by it. To reassert the English crown's prerogative under William and
Mary (1692), the colony was made a royal province,[1] and its governor was
court-appointed. However, since the governor's salary and budget depended on the colonial assembly's appropriation, the governor was
powerless without the assembly. The crown's attempt to remedy its
mistake precipitated conflict and suspicion between England and the
colonies.

Nonetheless, English administrative control over the colonies increased progressively, particularly when its governors became empowered
to set up the system of justice and appoint judges. Customs duties and taxes
were introduced, laws annulled, and through its crown officials, England
wielded arbitrary power in the colonies, which often protested by invoking
constitutional rights. In 1767 [1717] New York declared that taxation
without representation violated natural rights.

Despite their growing grievances, the colonies remained loyal to the
mother country. And when the British-French war broke out over Canada
in 1754, the colonies supported the British side for sixteen years with arms
and money, thus ensuring British possession of Canada. The American
colonies rightly expected that after the war (1760), in recognition of their
sacrifices, England would restore their ancient rights, or would at least
desist from violating current ones. Instead, in less than two years, the
colonies were faced with greater burdens. The British Empire's victories on
land and sea in order to secure the key to world commerce imposed a
tremendous debt on the nation. To repay it, the imperial government
turned its attention to the American colonies.

Gaining control over the West Indies, England secured a crucial source
of trade. But to maintain its commercial supremacy, England had to
prevent the colonies from trading with the West Indies. To this end, the
colonies were forced to buy in England goods available to them close by and
even ship them in English-owned and English-operated vessels. To
discourage colonial manufacture and trade, England began to levy duties on
goods leaving American ports, and shipped goods there in English vessels

without allowing the Americans to trade with the neighboring colonies. In addition, England imposed numerous taxes, duties, and unfair prices while crown officials mercilessly fleeced the population and suppressed its rights with impunity.

Emboldened by the American people's long patience, the English government, on George Grenville's[2] recommendation, introduced in 1765 the Stamp Act. The bill ordered that revenue stamps be affixed to legal forms, commerical papers, newspapers, wills, and all administrative documents. The Stamp Act incensed the Americans. The vocal protest precipitated various debating circles whose embittered members burned the offending bill in the marketplaces at Boston and Rhode Island, while in Connecticut the hangman publically executed the bill.

The people of Massachusetts in particular distinguished themselves in protesting against the unjust act. Their rights violated, the colonies sent delegates to New York to discuss the affairs of the nation. The [Continental] Congress drew up an enthusiastic declaration of colonial rights, stated its grievances against England, and drew up a petition to the king and Parliament. Benjamin Franklin, accompanied by two ambassadors, was dispatched to present the petition. The king and his ministers interpreted it as a sign of rebellion. To humiliate him, Franklin was summoned before Parliament. He refuted the crown's contention and stated convincingly the unjust acts of the king and Parliament.

Realizing its mistake in acting hastily, the English government, on the recommendation of Minister Grafton,[3] repealed the Stamp Act and in its place introduced a new series of customs duties on printers' colors, spices, and tea, and dispatched two regiments of troops to Boston for the enforcement of the act. The soldiers' destructive and obnoxious behavior, haughty indifference of colonial officials, and the violation of popular rights increased year by year. The colonial grievances voiced and petitioned remained unanswered.

Then a new event intruded into the already oppressive atmosphere. For its monopolistic control of tea trade in England, the East India Company paid substantial taxes to the government. But in 1770 the company had piled up a seventeen-million-pound surplus it was unable to sell. The English government, on the initiative of Lord North,[4] gave the company the right to export and sell the untaxed surplus tea directly to the colonies, bypassing local merchants. The American merchants and people protested against paying taxes to a privileged monopolistic company without avail.

The hardly healed wounds reopened again, particularly in Boston, whose citizens swore not to drink tea or allow its importation and pledged to return tea ships to England unloaded. The citizenry of Boston pledged its life and property to enforce the resolution. Whenever patriotic meetings were held, they were met by armed soldiers, leading to many minor clashes.

During the conflict over tea, which spread to other colonies, in 1773 some Bostonians boarded the tea ships and threw the tea overboard. This act wounded British pride and Parliament passed newer and newer measures to punish the rebellious colonies. The Boston port was closed, the city itself came under military command, Massachusetts's liberties were suspended, commerce was banned in the coastal colonies, including fishing in Massachusetts and New Hampshire. In addition troops were dispatched to enforce the measures.

The draconian measures sparked the smoldering flames in all the colonies, which began to unite. The British troops took drastic steps to thwart and subvert the popular and widespread support on behalf of Boston. When Massachusetts called an assembly in Concord, the English general, Gage, marched eighteen hundred soldiers to suppress it. On their way to Concord, at Lexington they fired on some armed American patriots, killing eight. This was the first citizen blood shed in the famous war. The news of the bloodshed roused the citizenry of Massachusetts, who attacked the British at Concord, killing two hundred fifty soldiers. The Americans lost only fifty men.

The armed clash was a call to revolution. The colonies armed, the people united and besieged the English troops in Boston. Realizing the strength of their despised enemy, the English government landed a twelve-thousand-man army to discipline the colonies. This precipitated the famous war which lead to the American Declaration of Independence in 1776, followed by ten years of bloody fighting leading to the ultimate American victory in 1782 and independence. The war cost England ₤129,123,091, of which ₤93,869,992 in unpaid debt still hangs around the nation's neck.[5]

VIII. Travel in Massachusetts—American Hotels—The Declaration of Independence— Thököly in Boston

Journeying through Hinsdale, Peru, Worthington, and Chesterfield, we were so attracted by many new and surprising things that we had no time to reflect and analyze them. The imagination is boggled: an impenetrable wilderness stood here and perhaps not visited by anyone since Creation other than some fishing, hunting Indian tribes who frequent the nearby lakes. And now we passed by populous villages and towns, cultivated fields, meadows, and orchards. Everywhere we saw unmistakable evidence of industry and prosperity, and people schooled in liberty.

The area we traversed in Massachusetts in our three-day journey did not appear uniformly fertile. The rocky hills are good only for grazing and there are still great stretches of forest. However, the lowlands have a better yield of corn and buckwheat than in my country. The northern parts produce large quantities of Indian corn. Paradoxically, where the soil is poor one finds thriving communities, since an unyielding land forces the population into trade and industry.

The communities of Northampton, Hadley, and Hatfield date back to 1653, when they formed Massachusetts's outside boundary within which the Indian tribes ruled until the early 1700s. Hadley suffered greatly from Indians who destroyed it twice. At Amherst we found a college and university offering higher education and foreign languages. Passing through Belchertown, Brookfield, Spence, Leicester, and Worcester, we only stopped for short visits.

***

[*111*]

112   In America, as in England, the stagecoaches exchange fresh horses at large inns while the passengers rest and eat. I was greatly impressed by the American inns, which surpass the English in comfort and luxury. The American inns have one unique feature. Immediately at the entrance, the traveler walks straight into the parlor, tastefully furnished with sofas, chairs, and rocking chairs. The floors are carpeted, and in some parlors one can find a piano. The hotel parlors always contain some books, mostly travel handbooks, local statistical and geographic books, guidebooks, and newspapers on racks. The walls are decorated with portraits and with drawings of landscapes. But most welcome to all travelers are the excellent great maps on rollers, all in deluxe editions, and particularly the Union and state maps, and the reliable local geographic maps. Between the maps and paintings, usually in a prominent place, almost everywhere hangs a special document, the gold-framed and glass-covered Declaration of Independence, sometimes garlanded with evergreens.

The Constitution and Declaration are the political Bible of the Americans, indispensable items in all homes, and the handbook of every citizen. The Declaration is published in many sizes, shapes, and forms. The new deluxe editions are printed on large-sized paper or are lithographed. Some contain facsimile signatures of all fifty signers, including that of John Hancock. Others are printed with the lithographed portraits of the signers, their names numbered underneath. In the more expensive editions the paragraph beginnings and the important statements are gilt-lettered and, framed, they hang in private homes, in public buildings, and in schools.

This daring, carefully worded document of the Revolution saved America from being swallowed by England and secured the rights of mankind. With the outbreak of the war in 1775, England realized the seriousness of the challenge and took resolute measures to suppress the rebellion. In early 1776 it landed an army of ninety thousand men and in one decisive move occupied some southern and central-coastal colonies. The Americans rose in full force once more to meet the challenge which threatened them with annihilation. Unarmed, without money, and alone in this dangerous situation, the Americans again called the Congress together in Philadelphia. Embittered by tyranny and oppression, the Congress, during the debates, for the first time raised the issue of independence, already advocated in passionately convincing language by Thomas Paine in his famous pamphlet, *Common Sense*. Recommending independence and a declaration of human rights, Paine expressed the citizenry's true sentiment[1] and design and they urged its realization. The Congress chose Franklin, Jefferson, and Adams to draft a declaration. The majority accepted Jefferson's version, which was adopted on July 4, 1776, in Philadelphia and signed first by the delegates of seven and later of all thirteen states.

This document, the cornerstone of American faith, despite its simplicity is strikingly original and unique. Its uniqueness becomes apparent when compared with European historical declarations of rights and charters of freedom which, by and large, were royal grants of historical rights. In essence the royal charter proclaimed to the people, this much will be yours and the rest belongs to us. At best, these charters of freedom, full of contrived smooth clauses, are but compacts between two contending parties. But this document summons Americans to a political creation, to the framing of a just government. It declares that just power derives from the consent of the people who entrust some rights to the government. The language of the Declaration is not the language of diplomacy but the language of natural law.

For Americans today, this document has retained its original magic from when it was first declared. Every year on July 4 the whole nation celebrates its independence and the Declaration is read in churches, in public places, at meetings, and in private homes. In school the children must learn it by heart, and practice foreign languages by translating it.[2]

***

We arrived at Boston in the evening. On the outskirts of the city in an illuminated liquor store I noticed a toy on whose label, in large block letters, was written: "Tekeli, the Hungarian Prince." I was pleasantly surprised by such an encounter with my country's memory. However, upon further inquiry I sadly learned that some French vaudeville troupe is putting on a rather mediocre skit about Imre Thököly,[3] who, when besieged by German troops in a mill, escaped hidden in a flour sack.

IX. Boston—Alexander Everett—American Etiquette—Introductions—Athenaeum —Navy Yard—Bunker Hill

*I*n Boston we checked into the Marlborough Hotel and early next morning, without any plans, went sightseeing in the streets. Americans claim that in Boston and Philadelphia reside the wealthiest, most educated, and intellectually influential people. In fact, these two cities not only play the same leading role in the nation's political and intellectual life as New York and New Orleans play in its commercial life but Boston and Philadelphia, as seats of scientific and political institutions, enjoy an intellectual leadership over other cities. Judging by its streets and buildings, one can easily imagine being in the more modern parts of London suburbia. Most of the private and public buildings here are built of white marble, and the entrance staircases in English style have polished brass railings. There is a Dutch cleanliness about the buildings. Although during the Revolution Boston's population declined to 15,320, it underwent phenomenal growth, reaching today 91,392 people.[1]

Later we visited Alexander Everett to present our letters of introduction. As former ambassador to Holland and Spain, Mr. Everett lived for some time in Europe and is the author of two acclaimed books, *America* and *Europe*, both translated and published in Europe.[2] At present Mr. Everett is a Massachusetts state senator, and his brother Edward Everett,[3] the widely traveled Harvard professor, serves in the Congress.

Mr. Everett received us in his study. The rich library, different maps, busts of famous people, the conspicuously framed Declaration, and books and manuscripts in every corner immediately revealed a man of learning. But even the appealing disorder of books and manuscripts spoke of a scholar

who combined knowledge and aesthetic taste. At first Mr. Everett appeared
reserved and distant. But during our conversation he relaxed, a typical
character trait of Americans.

***

Those who are accustomed to the Old French conversational etiquette
might be surprised at first about the impersonal republican manners.
Americans are untutored in refined etiquette, unschooled in facial expressions, and unfamiliar with the stiff gestures and deportment requisite in
culturally refined European circles. Americans are rather plain. Their form
of hospitality and welcome is a strong handshake. Yet behind the
unpolished stiffness, the face and eyes betray a simpler inner dignity and
simplicity of manners and sincere feelings that learned taste can never
acquire.

If one is acquainted with America's political principles, there is a
natural explanation for what appear as cold and reserved social habits.
Political freedom and refined cultural manners are compatible, not
exclusive. A comparison of different nations' social habits seems to indicate
that human intercourse is more formal under a monarchy than in free
societies. The monarchical system's enforced self-effacement and servile
mentality affects all classes and permeates the whole nation. When court
politics colors and shapes the administrative and often the intellectual life,
then it colors and shapes national life, whose true inner feelings give way to
assumed, formal attitudes and behavior. No matter how learned and
rehearsed the pleasures of easy flowing conversation, it exacts a high price.
By sacrificing our sacred inner self, our freedom, and our sense of justice,
we inevitably form a false conception of life.

By and large for most people in America the opposite is true. The
constitutional right of every individual to deliberate and participate ensures
the public's jealous concern that issues appear in their true reality without
theatricals. Independent in thought and judgment, Americans are particularly careful to respect each other's equal rights. It is literally true that the
Americans' preoccupation with truth and honesty in public life leaves them
no time to learn flattery and exaggeration. No nation, with the possible
exception of one class in England, has shown greater awareness of and
respect for mankind's universal rights than Americans. Experience has
shown that a stable society characterized by free and mutually compassionate and authentic social intercourse is predicated on equal respect for each
other's equal rights.[4]

***

In the afternoon Mr. Everett introduced us to his acquaintances and to
some city officials. Introductions here are simple and brief. The host takes
you to the house where he wants to introduce you and there his and your
namecards, with the current address, are sent in. That completes the

116   ceremony. If the master of the house wishes to see you, his namecard or invitation arrives, usually the same day, at your place, indicating he would be pleased to meet you or stating he is busy and not disposed to receive visitors. This way all concerned spare themselves many boring ceremonies.

Later we visited some institutions in Boston, among them the Athenaeum, one of the oldest and most prestigious literary societies in New England. Founded by private subscription, the Athenaeum has a twenty-three-thousand-book library and, among other things, extensive collections in coins, paintings, and statues. It subscribes to all the influential European and American newspapers. During the winter months, scientific and scholarly papers are read there and discussed. The library is open to nonmembers if introduced by a member. There are hardly any towns in America without similar institutions.

The state house is the most famous public building in Boston. Located on high grounds, it is surrounded by lawns and tree-lined walks. In 1827 the capitol building received a valuable art treasure. With money raised by subscription, the English artist, Chantrey, was commissioned to make a statue of George Washington. The $16,000 statue, a real masterpiece, is the pride and joy of the people of Massachusetts.

* * *

Through our distributed namecards we became acquainted with various people, many of whom offered their homes during our visit. Among these acquaintances, Messrs. Gray and Sweet were particularly helpful. Mr. Sweet took us to Charlestown, famous among other things for the Navy Yard, financed and maintained by the federal government. Two frigates, the battleships *Independence* and *Columbus,* each with seventy-four guns, and *Constitution* with forty-four guns were in the harbor. Several smaller frigates were under construction and one enormous ship, already under construction for five years, will carry one hundred twenty guns. We inspected several depots containing military weapons, including the recently constructed granite drydock.

Behind the Navy Yard rose Bunker Hill, a famous spot in American history. After the first battle of Lexington in 1775 some thirty thousand Massachusetts patriots besieged the British garrison in Boston for two weeks. Their artillery trained on Bunker Hill's dugouts, they made several small successful attacks on the enemy. As a diversionary tactic, the British set fire to Charlestown and made two assaults on the Bunker Hill defenders but were repelled with great losses. The third assault left many dead on both sides, including many prominent citizens of Boston, among them the popular General Warren. Mr. Sweet, an author on the battle of Bunker Hill, showed us the exact position of the warring forces, the lines of attack, and the strategic moves. Bunker Hill is a bloody but sacred ground to Bostonians and Americans.

Sándor Bölöni Farkas

By voluntary subscription great sums were raised to erect a national
monument on this spot. On June 17, 1825, the nation commemorated the
fiftieth anniversary of the famous battle. Many veterans of the Revolution
were invited, including General Lafayette,[5] the honored guest, to lay the
cornerstone of the Bunker Hill Memorial. The dedicatory event was
attended by large numbers of delegates from all states. Congressman Daniel
Webster[6] delivered an eloquent oration. Webster's anniversary address is a
masterpiece of patriotic oratory and spirited republicanism. Only the
length of his oration prevents me from succumbing to the temptation to
reproduce it here.

X. Charlestown—Discourse on Penal Code—Auburn and Pennsylvania Penal Systems—State Penitentiary and Treatment of Prisoners—Mr. Everett's Tea Party

*O*ne day we visited the state penitentiary in Charlestown. Of the many philanthropic institutions developed and perfected in America, the penitentiary attracted the most interest of European governments. The early American settlers brought over and introduced here the English civil and criminal codes. Although in the colonial period English civil law remained unchanged, Americans found the mother country's criminal code too cruel.

William Penn[1] and his Quakers were the first to question capital punishment in Pennsylvania. Parliament, however, resolutely opposed their attempts to introduce a more humane and effective penal code. After the Revolution, largely due to Penn's philanthropic disciples Franklin, [William] Bradford, and Lowndes, capital punishment was abolished for many crimes but retained for premeditated murder and poisoning. Corporal punishment, cruel physical and spiritual torture and humiliation were replaced by penology, which sought to reform criminals through penal labor.

This humane penal system, first introduced in Pennsylvania in 1793, prompted a controversial and lively debate in states which adopted it. Not only state governments but many humanitarian organizations, foremost among them the Quakers, scholars, and individuals debated the issue; the debates were followed by the publication of influential reform works. The psychoanalytic correlation of crime and the offender's educational level, the forms and degrees of punishment, the individual's moral well-being, and the rationale for punishment all became subjects for philosophical analysis.

During the passionate debates and discussions, many philanthropic associations, undeterred by cost, undertook various prison experiments on inmates. The published penological works made an invaluable contribution to the scientific understanding of human behavior.

These theoretical treatises and successful penal experiments gave rise to two fashionable schools of penal philosophy: the Pennsylvania and the Auburn systems. Both introduced solitary confinement and abolished capital punishment. In the Pennsylvania system the inmate is completely isolated day and night and, being excluded not only from the nation but from the whole world, works in total silence. During his solitary confinement he receives moral instruction, and work is the prisoner's reward for good conduct.[2] The Auburn system was first introduced at the Auburn model prison in New York state in 1817 [actually 1825]. According to this system, the prisoners in solitary confinement can work together but cannot talk or communicate with each other.[3] Most states, except Pennsylvania, adopted the Auburn system.

The Charlestown state prison in Massachusetts is based on the Auburn system. When we arrived, Mr. Gray, the chief warden, was already waiting for us. We met the two French magistrates [Alexis de Tocqueville and Gustave de Beaumont] sent over by the French government to study American prisons and penal system for possible adoption in France. After a tour of the guards' quarters in the old penitentiary, we visited the new prison.

Since the Auburn system prescribes a solitary cell for each inmate, the state had built a new model prison, a square building two hundred by forty-six by thirty-three feet, with 245 windows. In the center, six feet from the wall, the 307 cells are piled in tiers in a single building four stories high, and staircases connect the floors. The circular corridors contain the cells, about seven feet in height and length and three and a half feet wide. The grid-windowed iron doors open to the corridor. Each cell has a cord-pleated convertible bed tied to the wall during the day with broad straps. The cell furniture consists of a chair, a drinking mug, knife, fork, and spoon, a comb, and the Bible. Immediately to the right of the building is the chapel, on the left the kitchen, and across the big yard the workshops and a big shed for cutting stones.

When the prisoner is first brought here, he must take a bath, then is garbed in a strange prison outfit, one leg of his pants is red, the other gray or black, his jacket and cap are also of mixed color so he can be immediately identified upon escape. Informed of his crime and punishment, he is then made acquainted with the prison rules and is told that bad conduct increases and good conduct reduces his sentence. Then he is locked up in a solitary cell, silent and unvisited. The next few days the rules and regulations are repeated to him, accompanied by the prison chaplain's moral instructions. Subsequent to the prisoner's first days, he is assigned to a workshop where he can use his trade or skill. If untrained, he will get a job suitable to his

120   physique, the first year either in the smithy or in the stone-cutting shed, where, from that day on, he works with others.

The prisoner's daily schedule is as follows. The day begins at dawn. At the sound of a bell the cell doors open, the prisoners line up in the corridor, the chaplain prays and delivers a moral sermon. At the guard's signal, the prisoners march out to the prison yard to wash. On command, twenty-five to thirty form up Indian file and, their eyes fixed on the guard, are led to the workshops. In addition to the blacksmith and stone-cutting shed, there are sheds for cobblers, carpenters, plumbers, tailors, tinkers, and other trades. The shop guards are skilled workmen who not only assign and supervise work but also train new, unskilled prison-workers. The prisoners sit in a row, their backs against the wall, constantly facing the guards. They are forbidden to communicate with each other, and can ask instruction only from the guards. They cannot signal or look at each other.

When the bell sounds at a given hour, all work stops and, once more, the prisoners line up closely in the yard, hands pressed against thighs, eyes fixed on the guards, lest they communicate or signal to each other. At a signal, they move mechanically to the main entrance, where, through an opening, one by one plates are handed out with the breakfast. Mess plate in hand, each prisoner stops before his cell, waits, and enters on signal. The door is locked, and the prisoner eats his breakfast in complete silence. Twenty minutes later the bell sounds, and the prison column marches mechanically, under guard, to the shops. They work there till noon in uninterrupted silence, each prisoner sunk in his own solitary thought. At noon the same, sad mechanical march to the kitchen, then solitary lunch in the solitary cell. In one hour the prisoners are back at the shops to work uninterrupted till evening.

The only change in the mechanical routine occurs in the evening, when the prisoners wash up in the yard. After a solitary dinner in solitary cells, they line up in front of the cell doors and listen to the chaplain's prayer and moral sermon. At the sound of the bell, they climb into their beds, spend the night in deep, eternal silence, and wake at dawn to resume yesterday's mechanical routine. At night lanterns burn in the corridors to light up the cells. The guards stand at their posts in soft-soled boots, attentive to the smallest noise and movement in the cells they can see from their posts. Twice on Sundays the prisoners listen to moral sermons in the chapel. Other than those who wish to talk to the chaplain in their solitary cells, on Sundays the rest of the inmates spend the day alone or read the Bible. For the illiterate there are Sunday schools to teach reading and writing. Sometimes even the literate must practice writing.[4]

While Mr. Gray was explaining to us and the French magistrates the prison rules, we visited some cell rows, the kitchen, the chapel, the magazines, and workshops. Grave silence greeted our entry in the workshops. Every prisoner seemed to concentrate intently on his work. In some shops we paused, asked some questions about the work, but not one single prisoner looked at us. Absorbed in their silent world, they ignored our presence. Eternal silence being the enforced norm, and its violation the chief offense, the inmates are very careful not to break it. If the inmate, unable to resist the temptation, talks to his fellow inmates, he will be confined to his cell for days to contemplate on bread and water his sin, thus depriving himself of work—his only link to humanity.

In solitary confinement the prisoners do not wear chains or suffer corporal punishment, which is legally abolished. Records are kept of the violators of rules, and also of unconscientious work. Recorded infractions lengthen and conscientious work shortens the offender's prison term. Every year the prisoner's record is reviewed. The governor is authorized by law to reduce the prisoner's sentence for good behavior, including life sentences, if the offender shows promise of rehabilitation. The hope that the offender can return to the road of virtue, that he is not shut off from the world forever, is a powerful incentive for good conduct.

At the noon bell we watched the prisoners line up in the yard. They took their mess plates to the cells mechanically and an hour later marched off to work. The inmates get three meals a day, and always get meat at dinner. The daily food ration per person is one pound with plenty of bread. In some workshops the wages are auctioned to contractors, who supply the raw material. Contractors prefer prison-labor because it is under constant supervision. The contractor's average wage for prison-labor is thirty to thirty-five cents a day. Since the state spends seven to ten cents a day on a prisoner, his earnings not only cover his upkeep but defray the salary of the prison staff and other expenses. In fact, almost every year the state derives a profit from its penitentiaries, which is used for the temporary support of released prisoners.

The prison infirmary we visited had only five patients out of two hundred sixty prisoners. Unlike the prison, here inmates share a room and can talk. The infirmary was clean, quiet, pleasant, and its medical care similar to that in other philanthropic institutions.

***

This unique prison system has many other aspects which, in one way or other, seek to prevent crime and aim to show the moral road to the criminal rather than inflict society's vengeance on him. I have visited penitentiaries in France and England, and know something about our own prison system. It was natural, therefore, that hearing so much praise about America, I expected to find erring men confined here in more comfortable, nicer-looking, and better-kept prisons. But I had never imagined a mechanism could be invented to reform human reason and the soul, nor did I believe these moral machines could wield such an influence even on the born wrongdoer.

In my country the prisons are refuse dumps of the morally diseased, places where for a time society dumps its rotten parts. Our prisons are

122 houses of evil, where inmates bored mindless effectively and skillfully reeducate each other in crime at society's expense. The knout instills in the prisoner hatred against the law. Humiliated, he secedes from mankind only to return later to society, bitter and ready to avenge his tormentors. By contrast, the American penal system attempts to teach the criminal, irrespective of his previous life, to cope with his inner life, to come to terms with his conscience, and to reflect on his wrongdoing. He learns the discipline, order, and obedience he may have flouted in society. He learns moderation and industry, he discovers remedies for sources of indolence, he is taught cleanliness and punctuality, which were probably unknown to him. The prisoner is excluded from degenerate company, from seeing or hearing amoral things that corrupt even what was not corrupted in him before. Above all, twelve hours of uninterrupted silent labor leaves him twelve hours of free time, of which at least one hour he surely devotes to himself to reflect on his life, analyze his prison experience, sketch the still-open future and the possibility of reconciling himself to the society he offended. In the end, very likely he will resolve never to give cause for returning to such an institution.

***

We spent most of the day in Charlestown. In the evening we were due in Boston to attend Mr. Everett's tea party. We found there a large company and the same luxury and customs that are fashionable at English tea parties or French soirees. Before and after tea, the people formed groups and discussed various topics and issues. Just as a visitor is curious about his host country, so its people are curious and want to hear about the visitor's country. To a guest I praised what I have seen so far in America; its laws, its schools, its prison system, and various institutions. Then the conversation turned to my country and the guests wanted to know how these things compared in my distant country. What are the main constitutional principles and guarantees of our liberties? What is the quality of our schools and learning? Is the national language German, Latin, or some dialect of both? On what system are our prisons based? What are the leading institutions which promote human and national progress?

Under these questions my situation was not unlike the person who, caught in a dishonest act, is asked upon his honor to give an honest explanation. Suddenly and crushingly I felt, under the weight of these questions, the tremendous contrast between my country and America. How I wished for an honorable retreat. But it would have put me in the position of appearing either ignorant of my country, or having to lie and blush before the Americans. I tried to shift the topic to what I have seen in Europe and in other countries. But they already knew about Europe and were in the dark about my country. Finally, I had to answer the painful questions.

I am afraid my hesitation did not leave a good impression on the guests and I left the host's house sad and depressed. But a Hungarian traveler abroad is often dejected and distressed, particularly if he carries with him the memory of his land, and if he wants to praise not only its fertility but its culture. The memory of my embarrassment at the tea party tormented me endlessly. How painful it was to reflect on my country's condition, survey its literary, scientific, and cultural accomplishments, the prejudices and lack of knowledge about us abroad. Are Hungarians responsible for our backwardness in the civilized world? Why is this nation consumed by eternal millennial yearning? Why that veiled torment and melancholy mortification so characteristic of many of our writers? What is it that the best Hungarian minds seek to express in a thousand ways to help national enlightenment yet are unable to find the proper words for? Suspended between despair and defiance, the soul finds solace only in the promised future.

XI. The Condition of Schools in Boston— Harvard University at Cambridge—Theological Seminaries—Count Moric Benyovszky—American Comforts

*O*f the many institutions in Boston and Massachusetts devoted to intellectual and moral progress, the schools deserve special attention. After the Revolution, the citizens of Boston were the first to advocate the necessity of popular education and enlightenment, and took resolute steps in that direction, which produced excellent results. With other states following Massachusetts's lead, education became the overriding national concern and was conceived of as the chief means to maintain the republican form of government and principles of freedom. Bostonians are rightly proud of their educational institutions. Although Americans dislike taxes, for education every citizen, even if childless, readily pays taxes on his net income. By this method the poor enjoy almost free education on a school revenue derived mostly from the taxes of the well-to-do. There is indeed a great concern in the state that every child receive an education. Parents who neglect their children's education must pay a fine to the school budget. An old state ordinance requires every township of fifty households to commission someone to teach reading and writing. The local governments are empowered to raise revenue for the maintenance of schools. In 1830 Boston had 235 schools, 80 of which were public and 155 private, with an enrollment of 11,448 students and an annual budget of $196,000.[1]

Harvard College is the oldest educational institution in the United States. Founded in the colonial period in 1636 by a minister, John Harvard, it is located two miles from Boston at Cambridge. We visited the college and presented our letters to Mr. Ware,[2] who has just recently returned from a European tour, and is one of the professors at the Harvard Divinity School.

He showed us the buildings, the twenty-thousand-book library, and he took us around to see the special collections in astronomy, mathematics, chemistry, surgery, and anatomy. He told us the college's history and described its current policies and organizational setup. The college consists of eight separate large buildings connected by beautiful tree-lined walks, which give the whole place the appearance of a lovely English park. The college enrolls about four hundred students, who are instructed by thirty-five professors most of whose chairs are privately endowed, while the rest comes from state funds. I found it quite interesting that American colleges, unlike ours, are not surrounded by high walls. Despite its picket fence, the students, we are told, are under strict discipline. Annexed to the campus buildings was the Unitarian Divinity School and chapel, where twice on Sundays the students attend lectures.

Though the majority of the professors are Unitarians, Harvard itself is not a Unitarian college but a public institution designed to train all youth irrespective of their religious affiliation. Despite the great number of schools and colleges in America, none of the many religions dominates any private or public school. That so many students can study together without religious conflict and friction is once more attributable to a very simple cause.

According to the Constitution, religion is the citizen's private and exclusive affair, and the children's religious education is the task and responsibility of parents and priests. The schools and colleges teach only disciplines that are the common concern of all, and none of the religious principles is treated as science. Courses in religion and biblical history present only principles common to all Christians. Specific religious instruction is left to parents or is given by particular ministers in the specifically designed Sunday schools. This has the salutary result that American students and teachers in the same school can have various religious affiliations without ever raising questions about them.

To instruct the faithful and prepare the youth for religious careers, privately funded seminaries are set up. Consequently, the Calvinists have a seminary in Connecticut, the Presbyterians in Auburn, the Unitarians at Cambridge, the Episcopalians at New York, the Baptists at Hamilton, the Catholics at Baltimore, the Lutherans at Hartwick, the Methodists at Madison, and so on.

***

Returning from Cambridge, we attended a dinner given by Mr. Winthrop, lieutenant governor of Massachusetts. The guests included state and city officials, and some visiting foreigners. The old gentleman greeted us warmly. He mentioned enthusiastically that he knew well and became friends with our countryman, Count Moric Benyovszky,[3] during his American visit. We were gratified to hear such praise of our countryman but somewhat embarrassed to learn about this episode in Benyovszky's life here

126   in America. We consulted some books to learn that Benyovszky came to America from France in 1783 and settled in Baltimore. He entered into a business partnership with some local merchants to the effect that if they helped him to take Madagascar he would grant them some trading privileges on the island. Accordingly the Baltimore merchants equipped the frigate *Intrepid*, on which Benyovszky sailed to Madagascar in 1785. He died there the next year fighting the French.

Mr. Winthrop's dinner table was laid in English style, and the choice and expensive cuisine vied with that of any European aristocrat's dinner table. The wealthy Boston citizen's life recalls the privileged few in England and France. Those who believe that the comforts of life, secured and attained by wealth, will erode republican values, and sooner or later introduce aristocratic luxury, can indeed fear that people who walk on English and Chinese rugs in rooms decorated with priceless art, whose table sparkles with the choice wines of Spain, Portugal, and the islands, such leisure class will not maintain for long its independence. This apprehension would be legitimate only if this wealth were based on feudal privilege, on serfs' sweat, derived from monopolistic practices, or inherited through discriminatory inheritance laws. But in America wealth and property are the legitimate offspring of Freedom, Enterprise, and Industry. In America only the aristocracy of endeavor and individual resourcefulness will perpetuate themselves. Despite his comforts, the American is very economical. He knows well that individual initiative is his sole source of income. He cannot count on Fortune's smile or expect exclusive privileges from the law. The proud self-realization that wealth and its enjoyment derive from individual initiative increases his pleasure.

Europeans, notably the English, like to prophesy that pure as the democratic principles in America might appear, and notwithstanding all conceivable legal guarantees of democratic equality to prevent the emergence of some powerful individuals, still, in time the growing number of the wealthy will mark the triumph of aristocracy there. Thus America will parallel the destiny of Athens and Rome. Unpredictable as the web of the future and changeable as history may be, at least contemporary American conditions are such that even if a man, renowned for his wealth or achievement, dared to stand up among his fellow citizens to claim personal privileges or to bid for tyrannical power, he would inevitably incur public contempt and indignation.[4]

XII. Lowell and Its Factories—Travel Books—State of New Hampshire—Unitarians in the Northern States

A lthough there were still many things to see and visit in Boston, we had to leave for Canada. Boston's countryside is so populous, its well-to-do citizen's summer homes so comfortable that traveling here for a few miles is like traveling around London and Paris.

Lowell, located twelve miles from Boston on the Merrimack River, is one of the major industrial centers in America. Its progress was phenomenal. As late as 1812, the densely wooded area around the Merrimack River was still possessed and controlled by an Indian tribe. Unfit for farming, the unyielding wilderness was used for grazing and hunting. As discovered by a textile company in 1813, and revealed by subsequent land surveys in the area, the Merrimack over a distance of several hundred feet has a thirty-two-foot fall, and thus the mainstream could easily be diverted into a canal system whose fall would generate abundant waterpower. The same year, the land was purchased cheaply from the Indians, and the first mill, constructed from wood, was built with a capital of $3,000. The experiment proved successful, and in 1818 the second mill was added, soon the third, and finally the sixth, each with thirty-five hundred spindles. Later a carpet factory, a power plant, and other factory buildings were built.

Suddenly the desolate wilderness gave way to buildings, churches, shops, inns, and lovely residential homes. The community's population of 6,474 hums with activity on the brand-new, tree-lined streets. Well-built roads have aided the community's growth, and a company has invested $120,000 to complete a canal system to Boston to transport goods. It is estimated that there is enough waterpower to serve fifty mills with thirty-five hundred spindles each. By 1827, the mills had already spun 450,000 pounds of cotton, producing 1.2 million meters of textile. In the United States, particularly in the new states, there are many instances of such rapid progress.

From Boston we had a letter of introduction to one of the directors of the textile mill; he showed us around, explaining in detail the workings of the mill. On the first floor, steam-driven machines cut, card, and comb the cotton. Conveyors carry it from there to the second floor, where rollers draw out the strands and wind them on spindles. On the third floor, the yarn is condensed into spools, which are in turn woven into fabrics on the fourth floor. The raw and impure cotton bales, still on the first floor in the morning, are by evening woven into textile. Mostly women, boys, and girls handle the spindles, rollers, and the yarn on the factory floor. The finished textile is bleached, dyed, and finally submitted to the printing process. In ten days the loveliest and most colorful textile materials are produced and then stacked in warehouses. Later we visited the carpet factory and the power plant.

The textile mills give jobs and livings to about two thousand workers. Newly arrived immigrants comprise most of the labor force, particularly the poverty-driven Irish immigrants, who, if they are thrifty, can save enough in two to three years on their high wages to buy a few acres of very cheap land, and thus become farmers. To a settled and propertied citizen every opportunity is open. According to the latest science of politics, high wages are a sign of a prosperous nation because where the number of wage earners increases, the number of poor declines.[1] In America the daily wage is usually $1 and at busier places $2, of which a frugal person can save half.

***

During our second day in Lowell, we studied the travel books we carried with us and, comparing their entries and our observations, discovered that in America no statistical data, no matter how accurate, remain relevant after five years. The phenomenal population growth, economic and educational changes each year simply outstrip statistical information. Hence last year's facts about a place or thing are no longer useful the next year. Only the eternal truth of the Constitution and its progeny, civil society, are immutable. Ironically, the same could be said about the travel writers. Those who rely in particular on the English travelers' observations will be, for the most part, disappointed.[2] The English traveler comes to America full of prejudices and hatred. He cannot forget how this handful of people has triumphantly freed itself from England's huge, iron clutches, only to become its envied mighty competitor, surpassing it in many things. Anyone who has read a traveler's work and then retraced his footsteps soon learns to guess his predecessor's mind and feelings, and comes to know his personal biases. We have consulted the following four travel books, which differ from each other in judgment and viewpoint, just as we differ from theirs.

1. A. Levasseur, *Lafayette en Amerique en 1824 et 1825: Journal d'un voyage aux Etats-Unis*, 2 vols. (Paris, 1829).

Upon his triumphant return, Lafayette traveled in America from one celebration and reception to another. Even by the Americans' own admission, Levasseur's account of the visit is not exaggerated. However, a traveler who visits a noncelebrant America will find a different people and society.

2. His Highness Bernhard, Duke of Saxe-Weimar-Eisenach, *Travels through North America during the Years 1825 and 1826*, 2 vols. (Philadelphia, 1828).

Carrying with him his title and high rank, fully aware of his pedigreed birth, the duke obviously disliked many things here. His dry, two-volume descriptions are impressionistic and pedantically gossipy. The duke was critical of things and complained incessantly of the servants' slovenly service. Apparently he was either unaware of or not interested in the American Constitution and its civic society because he is completely silent about them.

3. *The Northern Traveller* (New York: Harper, 1830).

This reliable geographical, statistical handbook on the northern states was very helpful to us.

4. S.v.N. Aarau, *Mein Besuch Amerikas im Sommer 1824* (H. R. Sauerlander, 1827).

An account of America by an enthusiastically compassionate youth who only knows the nobler aspects of mankind. His language is ornate, his descriptions fragmented, and he is indignant about everything in Europe which stands in the way of introducing the American system. His daring comparisons reveal a sensitive soul, although many things in America fall short of his idealization.

5. Captain Francis Hall, *Travels in North America in the Years 1827 and 1828*, 3 vols. (Edinburgh, 1829).

Captain Hall is a man of considerable learning. Widely traveled, he writes analytically and his work betrays intimate knowledge. At the same time he is a stereotype of haughty British condescension, of unfounded prejudices and hatred of America and its people. He never misses an opportunity to discover and depict the weak side of Americans. He reaches his erroneous conclusions in appealing syllogisms. He achieves his caricature by holding the simpler American democracy and social life up to the English aristocratic light. Washington Irving rightly observed:[3]

> English travellers are the best and the worst in the world. Where no motives of pride and interest intervene none can equal them for profound and philosophical views of society, or faithful and graphic description of external objects. But when either the interest or reputation of their own country comes into collision with that of another, they go to the opposite extreme, and forget their usual

probity and candour, in their indulgence of splenetic remark, and an illiberal spirit of ridicule.

***

The next day we hired a very expensive carriage at Lowell because stagecoaches in America, as in England, seldom travel on Sundays. In no time we drove into the state of New Hampshire, completely unaware of it until the coachman mentioned it. America might be the only place in the civilized world where state boundaries can be crossed free, without passports, without police, customs, and detailed questionings. Toward Londonderry we crossed the Merrimack River and although there were no villages, our carriage passed by settled dwellings. Only in England and Belgium can the traveler enjoy the pleasure of journeying past houses as if he were in a garden. The whole state is parceled out into small holdings, mostly cultivated by private farmers whose houses and adjacent farm buildings are built, whenever possible, close to the road. Consequently the traveler comes upon, after every one hundred acres or so, new settlements and, interspersed, comfortable hotels. In Europe, on the other hand, as soon as the traveler leaves a village or town behind, he is on his own and feels solitary until the next village.[4]

Approaching the New Hampshire capital, Concord, we found the road jammed with carriages. Folks from the nearby farms were driving to church in Concord. Americans observe Sunday with something of a bigoted devotion. On weekdays none of the faithful frequents the churches, but on Sunday they may attend thrice. In the last thirty years the six northern states have undergone great religious changes. The descendants of the first settlers remained strict Puritans, while the Episcopalian church had few followers. During and after the Revolution, religious matters underwent new changes. Partly dissatisfied with Puritanism's opposition to democratic ideas, and partly craving more intellectual freedom in religion, the majority of settlers established new churches under Congregationalist and independent denominations.

In 1794 Joseph Priestley, the scientist, persecuted by the Episcopalians, left England together with other Unitarian ministers and settled in Boston [actually in Northumberland, Pa.], where his scientific writings and Unitarian principles converted many to Unitarianism. In consequence of the discord among the Congregationalists, many Bostonian intellectuals have participated in the ensuing theological debate. The victorious side, including President John Adams, took refuge in Unitarianism, which soon claimed many followers in Boston and from there expanded into the six [five] other northern states. Some Congregationalists in later years converted to the Anglican, Baptist, and Universalist faiths.

In Europe religious conversion is viewed differently than in England and America. For obvious reasons, in Europe religious conversion is a sign of an unstable character. But the Anglo-American tradition holds that increased knowledge of political institutions molds and perfects man, correspondingly an informed and enlightened human conscience will mold and perfect religious principles to harmonize reason and conscience and thus offer hope and solace for both.

XIII. Concord—American Constitutions —New Hampshire Constitution

A rriving at Concord on Sunday, when everything was closed, we could not visit any public institutions or even continue on our journey. Though a state capital, the city is not as populous as the other coastal towns. The buildings, the state capitol, the academy, and the churches were all very impressive. Three newspapers and one journal are published in Concord.

The rest of the day we spent in enthusiastic reading of the New Hampshire Constitution, ratified at Concord. New Hampshire was the first, after Boston, to declare illegal the Stamp and Tea acts, and was among the first to send armed men to aid Bostonians at the outbreak of the Revolution. After Pennsylvania and Massachusetts, the state issued a daring declaration of human rights and drafted its constitution.

In a discussion of the history of American constitutions, it should be noted that there are two kinds of constitutions: first, state constitutions, i.e., each of the twenty-four states has a separate constitution; and second, the federal Constitution binding on all twenty-four states. With the Declaration of Independence in 1776, all thirteen colonies formed self-governments, each independent of the others. At the same time the constitutions of all thirteen colonies, like those of the twenty-four states today and of the four territories, shared some fundamental principles, even though some state governments differ in form. Having drawn up their state constitutions, the states entered the Articles of Union and jointly created the Congress. The Congress is authorized to enter into treaties and alliances with other nations, establish foreign relations, and act in matters concerning the interests of the United States.

To illustrate this, let me present the New Hampshire Constitution, not only the oldest constitution (1784) but similar in its main principles to other state constitutions.

***

[Farkas translates into Hungarian the New Hampshire Constitution and then adds the following paragraph.]

In conclusion, if experience mandates change, to amend or abrogate some articles of the constitution, the initiative comes from the legislature and if the majority approves the amendment, it is submitted to the citizenry for vote. If two-thirds majority of two successive legislatures approves the amendment, and if approved by direct popular vote, the amendment becomes law.

XIV. Granite Quarry—State of Vermont —U.S. Population—Burlington—Lake Champlain—Canada—St. Lawrence River —Montreal—Quebec—Colonial Rule in Canada—The *John Bull*

*F*rom Concord we traveled via Enfield and Hanover toward Canada. Here there are only roadside settlements, while inland stretches the desolate wilderness. The region is well known to geologists for its high-quality granite ranges. There is not a crack in the huge blocks of four hundred to six hundred yards of granite. These geologic sites attract many visitors and granite quarrying constitutes the main source of income for the local population. The granite slabs are shipped on the Merrimack and Connecticut rivers to Boston, New York, and the seaboard towns.

At Haverhill we entered the state of Vermont and stopped at Montpelier, the state capital, for some sightseeing. Although favorably located on the banks of the Onion River, the town has a small population, since Dorset was the former capital. The first settlement in Vermont dates from 1731 and in a century its population increased to 280,465 [adjusted according to Table 9]. However, this growth is less spectacular than population growth in the northern and central and western states. At the beginning of the Revolution, the United States population hardly reached three million, which in half a century increased to thirteen million. The states every five years take a population census, while Congress conducts a census every ten years because state and congressional representation in the United States is based on population figures.

Table 9. Population Growth in the United States

	Farkas's figures	U.S. Census*
1790	3,929,228	3,921,328
1800	5,306,038	5,316,577

Table 9. Population Growth in the United States (Continued)

	Farkas's figures	U.S. Census*
1810	7,239,903	7,239,903
1820	9,625,734	9,637,999
1830	12,836,426	12,856,165

*One plausible explanation for the discrepancies here and in Table 9 is Farkas's attempt to compute in the total population figure the number of Indians and Negroes. Since America of the 1830s was still the white man's country infused with a substantial dose of what Alexis de Tocqueville called "le patriotisme irritable," population figures on Indians and Negroes were unreliable. Farkas's totals in Table 9 often deviate from figures in columns 1 and 2. Asterisks mark Farkas's errors.

Table 10.   Population Census of the United States[1]

	Whites	Indians, Negroes	Total
1. Maine	398,255	1,207	399,462
2. New Hampshire	268,910	623	269,533
3. Vermont	279,780	685	280,665*
4. Massachusetts	603,094	7,006	610,100
5. Rhode Island	93,631	3,579	97,211*
6. Connecticut	289,624	8,087	297,711
7. New York	1,878,000	45,522	1,923,522
8. New Jersey	300,226	20,555	320,779*
9. Pennsylvania	1,291,906	38,128	1,330,034
10. Delaware	57,605	19,134	76,739
11. Maryland	291,093	155,000	446,913*
12. Virginia	663,514	550,000	1,213,514
13. North Carolina	427,433	266,037	693,470
14. South Carolina	270,000	290,000	560,000
15. Georgia	308,337	210,000	518,337
16. Alabama	190,171	119,035	309,206
17. Mississippi	58,000	52,000	110,000
18. Louisiana	89,101	126,374	215,575*
19. Tennessee	537,930	146,289	684,822*
20. Kentucky	510,000	210,000	720,000
21. Ohio	928,093	9,586	937,679
22. Indiana	338,020	3,562	341,582
23. Illinois	159,000	2,053	161,055*
24. Missouri	112,065	12,362	137,427*
1. District of Columbia	27,635	12,223	39,858
2. Michigan Territory	30,848	280	31,128
3. Arkansas Territory	20,000	10,380	30,380
4. Florida Territory	18,385	16,340	34,725
Total	10,485,746	2,350,680	12,836,426

[The actual total in column 1 is 10,440,656; in column 2, 2,336,047; in column 3, 12,776,703.]

Following the beautiful Onion River, from Montpelier we traveled through Middlesex, Waterbury, Richmond, Dartmouth[?], and through Williston reached Burlington, the last town on the shore of Lake

Champlain. Burlington is noted for its scenic spots along Lake Champlain. Unfortunately we arrived late in the evening and soon after supper went to the harbor to wait for our boat.

The *Phoenix* sailed late at night and after boarding, we were soon on Lake Champlain. The next morning we awoke at Heron Island. Not far from here, on the western bank, is the Rouses Point Fortress, which the Treaty of Ghent, signed by America and Britain, designates as the boundary between the United States and Canada. About eleven miles from the fortress, our ship anchored at the first Canadian city, Saint Johns, where we went ashore. The guards at the fortress and in the city already indicated we have left behind a free country and were, once more, under a monarchical government. In the United States no public official, not even the president, has a military guard. But on these shores, there is already customs inspection.

Other than the fortress, Saint Johns lacks anything noteworthy. Leaving the town, we were in the midst of typical countryside. The monotony of travel is not relieved by settlements, orchards, gardens, or the variety of roadside buildings of prosperous farmers. Only plowed fields, divided by furrows, meet the horizon. The peasants, clad in coarse, homespun garments, work in groups. Their very appearance, submissive greetings, vacant stare, and listless movement indicate that they are engaged in corvée work.

Britain's North American dominions comprise Newfoundland, Nova Scotia, New Brunswick, Cape Breton Island, the two Canadas, Labrador, and Isle Saint John. Canada itself is divided into Upper and Lower Canada. Most Canadians are descendants of French settlers who emigrated during the reign of Louis XIV. According to the prevailing feudal custom, Lower Canada was parceled out through donations to French barons, marquises, monasteries, and bishoprics. Although in 1763 it became a British dominion, the feudal seigneurial system has remained intact to this day. The inhabitant, or *cottier*, pays different taxes, and 12 percent of the property's purchase and sale price goes to the seigneur or monastery. The land and its inhabitants stagnate. The French language, religion, science, and customs still reflect the early-eighteenth-century influence. One of the revealing signs of backwardness here is that in the free states and along the Canadian border, the same land on the New York or Vermont side costs ten to fifteen schillings per acre, while on the Canadian side, even though divided only by water or a signpost, the same acre is valued at one to one and a half schillings. Such then is the magic power of the Constitution and such is freedom's contribution to land values.[2]

***

Traversing the monotonous region, at noon we reached Laprairie, from whose hills we looked at the St. Lawrence, the second largest waterway in the world. The eyes absorb, the emotions heighten at the sight of this majestic, giant river. About two miles in the distance loom the

mountains and Montreal's proud church spires. The slow stream decep-
tively hides its enormous depth, and one gazes in silent wonder at this
massive water which conjures the great ocean and the wonders of nature.
Filled with its image, we journeyed across Laprairie. The town's chief
attraction is the gray nuns' cloister, which possesses most of the countryside.

At the shore, we boarded the steamer *La Prairie* and entered the St.
Lawrence. The Laprairie-Montreal crossing is difficult and dangerous, and
only skilled pilots can avoid the St. Lawrence's numerous rapids and
hidden rocks. The rapids have claimed many ships. At midstream the
nearly transparent river reveals the terrifying, jagged rocks. In two hours
we arrived at Montreal, Lower Canada's most populous city.

***

Among the joys of traveling are those first hours when the traveler,
unacquainted with the inhabitants, arrives in a strange town and, by
comparing faces, customs, and architecture, forms impressions about the
place. These first impressions are often indelible even though later
experience contradicts them. Traveling for a period of time, during which
the same objects can be seen in different settings, can quickly exhaust the
sensation of the first impressions, particularly if one travels alone. Lasting
and even new impressions in the midst of change can only derive from
familiarity with and knowledge of popular institutions and of social life and
its inner and external organizations. Those who travel out of necessity, to
fulfill their vanity or relieve depression, will have the same travel experience
as the proverbial globe-trotter from Praque who summed up the years of his
odyssey in one sentence: "I have seen many people, many cities, and many
tall churches." His conclusion can almost apply to our impressions of
Montreal, which, without any acquaintances, on our return trip we visited,
sampling its buildings and streets, and can only say, "We were in Montreal
twice."

In the evening we boarded the packet *John Molosson* to travel the St.
Lawrence to Quebec, the capital of Lower Canada. At Trois-Rivières we
stopped to take on firewood and new passengers. In the cold, windswept
rainy day we could hardly catch a glimpse of the shores. The St. Lawrence
is always busy with various ships, and particularly the huge log-booms
which, cut in Canada's vast forest, are floated down to Quebec and then
shipped to England.

On the third morning we reached Quebec port. The St. Lawrence is so
wide here that the opposite shores are but a blue line. Countless ships ply up
and down. As in most large commercial ports, the town's waterfront section
consists of narrow, muddy streets and merchant warehouses. Of particular
interest are the Hudson Company and the Labrador Company's fur trading
posts, and shops containing Indian handicrafts and dresses. The town itself
is divided into what is called the lower and the upper section, the latter built
on a steep incline with the same marvelous ingenuity as Edinburgh in

138 Scotland. On a high rock in the upper town is the famous fortress, which, like Gibraltar, is claimed to be inaccessible and impregnable.

After we presented our letters of introduction to the commander of the fortress, Harris Corner, whose hands were shot away, he granted us permission to inspect the fortification. Through winding streets, amid gun emplacements, casemates, and dugouts, finally we reached the so-called Cape Diamond. After the English took the fortress from the French, most of the buildings were reconstructed according to a new plan, and today ₤5,000 annually is spent on further construction. Cape Diamond, a precipitous rock, juts defiantly from the mountain ranges into the St. Lawrence. From the waterfront it towers a terrifying 348 feet high, and on its two-thirds-of-an-acre plateau the fortification is built. Standing on the uppermost rampart of the fortress, one becomes absorbed in the diverse panorama. Below, the mighty St. Lawrence teems with bobbing ships, in the distance the bluish mountain wilderness, and all around the stunning works of the human mind.

A soldier guided us through the fortress. In every stronghold there were gun emplacements and various devices to repel hostile armies. Behind the fortress is the so-called Plains of Abraham, where the English general Wolfe[3] and the French general Marquis de Montcalm[4] clashed in mortal combat in 1759 and died. Consequently the French had to surrender not only the fortress but the whole of Canada.

Below the fortress, right on the St. Lawrence, stands the splendid residence of the English governor-general who, as representative of the English king, rules both Upper and Lower Canada. Currently Lord Aylmer is the governor-general. Though Canada has a parliament, its upper house, in accordance with aristocratic principles, is composed of peers whose interests constantly clash and are diametrically opposite to the interests of the democratic lower house. Enacted laws can be implemented only upon the approval of the English monarch and the governor-general. Canadian politics is based on English colonial laws. Canada cannot maintain its own army, and its garrison forces are sent over and financed by England, which maintains at Quebec two and at other fortresses four regiments. The English government, opposed to the arming of the local population, also maintains a naval force composed of English ships and crew.

These colonies do not pay any direct taxes to England. Although the upkeep of the fortresses, the maintenance of colonial officials and soldiers, and taking care of virtually all colonial needs constitute a tremendous burden to the British crown, they are nonetheless justified for naval and commercial reasons. Since all the colonial products are shipped out and sold worldwide by England, which also dumps her finished products and those of other colonies here, England reaps great profit from these commercial transactions.

Though favorably located, neither Quebec nor the whole of Lower Canada is populous—and for various reasons. Most immigrant settlers prefer Upper Canada, where feudalism is absent and where the settler can claim his purchased land as his private property. In Lower Canada the monasteries and priests, in addition to controlling large tracts of land and wealth, also wield total power over the people. Consequently neither the schools nor education can spread and progress. The English Parliament's many attempts to limit the French language and to neutralize the priests' power met with little success, mainly because of the system of donating clerical reserve lands. But now, at national expense and from private donations of the well-to-do English families, they started to build schools, and the government finally decided to allocate some of the clergy's revenue to schools.

According to the 1784 census, Lower Canada had a population of 65,338 while Upper Canada was virtually unsettled. The 1831 census shows Lower Canada with 544,000 population, Upper Canada with 200,000; together with the other British colonies the population of Canada is 1,054,000. This increase is mostly due to the large number of Irish immigrants who are brought over here mostly at government expense. In 1829, immigration rose to 15,924, in 1830 to 28,000, and in 1831, 56,169 emigrants came from England, Ireland, and Scotland. However, in due time, some seeped down to the United States.

In front of the governor-general's residence a lovely memorial commemorates General Wolfe. The other noteworthy things in the town are the numerous churches and monasteries. Their architecture is commonplace, their interior is piled with gaudy, tasteless holy paintings, and at virtually every step is the inevitable confession booth.

After two days of sightseeing, we boarded the steamboat *Hercules* and proceeded down the St. Lawrence. The steamer was crowded with European emigrants, all anxious to settle in Upper Canada. In addition to our immigrants, the *Hercules* towed two sailboats. Though the weather was lovely, our slow progress and the jostling of immigrants irritated me. At Trois-Rivières we docked to take on firewood and new passengers. Then for a few hours we stopped at Sorel, which, located at the estuary of the Richelieu River, engages in a flourishing upstream trade. Its inhabitants are French and the place boasts the governor's summer residence and a garrison camp. In the afternoon we encountered the steamboat *John Bull*, one of the largest of its kind. It measures 189 feet in length, 70 feet across, and can carry eighteen hundred tons of cargo, or thirty-six thousand metric tons. We watched enviously as the powerful *John Bull* glided by our struggling *Hercules*, which arrived at Montreal late at night.

XV. The Dangers of Navigation on the St. Lawrence—Rapids—Kingston—Mississauga Indians—Fate of Immigrants—An Austrian Butcher in Kingston—Ontario and the Great Lakes—The Canadian Situation

*T*o reach Niagara from Montreal we either had to cross Lake Champlain or travel 392 miles straight on the St. Lawrence in the direction of the rather uninteresting regions of Upper Canada. Although we knew well the boredom of a steamboat journey, the shorter distance convinced us to take the St. Lawrence route. Between Montreal and Lachine for nine miles the St. Lawrence is so swift and its rapids so treacherous and full of snags that larger ships and steamboats, clearing more than three feet of water, invite sure danger here. The surging rapids between cliffs are a terrifying spectacle of nature.

From Lake Ontario to Trois-Rivières, the St. Lawrence has a descent of 218 feet, and while in places it flows placidly, suddenly, as if released from a dam, it surges forth with a roar, its high waves lashing the opposing rocks. At other places it forms whirlpools whose violent rush twists objects and swallows them without a trace. Long and bitter experience has taught the shipmen how to clear the rapids of the St. Lawrence, and nowadays with specially built longer boats, they can skillfully avoid the dangers.

But woe to a boat that drifts into a whirlpool! Larger vessels dare not challenge the rapids because, even if they bypass the whirlpools, the hidden rock snags are still uncharted. To avoid the Montreal rapids, we took a carriage to Lachine. The packet which was to depart immediately upon our arrival needed some repairs, and thus we visited Lachine. Only a few houses constitute the village, whose main livelihood is fishing, and it still struggles with the forest. Across the St. Lawrence is the Indian village Caughnawaga, and during our visit a few Indians paddled across in canoes, merrily swigging whiskey.

No sooner was our packet ready when, after a few hundred yards, it broke down and we had to board the *King William*. As we passed downstream, shipmen and passengers pointed to some rapids and told stories about the incidents that occurred there, which forced us to pay more attention as we proceeded to this awesome display of nature. Toward evening we reached Cascades [?] and because of the rapids we continued our journey by carriage, in the dark and muddy night, till Coteau-du-Lac, where the same night we boarded a packet on the St. Lawrence and next morning arrived at Cornwall.

At Cornwall we entered Upper Canada. But once more, facing the ever-present rapids, we hired a carriage. All day long we struggled in the cold, rainy, and windy weather, along the St. Lawrence on terrible roads and in the midst of endless forest. We spent the night in a lonely and crowded forest-inn, and arrived next day in Prescott to board the packet *James Kempt*. Most of our fellow passengers were immigrants. Leaving behind the dangerous rapids, our excursion was enlivened by the so-called Thousand Islands that dot the St. Lawrence from Prescott to Kingston. Some are inhabited by Indians, while others are used for fishing and hunting. By evening, from the movement of the steamboat we felt that the water gained depth, the waves increased, all of which indicated the closeness of Lake Ontario. It was dark when we disembarked at Kingston on Lake Ontario.

At Kingston we waited all day long for the arrival of the steamboat *Lady Dalhousie* from its run to Niagara. But its delay by unfavorable winds gave us time to visit the town, a fairly recent settlement. Allegedly the first settler bought the land on which Kingston is located from an Indian for a bottle of whiskey. Today, however, the town has a population of six thousand, and carries on a thriving water-bound commerce on Lake Ontario. The British government's Upper Canada fleet is tied up in the harbor, and there is also a one-regiment garrison stationed here.

As we waited for our boat on the shore, a couple of canoes approached and tied up at the embankment. They were the Mississauga Indians, who, on a hunting trip, stopped at Kingston to buy some food. Their canoes, built of thin planks and covered with bark, are unlike the white man's boats. Each canoe seated a family with children and hunting dogs, and was loaded with weapons, tents, furs, and provisions. The Indians' skin is of red copper tint; their long, jet-black hair very smooth; and their bodies bony. The men, handsomely attired in animal furs, homespun vestments, and wearing moccasins, came ashore to buy some provisions. The women remained seated in the canoes. Their color is also copper, and their smooth black hair, plaited with small colorful shells and trinkets, cascades over their shoulders. Some wore long earrings made of shells and trinkets, some had decorative emblems on their breasts and around their waists, and they all wore moccasins. When the men returned, and all were seated in the canoes, they rowed away in file, following the chief. Poor Indians!

142   Strangers in your own land! Your enemies, who murdered your forefathers, already treat you as foreign intruders!

Along the bank a few hundred immigrants waited for the steamboat. They sat among their belongings under the open sky. Strangers in a strange land. They left behind their native lands without knowing anything about their new country. Some came over under the English government's financial arrangement, particularly the Irish, who are brought over to settle the crown lands in Upper Canada. Others came on their own from England, Scotland, and various parts of Europe, and were on their way to Oswego to find a new country in the free states. What a strange sight to see so many immigrants on ships and on the shores. Most of them cannot afford a berth for their ocean crossing, and are transported in the ship's midsection, where, amid their belongings, they huddle and crowd. They have to provide their own food for the transatlantic crossing, which gets scarce toward the end of the journey or completely disappears. When they land they are still far from their destination and must treck far inland to find some cheap land to settle on.

During our ocean crossing and later on we had to travel on several occasions with immigrants. Each time I looked at them my heart sank, for I could not help imagining myself in their place. What a terrible thing to leave behind out of necessity one's own country. Woe to him who carries in his heart and soul the memory of his native land. Woe to anyone who devotes his night dreams, waking yearnings, and the happiest moments of his thoughts to his native country. Mercy to him who carries his country's memory even beyond the grave. I cannot imagine a more tragic fate than when a patriotic heart leaves his country and, exiled under a foreign sky, entombed in a foreign language, he lives in eternal struggle with his painful memories.

These immigrants may have taken the fateful step for various reasons. Perhaps it was unrelieved poverty under whose crushing weight they could not develop patriotic feelings. Perhaps they had no attachment to the land which from birth denied their rights, and could only count as their property the food and drink they took. Maybe persecution by the powerful, oppression by the privileged, and wanton denial of their freedom of conscience forced them to seek a freer homeland to exercise their natural rights. It is also conceivable that misjudgment or a momentary lapse of moral conscience led some astray, and now they hasten from the place where their name is branded, and hope to return to the road of virtue in distant seclusion. And who knows! Perhaps the superior intellectual, spiritual, and innate talents of some have invited the envy and calumny of others and he, lacking the spiritual strength or just being tired of fighting the philistines, now seeks a field where he can breathe more freely. They may even be members of a politically vanquished party who, hounded and pushed around by the victors, come to this country—the country of all political parties and haven of all mankind.

Sándor Bölöni Farkas

Among the immigrants we discovered Mr. Grassy with his whole family. Member of a well-known Italian family, he is a graduate of Napoleon's Polytechnique. Changing circumstances forced him to leave his country and settle here on crown reserve lands in Upper Canada. Our Kingston innkeeper also emigrated from Italy but he is already completely English.

During a boring day we made an interesting acquaintance at the inn. The wheel of fortune cast an Austrian butcher here whose livelihood depended on making sausages and on other speculative transactions in the meat business. The poor man, a good neighbor, pestered us all day with his compatriotic sentiments, urging us to immigrate, for, as he put it, here one pays taxes to neither the emperor nor the king.

At night the *Lady Dalhousie* arrived, together with other ships from downstream. We boarded early in the morning but the gusty winds from Lake Ontario proved too much for our weak ship, which tried in vain to pull out of the harbor. Together with other ships, we anchored and waited for the wind to change. Finally from downstream the powerful *Great Britain* arrived, churning big waves. Built recently, its powerful engines surpassing others in horsepower, the *Great Britain* measured 140 feet in length, 60 feet across, and drew 11 feet of water. We arranged with the captain to transfer from our packet to the *Great Britain* and soon, despite the gusty winds, we pulled out into the bay, leaving our powerless passengers behind. In less than an hour we were on Ontario and the gusty winds continued till noon.

***

Ontario and the four interconnected lakes are strange phenomena of nature. Looking at a map of America reveals that nature has blessed this part of the globe not only with great rivers but with lakes which, from one distant part to another, greatly facilitate communication and commerce. Among these are the so-called Five Western Lakes: Superior, Michigan, Huron, Erie, and Ontario. The headwater of the interconnected lakes and their massive body of water is Lake Superior. It forms a crescent five degrees south, reaches a maximum depth of 900 feet [1,330], has a length of 450 miles, and is 109 miles across. It discharges into Lake Michigan, which, occupying an area of 400 by 40 miles, flows into Huron that covers an area of 250 by 115 miles. It connects with Erie, which has a mean depth of 200 feet and measures 270 miles in length and 60 miles across. This massive body of water rushes off at Niagara over a 174-foot-high perpendicular cliff, the world-famous Niagara Falls that form the 500-foot-deep Lake Ontario, extending over an area of 180 by 40 miles. Originating in Ontario at Kingston, the 590-mile-long mighty St. Lawrence flows, from Lake Superior, over 2,000 miles before it empties into the Atlantic below Quebec.[1]

***

144   In the afternoon we arrived at Oswego, where that section of the Erie canal which originates at Albany empties, joining Lake Ontario and the Hudson. Immigrants bound for the United States disembarked here. We took on new passengers and, after a rough passage, arrived at noon the next day in York, the capital of Upper Canada.

York harbor has a very favorable location, and the town's buildings are brand-new. The governor's residence, the colonial courthouse, King's College, military headquarters, and a few churches comprise the public buildings. The streets are still marked with huge tree stumps, and within half a mile the eternal forest awaits its new settlers. The British government encourages and supports actively the settlement of Upper Canada. As in the United States, the land and town sites are first inspected and then surveyed. Generally, a homestead consists of one hundred acres, sold at two to three schillings per acre. Retired militiamen are entitled to freehold grants; an enlisted man receives one hundred acres, a sublieutenant two hundred and over, and a colonel twelve hundred acres. In addition, the immigrant's transatlantic passage is government-financed, and upon arrival he receives £5 to help him start homesteading. By these incentives many thousand Irish, English, and Scottish immigrants are brought over each year. Thus England not only disposes of its surplus population but, at the same time, builds up a counterpower against the fast-growing neighbor, the United States.

But no matter how attractive the English government's settlement policies are, Canadian settlers are still attracted to and look with undisguised yearning at the constitutional life of the neighboring free states. Despite the dept of gratitude to the mother country, they cannot hide their feeling of political nonexistence. At recent meetings they quite bluntly informed the English government that their predecessors' free land gifts and allegiance to the mother country cannot mortgage or bind the freedom of the present generation.[2] At the 1831 assembly a committee was appointed to investigate the obstacles that stand in the way of popular representation, and also to recommend a means to introduce a true, constitutionally representative government.[3]

In the evening we departed from York and gusty winds shook our steamboat as if we were on the high seas. But two of our distinguished fellow passengers, a republican from the free states and Mr. Mackenzie,[4] a member of the assembly (York) and a journalist, engaged in a lively and learned debate on the two countries' political affairs that made us forget the ship's roll and pitch.

The debate continued late into the night. It was so interesting and informative that we gladly would have sacrificed our sleep. At Queenston, because of the pouring rain, we remained on board and occupied ourselves till dawn with our forthcoming visit to Niagara Falls.

XVI. Queenston—Niagara Falls and Nature's Miracles—Count Leon—Return to the United States

On October 4 [1831] in Queenston we took a stagecoach to drive to the famous Niagara Falls. When from the mountaintops I saw the hills of the United States on the other side, it was like returning from a long journey to my own country. One more thing made this day a holiday for me. On the overcast, windy day, we could not hear Niagara's thunder, which on a clear day is audible for fifteen miles. At every turn of the road, on each hilltop, at every forest clearing, we fully expected to catch sight of the great scene. Among the passengers, Niagara and its thousand wonders were the sole topic of conversation. All eyes riveted, everybody wanted to be the first to shout: There, the great wonder!

There is hardly a soul who in his younger, dreaming days did not imagine or expect to make great voyages. How well I recall my daydreaming during geography lessons. I remember my grand visions of Niagara, and when in my reveries I sketched the things I wished to see in the world, miraculously America and Niagara always were part of that grand vision. Maturing years faded many contours of the grand vision, others were compressed, and I erased the fancier ones. And Niagara appeared to fade with the fancy ones. But now I am approaching its shores full of childish joy, amid my revived youthful dreams.

Finally, in anxious expectation we got off the stagecoach and checked into the magnificent Niagara Falls Pavilion. The inns around Niagara are built on sites so that they offer a view of the waterfall. The inn windows, opening from the corridor, face the cataract, and the top of the four-storied building is converted into a huge promenade. We hurried to the upper-story

146   corridor to look at the swirling water. A deep, terrifying rumble swelled from below, clouds of mist rose and towered over the abyss. A whole ocean plunged over the cliffs and seethed in milky pools among the rocks below. After watching for half an hour or so, we came down with the same feeling as a man, suddenly surprised and unable to express inner feelings, who withdraws into himself to analyze and find his emotional bearings.

In the afternoon we hired a guide and set out to explore the shores. From the inn a winding path descends over steep, wooded hills. In the deliberately untouched natural setting, now and then we could catch among the trees glimpses of the waterfall. The guide first took us to a spot called Table Rock, where we unexpectedly found ourselves standing on the frightening cliffs, and the seething, storm-tossed ocean flashed through my mind. We looked upstream at the river which, like water released from a dam, rushed in a bluish mass over the edge of the cliff and plunged in variegated columns into the dizzying gorge, pulling magnetlike the unwilling eyes. We looked into the gorge where the sky-blue water churned in milky foams. We gazed into the terrifying abyss which, like an approaching thunderstorm, rumbled, swirled, bubbled, and fermented, and waves chased and strangled each other. Spellbound, we watched from different spots the awesome display of nature. Our absorbed stare increased with each new discovery of spectacular scenes.

I left the place numb, convinced that what I have seen and heard here I will never be able to describe or write down. The drawings and paintings I have seen so far of Niagara seemed but amateur dabblings compared to the iginal, whose description spells futility.

We spent two days on the Canadian side and each day, from different vantage points, discovered new scenes to marvel at. We have advanced along the bank to the point where the Niagara rapids originate, close to Lake Erie. About half a mile upstream from the falls, the great river flows hushed. But its placid surface intimates enormous depth and the great mass of water that downstream forms the falls, Lake Ontario, and later the mighty St. Lawrence that constantly replenishes the ocean with fresh water. The river here is hardly a mile across, but downstream the banks progressively narrow, rocks break the surface and send the stream thundering on. At every step the river gathers speed and woe to anyone caught in its swirling sweep. At the rapids, Goat Island's upstream tip divides the river and forms the Canadian Fall, or Horseshoe Fall, and the American Fall. At the tip of the island, the cliffs-constrained stream surges like an unsluiced millstream, and plunges over a 174-foot precipitous rock. The quantity of water is easily double any European river's volume. According to the famous Dr. Wright's estimate, about eighty-five million tons of water falls each hour.

But the most breathtakingly terrifying view is from below the cataract. From the guides who live on the shore, one can rent waterproof gowns for the descent. We wrapped ourselves in the gowns which, tied like sacks, leave openings only for the eyes. The spiral staircase was covered lest the weaker suffer dizzy spells. Going down was like descending into a well. Amid deep thunder we wound our way down the steps for a while until we reached light, only thirty feet from the waterfall. What a sight suddenly numbs all feelings. Stepping into the daylight of dazzling, terrifying scenery, one is gripped with a sensation as in dreams when, facing imminent danger on a cliff or dying, with last desperate effort one lunges for escape. The heart appears to stop and, rooted to the spot, one casts a searching look for help. Words no longer can be heard, and one communicates with signs.

Slowly our fears dissipated, and we gazed upward where, as if from clouds, cascades of water streamed. Then we watched in the gorge below the rumbling, foamy swirl. Cautiously we approached the great waterfall even though the strewn rocks make this very dangerous and scary. At every step the guide cautioned us, and we could vividly imagine the accidents we heard about, including that of Chateaubriand,[1] who broke his arm here. One of the many natural wonders Niagara abounds in is the three-foot-wide cave that the waterfall tunneled under the cliff it plunges over. The cataract does not plunge straight but rather forms an arc, thus creating a space between the cave entrance and the fall. The cavern is constantly sprayed with windy mist. Those brave and resolute enough can, on a quiet day, crawl into the tunnel. I approached it and proceeded for a few yards when a sudden windy mist hit me and, half breathless, I made a hasty retreat. No tongue or brush can capture nature's scenery here.

When we climbed back to the bank, despite our waterproof gowns, we were soaked through, and our minds and imaginations filled with images one seldom finds in life. There is a museum on the shore noted for its collection of birds, snakes, butterflies, minerals, Indian dresses and household items. Among other things, under a glass we saw a bird with a fancy label: English Magpie. This bird resembles our common magpie, and we could not figure out what was so special about it. We were informed by the museum owner that in America there are no magpies and sparrows and hence the novelty.[2]

***

No American will have complete knowledge of his country until he has seen Niagara, whose shores all summer long are crowded with Americans and visitors from all parts of the globe. This year alone almost ten pages of our hotel's guestbook were filled with names. With particular delight I turned the guestbook pages. So many names from all over the world, and in so many languages, and among them our names in Hungarian. In an entry a few days' old I read the following: "Count Leon and party. An emigrant from Germany in the United States." Newspapers have written extensively about Count Leon's[3] immigration. The count had vast estates around the Rhine and Frankfurt in Germany. Supporter of the 1830–1831 liberal

148   movements there, he had to leave his country, sell his estates, and emigrate with fifty of his followers to a country where no opinion is persecuted. Right now he was looking for a place to settle in some state. Germany has lost fifty of its citizens and about 7 million florints [$3.5 million], just because he held different opinions, while America has gained fifty citizens and 7 million florints.

***

Once more we visited the Canadian Fall, and went down to the ferry to cross to the American side. On our way we discovered new scenic spots. The ferry crossing below the waterfall can be reached on foot in half a hour. With great effort a footpath was cleared on the steep, rocky embankment which can be descended without danger. Here too we found a museum containing minerals and in particular rocks from around Niagara, ancient roots, and other various curiosities. All visitors eagerly buy objects as mementos of the place. Seated in the boat, we looked back on the cataract. The river is still very swift and only an experienced ferryman can cope with it. Although not wide, its depth is 175 feet. On the other side we climbed a spiral staircase to the plateau and stepped, once more, into the United States.

On the bank of the American Fall is a handsome village, Manchester, with about fourteen hundred inhabitants. Nearly all the buildings are new and the hotels are especially attractive. We lodged at the Cataract Hotel and, incredibly enough, for the fifth time during our journey, met there a Philadelphia clergyman by the name of Lewis.

Though the American side of the falls, divided by Goat Island, carries less water than the Canadian Fall, it plunges from a greater height. The bridge leading to Goat Island is the most daring construction of its kind. The bridge pillars rest on huge midstream boulders, and one can cross the bridge safely. At the island bridgehead are located some baths, billiard rooms, nightclubs, and one shop stocked with Indian dresses, seashells, and mineral rocks. Goat Island covers an area of about seventy-two acres, left in its natural state save for some cleared paths. Its owner, Mr. Porter, has posted a sign offering to sell the island for $10,000.

After some turns on the island we were once more on the American side of the great fall. On this clear, sunny day three rainbows arched over the gorge below. On sunny days the rising vapors from below form a constant rainbow for the visitors. From the scenic spots two or three rainbows can be observed, and the same spectacle appears on moonlit nights. We descended the spiral staircase to the bottom and had to crawl under even more dangerous rocks. We struggled to the cataract's edge, but could not get under it. Below us the frightful abyss roared, defying hitherto all human ingenuity. Man has conquered the angry sea, charted its vast expanse, and learned about its hidden depths. But his boiling abyss has defied the human mind. No man has yet explored and unlocked the forces working in its hidden depths.

Climbing to the steep bank, finally we mustered enough courage to stand on the terrifying point. At the American Fall, exactly at the cliff's edge, where the water plunges down, six years ago a huge boulder got stuck a few feet from the bank. Even the powerful current could not topple the boulder. A Philadelphia citizen, by the name of Mr. Biddle, with great ingenuity laid across the boulder two huge beams and nailed a handrail to it, to be used as a catwalk.

Those who trust their heads can walk across the catwalk to the most intimidating vantage point. Not without trembling we crossed the catwalk and, gripping the handrail, gazed into the abyss below our feet. What a chilling view. One step, one resolute move, and then the dreadful plunge into the gorge whence no mortal has ever returned. There are moments in life when the despairing heart counsels such a step. Ascetism has discovered many methods of self-mortification to embitter life by contemplating death in life, and has taught constant readiness void of earthly attachments. But this contrived morality must be fed constantly with new images. One look from this catwalk, and the hopelessly resigned soul sees with clarity the whole futility of life.

***

Niagara is famous for various incidents. The story of a young Indian lad is well known to the local people. At the upper rapids a few years back stood an Indian village of the Chipewa tribe. In a canoe tied to the shore dozed a young Indian. A girl, jilted by the lad, stealthily approached the canoe and, under a spurt of vengeance, untied it and sent it downstream with its sleeping cargo. The canoe slowly glided until it reached the rapids. The people on the shoreline saw it without guessing its cargo. The rapids woke the lad, but too late. With resigned desperation he clung to the canoe that plunged into the abyss whence neither he nor any mortal has ever returned. Mercy to a man or animal swept into the surging current which dooms all. Birds that plummet into it are entombed or cast out downstream as battered carcasses. In 1827 the rapids swept under a boat with two men who never surfaced.

In the same year some visitors conceived a cruel game. They loaded the schooner *Michigan* with wild and domestic animals, and with a steamboat towed the cargo to the rapids, and released it to its fate. A huge crowd gathered on the shores. The schooner cleared the first rapids but snagged on the next rock. Its mast broken, it hovered momentarily and then was swept downstream, and disappeared, its plunge unseen. Moments later the swirling waters yielded the schooner's shattered fragments. Only a cat and a goose surfaced alive. In 1829 the famous jumper, Samuel Patch, jumped from a 125-foot-high ladder at the bottom of the cataract and survived. But soon he paid the price for his daring act, for at his next try at Genesee he jumped into the abyss and has never returned.

It seems that nature has blessed Niagara and its area with vastness and beauty. Huge rocks form the shorelines, everywhere various species of

150 flowers bloom, and the vaporous climate turns grass into velvety green. Sycamores, cedar, wild walnuts, and on thick vines a profusion of blue-clustered grapes grow all over the place. If a free constitution, favorable climate, and fertile soil can make anyone happy, then man can find it here. And only a resourceful mind, buoyant spirit, and pure conscience are required to make man the happiest of mortals in this place.

XVII. Buffalo—Iroquois Indians—Indian Tribes in the United States—Indian Schools —Buffalo Hotel—Lafayette's Last Visit to America

*A*fter three days of sightseeing, we went to see and say good-bye to the great miracle of nature. The road from Manchester follows the bank all the way to Buffalo. The whole area around here is fertile lowland, but is still covered with dense forest. What a paradise will this be, once it is completely cultivated. At the end of Grand Island we saw for the third time the Erie Canal, extending 165 miles from Albany. We saw many canalboats plying up and down, and crowded with passengers. At Black Rock we reached Lake Erie. The canal follows the Erie shore, separated by locks from the great lake. By noon we were in Buffalo.

Where Buffalo is located today with its 8,633 inhabitants, only sixty years ago wilderness stood in place of the streets, and the whole region was controlled by the fierce Iroquois, and occasionally a hunting Indian might have ventured here. The fierce and savage Iroquois possessed the vast areas between Lakes Erie and Ontario. The Iroquois League was comprised of six tribes: the Oneida, Cayuga, Mohawk, Seneca, Tuscarora, and Onondaga. During the early settlement of New York state, they must have numbered several hundred thousand because in 1610 they could arm twenty thousand men. To the first settlers the Iroquois were a terrifying tribe, the largest and cruelest among the Indian tribes. In warring with the white man, the Iroquois were often victorious and only gifts kept up a good neighborly relationship.

The fierce neighbors presented a serious problem to the white settlers bent on expanding their land possessions. But the Indians' revenge for injustice militated against using force against them. The two neighbors

152 signed frequent peace treaties but the white with shameless infamy violated and cheated on them, which in turn invited the blind revenge of the Indians, who killed and burned the whites. In the end the cunning white man triumphed over the simpleminded savage. Provoked into intertribal warfare, the Indians were corrupted and progressively decimated by gifts and whiskey, to the great relief of the whites. During the American Revolution, some Iroquois tribes, incited by the English, armed themselves and attacked the free states. Major General Sullivan[1] defeated the armed enemy tribes in 1779, and the rest destroyed each other in the following years. At the end of the Revolution the Indians could arm only fifteen hundred men.

Destroyed by their own hands and by the whites, they finally submitted to being preyed upon by white men. The victor seized and plundered their ancestral lands, and the Indians, helpless and full of irrevocable hatred against the whites, withdrew farther inland. For whiskey, guns, and trinkets the white settlers bought huge tracts of land from the morally corrupt, demoralized, pitiful remnants of a once proud and strong nation. Cunning and force, duplicity and dishonesty divested them of their ancestral lands. Since the Erie Canal had to cross some tribal lands, in 1818 the Indians sold, or were forced to sell, the land to the whites. Today 5,143 Indians live on 246,675 acres around Buffalo.

The history of many other American Indian tribes is similar to that of the Iroquois. To the first settlers, force was the accepted means to secure property. Property contracts were frequently written in blood and secured by cunning. This proved an efficient method against the demoralized, bribed, impoverished, and simpleminded savage, who in the end left his land or sold it for a pittance. Scattered over 77,402,718 [76,429,358] acres, sixty-nine Indian tribes live in the United States. The Congress entered into various agreements with the tribes. Some surrendered their land for payment and simply withdrew into the Missouri wilderness. Others remained in the Union and drew fixed payments from the government for the sold land. Still others, like the mighty Cherokee[2] and Choctaw nations, refuse any contact with the white man. They are self-governing republics, have separate schools, and have turned to agriculture and trade.

Table 11. Indian Tribes

Tribe	Residence	Population	Payment ($)	Acres of Land [Not given by Farkas.]
Passamaquoddy, Penobscot	Maine	956	—	92,260
Marshpee	Massachusetts	750*	—	—
Narraganset	Rhode Island	420	—	3,000
Mohegan	Connecticut	400	—	4,300
Seneca, Tuscarora, Oneida, Onondaga, Cayuga, Stockbridge	New York	5,143*	4,709	246,675

Table 11. Indian Tribes (Continued)

Tribe	Residence	Population	Payment ($)	Acres of Land [Not given by Farkas.]
Nottaway, Catawha	Virginia, South Carolina	497	—	171,000
Wyandot, Shawnee, Ottawa, Seneca,	Ohio	1,853	10,785 6,800	222,301
Delaware			5,600	
Wyandott, Potawatomi, Chippewa, Ottawa, Winnebago	Michigan	28,316	61,165	7,057,920
Miami	Indiana	1,073*	30,120	10,104,000
Kaska, Sauk, Menomini	Illinois	6,706	6,500	5,314,560
Potawatomi, Chippewa	Indiana, Illinois	3,900	6,800	—
Creek	Georgia	20,000	34,500	9,537,920
Cherokee	Georgia, Tennessee	9,000*	12,000	7,272,576
Choctaw	Mississippi	21,000	24,300	—
Seminoles and others	Florida	5,000	7,000	4,302,640
13 Tribes	Louisiana	1,313	—	—
5 Tribes	Missouri	5,810	—	44,806
Osage, Piankashaw	Missouri, Arkansas	5,407	8,500	3,491,840
Cherokee, Choctaw	Arkansas	6,700	—	12,858,560
Chickasaw	Mississippi	3,625*	—	15,705,000
Wea, Piankashaw, Quapaw, Winnebago	Mississippi	300,000*	39,000	—
Christian Indians		—	400	—
Total		427,869	$258,179	76,429,358

Not far from Buffalo there are three Indian villages (wigwams). In one of them an Indian missionary society has built a school and a church. We decided to make a trip to the village. The road leading to it, over a marshy and wooded region, is bad. On our way we met a few Indians, mostly on horseback, heading toward Buffalo. Though their outfits were mostly white men's castoffs, they have retained some tribal fashions. Their hats were decorated with silver brooches, or other objects. Their split earlobes swung like a pendulum, and they wore wide, homespun belts, mostly red and tied in a bow. Some carry broad-bladed knives sheathed in their belts, and twirl tomahawks in sinewy hands. The women's breasts are richly decorated, their earrings an enormous bouquet, and they wear colorfully embroidered moccasins.

Scattered log cabins comprise the village. In the gardens maize and potatoes grow. First we visited the school. The children were already dismissed when the teacher showed us the school and explained the curriculum. In reading and writing they use the Lancaster method but, on the whole, the children are taught the Christian faith and its theology. Later we went to the church. The village Indians are Presbyterians. We also stopped at some homes where the elders always shook hands and then resumed their former positions.

Despite all the missionary and civilizing efforts, the Indian cannot find his place among white men against whom he harbors a deep, residual hatred. To the Indian the white man is a double-crosser whose force and fraud deprived him of his ancestral land, killed his father and grandfather, and banished his descendants even from the ancestral burial grounds. He rejects the white man's education, which he considers the science of cunning. The Indian's soul is so hardened with hatred that he suspects double-crossing even when the white man means well. Progressively, the Indians are renouncing religion and all civilization, and are withdrawing into the northern wilderness, unoccupied by whites. The proud Indian will die of hunger rather than serve the whites.

In the last thirty years or so, the U.S. Congress has paid special attention to the Indians, partly because of strong public sentiment and partly out of fear of Indians. Some tribal lands were bought for cash, and the Indians withdrew voluntarily beyond the Mississippi. Recently, in exchange for their ancestral lands, they received one hundred million acres in the Missouri Territory, where in 1830 eight tribes[4] had already settled. The Congress seeks to persuade the Indians to resettle progressively in the exchanged territory and, through religion and education, bring the rest over to the white cause. But if the reservation Indian continues his savage way of life, he still remains a feared neighbor. Hence missionaries are dispatched to convert them, government agents are sent, and schools are maintained in the Indian territories. Annually these programs cost the United States $700,000.

Table 12. Education of Indian Children[5]

	Number of Children Educated
1822	468
1823	789
1824	916
1825	1,169
1826	1,194
1827	1,191
1828	1,238
1829	1,830
1830	1,512

Although the number of Indians in the Missouri Territory and beyond is not known, a general estimate puts it at two million.[6] But this number declines each year due to the constant intertribal rivalries.

***

From the Indian village we returned to Buffalo. Those who visit the Erie Canal region can see with their own eyes the truth of the statement that "in America villages and cities grow like crops." It is unlikely that anyone who traveled through Buffalo twenty years ago would recognize it today. Because it is endowed with a natural harbor, right after the Revolution some merchants settled around Erie bay. In 1814 the English burned down the city completely, save a widow's log cabin. Uninhabited and deserted for a long time, only a few merchant warehouses stood on the shores, behind which stretched the desolate wilderness. The opening of the Erie Canal gave new life to the region. With the appearance of the first canalboat in 1825, Buffalo has joined the five Great Lakes, the St. Lawrence, the Hudson, and the ocean. The rich area attracted hordes of speculators, followed by tradesmen and merchants of all kinds. They cleared the forest for streets, churches, houses, stores, and hotels. Already a classical-style public building stands in the center. Squares are left for public schools, and barrel-sized stumps stand in mute testimony to the wilderness that reigned here. Streets are measured and staked out far into the forest, and street names are scribbled on long poles even though everywhere felled trees are piled. Wherever one looks, one sees rising buildings that are being roofed, painted, or furnished. The ceaseless activity of carpenters, the hustle and bustle of industry and enterprise—what a beautiful sight for the human eyes to behold.

Even more remarkable are the architectural style and the appearance of these villages and towns, unparalleled in Europe or anywhere else. Attractive as some buildings or districts may be in Europe, invariably they have twice as many dirty streets immediately next to them or in other parts of the city, even in Paris and London. Here, on the other hand, architectural beauty runs in the blood, as it were. The settler may only construct a modest log house, but he will give a Greek or Italian touch to its facade, and tries to outdo his neighbor in neatness and comfort. Yet neither an architectural committee nor the police issue any directives on how to build.

***

In Buffalo we stayed at the Eagle Tavern, which in appearance and style, comfort and size, few hotels can match even in England. Not only can it regularly accommodate two hundred guests with comfort but every floor has richly furnished parlors, dining halls, reading rooms, bathrooms, and other conveniences that make a home comfortable.

The owner of the hotel is especially proud that Lafayette stayed here during his 1825 visit. The room he stayed in still contains his portrait, and the furniture and other objects are left as Lafayette left them.

Lafayette's 1824–1825 visit is a significant chapter in American history. During our travels we have found a great deal of evidence for that from people and in monuments of Lafayette's visit, recounted and remembered with pride to the most minute detail. Ever since the fall of the Greek and Roman republics, history cannot attest to greater and truer democratic men than Washington, Lafayette, and Bolívar.[7] The American revolutions they led are important and famous not because they established a new form of government, but because they transformed the prevailing

156 theory of governing and have inspired mankind to new ideas. Confined to the court and some personnel changes, previous revolutions failed to influence the people. But the American Revolution was fought for the reinstitution of natural rights, rather than for personal aggrandizement.

Lafayette played a significant role in the American Revolution, and he is remembered with an almost religious devotion. Only twenty years old, he joined the Revolution in early 1777, and fought to the end for liberty and independence, risking his life and fortune, and sacrificing his welfare. Born into a leading French family, cradled by fortune, endowed with splendid physical attributes, he had within his reach beauty, privilege, and the sensual pleasures of a glittering court that attracted the vanity-crazed, gilded youth. In the bloom of his youth, he rejected all this to brave for seven years the American wilderness. Indifferent to all personal gain, he came to fight for liberty and natural rights. He came to join a nameless, struggling, credit-burdened, and hard pressed but peerlessly determined handful of people to fight for liberty. He came when the chances for a successful outcome were small, when liberty was banished from the face of the earth, and the oppressed, servile people were scared even to think. He came here when reason itself and the free, unshackled expression of an idea were signs of rebellion. And the mere mention of or sympathy to the rights of man was persecuted and often rewarded with exile or death.

In such intimidating circumstances was Lafayette born, and made his unwavering commitment to liberty. In these adverse times Lafayette set forth his theories of liberty and man's rights. Renouncing fortune's appeal, he sacrificed wealth and possessions to make his unprecedented unselfish devotion to the cause of mankind. If a mortal man can be called upright and manly for standing firmly by his principled convictions, which he defends and upholds despite all temptations, and for risking everything, then Lafayette is rightfully considered a man of character. He remained the same character; whether in a seductive glittering court, in the American wilderness, where he could deliberate at will over France's unfolding destiny amid the uncertainties of the French Revolution, or even during his exile enforced by his own countrymen. Even in the Olmütz dungeon during the triumphant monarchy and the Restoration's witch-hunt, he remained a stubborn, unswerving republican. Lafayette's whole life is but a sequence of consistent principles. When he said farewell to America after the Revolution (1783), he concluded, before the Congress, with these words: "May this great moment, raised to Liberty, serve as a lesson to the oppressor and an example to the oppressed. May this nation remain the eternal haven of natural rights."[8] And liberty remained Lafayette's religion throughout his life.

Forty years have passed since Lafayette's last visit to America, the country of his fame. The ideals he was faithful to underwent many changes in Europe, where he had witnessed the intermittent triumph of his soul-nurtured ideals and their demise and oppression. Undeterred, he looked expectantly to America, among whose happy people the seeds he planted were nurtured into a mighty tree, but which never took root in Europe. A whole generation has passed in America since then and has laid to rest the champions of liberty. But in the new generation the seeds he planted grow more luxuriant and bear stronger fruit than ever before. Hence the grateful new generation honors and respects ever more the veteran of liberty. For the last time they and the whole nation wanted to see him, to express their gratitude and be blessed by him. Responding to the long-held wishes of the nation, the Congress invited Lafayette to visit America once more. He was moved by the nation's gratitude because he knew that the American people are not noted for sudden compliments for transient reasons. In a letter to President Monroe, Lafayette accepted the invitation but not the offer to avail himself of a special frigate sent by the nation.

He arrived in New York on August 6, 1824, to an indescribable public reception. Every state and city wished to see and share the nation's guest. Delegations flooded him with invitations, and he traveled for a year and a half in a celebrating nation. Officials and plowmen, tradesmen and schoolchildren, mothers with babes in their arms, Indians and Negroes, and the whole nation, in fact, forgot its business and came as pilgrims from far corners to see the hero of liberty, the man to whom they owed their prosperity. No ruler can boast of such a triumph. The triumphant reception was neither arranged by the police nor was it from-above-inspired gratitude. It was the warm handshake of a boundlessly grateful nation in which poor and rich vied to participate.

Levasseur, Lafayette's secretary, described in moving detail the whole trip; the welcoming speeches and the crowded events. The work is translated into English, and the Americans claim it is a true account of the actual events.

Lafayette returned to France in 1825. The newspapers have already spread his triumphant American tour, and upon landing, he was welcomed back with accusations and envy. One part of the world reproaches and maligns him for convictions that earn him grateful laurels in the other part of the world. History alone will answer this riddle.

XVIII. Sailing on Lake Erie—Ferenc Muller, a Compatriot from Pozsony—Pennsylvania—City of Erie—Sunday in America—Different Religions in America—Monroe's Speech on Religion

*A*t Buffalo we boarded the steamboat *Thompson* to take an excursion on Lake Erie and then, either from Sandusky or Erie harbor, to descend to the Southern states. The *Thompson* was an old ship, its engines weak, and, in addition to the heavy cargo, it was crowded with merchants, immigrants, and some Seneca Indians with their families. One could hardly move among the five hundred or so crowded passengers. We had sailed for barely two hours when a headwind rose and forced the ship into a zigzag course. All day we stayed on the upper deck with other passengers. We struck up a conversation with the poor Indians, who just sold their land in New York and were on their way to join the Indian aborigines beyond the Mississippi. Some spoke good English and were nicely dressed, only their red belts and weapons betrayed their Indian origins.

On a boring day aboard a packet one tries everything and talks to everybody. Among the passengers I noticed a handsome young man who always followed us and listened intently to our conversation. Finally, he drew me aside and, after a lengthy apology, asked me if I was Hungarian.

"Yes, I am."

"Thanks to God!" he exclaimed in broken Hungarian. "I guessed right away," he said, "from your mustache and the Latin[1] pronunciation of your English that you must be a Hungarian."

What a great surprise to hear Hungarian spoken in the middle of Lake Erie on the other side of the globe. Immediately we got into a lively conversation, exchanged biographical information and the circumstances of our visit. He was born in Pozsony [Pressburg], went to school there, and learned Hungarian in other schools in the country. His name was Ferenc Muller. His relatives, István Bock, came to Louisiana sixteen years ago and now trades in furs in New Orleans. Childless himself, he brought Muller to America years ago. The young Muller was just returning from a business trip to Canada, financed by his relative, and was on his way to New Orleans.

Although Muller had forgotten much of his native language, he was delighted to hear Hungarian spoken and tried to speak it only. To me his quaint, broken Hungarian sounded sweeter than any eloquent sermon at home. We talked only about Hungary, and he asked me countless questions about his native country. He repeated excitedly: if only the American Constitution could be planted in Hungary, then it would be the happiest land on earth. He wished not to die abroad but to return when the moment comes.

The sun had set and the wind increased. Around midnight at Portland a violent headwind forced us about twenty-five miles back to Dunkirk. Unable to press ahead, we plied up and down before Dunkirk harbor. Reluctant to stay below the deck among the great throng, I located Muller and we spent the night on the upper deck. Again we talked about Hungary and compared it with other countries. I was delighted to hear from him that he still keeps a Hungarian prayer book, from which on Sundays he reads to his brother lest they forget the language. He asked me if I could give him any Hungarian books. To my great regret I had none.

Behold the magic of language that unites natives of the same country, and even abroad we greet each other by the common bond of language. Travel experience has taught me that native-born Hungarians, scattered throughout Europe, are united not by the fact that they are born under one sky but by speaking one common language. To me this is a practical truth: a person who fails or refuses to learn the language of the country where he was born and lives is either very stupid or he despises his own country. Such a person will never identify with his native land or its people. A man who considers his native land but a pasture, such a man deserves contempt at home and abroad.

***

Afraid to approach the harbor, the captain kept our ship before Dunkirk till noon. In the end we decided to leave the crowded steamboat and continue our journey on land. The captain disapproved of our plan, fearing the waves might be too much for our rowboat. But frankly we preferred half an hour of danger to daylong idle anxiety on the steamboat. No sooner had we gotten into the boat than poor Muller burst into tears. He helped us with the luggage and wished us many an emotional bon voyage as though he parted from his brothers. Once more he shook our hands, choked up, and big tears welled in his eyes. I know those tears came from his heart and were induced by the memory of his great country.

160　　　　After half an hour of anxious storm-tossing, we reached the shore. I looked back at the steamboat. Poor Muller stood on the upper deck waving a handkerchief. At Dunkirk we took a stagecoach and, traveling in the direction of Fredonia and Portland, after Westfield we entered the upper corner of Pennsylvania. Driving by fertile, well-cultivated fields and beautiful orchards, by evening we arrived at Erie, where we met Count Leon and his retinue. He has already hired for the next day all the carriages for his large company, and we had no choice but to spend the next day here.

Built on the Erie shore in the upper corner of Pennsylvania, the city of Erie has a favorable location and is the capital of Erie County. But other than its college and the city hall, it has no other attractions. To a European traveler, however, it is significant that a city with barely six thousand people has several churches belonging to various denominations. It was Sunday and I watched in amazement with what religious bustle the people hurried to their respective churches. On Sundays, when people attend three services, hardly a soul can be found at home. To a European this is all the more remarkable inasmuch as in American states there is no holiday ordinance or administrative measure to make church attendance mandatory. To this must be added the absence of state religion, which to an incredulous European spells danger to the state and breeds public indifference; the equal rights of all conceivable religions, already numbering over fifty; the complete divestiture of the clergy of state authority; and finally, every citizen can freely choose his religion, or even establish one consistent with his convictions.

Indeed, these are astonishing, even contradictory, facts. Yet this is how matters of religion stand in America. The dogmatic verities written through the centuries in the blood of millions America has contradicted in half a century. Among many proofs, the most compelling is the large number of different and autonomous religions—while in any European country two religions suffice to make life nasty and brutish.

Table 13.　Religious Denominations in the United States[2]

Denomination	Membership	Number of Priests	Churches
1. Episcopalian or Conformist	1,200,000	—	1,777
2. Methodist Episcopalian	1,176,000	1,900	—
3. Protestant	600,000	528	—
4. Calvinist	1,304,827	2,914	4,384
5. Christian Community	375,000	300	1,000
6. Freewill Baptist	116,500	300	—
7. Mennonite or Anabaptist	120,000	250	—
8. Seventh-Day Baptist	20,000	30	—
9. Free Communionist	30,500	—	—
10. Universal Baptist	—	—	—
11. Baptists of Six Dogmas	20,000	125	—
12. Dunker	30,000	40	—
13. Sabbatarian	—	12	—
14. Emancipator	4,500	115	—

Table 13. Religious Denominations in the United States[2] (Continued)

Denomination	Membership	Number of Priests	Churches
15. Methodist	300,000	3,440	1,900
16. Seceder or separatist	—	—	32
17. Hutterian Brethren	5,000	—	—
18. Sandemanian	3,400	—	—
19. Naturalist or Owen Follower	2,500	None	—
20. Bible Christian	—	—	—
21. Mormons of New Bible	—	—	—
22. Independent	—	—	—
23. Unitarian	95,000	194	160
24. Congregational Unitarian	1,120,000	800	1,000
25. Presbyterian or Noncomformist	1,173,329	1,491	2,158
26. Associated Presbyterian	80,000	72	104
27. Protestant Presbyterian or Covenanter	—	—	—
28. Cumberland Presbyterian	100,000	—	—
29. Scottish Presbyterian	—	—	—
30. New England Enlightened Christian Ecclesiast	—	—	—
31. Roman Catholic	500,000	230	—
32. Quaker	200,000	None	500
33. Free Quaker or Nikolate	—	—	—
34. Dutch Reformed Protestant Church	107,130	—	185
35. German Protestant	200,000	120	500
36. Lutheran	200,000	230	—
37. Swedish Lutheran	—	—	—
38. Freethinkers	—	—	—
39. Manitou Worshipper (Hindu)	129,266	—	—
40. Jews	3,000	—	—
41. Moravian or United Brethren	7,000	23	23
42. New Jerusalem Ecclesia or Swedenborgian	5,000	29	30
43. Shakers or Millenarian	12,000	None	16
44. Rappite or Harmonite	800	1	1
45. Universalist	500,000	150	500
46. Swenkfeldian	—	—	—

But these numbers are not final because from time to time new religions are formed. Nonetheless, they cancel the scriptural millennium of "One herd, one shepherd." In America such hope is vain. Denied state support for one ascendant religion, the clergy by definition is left to its own resources to work out a peaceful religious coexistence, promote faith consistent with the principles of freedom, morality, and education. Religion being a congregation of believers, a priest cannot use coercion. They know only too well that enforced church attendance is a prelude to anticlericalism and the substitution of feigned religiousness for true religious ethics.[3]

At Erie I visited a few churches unaware of what religion they belonged to, not that one could tell from the service. There was no time to sit through each priest's sermon. What struck me is that despite the unique nature of religions, or, to put it in European terms, among these lawless

162   religions, the churches were full of devout worshipers. The American people are fully aware of how opposite we stand on religious matters. They asked sadly whether the Old World had changed its position on religion. On many occasions I heard this expressed even from the pulpit. Here the ministers often conclude their prayer: "O Lord, keep our religious and political freedoms. Give strength to our distant fellow brethren to win these freedoms and thus inherit thy bountiful kingdom."

The American principles of interreligious relations were summed up by President Monroe before the Congress as follows:[4]

> It is an undeniable truth that our religion and external worship of God can only be determined by reason and conscience rather than compulsion. Everyone has a right to follow the religion of his own conscience. This right is natural and inalienable. Though it is our duty to worship our Creator, we can only do it in a manner we judge pleasing to him. The citizen's religious rights are not subject to state authority but completely independent from it. The state is but the institution of laws, of property, of personal valor, and of civil life. No earthly power but God alone can judge one's spiritual relations with him.
>
> All men are born free and independent and, entering society on equal conditions, enjoy equal rights. Upon entering society, they retain the right of conscience which entitles them to equal freedom. This freedom must be granted even to those whose soul lacks the conviction of this truth. If a person abuses this freedom, let no man but God punish him who is accountable to God alone.
>
> What influence did priestly institutions wield in civic life? We saw how priestly tyranny ruined civil power, and we have witnessed all too frequently how the clergy aid political tyranny. But we have never witnessed it champion popular rights. The public oppressors of freedom can count unfailingly on the clergy's support. Experience has shown that governmental stability is predicated on the defense of the citizens' religious rights, just as it is predicated on personal property rights. A government is just when it respects equally all religious rights and none is favored over the others.
>
> Suppression of religious heresies and controversies produced bloodbaths in the Old World. Time has proved that only the cessation of persecution can tame the evil. America has proved that even if unlimited religious freedom could not exclude the clergy's adverse influence on the state, at least it can be effectively tamed.

XIX. Springfield—Election of Public Officials—State of Ohio—Newspaper Delivery—Ohio's Fastest Population Growth— Ohio River—Statistical Data

*F*rom Erie we took a stagecoach to the state of Ohio, traveling in the direction of Fairview. We drove only a few hours when the coach's axle broke. We walked to the village of Springfield, busy with district elections, which coincided with county elections. On that day, the sheriff, auditor, commissioner, assemblyman, and trustees of Erie College were elected. Springfield County comprises several villages. The voters gathered in groups before the assembly hall while their carriages lined the streets with horses tied to fence posts or other carriages. The whole scene was reminiscent of our county meetings and, in fact, we fully expected to see and hear the same thing as in our county elections. But here, despite three hours of watching and observing, things were completely different. No noise, no tempered squabblings, no violent clashes. When his turn came, the registered voter calmly entered the ballot room and calmly cast his vote into the ballot box. That was the end of the great thing. Yet the citizens have just fulfilled their fundamental duty in a republican government by electing administrative officials responsible for the county and state's happiness, or unhappiness, until the next elections.

In a constitutional republic the electoral laws are the bedrock of the governmental system and the cornerstone of civil liberties. The fall of Greece and Rome resides in the class restriction of the electorate, the disfranchisement of the people, and the establishment of permanent officeholders. These historical lessons greatly influenced the framers of the American Constitution, who with one stroke of the pen established the self-evident truth that in civil society individuals enjoy equal rights. From

164   this it logically followed that privilege, ancient custom, aristocratic and other monopolistic rights have gone with the wind. It also became self-evident that every citizen had a right to choose according to his conscience representatives and keep them in office only as long as they deserve the trust placed in them.

Opponents of republican principles who claim to see the rebirth of a national aristocracy, and to whom administrators are the necessary product of a higher power's secret decisions, find this system incomprehensible. Convinced that the electorate is always faction-ridden, they prophesy the collapse of the whole system. Yet in America no one seems to fear this for the simple reason that here the people constitute the government and not the government the people. The Americans, charged with the constant responsibility to elect representatives and judge constantly governmental policies, are trained to view themselves as active members of government. So inborn is this that every individual considers the national interest his interest. They jealously guard and maintain national greatness considered by the citizens as their own creation. This self-conscious pride of citizens establishes a cohesive public spirit.[1]

Whenever a public office is lawfully vacated, all citizens participate in choosing the best candidate to fill it. To reduce the cost of traveling to assemble as electors and to speed up the election returns, the citizens assemble in towns, districts, and villages in wards. Everywhere the elections are held on the same day. Every district sends its ballot results to a designated place where they are tallied, and those who receive the majority vote are declared winners. To close the avenue to all human frailties, elections are based on secret ballot. Public offices not being hereditary but subject to annual elections, office-hunting is not so irritating. To gain public office by majority vote of one's fellow citizens is a distinct honor to every citizen.

Here too, despite the strict electoral laws and a strong sense of justice, vanity, hunger for power, and cunning could twist elections to ends to which they are twisted in many places in Europe, despite flawless laws. But a powerful guardian watches here over civil liberties and laws, ready to strike with its sharp weapon the violator of the law making his first move. That guardian is the freedom of the press. A speaker once said in the English Parliament that should a tyrant ever suppress the Englishman's rights yet the freedom of the press remained, then in two years all rights would be restored.

We had hardly left Springfield when our bad carriage broke down again—but for the last time. We reached Ohio on foot and arrived at Salem in the dark.

We traveled in Ohio for three days, winding our way down to Monroe, Andover, Vernon, toward Brookfield and Poland. But none of these places offered any attraction and we stopped only briefly. These parts of Ohio are mostly flat lowlands covered with dense forest. The road cleared through the untracked wilderness a few years back is still in its original state. Not unlike log fortresses, felled trees are piled up along the roadside and in the middle of the sticky muddy road. An occasional roadside settlement is ringed by burned forest, and among the tall charred trunks cattle graze on the velvet green grass. Farther off one sees houses and farm buildings just under construction. Then the wilderness, and again a new settlement. In between one comes across an inn which matches in comfort those in cities. Then the same vast forest in the midst of which a poor settler struggles with the wilderness—felling, burning, and destroying to build himself a modest log cabin. Such scenes greet the traveler in this region of Ohio. Traveling in the midwestern American states is not unlike traveling in fairy-tale stories where the traveler, by magic, comes upon at the edge of dense forest shining cities, then again vast forest where by the lakeside he finds inns resembling splendid castles.

***

The stagecoaches in America carry newspapers, whose manner of distribution in the wilderness delighted and surprised me. Remote from civilization and poor as he may be, every settler reads a newspaper. Approaching a clearing, the stagecoach sounds a horn, indicating the nearness of some settlement. The box under the driver's seat is packed with newspapers. Nearing the settlement, he sounds the horn once more to indicate delivery. Without stopping, the driver tosses the newspapers by the roadside. The scene repeats itself all day—newspapers are tossed out at settlements to the left and right.

***

Of the twenty-four states, Ohio's population has increased the fastest. These regions around the waters, virtually unknown till 1780, were possessed by Indian tribes, the so-called Western Territories. The same year some forty-seven settlers came from New England and at auction for $59 bought the whole region where Cincinnati, the capital, is located. Cincinnati, because of its closeness to the Ohio River, its fertile soil, and moderate climate, attracts swarms of settlers. Its spectacular growth through individual enterprise is unprecedented in human history.

Table 14. Cincinnati's Population Growth

1795	560
1810	2,540
1813	4,000
1820	9,733
1831	31,000

Table 15.   Ohio's Population Growth[2]

1780	81
1790	3,000
1800	42,150
1810	230,760
1820	581,434
1830	937,679

The daily increase in population, mostly European immigrants, is not due to fertile cheap lands or moderate climate. After all, Europe has enough cheap and fertile lands. As everywhere, here too work and human initiative create wealth. But people are drawn irresistibly by a magic, the magic of [constitutional rights], which to a man mean more than all the wealth and cheap, fertile land.

***

At Beaver we crossed again into Pennsylvania, and followed the beautiful Ohio River. Ranked the largest in the United States, it flows through the central states and joins, via the Mississippi, the Gulf of Mexico and through Pennsylvania and the Ohio Canal it links the ocean and the upper lakes. The Ohio River's commercial importance grows daily. It serves the fertile central states, whose products and goods reach all the ports by water-bound traffic. Some 198 steamboats service daily the Ohio River. To illustrate the American reliance on exact statistical data, I list the compiled statistics of the Ohio packet service.

Table 16.   Steamboat Construction and Service on the Ohio River

Year Built	Number	In Service	Lost
1811	1	—	1
1814	4	—	4
1815	3	—	3
1816	2	—	2
1817	9	—	9
1818	23	—	23
1819	29	—	29
1820	7	1	6
1821	6	1	5
1822	7	—	7
1823	13	1	12
1824	13	1	12
1825	31	19	12
1826	52	36	16
1827	25	19	6
1828	31	28	3
1829	53	53	—
1830	30	30	—
1831	9	9	—
Total	348	198	150

According to the figures, since 1811, when the steamboat service   *167*
began, 348 steamers serviced Ohio. Of that number 198 are still in service
and 150 were lost or retired.

Table 17.   Nature of Steamboat Losses[3]

Retired	63
Shipwrecked on snags	36
Burned	14
Collision, sank	3
Other accidents	34
Total	150

America has greatly surpassed the European states in preparing such
statistical data. Each state publishes an annual almanac of comprehensive
and detailed public information which vies with the information provided
by the newspapers. A visiting foreigner can see in it as if in a mirror a state's
geography and its statistical data. Even a solitary backwoodsman, remote
from civilization, is well informed of his state's annual progress.

XX. Economy—Rapp's Community and Its History—Economy's Social Institutions— American Wines—Owen's Community

*F*rom Beaver we journeyed to Economy to visit the famous Harmony or Rappite Society. During our journey we heard many diverse opinions about Rapp and his society. Even more controversial are the European accounts.[1] Some describe the Rappites as a model commune of human enterprise based on perfect equality and the purest ethical life. Others view them as a bunch of simpleminded Germans, purblindly accepting Rapp's humbug mysticism, cunningly manipulated, intellectually oppressed by Rapp, upon whose death the society will dissolve. Others stress the society's absurdly antidemocratic and promonarchical leanings, which endanger republican principles and restrict individual liberties.

The Rappites' or Harmonites' main tenets are: perfect equality and repudiation of private possessions in favor of communal ownership. The undivided communal property is shared and used equally, and all members are enjoined to work and strive for the increase of property. Idlers are disqualified from joining, and members must work according to their ability and skill.

Approaching Economy, we inquired from our fellow passengers about the commune. Among the controversial opinions some dwelt on the bizarre aspect of the society. During our conversation one passenger, at first talkative but then somberly silent, said that as a member of the commune, he could best answer our questions. His statement silenced us for obvious reasons. Progressively our man became calm and, when we approached him with different questions, he answered readily, noting how unfortunate it is that we visit his society full of prejudices.

At Beaver the Ohio countryside turned mountainous and rocky, relieved by flat lowlands along the riverbank. In places the Ohio was wedged between rocky, wooded mountains. Near Economy the countryside turned flat and only the riverbanks were cleared of forest. As we left the wooded area behind, the road turned and twisted to reveal a scene unique in America. Plowed fields, fenced meadows, and fields interspersed with fruit trees recalled the German countryside. "The fields of Economy!" remarked our Rappite companion with a touch of satisfaction. As far as the eye could see stretched fenced fields. We drove through a fenced orchard gate virtually unknown in America, where the fields are open. Our astonishment grew with each step. On the huge fields fifty to sixty plows were at work; farther off, choice cattle grazed in the fenced pastures, and close by, a flock of merino sheep, then some colts. Just as on the great Hungarian estates, the herds of cattle were grouped and fenced off separately. On the road we met a group of peasants who wore Swabian- and German-style outfits typical of the Rhineland district. Haystacks, strawricks, brick kilns, and other farm buildings were scattered in the fields. Seeing all this, we could easily imagine that we were on a prosperous aristocrat's estate.

We drove into Economy and our surprise grew. There were beautiful, wide village streets with a double row of trees, and uniformly built two-story houses in the old German style. Every house had an identical truck garden; in the back at the riverbank stood some large buildings. A splendid inn and a simple church were in the center of the village. In appearance and arrangement the whole place recalls European cities.

At the inn our Rappite companion greeted us and introduced himself as the innkeeper and member of the society. He seemed to have forgotten the unpleasant questions and discussions we had en route. Instead he readily offered his services and acquainted us with the inn's schedule. In a few minutes the innkeeper returned saying Rapp Jr. would like to see us.

The innkeeper must have concluded from our German conversation that we belonged to Count Leon's immigrant party.[2] Count Leon had been expected for some time and, in fact, his secretary was already here. Rapp Jr. received us in the parlor, a tall, stocky man abut forty years old, and one detected sincerity in his face, clothes, and countenance. He greeted us in German. It took a while to convince him that we did not belong to Count Leon's group. We expressed our surprise at what we had seen and stated the purpose of our visit, and indicated we wished to meet the elder Rapp and his followers. He readily offered his services and led us to his father.

We knew already about the elder Rapp's troubled history and how, like a prophet, he brought twelve hundred emigrants over from Württemberg to forge a community in the wilderness based on his unique principles. His intellectual and spiritual leadership united the commune, turning poverty into prosperity. We fully expected to see an extraordinary man full of aristocratic *gravitas*. And then a gray-haired man, about seventy enters in a

170   long, old-fashioned buttoned overcoat, leaning on a brass-handled cane. His steps are energetic, his blue eyes sparkle under thick, bushy gray eyebrows. He had a remarkable face: smiling cheeks and simple gestures. The old patriarch greeted us in German, and after a hearty handshake bade us to sit down. Although he lacked the lordly aristocratic mannerisms, something in this simple old man inspired trust and attracted our attention. The old man spoke a German dialect resonantly and with an unusual accent. After the customary pleasantries, we told him of our intention to stay for a while to learn more about the commune and its history. The old patriarch readily complied, sat up in his armchair as if to prepare for a festive lecture, and with a radiant face told us the following story.

"From early childhood I was attracted to religion and felt curious concerning religious sentiments. I was a devoted reader of the Scriptures and the history of religions. I realized that the Christian religion has, in many ways, deviated from its original moral simplicity. Aware of its deficiencies, I felt that religion must be made purer and simpler if it is to influence man's moral life. In my former country in Württemberg, I communicated these thoughts to my fellow citizens. I found many Catholic and Lutheran brethren who agreed with and joined me. I began to spread my ideas and preached in public places. Soon there were all kinds of believers in large numbers at my meetings, which of course attracted the attention of the priests, who used all sorts of means to denounce and persecute me. First anathema rained down on me from the pulpits, then they complained to the authorities, who, in response to the hue and cry, finally forbade my public sermons.

"Tired of the priestly accusations, I withdrew and secluded myself. But no matter how I wished to seclude myself from the public, the people and my persecuted followers visited me. Consequently, it got to the point that I was threatened with arrest. Under such pressures, my convictions and conscience forced upon me the thought of leaving Germany and settling in a colony where I could worship my God according to my beliefs. In 1802 I wrote to Napoleon, then first consul, to secure me and my followers a place in Louisiana, then a French colony. In time through the embassy I received Napoleon's reply granting us a place to settle in Louisiana, where we could sail soon in two French ships. About fifteen hundred of us planned to leave. But the authorities threw many obstacles in our way and in the meantime, in 1803, Napoleon sold Louisiana to the United States. Consequently he informed us we could settle in France, close to the Pyrenees.

"For a variety of reasons we could not accept this offer, and we decided to emigrate to the United States. But, having no acquaintances there, my society chose me and two of my followers to come over and find a place. For a year we traveled in America on scant financial resources. Without a $2,000 contribution from Philadelphia and Baltimore, and $800 for my sermons from our German compatriots in Philadelphia, it would have been almost impossible to carry out our plan. With this money we bought some land close to Pittsburgh in Pennsylvania, and then wrote to our followers and, overcoming many obstacles, gradually twelve hundred of them arrived.

"The purchased land was a trackless forest, which we cleared with great effort. Poverty made us realize that we could only succeed collectively. By mutual agreement we decided to organize into a permanent commune, share our possessions and earnings. The commune was named Harmony. At the beginning we lived in great poverty, a little farming and cattle raising were our only sources of income. Through our efforts we progressed and could buy, in place of our small, barren village, a larger and more fertile tract of land in Indiana, which we called New Harmony. There our enterprise was even more successful. Our large-scale farming and cattle raising proved very profitable. But the hot climate was unhealthy for our brethren, accustomed as they were to the colder weather in Württemberg, and many died of malaria. These circumstances forced us to sell New Harmony to Robert Owens and his followers in 1824 for $120,000. Then we moved to this place we call Economy. The land here too was a wilderness but, as you gentlemen can see, we have prospered by our efforts."

With polite simplicity he related many smaller circumstances of his commune. The old patriarch then invited us to dinner. In the meantime Rapp Jr. showed us around the commune.

At its previous locations, the commune engaged almost exclusively in farming and cattle breeding. Here, however, they diversified;[3] built cotton, cloth, hemp-dressing factories, a steam plant, beer and whiskey distilleries, and a large gristmill. The factories and workshops were all steam-powered, mostly by English- and partly by American-made engines. While the factory buildings were under construction, the commune sent some of its picked members on a study trip to well-known factories in Europe and America. Then at considerable cost, experts were hired to help them train factory hands when the factory opened, but today almost all work is done by the members.

First we visited the cotton and cloth factories. The machines here, as in the nearby flour mill, are steam-driven. The factories produce an annual net profit of $32,000 and they also supply the members with clothes.

We also stopped at the museum, supervised by Dr. Muller, a charming old gentleman who came over with the first group of settlers. The museum has a small library, mostly German works, and other rare items all collected by Dr. Muller, who described with innocent pride the history of each item. Directly above the museum is the music room, where on Sundays the members assemble, particularly the girls, to sing spiritual songs.

Count Leon's secretary [Johann Georg Goentgen] and Dr. Muller joined us at dinner. Before the meal, the elder Rapp offered us several kinds of wine produced by the commune at its previous place on the banks of the Wabash. American wine resembles strong Hungarian wine, though a bit

172   heavier and oilier, and thus difficult to transport. Grape growing has not yet
       progressed much in America. Though Economy shares the same longitude
       as Italy and its climate is just as warm, the close proximity of vast forests
       and the nearby waters are responsible for the sudden cold spells and the
       many chilly nights, all of which have adverse effects on the grapes that
       suffer from oidium. But with the eventual clearing of the forest, America
       here too will triumph over nature. During dinner the elder Rapp with great
       charm regaled us with many old stories. The table was laid with a mixture
       of German and English dishes, more abundant and luxurious than I would
       have expected from an old patriarch. After dinner, Miss Gertrude, Rapp's
       granddaughter, played the clavier and sang.

           The next day we inspected the farm buildings. The granaries are well
       stocked; the threshing, seeding, and flax-breaking machines all steam-
       driven; the barns and several big farm buildings so advanced, the farming so
       intensive, that this economic pursuit of the commune could serve as a
       model. Most of the males are divided into special work units, which
       compete with each other. There are workshops for virtually all kinds of
       handicrafts, and the products are stored in warehouses, which also supply
       all the needs of the members. If a member needs a piece of clothing or other
       necessity, he receives it from the communal warehouse. Though personal
       needs are not defined by law, the collective spirit is so strong that no one
       appears to abuse the communal fund. I even heard that members compete
       with each other to see just how little one or the other can get by on from the
       communal store. Every morning the butcher and the miller deliver to the
       families their quota of meat and flour. Vegetables are supplied from the
       small family gardens, and goods not produced by the commune are
       supplied from the warehouse.

           We also visited the silk factory, built three years ago, when, following
       the elder Rapp's initiative, the commune planted mulberries. Silk produc-
       tion is still modest, and Rapp, Miss Gertrude, and the schoolchildren take
       care of the silkworms. During the last two years the new factory has
       produced some pieces of silk textile. The Pennsylvania Chamber of
       Commerce and government officials here too provided a telling example of
       how to encourage human enterprise. Informed of Rapp's initiative in
       silkworm raising and silk production, government officials decided that, in
       order to boost domestic silk production, at the next assembly meeting all
       officials should appear wearing silk scarves, silk vests, pants, and jackets
       made from Rapp's manufactured silk. It was during our stay that the silk
       scarves were woven; the vests were already made.

           We also inspected some houses to see the interior arrangement. They
       are all uniform; comprising two big and two small rooms, in addition to a
       pantry and cellar. During the day only the old people and children are at
       home. At the morning bell, everybody hurries[4] to his work, which is
       unsupervised and without command. Some members are entrusted with
       the marketing of goods and products, and salesmen are elected annually

who are accountable for all their commercial transactions. Rapp Jr., an astute and resourceful businessman, is in charge of all business activities. The commune's liquid and other property holdings are assessed at over $2 million, which accumulates undivided.

Great care is taken of education and schooling. Without exception, all children must attend school, where, in addition to reading and writing, they are instructed in history, science, technology, and economics. The commune does not have a single illiterate member. To train the children early for work, the students every day work one hour under the teacher's supervision. In the spring they pick mulberry leaves, gooseberries, raspberries, and fruits. Instruction in the school is based on the Lancaster method under the supervision of Dr. Muller. The schoolbooks are printed in the commune's own printing shop.

Almost all members of the commune are German; they speak the Swabian dialect and dress according to the old custom. Englishmen hardly ever join the commune, although there is one Negro family. Freed from slavery by the commune itself, the family members are now free human beings. New members undergo a one-year probation period and then, if one is dissatisfied with communal life, he can leave and take his original possessions.

Finally we walked up to the hillside vineyards, planted by the Württemberg method whereby vines are planted in rock terraces that girdle the slope. The grape plants are imported from France, but mostly from Hungary. Rapp Jr. praised Hungary's fertility and expressed great interest in our country. Although it was gratifying to talk about Hungary, it reopened my wound that everyone knows Hungary only by its fertility. Whenever I have come across geography books in America, invariably I look up Hungary, which is either listed under Austria or casually referred to as "a very fertile country."

Coming down from the vineyards, Rapp Jr. described his great plans for the commune's growth. He expressed the conviction that the commune will not break up, provided its members continue their simple way of life, refrain from mixing in politics, and the American Constitution remains unchanged. He complained of the misconceptions spread about them, particularly in Germany—the *Brockhaus Lexikon* characterized them as dreamers. Bernhard, Duke of Saxe-Weimar-Eisenach, whom they received warmly in 1826, in his travel accounts describing Owen's community spread false[5] information about the Rappites. Rapp Jr. indicated he planned to refute the charges in his forthcoming work.

When Owen was mentioned during the conversation—he bought New Harmony from Rapp and, like him, based his community on communal ownership—we inquired about him. But because of the controversial purchase, Rapp Jr. was critical of him.

The Owenite communal experiment is a peculiar phenomenon in America and, in many respects, similar to the Rappite one. Owen was born

174   in Wales and became famous for his educational reforms. In Manchester he made famous the New Lanark cotton mills he bought, and organized a unique colony of workers there. He put in school children picked from poorhouses and educated them according to the ideas of Rousseau's *Emile*[6] and Defoe's *Robinson Crusoe*. His colony soon numbered twenty-three hundred members, and in 1813 he expounded his educational theories in a book, *A New View of Society*.[7] Owen wanted to organize the whole of mankind into working-family communes. But his hostility to received religions incensed the clergy, with whom he engaged in extensive pamphleteering. Finally he had to leave Great Britain and turned to America to realize his great ideals. In 1824 he bought New Harmony from Rapp and built his commune there.

    Communal ownership is the cornerstone of the Owenite community as well. Hostile to all religions, whose different forms caused so much evil in the world, Owen stressed man's conscience as a guide to belief and made pure deism the religion of his commune. Rights are equal but so are the duties of maintaining communal existence, which encourages the personal well-being of all. Although Rapp's communitarian ideals are similar concerning the need for communal unity, he stresses not only individual well-being but religious ties, which are completely ignored by Owen.

    The Shaker, Rappite, and Owenite communities are three unique phenomena in human history.[8] If they can maintain themselves for another half a century, they will distill great philosophical lessons, and refute many political theories. In all respects the honor for what may follow belongs to the American Constitution, which allows time and gives testing ground for diverse thinking and ideas. It sanctions the soul's many-sided quest without fear of imperiling the system of government and the Constitution.

    Returning to Economy, we visited Rapp's garden too. In the small plot are heaped America's rare plants that would delight a botanist for days. In a corner under a trellis stands the statue of Harmony, commissioned recently in Philadelphia. Though Rapp continues his usual busy schedule, he still finds time to cultivate his garden.

***

    Our three days here were full of visits and inquiries. But much remained to be seen and learned. Economy is the great school of practical life and pragmatic philosophy. What is done here is clear and logical: these simple morals, this bucolic domesticity, this disregard of worldly luxury, balanced by full enjoyment of life's rich offerings—all this would seem pious dreams had we not seen it to be convinced of its existence. Does communitarian existence impede the higher strivings of reason; or throw obstacles to human achievement; and does it mortgage the vaunted, proud free will? And do these simple patriarchal pleasures, this secure wealth, and this spurning of worldly vanities satisfy the soul amid all this ceaseless toil? All this different men will judge differently in different situations. I left this place in awe, enriched by a new philosophical discovery: I rejoice in and prefer what I have seen to the secrets that can be learned in all salons.

We came finally to say farewell to the elder Rapp, and to have a last look at this remarkable man. In the style of ancient hospitality the patriarch had his Wabash wine brought forth, offered it to us, and wished us Godspeed for our journey. We left the place full of remembrances of things and people, and enriched by the memories.

XXI. Pittsburgh—Meeting Farkas Wesselényi and Pál Balog—Allegheny and Monongahela Rivers—Allegheny Mountains—State of Maryland—Slavery

*A*s soon as we left behind Economy's boundaries, we were in the midst of scenic woodlands. The road along the steep Ohio bank was bad, and we arrived after dark in Pittsburgh. Inadvertently, the coachman took us to a hotel other than the recommended one, and only the darkness prevented us from turning back. But our coachman's mistake had a pleasant consequence. As soon as we removed our luggage, I hurried into the parlor to register and get our room numbers. But behold! The last-registered names were those of Baron Farkas Wesselényi and Pál Balog. In fact, their rooms were next to ours. We rushed to their rooms, but they were dining out. We waited for two hours on the terrace, resolved to greet them, as a surprise, in Hungarian. When they returned, our joyful and noisy reunion brought out the reserved Americans from their rooms to see the commotion. After we separated at Sing Sing, we traveled to the north, they to the south, and then planned to meet in New York in December. It was so inconceivable that we would encounter each other so unexpectedly once more, right on the spot we resolved never to separate again.

The next day Wesselényi and Balog set out for Economy and we presented our letter of introduction to Messrs. Dobbin and Irwin, two businessmen in whose company we toured the city and the factories.

Pittsburgh is at the confluence of the great Allegheny and Monongahela rivers, which form the Ohio River. The Allegheny and Monongahela originate in two separate regions of America; the Allegheny in the north, below Lake Erie, the Monongahela in the Laurel Mountains in Virginia. Gathering several rivers, they join at Pittsburgh to form the Ohio

River, which, after two hundred miles of meandering, issues into the
Mississippi and finally empties into the Gulf of Mexico. These waterways
give Pittsburgh the key to the north, south and west, while the three-
hundred-mile-long Pennsylvania Canal opens the door to the Eastern
seaboard. In addition to its good location, nature has endowed Pittsburgh
richly: the greatest iron ore, coal, and salt deposits in the surrounding
mountains make the city a natural industrial center.

After the Revolution, Americans quickly discovered the natural
wealth and favorable location of the city, and soon settlers arrived both
from Europe and America, mostly skilled workers.

Table 18. Pittsburgh's Population Growth[1]

Year	Population
1800	1,565
1810	4,768
1820	7,242
1825	12,542
1830	17,000

Besides the Americans, English, Scottish, Irish, and Germans have
contributed to the population growth, but already the many nationalities
are completely Americanized. Where the law does not divide the people
into classes, where all enjoy equal rights, there liberty turns the individual
into a citizen eager to learn the language and become a patriot by
naturalizing his name.

In appearance Pittsburgh is unlike the other colorful, pleasant
American cities. It rather resembles Manchester and Birmingham in
England. Eternal coal smoke blankets the city, its buildings, and factories
are plastered in soot, the streets and riverbanks throng with loaded,
rumbling wagons. The constant loading and unloading, the incessant din of
forges and factories—that's Pittsburgh.

All the factories we have visited used steam power. Some claim that no
English city makes such extensive and wide use of steam power. Among
other things, we toured a bakery where the same steam power that sifts the
flour also kneads and cuts the dough into small, round crackers. Seven
factories alone specialize in casting and assembling steam engines. And nine
furnaces supply the iron for the eight rolling mills which produce iron
ingots, slabs, and sheets. Ten factories, all steam-driven, manufacture nails
and have a thirty-six-thousand-pound output per day[2] by a novel American
method recently patented. In addition, there are several saw and flour mills,
and textile, carding, and glass-cutting factories, most of which utilize steam
power.

In the afternoon we visited the city's famed bridges, whose spans over
two rivers are an engineering marvel. The long bridge on the Monongahela,
built specifically to span the Pennsylvania Canal, is unique. It rises about
two fathoms above the water level, as wide as the Danube at Buda-Pest.
The bridge is supported by eight tiers with seven spans. The boats cross
under this bridge and ply up and down the canal.

When Balog and his group returned from Economy in the evening, we decided to travel through the central states to visit Baltimore, Washington, and Philadelphia. Early next morning we took the stagecoach because the road to Baltimore through the famous Allegheny Mountains was long and difficult. But the burden of the journey was somewhat relieved by recounting to each other our travel experiences. Toward Wilkinsburg, Howardsburg, and Adamsburg we reached the Allegheny Mountains, whose ranges stretch from South Carolina to Lake Erie, and the journey from Pittsburgh to Baltimore takes three days. Wherever one looks from the lofty mountain passes one sees vast forests and new chains of mountains. Settlements are rare, and sometimes one must travel two to three hours before finding an inn. Greensburg, Youngstown, Ligonier, Stoyestown, and Bloody Run are rather nondescript places and we traveled nonstop for two days, climbing and descending mountains.

Before the Revolution, the Allegheny Mountains were hardly explored and were possessed by some fabled Indian tribes; it was rather risky to cross them alone. Nowadays, however, one can travel safely on the rough but well-traveled road. We walked on foot to higher mountains. After the third day as we passed through St. Thomas and Chambersburg, we entered the densely populated regions in the state of Maryland.

***

As soon as we entered Maryland we saw more Negroes than in any other states. Everywhere blacks worked in the fields. The reason did not dawn on us until we saw a notice posted on an inn door which read: "On October 28th this year the goods of Jacob Caldwell debtor, including two male and one female Negro slaves will be sold at an auction to the highest bidder." Reading this, I felt as if an icy hand gripped my heart. I sighed in sorrow—we had arrived in the land of slavery!

During our travels we heard a lot about slaves, the constant topic of controversy between the free and the slave-owning states. Having observed the unprecedented free civil life secured by this great country's Constitution, based on the principle of natural law, its many institutions devoted to the advancement of mankind, I found the contrast between noble ideals and despicable praxis always incomprehensible. To excuse my American ideals I rationalized by recalling that in our country it was only recently that the decree of Joseph[3] broke the eternal chains of serfdom. Even now when some members of the nobility read the old laws they heave a nostalgic sigh about the good old pre-Joseph era. In some of our countries to this day the humanitarian supporters of *urbarium* are denounced as law breakers. I weighed all these facts, but they exonerated from shame neither my country nor America.

To me the saddest and most shameful aspect of moral philosophy is man's willingness to abuse power and reason when wielding intellectual and political power over the powerless and the uneducated. Perhaps no individual and no nation can be considered truly enlightened unless they irrevocably renounce or curb this tendency, and pledge to respect the rights of the uneducated and powerless as their own. But how many individuals and nations can boast of the abrogation or at least disuse of this evil tendency so that we have a guarantee against relapse? If approaching an ideal can be scaled on a thermometer, then America, including her treatment of slaves in historical perspective, has reached the highest degree of esteem in my heart.[4]

In Europe slavery began with the dawn of history. The first shipload of captured African Negroes was brought to Virginia in a Dutch ship in 1622 [actually 1619] and, like beasts of burden, they were cold-bloodedly sold for cash. The prevailing opinions held that God created the Negro, unlike the whites, from inferior clay. And being but a heathen savage, he did not deserve the name of human being. Greedy for new profits, the English too shipped Negroes as if they were beasts of burden by the thousands to the American wilderness. To all European nations this profitable trade appeared legal. Virginians were the first in whom human conscience awakened and in 1680 they submitted a strongly worded, compassionate petition to the English court to terminate the shameful trade in human flesh. Several colonies supported the petition. In response, Parliament callously argued[5] that its slave trade was too profitable to renounce for the sake of Americans. In 1699 they renewed their appeal but the government, instead of abolishing the slave trade, levied certain taxes on slave-traders in order to share in the infamous profit.[6]

The issue remained deadlocked until the colonies removed the English yoke. With the Declaration of Independence, the states' attention first turned to the issue of slavery. Unfortunately, the cursed custom through generations had taken deep roots. It hardened into a human trait, particularly in the Southern states, where slaves comprised one-third of the population, and thus emancipation was considered dangerous. Shortly before independence, Virginia became the first to prohibit[7] legally the importation of slaves. Pennsylvania went one step farther by declaring all slaves born after the promulgation of the law to be free men.[8] The state of New York set twenty years for the abolition of all slavery. In response to these noble examples, eight of the thirteen states abolished all slavery. Finally the congress in 1808, to the embarrassment of European powers,[9] declared the slave trade a piracy, and citizens caught in slave-trading could be punished by death.[10]

While the United States took these steps to abolish slavery, some big European powers continued to sanction the inhuman practice in their colonies. Thirteen of the twenty-four states have completely abolished slavery, and in the process 339,360 Negroes became free men. There remain the Southern states, where the evil habit has its deepest roots and where 2,011,320 Negroes are still slaves.[11] The number is indeed shocking.

180   But the Negro population's increase there is partly due to the climate. The planters are forced to employ Negroes because for six months out of the year the white man cannot work in the fields in the oppressive heat.[12] This also explains why the planter dreads to part with Negroes his predecessor bought and those he inherited like beasts of burden. But the so-called thirteen free states' resolute moral stand against the slave-owning eleven and the awakened public conscience will shortly end all slavery.[13]

In the thirteen free states a number of organizations have been formed for the emancipation of slaves. But one difficult and vexing question arose: What should become of the already freed and the yet to be freed slaves? Once more this presents a delicate issue, inconceivable to a European mind. The white man shows a certain reserve even toward the freed Negro, who possesses equal natural rights. Is this nature's ploy and play on color? Or is it more plausible that the white man finds it humiliating to socialize with those hitherto treated as beasts of burden and under the sway of his absolute power. Behold! One more instance of the weak side of the human soul which sways some American citizens just as it sways the proud European aristocrat. The logical sequence of this contempt is that the poor Negro is reluctant and hates to socialize with his former tyrannical masters.

Several methods were proposed to alleviate the problem. Among others, it was suggested that Negroes should be transported back to Santo Domingo, settle a colony with them beyond the Mississippi, or resettle them in Canada. Finally in 1815 Mr. Finley worked out a plan, modeled after the British Sierra Leone Company, to repatriate the Negroes in Africa.[14] The advocates of the plan met in 1817 [actually 1818] at the American Colonization Society's meeting, presided over by Henry Clay, and decided to colonize the free Negroes in Africa.[15] The society has collected sizable sums of money, and on the west coast of Africa at five and six degrees latitude, at Cape Mesurado Bay, bought a huge tract of land, called Liberia. Already in 1819 the United States shipped free Negroes to Liberia, distributed land to them, built houses for them, and advanced some capital for farming.

The first city founded in Liberia at Cape Mesurado Bay the new citizens named Monrovia, after President Monroe. The United States has agents there and every year at government expense free Negroes are transported there. Monrovia has a few thousand inhabitants, who brought with them the American republican principles, laws, and the Constitution. Imbued with religious and moral values, the inhabitants have already built three churches in Monrovia. In 1826 a young printer, Mr. Force, arrived from Boston and set up a press which publishes the *Liberia Herald*. Its editor, John B. Russwurm,[16] is a Negro scholar. The new state has an army of five hundred soldiers. In 1831 the United States again shipped there 343 Negro colonists.[17] What new chapter will Liberia soon open in human history!

***

This, then, is the history of slavery in the United States and the noble
efforts for emancipation. Noble indeed because the history of human
frailties chronicles an all too human tendency to propound lofty principles
short of personal and property sacrifices. But no sooner does either of them
come into play than man immediately falls back on his inexhaustible
reservoir of syllogisms to bolster and color his interest. Only those sacrifice
property and personal interest for free principles who, like the Americans,
have a sacred commitment to liberty. The people of the United States are
pained and suffer under the reproach of slavery. I know and feel it because
in western Europe it is widely held that in Europe slavery only flourishes in
Russia and Hungary. This belief always hurt me deeply.

XXII. Baltimore—Statue of Washington —American Interest in Books—Railways— Negro Church—Journey to Washington

*B*altimore is the most populous city in Maryland. Built on the banks of the Patapsco River, it has ready access to the ocean. Although in 1765 it could only count fifty houses, after the Revolution its trade and population increased markedly, and today it has 80,625 inhabitants.

Among the city's public monuments we first visited the statue of Washington, ideally located on a hill in Howard Park and visible from all parts of the city. Modeled somewhat after the Napoleon pillar in Place Vendôme in Paris, the 176-foot-tall monument contains an interior spiral staircase leading to the white-marble statue of Washington. Erected by the state of Maryland, it is the finest of the Washington monuments in the United States. Not far from the monument there are still some ancient oaks from the original forest.

The buildings in Baltimore reveal good taste and aesthetic sensitivity. The Catholic, Unitarian, and Episcopalian churches are architectural marvels. The St. Paul Catholic Church is styled after the Roman Pantheon, the Unitarian Church resembles the Basilica of St. Peter with its columned entrance, and the Episcopalian Church is also made attractive by columns.

The bank, City Hall, the Peale Museum, the Athenaeum, and other public buildings are many testimonials to the citizens' fine taste. Baltimore's public institutions vie with other cities' institutions, and numerous societies promote here too education, learning, science, and trade.

Of the many remarkable things in America, I was always surprised to find even in the smallest town, at least in the city hall, a library. Sparsely populated as the place might be, invariably the city hall contains a library

with books at least on local things. Love of books is so widespread among
the citizens that even in the poorest homes one can find, if nothing else, the
Bible, the Constitution, and a book or two on the geography and history of
the United States. Among the well-to-do a library with handsomely bound
books is always part of the furniture. In addition, at least one newspaper is
an indispensable household item.

***

At Baltimore two railways are under construction—one to Ohio, the
other to Washington. Each line has already progressed a few miles. During
our stay in America we had a chance to inspect on a few occasions railroads
and the method of their construction. Most American railways are
horse-drawn rather than steam-powered as in Manchester. Each carriage
accommodates twenty-five to thirty passengers, and a horse can pull it
easily at a trot. If each year the present rate of railroad and canal
construction continues, then fifty years hence hardly a place in America
will have an ordinary horse-drawn carriage.

***

One evening I went to a local circus. A traveling troupe performed
some acts on horseback. The performance was mediocre, the audience
unenthusiastic. What attracted my attention, however, was that Negroes
sat segregated. On cheaper tickets, in addition to the price, is printed:
"Gallery for colored persons."

***

Although Baltimore is mostly a Catholic city, on Sundays it is like
other dour Puritan cities. Baltimore and New Orleans are mostly settled by
Catholics whose bishopric is in Baltimore. But this ceremonious religion is
just as inconspicuous here as any of the other twelve religions. By mere
chance I found myself in a Negro church, where all the worshipers were
Negroes. A handsome, well-built mulatto priest preached with surprising
elegance and vocal power. The two sexes, all neatly attired, sat separately
and most of the women wore white. The sermon, dwelling mostly on the
humble acceptance of earthly misery, I ignored, for I was more interested in
the members, who appeared to be quite taken by the priest and followed his
sermon with devotion. Being used to white faces, I could hardly take my
eyes off the interesting, colorful faces full of sincere piety for their new
religion. Respect and sorrow mixed in me as I reflected on what they would
have been in the burning African sands and what they are now. What
would make them happier? Freedom in the wilderness's savage bosom? Or
being handsomely attired, semieducated, and Christian?

For a century and a half the whites shared the common belief that the
Negro is made of inferior clay, that he is incapable of education and unripe
for liberty. And yet the freed Negroes of the United States in general, and

184 those of Santo Domingo in particular, have refuted this. Some of the Negroes in Liberia and Santo Domingo are as intelligent as the whites, and their government is based on the same enlightened principles as that of the United States. Paradoxically, fellow beings of the same race are slaves next to them. Indeed, they hardly differ from animals because, confined from birth to food and punishment, their human potential was stifled, and so from generation to generation they remained semisavages in this situation.

Despite all our theoretical postulates, it is indisputable: only freedom prepares man for liberty and enlightenment.

***

From Baltimore we journeyed to Washington, fully resolved to return and see the forthcoming horserace. The road to Washington was crowded with travelers. On the intensely cultivated land and extensive tobacco fields Negroes worked everywhere, and their sheds surrounded the planters' mansions. This is a very striking sight to travelers from the northern states.

It was dark when we crossed into the District of Columbia at Bladensburg. After the oppressive heat the cool moonlit night, the balmiest part of the day here, felt good. On the distant horizon a large white building loomed. "That's the Capitol," said our driver affectionately.

Approaching the Capitol and Washington, I was seized with childish joy in anticipation of seeing the capital of the United States. Not far from the Capitol, we checked into the National Hotel, which bears a strong resemblance in design and appearance to a big multistoried military barracks.

XXIII. Washington—The Capitol—Paintings in the Capitol—The House and the Senate—White House—Patent Office—Secretary of State Livingston—Introduction to the President

*A*nyone who imagines Washington to be like Paris, London, or any other European capital, with a splendid royal court, shining administrators, palace guards, liveried servants, theaters, an indulgent aristocracy, and gaping foreigners, will be very disappointed. This city is famed for its future-oriented design, its great public buildings, and being the legislative and executive seat of government. All these are important to a traveler, provided he does not come here for pleasure.

During the Revolutionary period, when the United States had no capital, the Congress met in New York, but mostly in Philadelphia. After the signing of the peace treaty, concern was expressed that the capital should be close to all the states without, however, belonging to any particular one, to prevent the benign influence of localism. Exempt from state jurisdiction, the capital should be autonomous and under federal administration. To this end, on the banks of the Potomac River at the present site of Washington, Georgetown, and Alexandria, the states of Maryland and Virginia turned over to the federal government about one hundred square miles of land. By consensus it was named the District of Columbia and put under direct congressional control with the provision that it would never form a separate state but would always belong to the Union.

Progressively the capital's plans were drawn up, the public buildings started in 1792, and by 1810 [1800] the Congress and the government moved here, where they have met ever since. In 1790 the present site of Washington was wilderness; today its population, together with

186 Georgetown's 30,250 and Alexandria's 9,608, is 39,858 inhabitants. Designed for a population of one million, the original plans of Washington called for grand avenues. On the highest hill stands the Capitol, surrounded by a wide park. It is the hub of broad avenues named after the twenty-four states, while the east-to-west streets are alphabetized. The great Pennsylvania Avenue, directly across from the Capitol, leads to the White House, built on a hill and already completed, together with other buildings. The buildings for the most part are scattered and the land beyond the capital is empty, except for stakes to mark the future streets. The haphazard construction gives a very strange appearance to the city, and many people are critical of the grandiose design. In particular, some object to the broad avenues, which, in addition to the tree-planted malls, leave a middle lane wide enough to accommodate three ordinary streets. All this spaciousness, some people hold, detracts from the community spirit.

The most important public buildings are the Capitol, the White House, the Departments of War and Navy, the Post Office, the Bureau of Archives, and the four cabinet secretaries' offices. Looming proudly over the others is the classically styled Capitol, the largest and most magnificent building in the United States. The open Capitol Hill grounds are divided into lovely parks full of rare American plants. An elegant marble staircase leads up to the Corinthian-columned entrance. The magnificent circular hall, the Rotunda, is illuminated from the domed ceiling. The Senate and House chambers occupy the two wings, which receive light from the glass ceiling. Other rooms contain the Library of Congress, the Supreme Court, the archives, and various congressional committee rooms.

We first entered the Rotunda from where corridors lead to the Senate and House chambers. The Rotunda was designed to display paintings depicting American historical events. Four pieces, each twelve feet in length, have already been painted by the famous American artist, Colonel John Trumbull. The first depicts Benjamin Franklin reading the Declaration of Independence before fifty-two congressmen in 1775. Members of the Congress are seated in rows around the hall, and only Franklin and two other figures stand. The faces appear to concentrate on the great issues, and, it is said, the figures are historically authentic. Of the original members of Congress, only Charles Carroll, age ninety-five, is still alive; he resides in Baltimore. The second painting depicts Burgoyne's surrender at Saratoga; the third portrays the defeated English army after the siege of Yorktown as it marches before General Washington and his staff on horseback, accompanied by the smiling young Lafayette. The fourth represents the historical moment when Washington resigned his commission before the Congress. What soul-lifting scenes, and with what pride can Americans view these paintings!

In addition to the four oil paintings, four excellent panels decorate the walls. The first, by [Antonio] Capellano, shows the famous Indian princess, Pocahontas, saving the life of Captain John Smith.[1] The second

panel, by [Enrico] Causici, shows the landing of the New England Pilgrims
at Plymouth. The third, by [Nicholas] Gevelot, represents William Penn making his famous treaty with the Indians in 1782 under a tree close to Philadelphia. The fourth panel, also by Causici, shows Daniel Boone fighting two Indians.[2]

From the Rotunda we entered the House of Representatives. The semicircular chamber, without ornament or pomp, has a certain dignity of its own. Fourteen columns support the gallery, reserved for accredited diplomats. In the center of the semicircle, close to the wall, is the speaker's chair facing the ascending, tiered chamber. Every congressman has a separate writing desk and the chamber's floor is carpeted. Lafayette's full-length portrait hangs on the west wall and opposite it will eventually hang Washington's portrait. In the other wing the Senate and the Supreme Court are identical.

The corridors leading to various rooms in the Capitol have different-styled columns. The ones in the Senate corridor are very original—maize twines upward from the pedestal and the columns trail with ripe ears of corn.

The capital [White House, etc.] cost the nation $1,646,717 and when it was nearly completed, the British captured Washington in 1814 and set fire to the Capitol, damaging its roof and the library. But a more magnificent structure rose from the ashes. During the few days of occupation, the British troops, under the command of General Ross, vandalized the city. Among other things, a beautiful memorial in the Armory, commemorating the American soldiers who fell at Algiers, was damaged together with other allegorical figures. With barbaric methods the British soldiers hacked to pieces the [Genius of] America and History. Today both allegorical figures stand on the Capitol staircase, still bearing the marks of British swords. On the pedestal is inscribed: "Mutilated by Britons in 1814."

***

Across from the Capitol is the White House, the second loveliest public building. Although not a luxurious royal palace, its simple classical style has its own appeal. Not far away are four identically long buildings, the four cabinet secretaries' offices, and in a separate building the Post Office and Patent Office.

Modeled after the French Conservatoire des Arts et des Métiers, the Patent Office was established by Congress in 1793. New inventions or the discovery of practical uses of things, if proved to the Congress, receive a patent for fourteen years. In return, the inventor must provide the U.S. Patent Office with an authentic prototype of his invention, including its technical description. In the last thirty years inventions increased phenomenally and now fill several rooms. Visitors interested in mechanical devices can spend many instructive and interesting days there.

***

188   After a tour of various parts of the city, we called upon Mr. Edward Livingston[3] to present our letter of introduction. In fact we only went to his office to inquire when and how we could see him. To our surprise, an official simply told us Mr. Livingston could be seen any time and, if we wished, we could call upon him at home. We found it rather peculiar just to drop in on him unceremoniously as if he was an ordinary citizen. Mustering some courage, we located Mr. Livingston's residence; cabinet members here do not live in hotels. A servant opened the door and without any announcement led us to Mr. Livingston. Although busy with work, he immediately put it aside and, having read our letters, received us warmly. For about half an hour we discussed various things, but neither his manner nor his statements betrayed his position as cabinet secretary. His rooms were not piled with documents and neither his appearance nor official demeanor suggested a powerful government official. He walked us to the staircase and took leave as if he was a private citizen.

Only after some distance from the residence did we remember the main purpose of our visit, i.e., to get permission to see President Jackson. Mr. Livingston had already left when we returned. This meant we could only see him the next day and postpone our visit to President Jackson. We discussed the problem. One suggested we should go and just announce our visit to the President. This sounded a bit daring and too citizenish. Debating the issue on all sides, we reached the White House, divided in opinion. Two votes favored a personal visit, two proposed to see Mr. Livingston first. The debate continued as we strolled up and down in front of the White House. Finally, one pro-Livingston advocate changed sides and the majority vote decided on an unannounced visit.

We entered the beautiful grounds. Nowhere in sight a guard, sentry, or liveried servant, and no one barred our way. We strolled for a while on the colonnaded entrance until a servant came out and we told him our purpose. Pleasantly he informed us we could see the President if we waited until he finished his business with the Danish ambassador. We gave the servant our namecards, saying we are Hungarians who wish to pay our respects to the President. Soon the servant returned and said, if we wished, the President would be pleased to see us at 11:00 A.M. the next day.

XXIV. President Jackson—Bleker Olsten's Story—The President's Constitutional Duties—Presidential Elections—Elections to the House and the Senate—Congressmen and Their Laws

*N*ext day we arrived on time at the White House. The servant ushered us into the waiting room, where two gentlemen sat on the couch waiting for the President. The middle-sized and rather unpretentious room was carpeted; chairs, couches, and a grandfather clock constituted the furniture, all tastefully arranged. There are moments in life when one awaits the imminent event with heartpounding anxiety that preoccupies his whole being. At the same time he is torn by inner doubt and anticipates the expected moment in fear and trembling. Those who have experienced such moments will understand my frame of mind and feelings at this auspicious hour. I was about to see a man elected to the highest office by the free vote of thirteen million people. Not birth, not wealth, or chance but personal attributes earned him this distinction.

Presently Mr. Jackson appeared—a tall, grayish, polite old man, in a plain black suit. As he entered we approached him, stated our names and nationality, and told him how much we wished to see him. Cordially he shook our hands, took a seat and seated us around him, and then introduced the other gentlemen. During our half an hour with the President he inquired about our country and the trip. The conversation then turned to America. Our praise of his country and its institutions pleased him. His direct statements and polite manners quickly made us forget we conversed with the first elected servant of thirteen million people. In the meantime several people entered the room and he greeted them as plainly as if he were in a private home. As we took our leave he shook our hands and invited us to see him if we returned to attend the session of Congress.

190   I will never forget how happy I felt when we left, knowing I met and talked to this famous man. His handshake made me prouder than any honor in this world, it enriched my memory with a treasure I will forever cherish.

***

We who are used to the notion that a country's chief magistrate is the elect of heaven, to be approached in fear and trembling, are also familiar with the spectacle of the elect of heaven's halo creating officials who surround themselves with glitter and splendor in order to be obeyed and feared by subjects. We can hardly comprehend the American administrators' direct simplicity. Our historical experience instills the belief that fear teaches obedience. But Americans have refuted our centuries-old experience and have completely contradicted our concept of administration. The following incident, related by Miss Wright[1] and repeated by Levasseur as authentic, gives some indication of the American president as the chief executive.

> Bleker Olsten, the Danish Minister-Ambassador, taking up his post at Washington, upon learning that Jefferson gives audience every day at 2 P.M., hurried to pay his respects to the head of the American government. Jefferson was so amiable and interesting that one hour passed before the ambassador noticed he had overstayed. When the conversation began to drag, the ambassador anxiously waited for the Presidential signal to terminate the visit. The ambassador waited but failed to detect the signal. Realizing he definitely overstayed, he wished to withdraw but feared it would violate etiquette. To the ambassador's great embarrassment dinner time was announced. To Jefferson's offer whether he would care to stay for a simple dinner he offered some excuses and left.
>
> The confused ambassador related the incident to an American acquaintance, adding in his own defense: "But how could I leave without the President indicating the audience was over? Is there no etiquette in this country? How can they maintain the prestige of public officials to lend majesty to government? Pray, teach me the rules I should follow in dealing with the President."
>
> The American advised Bleker Olsten to leave all formal etiquette in Europe. The American President's only privilege, when dealing with citizens, is that he is under no obligation to return visits because his busy schedule prohibits such practice.
>
> Later when Bleker Olsten was dining with Jefferson, he made excuses for his overstay the other day. Explaining his predicament, the ambassador ventured the observation that American formalities differ from those of European courts.
>
> "I know it is improper for a foreigner to criticize the custom of the host country. I am also aware that an incumbent president can ignore existing formalities. But my sympathy for this country compels me to disapprove of the informalities which, though they may set well with Jefferson, can be harmful to his successor. There are certain rules we must obey at all times and all places. Believe me, Mr. President, or believe the wisdom of ages on whose authority I can state: rules and etiquette cannot be ignored with impunity. The stability of administration demands that public officials be surrounded with a certain decorum and pomp to ensure the obedience of the masses."
>
> "I cannot dispute your observations, Mr. Ambassador," said Jefferson,

"concerning kings and their courts. But I am not a king. Let me explain the difference with an anecdote. I assume you have heard about a Neapolitan king who loved hunting. One fine day when the king was getting ready for his hunt he was obliged to hold a morning audience, which was larger than he anticipated. Fearing it might spoil his hunt, he turned impatiently to his foreign minister, the famous Caraccioli, saying he was tired of the boring ceremony.

"'Your Majesty forgets,' remarked Caraccioli respectfully, 'that your Majesty is but a ceremony.'"

***

What appears unique and so incomprehensible to a European about this country's public administration is very natural to an American. The people being sovereign, Americans cannot conceive of government officials as other then the executors of the public will. The Constitution clearly defines the power of all public officials. Prestigious and powerful as the presidential office may be, neither he nor members of his family can use it to acquire wealth and personal power. Article II of the Constitution, binding on all twenty-four states, concisely defines the president's executive and other duties.

Section 1

1. The executive Power shall be vested in a President of the United States of America. He shall hold his office during the Term of four Years, and . . . the Person receiv[ing] a Majority of the whole Number of Electors appointed.

5. No Person except a natural born Citizen, or a Citizen of the United States, at the time of the Adoption of this Constitution, shall be eligible to the Office of President; neither shall any Person be eligible to that Office who shall not have attained to the Age of thirty five Years, and been fourteen Years a Resident within the United States.

6. In case of the removal of the President from Office, or of his Death, Resignation or Inability to discharge the Powers and Duties of the said Office, the Same shall devolve on the Vice President, and the Congress may by Law provide for the Case of Removal, Death, Resignation or Inability, both of the President and Vice President, declaring what Officer shall then act as President, and such Officer shall act accordingly, until the Disability be removed, or a President shall be elected.

7. The President shall, at stated Times, receive for his Services, a Compensation, which shall neither be increased nor diminished during the Period for which he shall have been elected, and he shall not receive within that Period any other Emolument from the United States, or any of them.

8. Before he enter on the Execution of his Office, he shall take the following Oath or Affirmation: "I do solemnly swear (or affirm) that I will faithfully execute the Office of President of the United States, and will to the best of my Ability, preserve, protect and defend the Constitution of the United States."

Section 2
(Powers of the President)

1. The President shall be Commander in Chief of the Army and Navy of the United States, and the militia of the several States, when called into the actual Service of the United States ... he shall have Power to grant Reprieves and Pardons for Offenses against the United States, except in Cases of Impeachment.

2. He shall have Power, by and with the Advice and Consent of the Senate to make Treaties, provided two thirds of the Senators present concur; and he shall nominate, and by and with the Advice and Consent of the Senate, shall appoint Ambassadors, other public Ministers and Consuls, Judges of the supreme Court ...

3. The President shall have Power to fill up all Vacancies that may happen during the Recess of the Senate, by granting Commissions which shall expire at the End of their next Session.

Section 3
(Powers and Duties of the President)

He shall from time to time give to the Congress Information of the State of the Union, and recommend to their Consideration such Measures as he shall judge necessary and expedient; he may, on extraordinary Occasions, convene both Houses ... he shall reveive Ambassadors and other public Ministers; he shall take Care that the Laws be faithfully executed ...

Section 7 [Article I]

2. Every Bill which shall have passed the House of Representatives and the Senate, shall, before it become a Law, be presented to the President of the United States; If he approve he shall sign it, but if not he shall return it, with his Objections to the House in which it shall have originated, who shall enter the Objections at large on their Journal, and proceed to reconsider it. If after such Reconsideration two thirds of that House shall agree to pass the Bill, it shall be sent together with the Objections, to the other House, by which it shall likewise be reconsidered, and if approved by two thirds of that House, it shall become a Law. ... If any Bill shall not be returned by the President within ten Days ... after it shall have been presented to him, the Same shall be a Law, in like Manner as if he had signed it ...

Section 4 [Article II]
(Impeachment)

The President ... shall be removed from Office on Impeachment for, and Conviction of, Treason, Bribery, or other high Crimes and Misdemeanors.

These few articles define the power of the president and his duties. The failure of Europe has taught the American Constitution makers four great lessons of how to safeguard the Constitution, and until the same mistakes are repeated here, there is no cause for concern. The first fortunate idea was the abolishment of state religion; second, that of a standing army; third, the annulment of hereditary offices; fourth, and most important, the separation of executive and legislative powers. No one can serve the two branches simultaneously. This precludes either one person or any of the three branches of government usurping all power. Although the Constitution makes the president the chief executive, his power is confined by the Senate. He cannot constitute any danger to the other two branches, which preserve the Union and ensure a constitutional presidency and prevent the emergence of an arbitrary ruler.

Since all the citizens participate in the presidential elections, they constitute important events in America and mobilize almost the whole country on this occasion. Inasmuch as a whole nation, as prescribed by state laws, cannot assemble for an election every four years, thirty-four days before the first Sunday in December each state appoints a number of electors equal to the whole number of congressmen and senators to which the state is entitled in the two houses. The twenty-four states elect 288 electors, but officeholders cannot be chosen electors, whose duties are defined by constitutional amendment.

Amendment XII
(Election of President and Vice-President)

The Electors shall meet in their respective states and vote by ballot for President and Vice-President, one of whom, at least, shall not be an inhabitant of the same state with themselves; they shall name in their ballots the person voted for as President, and in distinct ballots the person voted for as Vice-President, and they shall make distinct lists of all persons voted for as President, and of all persons voted for as Vice-President, and of the number of votes for each, which lists they shall sign and certify, and transmit sealed to the seat of the government of the United States, directed to the President of the Senate;—The President of the Senate shall, in the presence of the Senate and House of Representatives, open all the certificates and the votes shall then be counted;—The person having the greatest number of votes for President, shall be the President, if such number be a majority of the whole number of Electors appointed. . . . The person having the greatest number of votes as Vice-President, shall be the Vice-President, if such number be a majority of the whole number of Electors appointed, and if no person have a majority, then from the two highest numbers on the list, the Senate shall choose the Vice-President; a quorum for the purpose shall consist of two-thirds of the whole number of

194   Senators, and a majority of the whole number shall be necessary to a choice.... But in choosing the President, the votes shall be taken by states, the representation from each state having one vote...

In elections so far the House of Representatives has only twice elected the president, in 1880 and 1825; in other elections the presidential candidate received the majority vote. In 1800 the Congress cast ballots thirty-six times in five days until Jefferson was elected. The Constitution limits the president's term to four years but he can be reelected for a second term. Since the framing of the Constitution, the following presidents have held office:

Table 19.   Presidents and Their Terms

Washington	1789–1797
John Adams	1797–1801
Jefferson	1801–1809
Madison	1809–1817
Monroe	1817–1825
John Quincy Adams	1825–1829
Jackson	1829–

The Constitution designates the president as the chief executive, but the people have taken the precaution that if by mistake an unworthy person is elected, or he abuses his power, then such a dangerous person should be countervailed by a popularly elected Congress.

The House and the Senate comprise the Congress. Every state elects two senators (today forty-eight) and one representative for every forty thousand people (today two hundred forty). The senators are elected for a six-year term and congressmen for a two-year term, and neither can hold any other office. The Congress convenes the first Monday in December every year. During the opening session both houses elect the speaker by secret ballot. Each house keeps a journal of its proceedings and publishes the same to inform the public. The powers of the Congress are those not specifically charged to the states, that is, powers entrusted to the Union, such as:

Article I
Section 8

1. The Congress shall have power to lay and collect Taxes, Duties, Imposts and Excises, to pay the Debts and provide for the common Defense and general Welfare of the United States...

2. To borrow money on the credit of the United States;

3. To regulate Commerce with foreign Nations, and among the several States, and with the Indian Tribes;

5. To coin Money, regulate the Value thereof...

7. To establish Post Offices and Post Roads;

8. To promote the Progress of Science and useful Arts, by securing for limited Times to Authors and Inventors the exclusive Right to their respective Writings and Discoveries;

9. To constitute Tribunals inferior to the supreme Court;

10. To define and punish Piracies and Felonies committed on the high Seas, and Offenses against the Law of Nations;

11. To declare War, grant Letters of Marque and Reprisal, and to make Rules concerning Captures on Land and Water;

12. To raise and support Armies, but no Appropriation of Money to that Use shall be for a longer Term than two Years;

13. To provide and maintain a Navy;

14. To make rules for the Government and Regulation of the land and naval Forces;

16. To provide for organizing, arming, and disciplining, the Militia, and for governing such Part of them as may be employed in the Service of the United States, reserving to the States respectively, the Appointment of the Officers, and the Authority of training the Militia according to the discipline prescribed by Congress . . .

Section 7

1. All Bills for raising Revenue shall originate in the House of Representatives; but the Senate may propose or concur with Amendments as on other bills.

Section 8

18. To make all Laws which shall be necessary and proper for carrying into Execution the foregoing Powers . . .

Section 9

1. The Migration or Importation of Such Persons as any of the States now existing shall think proper to admit, shall not be prohibited by the Congress . . .

5. No Tax or Duty shall be laid on Articles exported from any State.

6. No Preference shall be given by any Regulation of Commerce or Revenue . . .

7. No money shall be drawn from the Treasury, but in Consequence of Appropriations made by Law; and a regular Statement and Account of the Receipts and Expenditures of all public Money shall be published from time to time.

8. No Title of Nobility shall be granted by the United States: And no Person holding any Office of Profit or Trust under them, shall, without the Consent of the Congress, accept of any present, Emolument, Office, or Title, of any kind whatever, from any King, Prince, or foreign State.

Article IV
Section 2

1. The Citizens of each State shall be entitled to all Privileges and Immunities of Citizens in the several States.

Section 4

The United States shall guarantee to every State in this Union a Republican Form of government . . .

Amendments

1. Congress shall make no law respecting an establishment of religion, or prohibiting the free exercise thereof; or abridging the freedom of speech, or of the press; or the right of the people peaceably to assemble, and to petition the Government for a redress of grievances.
the Government for a redress of grievances.

2. A well regulated Militia, being necessary to the security of a free State, the right of the people to keep and bear Arms, shall not be infringed.

3. No Soldier shall, in time of peace be quartered in any house, without the consent of the Owner, nor in time of war, but in a manner to be prescribed by law.

4. The right of the people to be secure in their persons, houses, papers, and effects, against unreasonable searches and seizures, shall not be violated, and no Warrants shall issue, but upon probable cause, supported by Oath or affirmation, and particularly describing the place to be searched, and the persons or things to be seized.

9. The enumeration in the Constitution, of certain rights, shall not be construed to deny or disparage others retained by the people.

10. The powers not delegated to the United States by the Constitution, nor prohibited by it to the States, are reserved to the States respectively, or to the people.

Article VI

3. The Senators and Representatives ... shall be bound by Oath or Affirmation, to support this Constitution; but no religious Test shall ever be required as a Qualification to any Office or public Trust under the United States.

Article V

The Congress, whenever two-thirds of both Houses shall deem it necessary, shall propose Amendments to this Constitution, or, on the Application of the Legislatures of two thirds of the several States, shall call a Convention for proposing Amendments, which, in either Case, shall be valid to all Intents and Purposes, as part of this Constitution ...

On the first Monday in December the Congress assembles regularly without any advance notice. At the opening session the president delivers his State of the Union Message concerning his administration's policies and offers programs for debate. Then the secretaries of state, the treasury, navy, and army give a report on their departments, and present their budgets, which are analyzed by committees. All this is published to inform the nation. After the presidential message is discussed, various proposals are introduced. Every congressman's speech is listened to uninterrupted, no matter how boring it may be. Consequently legislative decisions are slowly reached. Annually half of the congressmen and one-third of the senators' terms expire, and new members are elected. Members of the

House during the session receive $7 per diem, from which they cover their living expenses.

The American Congress differs significantly from European parliaments in that no government official can be elected to the House. The framers of the Constitution had vivid memories of the English Parliament, where at times the people were merely a fictional sovereign, while de facto the executive arbitrarily ignored the minority of independently elected members and passed laws according to the wishes of the government.

In America it is easier than it is in Europe to prevent executive encroachment on the legislative branch. The absence of charters, diplomas, and ancient privileges means the absence of courtiers who, trained in the arcane executive branch, alone can divine the meaning of the former. The diploma of Americans is the law of nature, whose meaning can be interpreted by natural reason.

XXV. Revenue and Expenditures of the United States—The 1830 Budget—The Military—National Guard and Its Rules—Naval Ships

*T*he first weeks of the congressional session are taken up by debate on national revenue and expenditures. The annual budget figures are published in detail and in many copies; newspapers carry excerpts of it so citizens can learn how and for what public money is spent. Not to overburden the citizenry, economy is the guiding principle of the Republic. America has furnished a historically unprecedented example of frugal economy. By 1831 not only will it pay $362,719,701 into the tremendous national debt incurred during the War of Independence but it has undertaken various domestic programs. Not to overburden the citizenry, economy is the guiding principle of the Republic. America has furnished a historically unprecedented example of frugal economy. By 1831 not only will it pay $362,719,701 into the tremendous national debt incurred during the War of Independence but it has undertaken various domestic programs. Though personal income tax was abolished in 1818, still $12 million annually is paid into the national debt, which is expected to be paid off by 1834. On top of this, after expenditures the government shows a $12-million annual surplus without the citizens paying one penny of direct tax to the federal treasury. This is indeed a disheartening lesson for Europe.

Table 20. Revenue and Expenditures, 1830[1]

	Revenue
1. Customs	$22,681,965
2. Sale of Public lands	1,457,004
3. Post offices and mines	490,000
4. Dividends and sales of bank stock and bonus	138,150
5. Surplus from previous year	4,257,318
Total	$29,024,437

Sándor Bölöni Farkas

Table 20. Revenue and Expenditures (Continued)

	Expenditures
1. Members of Congress	$ 526,700
2. Cost of the House	136,600
3. Congressional Library	7,750
4. President's salary	25,000
5. Vice-President's salary	5,000
6. Cabinet secretaries' salaries	30,000
7. Salary of administrators, upkeep of offices	593,916
8. Ambassadors, consuls	207,003
9. National-debt payments	12,383,800
10. Military's salary	1,063,909
11. Fortifications	360,000
12. Military equipment	190,000
13. Military headquarters	407,000
14. West Point	100,000
15. Upkeep of military	752,270
16. Fortifications and buildings	1,004,600
17. Salaries of Navy officers and staff	463,449
18. Naval ship construction	2,120,909
19. Pensions of Revolutionary veterans	767,492
20. Military pensions	185,344
21. Indian Department	589,150
22. Harbor improvements	367,123
23. Internal improvements	1,600,000
24. Miscellaneous	570,656
Total	$25,456,688
Surplus	$ 4,566,760

As the figures indicate, even the four revenue sources give the United States a surplus of $12 million beyond 1834. Currently there is debate on what to do with it. The simple secret of national welfare is that no conspicuous court, indolent officialdom, useless army, and secret police are kept at public expense. The president, the chief executive officer, draws a salary of $25,000, which is munificent considering he does not keep a court, guards, or liveried servants. His main expense is giving dinners, if he desires, during the congressional session. The king of England alone draws twice as much as the expense of all administrative officials of America ($5 million, or ₤1 million). The king of France's expenses equal the expense of the federal government of America (12 million francs).

What makes the United States' unprecedented prosperity even more striking is that the government does not cost the public any money. How, then, can this society be dissatisfied with its government? The English vent their frustration against taxes in various satires and poems. Currently in England there circulates a funny poem on taxes, eagerly bought and read by the public and, printed on large parchment, it hangs in all pubs. Rumor has it Lord Chancellor Brougham[2] is its author.

Tax, heavy tax
on every food that goes into our mouth, covers our body, or shods our feet
Tax
on everything that pleases the eye, hearing, feeling and palate
Tax
on happiness, candlewax and household furniture

Tax
on everything on earth, underground artesian waters, on goods that
come from abroad or grow at home
Tax
on sauces that whet the appetite, seasonings that restore health
Tax
on judge's ermine, on hangman's rope, coffin nails, the bride's
ribbon, on tables, and on beds we sleep and wake
We must pay Tax

on school straps. Our beardless youth puts a taxed bridle on his taxed horse, and rides on taxed roads. The dying Englishman stirs his 7% taxed medicine with a 15% taxed spoon. He collapses on a 22% taxed bed, writes his will on notarized paper costing £8, gives up the ghost in the arms of the apothecary who paid £100 to usher his soul from this world. Then his property is taxed at 15%, he pays extra to the coroner, and large sums to be buried in God's acre. His virtues are inscribed for posterity on a taxed tombstone and, then, finally joins his ancestors—never to be taxed.

***

The bulk of Europe's national revenues is swallowed up by the military. A republican system dislikes war, and if left alone it has no cause for conquest. In addition to these republican principles, America's fortunate geographical location militates against maintaining a large army. Even the Constitution prohibits it. The states maintain no standing armies, and until 1821 the United States had only a 10,000-man army. Since then it has been reduced to four artillery and seven infantry regiments now consisting of 6,188 men, sufficient to guard seventy-two fortresses and keep the Indians in check. In the whole United States there is not one single honorary guard. The small voluntary army, serving five years, is well paid. The enlisted men receive $5 a month, and are supplied with uniforms and food.

Table 21. Salary of Officers

Major general	$6,535
Brigadier	4,441
Adjutant	3,234
Inspector	2,796
Colonel	2,958
Lieutenant colonel	2,460
Major	2,194
Captain	1,594
First lieutenant	1,350
Second lieutenant	1,290

If to the 6,188-man army are added the 1,054 navy officers, then the total United States Armed Forces comprise 7,242 men.

***

But America complements its small armed forces with an awesome military power, the National Guard, which numbered 1,190,000 men in 1831. In Europe, only France could command such a force and number.

During the Revolution the Americans reformed and invented a new concept of a national guard, which influenced Lafayette in organizing the French National Guard in 1789. [Duties of the National Guard as defined by an act of Congress are omitted.]

***

Next to the National Guard, America is building an even mightier naval power. Annually $2 million is spent on new ship construction. In the seven Navy Yards, ships are constantly under construction; built mostly from the famous live oaks, which do not shatter when fired upon, they are superior to the English warships. The United States has fifty-one naval vessels with 1,257 guns.[3] Right now the largest, the 140-gun warship *Pennsylvania*, is nearing completion.

XXVI. Mount Vernon—State of Virginia—Washington's Tomb—Story of Captain John Smith and Pocahontas[1]

*T*here is a sacred place in America frequented by citizens and foreigners full of noble feelings. The hallowed place is Mount Vernon, former residence and now shrine of the great George Washington. Mount Vernon is located twenty miles below Washington in Virginia; it would have been inexcusable not to visit the hallowed spot. We cruised in the steamboat *Essex* down the Potomac and in a few hours got off at Alexandria, the boundary of the District of Columbia.

Beyond the city one soon enters the state of Virginia. Only visitors who want to see Mount Vernon take the bad overland route through the forest, others take the river route. After seemingly endless winding through the forest, we came upon a picket fence which marked the Mount Vernon estate. The place had a very European appearance, the forest was once cleared and then reforested, and we saw corralled and open herds of cattle. Then we spotted the building on a hill, surrounded by forest. At the entrance gate stood some dilapidated English-style porters' lodges. A Negro porter let us in and for half an hour we strolled in the huge park, now and then catching sight of some buildings. The whole place appeared impoverished. Intermittently one could see patches of wheat and tobacco fields and in the meadows cattle grazing.

The hilltop mansion had a sweeping vista on the Potomac. The one-story mansion, built in a simple colonial style, was adjoined by farm buildings and a few Negro shacks. But the whole place exuded neglect, somewhat reminiscent of a once well-kept but deteriorating Hungarian nobleman's estate. Bushrod Washington, the owner, nephew and only male descendant of George Washington, lives mostly in the city and pays little attention to the mansion.

When we entered the grounds, Negroes volunteered to show us the grave. Not far from the mansion, on a hillside hidden by cedar and oaks, rests the great man in the tomb of a citizen-hero. Cut into the hillside, the average-sized vault's brick front has an ordinary gate. The vault itself is overgrown with tufts of grass and surrounded by oaks, cedar, and holly trees whose branches were stripped so bare the owner posted a sign begging the relic-seekers to spare the trees.

I have stood at the tombs of kings and famous men, reflecting on their deeds and memories. But only in the Pantheon and in Westminster have I been as ovecome with feelings that swelled up in me as I was when I stood before this vault. There flashed through my mind America's suffering and struggle, its triumphant happy present, and rich legacy to mankind. I felt my heart pound. The man in front of whose earthly remains we stood played an enormous role in all this. Only the cool counsel of reason kept me from prostrating myself before his grave.

Ignoring the posted sign, our Negro guide, for a small reward, let us break a cedar bough and gather a bouquet of holly. The vault for some time has been closed because the visitors kept chipping away at the outside coffin. It was last opened during Lafayette's visit. The old man entered the vault alone to visit his friend's tomb. He remained long, his sobbing heard outside.

We took one more stroll in the park. We found the garden house full of rare tropical plants, and returned to look at the buildings, which, it is claimed, remain untouched just as the great man left them. Evening was drawing close and we had no time to announce ourselves to Bushrod Washington to see the rooms he so graciously opens to visitors. Among other memorabilia, the rooms contain one unique item. When the Bastille was taken in 1790, Lafayette sent Washington its key with a note saying this was "the last key of European despotism." The key and the note are under glass, but the prophecy remained unfulfilled.

Farewell, hallowed spot! Rest in peace, great man. Your immortal name and character, devoted to national welfare and justice, I have worshiped since my dreaming childhood. Visiting your tomb, I come away like pilgrims from the Holy Land. In memory of this great man, let this be my last sacred emotion over cold reason.

XXVII. Horserace in Baltimore—Jockey Club's Reception—Napoleon's Descendants in America—Király, a Compatriot from Hungary—Chesapeake Bay—State of Delaware

*R*eturning from Virginia, we spent a day in Washington before attending the horseraces in Baltimore. In England we had already seen some horseraces and now wanted to compare the two. The three-day derby here is by and large an imitation of the English one not only in general appearance but in terms of rules, shape of the racecourse, and the dress worn. Only the Negro jockeys' black color and the large purses for the winners of trotting events made the derby different. The horses were of an English breed which apparently does not degenerate here. In fact, the Virginia breed is reputed to have improved the English stock. The native American horses bear close resemblance to the English pony.

Already in a few places in America they hold regular horseraces, the best-known are those at Charlotte [?] in Virginia and at Baltimore. I believe that horseracing, imported from England, will have a shaping influence on the American male character. Horace's poetic adage—*gaudet equis canibusque,* "dogs and horses please man"—contains a great practical truth. Those who visited England and have observed the Englishman's passionate devotion to horse breeding will attest to the truth of Horace's poetic wisdom. This manly, scientific and indefatigable nation, initiating the most daring challenges, could not be conceived of without horses. Obviously, insular existence and other historical circumstances shaped the development of the manly character but it was also influenced by horseback riding.

Those who are timid about or who eschew horses and riding will be skeptical when told that Americans' partial imitation of English horseracing is of major importance. To argue this is like debating the opponents of innovations, dueling, or marriage. Many people laughed when recently in Hungary and Transylvania two important books appeared on horses. People could not comprehend how an intelligent person, other than a veterinarian or a nobleman, could write let alone think about horses. Yet in England, by no means a frivolous nation, which knows and cares about its laws as much as our great aristocrats, even the king rides a horse, attends the horseraces, and enters his horses to win just as his ministers do. In fact many members of Parliament ride to sessions. It is not unusual to see government officials ride to their offices.

***

After the derby, the Maryland Jockey Club gave a magnificent ball, to which we were also invited. In typical English fashion the invitation card stated how the guests should be dressed. I wish the Americans did not imitate the English in this. Although such a request does not violate individual liberties because one can dress differently or simply remain home, still it complicates social intercourse. Many guests were already there when we arrived. Those who expect republican simplicity at social events in big American cities will be greatly disappointed. The ladies were dressed with great attention to the latest fashion journals and etiquette of Paris. Refreshments were served in great quantity in the adjoining rooms. The Negro band's music was atrocious; they played mostly *contredanses* and sometimes waltzes. The dancers, somewhat graceless and reserved, indicated that grand balls here are less frequent than in Europe.

Midway through the ball the ambassador of a European country, Mr. L.X.X., made his appearance. A gold-chained pince-nez dangled on his tailcoat, and his medal-studded chest was ablaze like a mirror. His appearance attracted great attention, groups formed wherever he stopped, and whispering smiles followed L.X.X. The dazzling medals were so conspicuously ridiculous that people stared at them, smiling.

***

The other important person who attracted great attention was the young Jérôme Charles Bonaparte, son of the former Westphalian king, Jérôme Bonaparte, from his first marriage to the Patterson girl. He soon withdrew to the bar to join a circle before the hearth to smoke his cigar. He bore a striking resemblance to Napoleon. He married the daughter of a wealthy Baltimore merchant, who was also at the ball. Two sons were born from this marriage. Had Napoleon succeeded, this young man might have sat on some European throne. The Bonaparte clan is large in America. In addition to Jérôme's two sons, the former king of Spain, Joseph Bonaparte, also lives here, as do Lucien Bonaparte, the duke of Canino who married Joseph's eldest daughter, and the unfortunate Marshal Murat's two headstrong sons.

Joseph lives at Bordentown in New Jersey. They say he lives under the name of Count Survilliers and leads a secluded life, accessible only to his

206 servants and close friends. Though he seldom appears in public, when he does he behaves like an ordinary citizen. He contributes generously to philanthropic and public causes, which earned him respect. A few years ago there was a great fire at Bordentown. In the newspaper Joseph had expressed his appreciation to his neighbors for helping him to put out the fire, adding nothing disappeared from his home during the confusion. The appreciation pleased his neighbors but the conclusion offended them. Eventually, however, Joseph's virtues compensated for the insult.[1]

***

One interesting acquaintance also made memorable our stay in Baltimore. One morning, strolling with Wesselényi in the Barnum Hotel's parlor, we noticed an elegantly dressed gentleman listening with interest to our conversation. Momentarily he addressed us, saying ever since he saw our name in the bar three days ago he wanted to get acquainted because he too was a Hungarian and his name is Király. The new acquaintance delighted us. Mr. Király spoke little Hungarian and passable German. He told us the adverse circumstance that brought him to America.

Király was born at Liszka [now is Czechoslovakia] in the Tokay district. While in Hungary he made business trips to Walachia, Constantinople, and Germany. Then for a while he served in the Prussian army and, upon leaving, resumed his business activities. He lived in Manchester for three years, came to America as a visitor, liked the place, and stayed. His parents and relatives still live in Hungary and he would like to see them once more.

Staying in the same hotel, we often met Mr. Király. His elegant suits and style of life indicated that he must have been a wealthy man. He changed his name to King. Although he told us many things about his life, we could not get a clear picture of his activities. Among other things he was in the jewelry business, and some of his manners intimated an international salesman.

Although Király always spoke glowingly about blessed Hungary and his early life there, it became apparent his country also carried bitter memories. He disliked the laws, customs, and noble privileges, and must have had some unpleasant fracas with a county official named György Józsa. Whenever he mentioned the name, Király got angry and reverted to broken Hungarian to lend native flavor to the dialogue.

"Here no Gijuri Josha shouts commands: 'Soldier, bring out the bench. Lie down, Király! Give him twenty-five lashes.'" These bitter memories visibly upset Király. Whenever the topic came up he got excited and, wildly gesticulating, repeated in broken Hungarian: "Here nix [no] Gijuri Josha! Here America! Here nix tyrannical county official!"

***

At Baltimore we boarded the packet *Charles Carroll* bound, via Chesapeake Bay, for Philadelphia. The Chesapeake shorelines are magnificent and we met some oceangoing ships too. At Frenchtown, where the Elk River joins Chesapeake Bay, we entered a tributary and went ashore at its intersection with the Chesapeake and Delaware Canal. We transferred our luggage to the canalboat and, via the state of Delaware, reached New Castle, boarded the packet *William Penn* and via the Delaware reached Philadelphia, where we checked into the Mansion House.

XXVIII. Philadelphia—Public Buildings —Institutions—Leimer—Philadelphia Museum—Quaker Church—Denominations in Philadelphia—Philadelphia Mint—Newspaper Reports about Hungary

*M*any travelers claim that Philadelphia is the loveliest city in the world. I have often heard such exclusive claim for many European cities and, even though I expected Philadelphia to be lovely, I hardly imagined that after ten days I would confess that Philadelphia indeed is the queen of cities. The first day we visited renowned streets and places. The more we saw the more awed I became, convinced I was in ancient Rome or Athens.

William Penn's original city plan, outlined in 1682, is perhaps the most original and the first since antiquity to design a city rather than let it evolve without a preconceived idea. Between the Delaware and Schuylkill rivers, covering two English square miles, 634 identically wide avenues progress east to west and south to north forming, at intersections, equal squares. The middle sections of the avenues are laid with square flagstones, while the larger streets are covered with macadam. The sidewalks on either side are of white marble and granite, and kept by the owners as clean as if they were palace floors. Most of the houses are built of white marble or granite and the entrance staircases decorated with polished brass. The city's strikingly beautiful buildings and the prevailing cleanliness impart great aesthetic pleasure.

Next to the residential homes, about two hundred public buildings and churches enhance the aesthetic beauty of Philadelphia. Foremost in beauty is the classical style of the United States Bank. It is modeled after the Athenian Parthenon, and from either side identical staircases lead up to the eight-Doric-columned portico. A spacious vestibule connects the main hall, illuminated from the dome and supported on either side by six Ionic columns. The floor is laid with Italian and American marble. The Girard Bank's Corinthian-columned portico and the Ionic-columned Pennsylvania Bank also reflect Greek style. The other nine banks are just as impressive.

In the center of the city stands the State House, where the Continental Congress met before it moved to Washington. In one of its rooms the Declaration of Independence was adopted, signed in 1776, and then read to the people from a balcony still in existence. This historical building is greatly revered. Behind it is a promenade, then the Park of Independence and Washington Square. The city hall, the universities, colleges, theaters, churches, hospitals, and so on are many architectural marvels seldom seen anywhere in the United States.

While commerce and politics dominate other American cities, Philadelphia is renowned for its educational and philanthropic institutions. One has to see to believe the unselfish and competitively spirited civic sacrifices of Philadelphia from early on for public institutions. Philanthropy is an inborn trait here, and with an amazing competitive spirit they endow different institutions and support various humanitarian causes. Each day we visited some but it would take months to see and study all. Over one hundred sixty societies[1] alone are devoted to the dissemination of useful knowledge and promoting charitable and other humanitarian causes. Some among them promote commerce, trade, mutual aid, handicraft associations and help immigrants and tourists.

Correspondingly, just as many institutions promote religion and morality. Although every religion has its own fellowship organization, there are twenty-five societies whose goal, irrespective of creed, is to attain pure religion, morality, education, and in particular the dissemination of the Bible.

The various branches of science shed the most illuminating light on Philadelphia, the center of scholarship and the cradle of learning. Perhaps nowhere is the love of books more pronounced than here. Not only does every private home boast a library but in addition to the various-sized libraries of schools and associations, the city has sixteen public libraries, the Philadelphia Library with sixty-four thousand books, not to mention the numerous newspaper reading rooms. About fifty · newspapers and magazines are published in the thirty-two printing shops alone. The American Philosophical Society, the leading scientific association founded by Franklin in 1743, has a famous library with extensive natural science and other collections. The society's purpose is to disseminate useful and scientific knowledge. Its rooms are always open for reading and lectures, and foreigners are welcome to join. The society holds its meetings on the first and third Friday of every month. The scientific papers read and discussed there are published each year. Other branches of knowledge also have similar societies and publish their works each year.

Many of the scientific societies are devoted to education. Nowhere in the world is education approached in a more philosophically rigorous way

210 and with more success. Learned societies are not satisfied with theoretical analysis only but have produced amazing practical results. In addition to the large, leading schools dedicated to the systematic study of all knowledge, particular attention is paid that every child in the town can at least read and write. Societies were formed to educate the poor [Adelphi School] and according to an 1831 report, that year alone 5,083 children received free education.

***

What strikes a foreigner is that the philanthropic, educational, and scientific institutions are founded and maintained by private donations rather than by government. To a European publicist, this has important implications. The American government's main concern is to protect the citizen's legal, personal rights, and the pursuit and attainment of happiness are left to individual initiative. Government allows great scope to individual endeavors, it protects the fruits of human labor, and individuals enjoy its fruits as they please. When Jean Colbert, Louis XIV's minister, asked the French merchants how the government could promote economic activity, they gave the celebrated reply: *Sire, laissez nous faire*, "Sir, let things alone." The French merchants' laconic response sums up the preconditions for individuals to create good and great things.[2]

Ferenc Müller, my acquaintance from Lake Erie, gave me a letter of introduction to a certain Mr. Leimer, a Hungarian born in Pest who left sixteen years ago and now is a rich wine-merchant here. Though he forgot the language, Mr. Leimer claims to be a Hungarian. Allegedly out of love for his native land, twice he tried to import Hungarian wine via Trieste, but on both occasions it arrived spoiled. He claims the Hungarian wine cannot compete in price and quality with the lighter French wine the American public prefers. Mr. Leimer knows many German immigrants, most of whom forgot their native language, while the second generation speaks only English and even their names are Americanized. He introduced us to a certain Mr. Ritter, owner of a bookstore, who imports German books published in Europe. Here only religious books, songbooks, and a newspaper are published in German.

***

The Philadelphia Museum, like the one in Baltimore, was founded by Mr. Peale, and has one of the richest collections of birds, shells, butterflies, one anaconda, devilfish, and a complete skeleton of a mammoth, the only one in the world, and it fills a whole room. One gallery displays contemporary oil portraits of famous Americans and Europeans. On the upper floor is an excellent collection of Indian dresses and weapons.

***

One outstanding project in Philadelphia is the Waterworks. With the city's growth, the need for water increased. Already Franklin had recommended and tried various projects to ensure the city's water supply, but none proved financially feasible. Finally, at great expense the Waterworks was built and, using the Schuylkill River located outside the city, it supplies a reservoir built at an elevation of 105 feet. Daily the Waterworks pumps 76 million cups of water into the reservoir, whence pipes lead to the city. Because of its elevation, the reservoir can supply water to even the third floor of the houses.

***

One Sunday I attended some churches, among them a Quaker one. Already in England the sect attracted my attention and earned my respect. The worshipers gathered in deep silence. Clad in black, the men sat separate. Wide-brimmed hats over their eyes, they gazed at the floor. The women were in separate rows. Wearing dark gowns, unfrilled tall bonnets, and vests, they sat motionless and silent. Entering, a foreigner could not tell whether he was in church. The walls are bare of religious attributes, there is neither an altar nor any external manifestations of religion. In the entombed silence one could almost hear one's own breathing. Each worshiper is preoccupied with his own self. The newly arrived pass unnoticed, and only the usher points silently to an empty seat for a foreigner.

One is greatly moved by so many different people sunk in deep meditation. The faces reveal that this is no pretense but truly the soul's inward dialogue and reflection. The solemn congregation remained seated, recounting its deeds to God, reviewing its past activities, and reflecting on its ethical obligations. No religious ceremony interrupts the worship, except on the rare occasion when someone, stirred by the Holy Spirit, verbally communicates it to the congregation that listens, standing up, and then resumes its former position. After a while the people get up and leave silently—and that's the end of the religious service.

I left the sacred place deeply moved by this simple religion, which has earned the world's high esteem. Once more I recalled the differences in religious worship, the ways in which man uses his inventive mind, cunning reason, and imagination to offer his heart to the Creator. What enlightened reason dares to decide whose worship is more pleasing, which invocation more effective in God's eyes? Who is it, dust and ashes, be it king, ecclesia, or state, who has the tenacity to arbitrate between the human soul and God? Whatever the form and nature of worship, it is impossible not to respect a religion's principles and followers who approximate the great ethical ideals and whose character in daily life is guided by moral precepts. Of the many religions in England and America one must single out for respect the Quakers, who stand foremost in the public eye for their integrity. The Quakers' word is sacred: in an agreement it is a binding contract, and in social relations, it shows a feeling heart. Whether it be charity, devotion to public welfare, or civic philanthropy, the Quakers are first. Indicative of the respect they enjoy before civil law, they are exempt from oath taking. Equal among themselves, social ranks and conventional rules unknown to

212   them, they also dislike systematizing theories. Most Quakers are educated
and cultured. For centuries it was held that no state can function without
kings and priests. Now the Quakers in the last century and a half and
America in the last fifty-four years have proved the exact opposite.

Strolling in the streets, I visited a few more churches because Sunday
is completely devoted to church affairs. Philadelphia is the place of many
denominations, as evident from the table below.

Table 22.   Denominational Churches in Philadelphia[3]

Religion	Number of Churches
1. Protestant Episcoplian	13
2. Roman Catholic	4
3. Presbyterian	19
4. Scottish Presbyterian	1
5. Covenanter	1
6. Baptist	6
7. Methodist	10
8. Quaker	6
9. Free Quaker	1
10. Unitarian	1
11. German Lutheran	5
12. Dutch Calvinist	3
13. German Calvinist	2
14. Universalist	2
15. Swedenborgian	1
16. Moravian	1
17. Swabish Lutheran	1
18. Saint Zion Ecclesiasts	1
19. Mennonite	1
20. Bible Christian Catholic	1
21. Seamen Church	1
22. Jews	2
23. Negro churches	10
Total	93

That all these denominations live in peaceful coexistence may be due to
their great diversity.

Many travelers noted that Philadelphia is a Quaker city. The drab
Quaker influences social life and imparts to it a certain dour uniformity.
Our short visit prevented us from forming any opinion about the social and
family life here. But this much is certain: the pleasure-seekers, interested in
splendid salons and a glittering social life, will quickly tire of Philadelphia.
Those, on the other hand, who seek the pleasures of the mind will find
inexhaustible inspiration sources in Philadelphia.

***

One day we visited the United States Mint. It was rather strange that
nobody supervised the handling of gold and silver. In a European
governmental department at least three individuals would watch each
other, to prevent stealing. Seeing our astonishment, the director of the mint
said: "We trust the individual. Our check on character and his private

possessions is based on trust which, in turn, compels honesty." Foreign coins are melted here and reminted, stamped with the American emblem. At this moment there were two barrels full of Mexican coins. Private citizens can bring in foreign coins; the gold or silver is reminted at government expense and returned to the owner at full value.

Every day our circle of acquaintances widened and with each passing day we enjoyed more things, until some unpleasant news spoiled our visit. One day the *Pennsylvania Inquirer* [title varies, *Philadelphia Inquirer*] reprinted an article from the *London Courier*, carrying the following news:

ATROCITIES IN HUNGARY

"We excerpt a few scenes from the popular uprising in northern Hungary, the atrocities and reprisals committed." The article then describes at length the well-known cholera epidemic and uprising in northern Hungary. The article concludes: "But enough of the atrocities. The bloody cruelties in Szepes and Zemplén counties forewarn what the barbarously oppressed, ignorant masses can do in blind hatred when momentarily freed from their chains."[4]

For nearly half a year we had received no news from home. Now this. Our country's name is so seldom in foreign newspapers, and now we appear in this damning light before the Americans. How sad all this is. Beset by a thousand suspicions, our travel spoiled, we decided to shorten our trip and leave Philadelphia, where my sad sighs will return forever![5]

XXIX. Return to New York—The Ship *Albany*—Ocean Voyage

A t Philadelphia we boarded the packet *Trenton* and, crossing the Delaware, got on dry land at Trenton in New Jersey. Several carriages waited on the shore for passengers who wished to continue their journey. In New Jersey we stopped only at Trenton and New Brunswick, where we boarded the packet *Swan* and, via Raritan and Long Island Sound, arrived in New York, thus completing the 2,450-mile route on land and water.

Our original plan was to spend the winter in the Southern states and depart for Europe in the spring from the tropical West Indies and the New Orleans. But the exaggerated news from Europe and Hungary hastened our departure. In the harbor, there was a ship nearing completion and ready to make its maiden voyage to Le Havre. Designed by a famous shipbuilder, under construction for three years, it excited our interest. We made our reservations on the ship, commanded by the famous Captain Hawkins, who spent twenty-two years at sea. The ship's interior was built in the latest fashion, the furniture and wall panels made of mahogany and white maple. The cabins were constructed to accommodate passengers comfortably in separate berths.

While the ship's interior was completed and the cargo loaded, we made short excursions into the countryside. One day we visited Sing Sing, which we could not see on the previous occasion. Then we made a short trip to New Jersey to see the Morris Canal at Newark. In New York our circle of acquaintances kept growing. At a dinner party given by Mr. de Rham, the banker, we met General Santander, former vice-president of Colombia, who has just returned from exile. Santander was found guilty and sentenced to die for his attempted assassination of Bolívar, who, however, commuted the death sentence to exile. Consequently Santander lived in France and, upon the death of Bolívar, was recalled by patriots. At the dinner party Santander was accompanied by Mssrs. Acosta and Gonzales.

***

Finally our ship was baptized *Albany* and the embarkation day arrived. When we first landed on these shores we were about to leave, amazement and joy mixed in us. Our short sojourn here richly rewarded our hopes and opened a bright chapter in our lives. I landed in America full of great expectations. I leave this country with boundless admiration yet with the sadness one feels leaving for long, or forever, an esteemed and beloved friend.

Its flags flapping, the lovely *Albany* anchored in the middle of the Hudson. The steamboat *Rufus King* stood by to ferry us across. We said good-bye to our friends who accompanied us to the shore, and on November 23 the *Rufus King* ferried us in a quarter of an hour to the waiting *Albany*. While its anchor was raised, we settled into our cabin. Although very comfortable, we could not hide our concern that we sailed on the ship's maiden voyage in the worst season of the year.

Due to unfavorable winds, the *Rufus King* towed us from the bay. We shared the cabin with one Parisian and two Lyonnais merchants, one of whom brought his young American wife, and a pickled old Bourbonist and a young Philadelphia man. The old Bourbonist left France after the July revolution and, disenchanted with the great freedom here, was now returning to France. Altogether there were ten cabin passengers and nobody in steerage. The captain, officers, crew, and servants brought the total to thirty-two. As a general rule, America-bound ships are crowded with passengers, while the returning ones sail virtually empty. The five-hundred-fifty-ton *Albany* was greatly overloaded with cotton and potash.

At Staten Island the *Rufus King* left us and, hoisting our sails, by noon we were at Sandy Hook. The water turned bluish, presaging the vast ocean and indicating we passed all danger points. When the pilot left our ship, we parted with the last American. We sailed into the vast ocean and the shores receded. I could hardly take my eyes off the bluish mountains. Amid feelings of grief and the emotions of a child I repeated my silent farewells to this beautiful country. I could not take my eyes away. The mountains turned faint blue. Farewell once more, glorious country! Remain mankind's eternal guardian and haven! Stand forever in stern warning to despots! May you remain forever the inspiring beacon to the oppressed.

Chapter Notes

Notes to Chapter III*

1. A. Levasseur, *Lafayette in America in 1824 and 1825, or Journal of a Voyage to the United States*, trans. John D. Godman (Philadelphia: Carey & Lea, 1829), 1:125.

2. *New York Annual Register*, ed. Edwin Williams (New York: J. Leavitt, 1831), p. 60.

3. No civilization has ever spent more on philanthropic purposes than the American. See Merle Curti, "American Philanthropy and National Character," *American Quarterly* 10 (Winter 1958): 37–42.

4. Alexander Lips, *Statistik von America* (Frankfurt: H. Wilmans, 1828), p. 163.

5. Extracts from the New York State Governor's Message, January 1831. See also extracts from the Report of the Committee of the Public School Society in New York City, February 1829.

The public school system that so impressed Farkas in Jacksonian America was based on the principle that the state, or the revenue from the school fund, would pay only a share of expenses. And at least an equal share, as the condition of receiving the state fund, would be assessed upon the property of the town. In addition, as a prerequisite to sharing and receiving public money, the inhabitants of each district were required to tax themselves for building schoolhouses and furnishing them, etc.

For instance, the estimated revenue (Table 4) shows that the revenue from the school fund, i.e., the amount derived from the state treasury, paid less than one-tenth of the annual expenses of public schools, another tenth was raised by tax upon property in towns, and two-tenths ($239,713) was comprised of school money. This explains why in New York state the student-population ratio in the 1830s was 1 to 3, in Prussia 1 to 7, in Bavaria 1 to 8, and in England 1 to 15.

6. Baron Farkas Wesselényi (1782–1851), lord lieutenant of Szolnok County, was the brother of Miklós Wesselényi, the principal leader of the reform generation and a close friend of Farkas.

7. Pál Balog (1794–1867) was a physician and a school friend of Farkas but later the two became estranged over political issues. Balog was the private physician of István Széchenyi, and was offered the editorship of the *Sunday Newspaper*, cosponsored by Farkas, but declined and retired to his country estate. Balog was also member of the Hungarian Academy and president of the Hungarian Medical Association.

Notes to Chapter IV

1. *New York Annual Register*, pp. 203, 208. The number of vessels entering New York harbor (Table 5) is from January 1 through December 31, 1830, inclusive.

2. Baron Lederer was Austrian consul in New York.

---

* Chapters I. and II. deal with Farkas's European travels and the Atlantic crossing. They are not included in this translation.

220 3. *New York Annual Register*, p. 103. The *Register* notes that of the 237 newspapers published in New York state, about 70 were favorable to the Jackson administration, 80 in opposition, and of the latter 48 were avowedly antimasonic. The 54 newspapers published in New York City had the following circulation:

11 daily	16,000 copies
10 semiweekly	18,000
26 weekly	50,000
6 semimonthly 1 monthly	2,000
54	86,800

4. Count Ferenc Béldi (1789–1881), a liberal Transylvanian aristocrat, was a close friend of Farkas and helped finance the American trip. Farkas dedicated the first edition of *Journey* to Béldi.

5. Cadwallader D. Colden, *The Life of Robert Fulton* (New York: Kirk & Mercein, 1817), pp. 167–68, 176. Farkas's Hungarian translation is inaccurate. Hence I used the original version.

6. *The Northern Traveller* (New York: Harper, 1830), p. 14.

Notes to Chapter V

1. Basil Hall, *Travels in North America in the Years 1827 and 1828* (Philadelphia: Carey & Lea, 1829), 1:49.

2. Thaddeus Kosciuszko (1746–1817), a Polish army officer and statesman, gained fame for his role in the American War of Independence and for his leadership in the national insurrection in his homeland.

3. A. Levasseur, *Lafayette in America*, 1:109. The citizens of Newburgh indeed "distinguished" themselves during Lafayette's visit. About thirty thousand persons waited on the shore for Lafayette, who was due at 7 A.M. but arrived at 3 P.M.

4. Stephen Van Rensselaer (1764–1839), eighth patroon, soldier, congressman, and president of the second canal commission, established at Troy a school dedicated to the "application of science to the common purpose of life." The school was later incorporated as Rensselaer Institute.

5. Farkas refers to the founding of the Rensselaer Polytechnic Institute in 1824. In 1965, with an endowment of $48 million and a faculty of 564, it enrolled forty-six hundred students.

6. Joseph Lancaster (1778–1838), educator, developed the system of mass education known as the Lancaster school, a monitorial or "mutual" approach in which bright and more proficient students were used to teach other children under the direction of an adult. Lancaster emigrated to the United States in 1818 and was warmly received. He lectured extensively and founded schools in Philadelphia, Baltimore, Boston, and Washington, D.C. In New York the Public School Society established more than sixty Lancaster schools.

7. *New York Annual Register*, p. 59

8. Although Thomas Jefferson proposed a national system of roads and canals which he believed could be authorized through an amendment to the Constitution, he found De Witt Clinton's proposal to connect the Hudson and Lake Erie with canals a century ahead of its time.

"'Why sir,' said Jefferson to Clinton, 'here is a canal for a few miles, projected by George Washington, which if completed, would render this a fine commercial city, which has languished for many years because the small sum of 200,000 dollars necessary to complete it, cannot be obtained from the general government, the state government, or from

individuals—and you talk about making a canal 350 miles through the wilderness—it is little
short of madness to think of it at this day.'" Quoted by David Hosack, *Memoir of De Witt Clinton*
(New York: J. Seymour, 1829), p. 346.
9. Canal Commissioner's Report to the New York Legislature, 1831. See also *New York Annual
Register*, pp. 124, 222.

Notes to Chapter VI

1. *A Revision and Confirmation of the Social Compact of the United Society Called Shakers*
(Harrodsburg, Ky., 1830). This pamphlet seeks to refute the erroneous opinions circulating
among the public about Shakers, and to lay before the public the true principles of the religion.

Notes to Chapter VII

1. Farkas is referring to the Plymouth colony which was left free to govern itself as a
self-constituted commonwealth until 1791, when William III joined it to Massachusetts Bay.
2. George Grenville (1712–1770) initiated his policy of taxing the American colonies by his
Revenue Act (1764) and the Stamp Act (1765), and started the train of events leading to the
American Revolution.
3. Augustus Fitzroy, Duke of Grafton (1735–1811) was prime minister in England and a
prominent figure in the period of the American Revolutionary War. Grafton, who favored
reconciliation toward the colonies, was lord privy seal under Lord North (1771–1775) and
again in the Shelburne-Rockingham ministry (1782–1783).
4. Frederick North, Earl of Guilford (1732–1792) was prime minister from 1770 to 1782, and
his vacillating leadership contributed to the loss of Britain's American colonies.
5. David Ramsay, *The History of the American Revolution* (Philadelphia: R. Aitken & Son, 1789),
2:335. See also Alexander Lips, *Statistik von Amerika*, p. 235.

Notes to Chapter VIII

1. According to David Ramsay, Paine's *Common Sense* pressed Scripture into service in his
argument, and the powers and even the name of the king were rendered odious in the eyes of
colonists, who read and studied the history of the Jews, as recorded in the Old Testament.
Ramsay states that "the change of the public mind of America, following the publication of
Paine's *Common Sense*, respecting the connection with Great Britain is without parallel." See
History of the American Revolution, 1:338.
2. A. Levasseur, *Lafayette in America*, 1:11.
3. Imre Thököly (1657–1705), a Protestant magnate, led the Kurucz insurrection against

Hapsburg oppression. Thököly also entered into an alliance with the Ottomans, but the defeat of the Turks at Vienna in 1683 doomed his insurrectionist movement. After the Hapsburgs took Transylvania, the Treaty of Karlowitz (1699) exiled Thököly to Turkey, where he died.

Notes to Chapter IX

1. *The American Almanac and Repository of Useful Knowledge for the Year 1831* (Boston: Gray & Bowen, 1831), p. 260. According to the fifth census of the United States, Boston's population in 1830 was 61,381, and not 91,392 as given by Farkas.

2. Alexander H. Everett, *Europa, oder, Übersicht der Lage der Europäischen Hauptmachte im Jahre 1821* (Bamberg: C. F. Kunz, 1823); *Amerika* (Hamburg: Hoffman & Campe, 1828).

3. Edward Everett (1794–1865) served in the House (1825–1835) and in the Senate (1853–1854). He is chiefly remembered for delivering the speech immediately preceding President Lincoln's Gettysburg Address—November 19, 1863—at the ceremony honoring the fallen soldiers of the U.S. Civil War.

   Emerson was pupil of Everett, see *The Complete Works of Ralph Waldo Emerson* (New York: Houghton Mifflin, 1903–1904), 10:330–35. Though he esteemed highly his former teacher, Emerson said Everett was "attracted by the vulgar prizes of politics" (*Journals, 1841–1844*, 4:255). In 1850, at the request of Webster, Everett drafted a letter defending the action of President Taylor in sending a special agent to report on the Hungarian Revolution of 1848.

4. James Fenimore Cooper, *Notions of the Americans: Picked Up by a Traveling Bachelor* (London: Henry Colburn, 1828), 1:210–11.

5. Marquis de Lafayette (1757–1834) fought with the American colonists against England in the American Revolution.

6. Daniel Webster (1782–1852), orator and politician, practiced prominently before the U.S. Supreme Court, and served as congressman, senator, and secretary of state. He is best known as an enthusiastic nationalist.

Notes to Chapter X

1. William Penn (1644–1718), Quaker leader and advocate of religious freedom, founded the American Commonwealth of Pennsylvania.

2. *Letter from Edward Livingston . . . to Robert Vaux, on the Advantage of the Pennsylvania System of Prison Discipline . . .* (Philadelphia: J. Harding, 1828).

3. Basil Hall, *Travels in North America*, 1:320.

4. *Laws of the Commonwealth for the Government of the Massachusetts State Prison* (Charlestown: Press of the Bunker Hill *Aurora*, 1830).

1. *American Almanac*, p. 186.

2. Henry Ware (1794–1843), secretary of the American Unitarian Association, opened correspondence with the Transylvanian brethren, and the widely traveled American Unitarian, George Sumner—younger brother of statesman Charles Sumner—visited Kolozsvár some years later. Ware gave Farkas extensive and detailed information on the history of Unitarianism and other religions in the United States, which Farkas submitted in his special report to the Transylvanian Unitarian Council.

For this and Ware's letter to Farkas, see "American-Hungarian Unitarian Contacts During the First Part of the Century," *Keresztény Magvetö* [Christian sower] 26 (1891): 10–35.

3. Count Moric Benyovszky (1741–1786) was a colorful buccaneer known chiefly for his memoirs and travels. He established a colony on Madagascar, became its king, and died fighting the French. His memoirs, published in 1790, were translated into Hungarian by Maurice More, the great Hungarian romantic writer. For the English version of Benyovszky's memoirs, see Captain Oliver Pasfield, *The Memoirs and Travels of Count Benyovszky* (London: T. Fisher Unwin, 1843). The definitive edition of his travel memoirs is *Benyovszky Moric emlékiratai: Ázsian át Madagaszkárig* [Memoirs of Moric Benyovszky: Through Asia to Madagascar] (Budapest: Móra Ferenc, 1956).

4. A. Levasseur, *Lafayette in America*, 2:155; and James Fenimore Cooper, *Notions of the Americans*, 1:229.

Notes to Chapter XII

1. It is instructive to compare Farkas's account of Lowell with that of Dickens. Dickens concludes his report on the textile mills by urging the reader to reflect "upon the difference between this town and those great haunts of desperate misery..." See Charles Dickens, *American Notes* (New York: P. F. Collier, n.d.), p. 76.

2. During Farkas's visit to America, *The New England Magazine* reprinted a typical English article from the *London Quarterly Review* to demonstrate the insufferable condescension of the English toward America. The article states: "From the hour that in an excess of passion, they chose to fling away from their king, and relinquish the immense benefits arising from a government checked by a powerful aristocracy, and allied with a church establishment, and trusted exclusively to the democratic branch of government, they have done nothing but propagate the species, and chop down forest timber, without advancing the cause of good government or of any branch of knowledge, science, or art, one jot." See *The New England Magazine* (July–December 1831): 416–17.

3. Washington Irving, "English Writers on America," in *The Works of Washington Irving* (New York: P. F. Collier, n.d.), 1:13. Irving notes that it has been a peculiar lot of America to be visited "by the worst kind of English travellers." But he argues that all the misrepresentation cannot conceal America's "rapidly growing importance and matchless prosperity." According to Irving, the latter are due not merely to local and physical causes, but to moral causes: to "both political liberty, and general diffusion of knowledge... and sound moral, and religious principles" (p. 14).

4. James Fenimore Cooper, *Notions of the Americans*, 1:78.

Notes to Chapter XIV

1. Farkas's census figures (Table 9) are based on the fifth census (1830). See *American Almanac*, p. 158.
2. *The Northern Traveller*, p. 196.
3. James Wolfe (1727–1759) was commander of the British army at the capture of Quebec from the French, a victory which led to British supremacy in Canada. Wolfe was William Pitt's choice to command the Quebec expedition. On September 13, 1759, Wolfe surprised the French on the Plains of Abraham. Wolfe, twice wounded early in the battle, died of a third wound, but not before he knew Quebec had fallen to his troops. Montcalm survived him by only a few hours.
4. Marquis de Montcalm (1712–1759) served as commander in chief of the French forces in Canada during the Seven Years' War, a worldwide struggle between Britain and France for colonial posssessions.

Notes to Chapter XV

1. *The Northern Traveller*, pp. 101–02.
2. By the 1830s there had arisen in all the provinces a demand for a government more responsive to the popular will. English radicals—many of whom Farkas knew personally, foremost among whom was Sir Francis Burdett—lent their support to Canadian radicals who demanded Canadian independence. The more radical Canadian leaders wanted adoption of an American form of government and hinted at separation from Britain.
3. First Report of the States on the Representation of the People of Upper Canada (York, 1831). I was unable to verify the existence of this report.
4. William Lyon Mackenzie and his journal, *Colonial Advocate*, were the battering ram of the reformers. He attacked the Tories, the clique of merchants, churches, and officials who dominated and dictated the policies in the province. He became the champion of the freeholders of Upper Canada, and in 1828 he was elected to the York assembly. When his journal accused the assembly of subservience to a mercenary executive, the assembly voted the article libelous and expelled Mackenzie from its midst. Four times he was reelected, only to be again expelled on each occasion. During the explosive situation of 1837, when in Lower Canada Louis Joseph Papineau was echoing the slogans of the American Revolution, Mackenzie, in close touch with Papineau, called upon the oppressed people to strike their blow for liberty.

Notes to Chapter XVI

1. Vicomte de Chateaubriand (1768–1848), diplomat and author, was one of the first great romantic figures in Europe. Refusing to join the Royalists, he sailed in 1791 for America—a stay memorable for his romantic account of fur-traders and Indians. Chateaubriand indeed

broke his arm at Niagara Falls, and it was sheer luck he did not fall into the roaring abyss. See Richart Switzer, *Chateaubriand's Travels in America* (Lexington: University of Kentucky Press, 1969).

2. It is difficult to establish just what kind of magpie Farkas saw displayed. The best-known species, the black-and-white bird with an iridescent blue gray tail, is common in western North America. However, the yellow-billed magpie, native to central California, might be the bird he refers to.

The same applies to sparrows. Old World sparrows were introduced almost worldwide. However, the Eurasian tree sparrow was introduced into the United States only in the 1870s and hence Farkas may have seen this species displayed as a novelty in the museum.

3. For the most exhaustive treatment of Count Leon's group and its disruptive relationship with George Rapp's Harmony Society, see Karl J. R. Arndt, *George Rapp's Harmony Society 1785–1847* (Philadelphia: University of Pennsylvania Press, 1965).

Notes to Chapter XVII

1. Farkas mistakenly attributed the victory to Philip John Schuyler. It was Major General John Sullivan who defeated the Iroquois in 1779.

2. Farkas's Rousseauean sympathies with the Indians are interesting inasmuch as he implies that the Indians had two choices: either emigrate beyond the Mississippi or face annihilation. Although the vision of a white nation was pervasive in early America, the notion of racial colonization—of removing free blacks to Africa and Indians beyond the Mississippi— emerged strongly in the Jacksonian era, which could tolerate a white-and-red nation but not a white-and-black America. See Bernard W. Sheehan, *Seeds of Extinction: Jeffersonian Philanthropy and the American Indian* (Chapel Hill: University of North Carolina Press, 1973); and Arthur H. De Rosier, Jr., *The Removal of the Choctaw Indians* (New York: Harper Torchbooks, 1972).

3. *The Quarterly Register of the American Educational Society* 3 (August 1830): 59. In compiling Table 10, Farkas places 300,000 Indians in the Mississippi area. However, the *Register* states that the whole "number of Indians within the limits of the United States, east and west of the Mississippi, is 300,000."

4. *Message of the Secretary of War, 1831* (Washington, D.C.: Government Printing Office, 1831).

5. *The National Calendar for 1831* by Peter Force (Washington, 1831), p. 107. The amount allowed from the Civilization Fund for Indian children's education in 1829 was $259. The American Board of the Commission for Foreign Missions had the following budget for the education of Indians:

Baptist	$2,000
Methodist	550
Jesuit	400
Protestant Episcopalian	300
United Brethren	250
	$3,500

Altogether 1,370 Indian students were educated in 1830 with $3,500 from the Civilization Fund.

6. Farkas's estimate is too high. *The Quarterly Register* 3 (August 1830) estimates that about 450,000 Indians can be found in the territories of the United States.

7. Simón Bolívar (1783–1830) was the soldier-statesman who freed six Latin American republics from Spanish rule. Upon his return from Europe and the United States, he became a leader in the newly formed Latin American independence movement and played an important

role in the events surrounding the initial declaration of Venezuelan independence from Spain (July 5, 1811).

8. Quoted by Thomas Paine, *Rights of Man* (Garden City, N.Y.: Doubleday, 1973), pp. 282–83.

Notes to Chapter XVIII

1. One of the anomalies of historical Hungary is that Latin remained the official language of administration till the 1840s, when linguistic nationalism gained ground.

2. *The Quarterly Register* 3 (February 1831): 189–227. Farkas also lists as his source *Sword's Pocket Magazine* (Boston, 1831).

3. Alexander Lips, *Statistik von Amerika*, p. 161.

4. The collected works, speeches, and letters of President Monroe contain no such address before the Congress. The speech Farkas ascribes to Monroe, of course, is a nice ploy against the Hungarian censor.

Notes to Chapter XIX

1. Alexander Lips, *Statistik von Amerika*, p. 147.

2. *The American Atlas* (Philadelphia: Carey & Lea, 1832).

3. *American Almanac*, p. 253.

Notes to Chapter XX

1. By the mid 1820s the Rappites were well known in Europe. Byron satirized them in *Don Juan* (canto 15, 35) in no uncertain terms:

> When Rapp the Harmonist embargoed Marriage
> In his harmonious settlement—(which flourishes
> Strangely enough as yet without miscarriage
> Because it breeds no more mouths than it nourishes,
> Without those sad expenses which disparage
> What Nature naturally most encourages)—
> Why called he "Harmony" a state *sans* wedlock?
> Now here I've got the preacher at a dead lock . . .

The Harmony society also served as a model for Goethe's *Auswanderstaat*, or emigrant state, which is outlined in *Wilhelm Meisters Wanderjahre*, esp. bk. 3, chs. 11–13. Goethe in turn bases his version on Bernhard Karl, Duke of Saxe-Weimar-Eisenach, *Durch Nord-Amerika in den Jahren 1825 und 1826*, 2 vols. (Weimar: W. Hoffmann, 1828). See Karl J. R. Arndt, "The Harmony Society and *Wilhelm Meisters Wanderjahre*," *Comparative Literature* 10 (Summer 1958): 193–202.

2. This confused identity and Rapp Jr.'s suspicion are of some historical interest. Count Leon indeed arrived at Economy in 1831 at the head of a little band of German followers. Eventually he succeeded in splitting up the Harmony Society, and about two hundred fifty members followed Count Leon; five hundred members remained true to George Rapp. See Mark Holloway, *Heavens on Earth*, 2d ed. (Philadelphia: University of Pennsylvania Press, 1970); and Karl J. R. Arndt, "The Life and Mission of Count Leon," *American German Review* 6 (June 1940): pt. 1, pp. 5–8; 6 (August 1940): pt. 2.

3. Friedrich List, the economist, approved of and praised these activities of George Rapp. See Margaret E. Hirst, *Life of Friedrich List* (London: Smith, Elder & Co., 1909), pp. 35–36.

4. Farkas's account of the Harmony Society is, by and large, accurate. However, it is interesting to note that William Pelham, an enthusiastic member of the society, in his letters noted that although the bell rings at 6 A.M. for work, "I believe few persons go to work till the 8 o'clock bell rings." See *New Harmony as Seen by Participants and Travelers: Letters of William Pelham* (Philadelphia: Porcupine Press, 1975).

5. Duke Bernhard wrote that Rapp had complete control over his members. It extended so far as to prevent his society from "too great an increase" and to forbid husbands from associating with their wives. Also he reports that George Rapp castrated a son who trangressed this law, and the son died under the operation. The duke assumed a sarcastic tone when he wrote: "The man of God, it appeared, took special care of himself; his house was by far the best in the place, surrounded by a garden with a flight of stone steps, and the only one furnished with a lightning rod." *Durch Nord-Amerika in den Jahren 1825 und 1826*, 2:105–24.

6. Whether Owen borrowed Rousseau's ideas has been discussed by scholars with somewhat inconclusive results. See Frank Podmore, *Robert Owen: A Biography* (New York: A. M. Kelley, 1968), pp. 126, 137, 150–52, 646. Although there is a general similarity of Owen's and Rousseau's educational ideas, there is no allusion to Rousseau in Owen's writings. Like Rousseau, Owen was a prophet of the essential goodness of human nature.

7. See also Robert Owen's speech on a new system of society delivered before the Congress of the United States in the presence of the President (March 7, 1825), in Oakley C. Johnson, *Robert Owen in the United States* (New York: Humanities Press, 1970), pp. 41–64.

8. It is instructive to contrast nineteenth- and twentieth-century views on cooperatives and experimental colonies. Toynbee includes utopias among the "arrested civilizations" and postulates that they are retrograde steps of a declining society. See Toynbee, *A Study of History* abr. D. C. Somervell (New York: Oxford University Press, 1946), pp. 183–85.

Notes to Chapter XXI

1. *American Almanac*, p. 206.

2. *The Northern Traveller*, pp. 398–99. For instance: "Juniata Works in Pittsburgh employed 55 persons, produced 26,000 weight of nails a day, consuming 425 bushels of coal."

3. Emperor Joseph II (1741–1790), the "hatted king" in popular language, admired Voltaire and personally called upon Rousseau. He wished to remove the hated names of bondsman and *urbarium* (defined the peasant's duties and obligations on seigneurial lands), abolished corvée, and introduced the duty of general taxation. He announced the unlimited right of free migration for the serfs, permitted them to marry, to learn professions, to go to school, and to enter learned professions without the permission of the landlord. All these measures greatly alarmed the Hungarian feudal lords, particularly since in some countries the peasants rose in

terrible revolt, as in Transylvania. See Oscar Jászi, *The Dissolution of the Habsburg Monarchy* (Chicago: University of Chicago Press, 1929). On Emperor Joseph, the people's emperor, see Paul K. Padover, *The Revolutionary Emperor: Joseph the Second, 1741–90* (New York: R. O. Ballou, 1934).

4. Farkas was genuinely puzzled by the conflict between slavery and the very meaning of the New World, which also preoccupied George Bancroft. Like the latter, Farkas faced the paradox: if American republicanism is the asylum of liberty and good government, then how is one to explain the growth of slavery, an institution so repugnant to the ideals and practices of free people? Farkas's answer, like that of Bancroft, was based on a sharp moral distinction between the original cause of American slavery, the selfish greed of European merchants and governments, and the conditions which led to its perpetuation. It is interesting to note that Farkas's comparative use of Emperor Joseph II enables him to employ a larger perspective to mitigate American guilt over slavery, a method also used by Bancroft in blaming slavery on guilt-sickened and profit-hungry Europe. See George Bancroft, *History of the United States of America* (New York: Appleton & Co., 1896), 1: ch. 8. Using this larger perspective, Bancroft concluded (3:408) that "in the midst of the horrors of slavery and slave trade, the masters had, in part at least, performed the office of advancing and civilizing the negro."

5. One of the staunch supporters of Virginia's antislavery stance was Samuel Johnson, who hated slavery. See Boswell, *Life of Johnson* (Oxford: Clarendon Press, 1887), 2:479–80: "Englishmen, as a nation, had no right to reproach their fellow subjects in America with being drivers of negroes; for England shared in the guilt and the gain of that infamous traffic."

6. A. Levasseur, *Lafayette in America*, 1:205–06.

7. The Virginia House of Burgesses enacted a prohibitive duty in 1772 on slave imports and requested the crown to accept this curtailment of a "Trade of great Inhumanity." The crown disallowed the bill. In 1778 Virginia prohibited the importation of slaves by statute, not by constitution.

8. In 1775 Philadelphia Quakers organized the Society for the Relief of Free Negroes Unlawfully Held in Bondage. In 1776 the local meetings of Friends were directed to disown any Quaker who resisted pleas to manumit his slaves.

9. Farkas refers to the Congress of Vienna's (1815) abstract declarations condemning the slave trade.

10. A. Levasseur, *Lafayette in America*, 1:206.

11. *New York Annual Register*, p. 333.

12. James Bryce, *The American Commonwealth* (New York: Macmillan, 1906), 2:859, uses the same argument as Farkas in employing slave labor on the plantations: "The Negro is doubtless a heavy burden for American civilizations to carry. . . . The Negro, however, is necessary to the South, for only he can till its hot and unhealthy lowlands . . ."

13. The Abolitionist Movement was strong during Farkas's visit (1831) and during the early 1830s it gave rise to newspapers like the *Liberator* and to organizations such as the American, New England, and New York City antislavery societies. See G. H. Barnes, *The Antislavery Impulse, 1830–1844* (New York: Harcourt, Brace, 1964), pp. 1–6, 33, 58, 107.

14. Robert Finley (1772–1817), the high priest of the great revival, was a radical evangelist and judged by many the most notable figure in the moral history of the nineteenth century. See Barnes, *Antislavery Impulse*, esp. ch. 1, and Lawrence J. Friedmann, *Inventors of the Promised Land* (New York: Knopf, 1975), ch. 6.

15. The project for colonizing free Negroes in Africa was formally initiated in Washington (December 21, 1816) at a meeting presided over by Henry Clay. See *National Intelligencer* (December 21, 1816). For Clay's speech and motion at the 1818 meeting of the American Colonization Society, see *The Papers of Henry Clay*, ed. James F. Hopkins (Lexington: University of Kentucky Press, 1961), 2:420–22.

16. John Russwurm, graduate of Bowdoin College, went to Liberia in 1829 to supervise the system of education. The country, however, was not yet ready for the kind of work he wanted to do. Hence he went into politics and served as governor of Maryland from 1836 to 1851. See

Benjamin Brawley, *A Social History of the American Negro* (New York: Natural History Press, 1970), pp. 161, 187, 189.
17. The most reliable study of the Maryland colony is John H. T. McPherson, "History of Liberia," *John Hopkins University Studies in History and Political Science* 9 (1891).

Notes to Chapter XXIII

1. Captain John Smith (1580–1631) was an explorer and the principal founder of the first settlement in North America at Jamestown. He played an equally important role as a cartographer and a prolific writer who vividly depicted the natural abundance of the New World, thus enticing the colonizers and prospective English settlers in the seventeenth century. In addition to his maps, his writings include *A Description of New England* (1616), which is a counterpart to his *Map of Virginia with Description of the Country . . .* (1612); *The Generall Historie of Virginia, New-England, and the Summer Isles* (1624); and *The True Travels, Adventures, and Observations of Captain John Smith in Europe, Asia, Africa, and America* (1630).
2. *The Northern Traveller,* p. 385.
3. Edward Livingston (1764–1836), lawyer, legislator, and statesman, codified criminal law and procedure. He was a Republican representative in Congress (1795–1801, 1823–1829) and a senator (1829–1831). He was secretary of state (1831–1833) under President Jackson, in which position he prepared the antinullification proclamation in 1832, concerning South Carolina's opposition to the protective tariff. He was also minister plenipotentiary to France (1833–1835).

Notes to Chapter XXIV

1. Frances Wright, *Views of Society and Manners in America* (London: Longman & Co., 1822), pp. 123–26.

Notes to Chapter XXV

1. *The National Calendar for 1831*, pp. 216–39.
2. Henry Peter Brougham (1778–1868), a prominent Whig politician, reformer, and chancellor of England (1830–1834), was also a noted orator, wit, and man of fashion. Before and during his tenure as chancellor he took the lead in creating the University of London—the first English nondenominational institution of higher learning. He also helped to found *Edinburgh Review* (1802), sponsored the Public Education Bill (1820), was an eloquent and strong antislavery advocate, and took a leading role in forcing the Reform Bill of 1831 through the House of Lords.
3. *The National Calendar for 1831*, p. 190.

Notes to Chapter XXVI

1. Farkas gives an account of Captain John Smith's adventures and exploits against the Turks in Hungary. Because of Smith's penchant for self-dramatization and Farkas's uncritical acceptance of his exploits, this part has been omitted.

Notes to Chapter XXVII

1. See James Fenimore Cooper, *Notions of the Americans*, 1:400–401. According to Frances Wright, *Views of Society and Manners in America*, p. 474, Count Survilliers wrote: "All the furniture, statues, pictures, money, plate, gold, jewels... have been most scrupulously delivered into the hands of my house. In the night of the fire, and during the next day, there were brought to me by labouring men drawers in which I have found the proper quantity of pieces of money, and medals of gold, and valuable jewels, which might have been taken with impunity."

Notes to Chapter XXVIII

1. James Mease, *Picture of Philadelphia* (Philadelphia: T. Town, 1823); and *The Pennsylvania Register* (Philadelphia, 1831).
2. Quoted by Alexander Everett, *America* (Philadelphia: Carey & Lea, 1827), p. 124.
3. James Mease, *Picture of Philadelphia*, pp. 36–54.
4. On the 1831 peasant uprising, see Zoltán Bodrogközy, *A magyar agrármozgalom története* [The history of the Hungarian agrarian movements] (Budapest: Királyi Magyar Egyetemi Nyomda, 1929), 1:259–71; and János Balásházy, *Az 1831 esztendöi felsö magyarországi zendüléseknek történeti leirása* [Historical description of the rebellions of 1831 in northern Hungary] (Pest: Trattner Karoly, 1832).
5. Farkas's childhood sweetheart, Jozefa Polcz, daughter of a wealthy merchant in Kolozsvár, married an American, James Swain, who was member of the American legation in Vienna. Swain took Jozefa to Philadelphia, where she died in childbirth in 1833. Romance has it that Jozefa's last wish was to name her son after Sándor Farkas.

Index

Index